DEDICATION

To those who have kept us fed

CHAPTER ONE

"Benny's piked off again." Otter's tone suggested complete indifference to this development, but Colonel Sir Orion Goddard—Rye, to his few remaining friends—saw worry in the boy's eyes.

"How long has he been gone?" Rye asked, with equally studied casualness.

"Nobody's seen 'im since last night. Missed 'is supper."

Hence, Otter's worry. No child in Rye's household willingly missed a meal or passed the night anywhere but in the safety of the dormitory.

"You've looked in the usual places?"

A terse nod. Otter—Theodoric William Goddard—was constitutionally incapable of fashioning an actual request for aid, but he had come to Rye's office asking for help nonetheless. In all likelihood, Otter and the other boys had been searching for Benny for most of the day. Sunset approached, and with it the unavoidable necessity of enlisting adult assistance.

A child alone on the London streets at night, even a lad as canny as Benny, was a child in danger. "Any idea why he'd wander away now?"

Otter's gaze slid around the room, which managed a credible impersonation of a gentleman's study. The ceiling bore a fresco of scantily clad goddesses, muscular gods, and snorting horses, and more than once, Rye had caught Otter lying on the couch, gawking at the artwork.

The rest of the room was nondescript. Grandpapa Goddard's portrait added a note of stern benevolence from a bygone era. Correspondence sat in neat stacks on the desk, and newspapers in French and English adorned the sideboard. The carpet bore a slightly faded design of roses and greenery, and the furniture hovered between comfortable and worn.

The only remarkable object in the room was Rye's cavalry sword, hung above the mantel and below Grandpapa's portrait. Rye kept it there, immediately across from his desk, as a reminder and a reproach.

"Benny disappeared for a few days last month," Otter said. "Away on business, according to him."

Rye mentally berated himself for not noticing that previous absence, but he did not eat with the boys. Enlisted men needed privacy from officers, and conversely.

"Did the magistrate take him up?"

"Mayhap. They'd hang a boy like that for sport," Otter said, "or sell him to a molly house and claim he'd been transported."

Some of the magistrates would. Of the six boys who called Rye's dwelling home, Benny was the tallest and the least robust. He had a lanky sort of grace, delicate features, and the quiet air of the scholar, even though he hated soap and water. Benny could read—read well, a quirk he didn't advertise to the others—and had a fondness for cats.

Otter, by contrast, was terrified of cats, a secret Rye would take to his grave. If the other boys knew, they exercised the curious diplomacy of the stews and ignored this gap in Otter's otherwise impregnable defenses.

"Did Benny intimate what sort of business had called him away?"

Otter pushed unruly dark hair from his eyes. "Hint, ya mean? Nah. Benny keeps mum on a good day."

One of Benny's many fine qualities. "I'll ask a few questions down at the pub and have a look around." Rye would search every alley and coal hole. "He won't be gone long. Tell the others I've been alerted, and they are not to worry."

Otter snorted and left the office on silent feet. The boy never offered greetings or partings, though he was learning to knock before entering when a door was closed. With the lads, Rye had found patience to be not merely a virtue, but a nonnegotiable necessity.

As was an ability to take each boy on his own merits. John was their songbird, with a tune for any occasion, most of his ditties too filthy and hilarious to have been learned anywhere but at the lowest taverns. Louis knew the streets, alleys, wynds, and sewers. Entire rivers flowed beneath London, and Louis carried a map of the whole city in his head.

Bertie knew the rooftops and could get onto them and traverse them with more agility than a squirrel. He frequently served as lookout for the others, a skill usually acquired in the housebreaker's trade.

And shy, fastidious Drew had a facility for math and memorization. He'd spout Bible verses at odd moments in odd contexts, and how he'd come by his store of proverbs, aphorisms, and quotes, nobody knew. He, too, abhorred soap and water, though somebody had put the table manners on him.

That the boys had already done their best to find their friend, with no results, was cause for panic. Most pickets who failed to come in from a night watch hadn't deserted.

Rye left the house by way of the back garden, stopping only to grab his top hat, riding crop, and gloves. He could look the part of a gentleman when necessary, not that it did him any good. Still, the uniform mattered, in business as in war, and thus he had dressed today in the finery of a prosperous merchant.

The boys were likely watching him, so he made straight for the stables, as if his plan was to trot from one watering hole to the next. Like a cat, Benny sought the warmth and safety of the mews when he wanted privacy, another secret Rye carried. He'd once found Benny poring over a primer in the hayloft and had spotted the boy sniggling out to the mews on many occasions thereafter, a book in hand.

Rye gave his eyes a moment to adjust to the stable's gloom. He kept two horses, an extravagance he excused as more vanity expected of a successful purveyor of fine wines. The truth was, old Agricola was getting on, though he still cut a dash under saddle, while Scipio was still prone to moments of youthful stupidity. They managed well enough together in harness, but a matched pair, they were not.

The horses looked up from their hay when Rye entered their domain. He paused to scratch Scipio's hairy ear and spared a pat for Agricola's velvety nose. Both geldings were calm of eye, and their stalls had recently been set fair, a routine Rye insisted on.

"Seen any wandering boys?" Rye asked softly.

Agricola craned his neck over the half door to nudge at Rye's pocket. He rewarded the horse with a bit of carrot left over from their morning hack.

Where were the cats? The stable had its share, and they were a lazy, arrogant lot. The swallows made sport of them, and if the felines had ever caught a mouse, they'd done so under a vow of secrecy.

Benny loved the worthless lot of them, though. Rye climbed the ladder to the hayloft silently, his riding crop between his teeth. A fat tabby watched his progress from a beam over the barn aisle. An equally grand marmalade specimen lay curled in a pile of hay, yawning as Rye stepped off the ladder. Benny's honor guard was keeping watch.

Threats welled, admonitions about boys who played silly games merely to get attention, foolish lads who set a whole household to needlessly worrying.

Except that Rye Goddard had once been a foolish lad unable to gain his papa's notice, and on a few memorable occasions, he'd been a very foolish man. He poked gently at the hay with his riding crop.

"I know you're in there," he said pleasantly. "Grabbing a nap when there's work to be done. Otter is worried about you, and if he's worried about you enough to bother me, then you've made your point." Not with fists, but with a more subtle weapon —absence.

The riding crop brushed against something solid.

"Go away." This directive was muttered from the middle of the pile of hay, and never had two words given Rye greater relief.

"I'd like to," he replied. "I'd like to get back to tallying up my revenues and expenses, like to create my income projections for the next quarter—a cheerful, hopeful exercise—but no. I am instead required to nanny a wayward lad who has probably fallen in love with a goose girl who rejects his tender sentiments. This happens, my boy. We all get our hearts broken, and it's the stuff of some of John's best melodies." Also the stuff of a commanding officer's worst nightmares.

"Go away." For Benny, that tone of voice qualified as a snarl. "I ain't talking to you."

"Did Otter threaten to make you take a bath?" Benny didn't stink, but neither did he regularly wash his face.

"Fetch the lady wot cooks at the Coventry. I'll talk to 'er."

Rye planted his arse on an overturned half barrel and considered the puzzle before him. Benny was not by nature a difficult or complicated fellow, but now he was talking in riddles.

"What lady who cooks for the Coventry?" The Coventry Club was a gaming hell doing business as a fancy supper club. Rye's sister Jeanette had, for reasons known only to her, married one of the club's co-owners several months ago. Multiple reconnaissance missions suggested the union was happy and the club thriving, which was ever so fortunate for the groom's continued welfare.

And no, Rye was not in the least jealous. Jeanette deserved every joy life had to offer, and if Sycamore Dorning counted among her joys, Rye would find a way to be cordial to the man—when Jeanette was on hand.

"Fetch the lady with the kind eyes," Benny said as the hay rustled. "I won't talk to you."

"Miss Pearson?" She was an assistant cook in the vast kitchens at the Coventry. Rye had met her once under less than ideal circumstances, but like Benny, he recalled the compassion in her green eyes.

"Aye, Miss Ann. She'll come."

Benny's tone rekindled Rye's worry. The boy wasn't having a mere pout, he was miserable. Rye nudged the hay aside with his hand.

"Benny, are you well?" More nudging and swiping at the hay revealed the boy lying on his side curled in a blanket. *Not well*, was the obvious answer, not well at all.

"Go away." Benny pulled the blanket up over his head. "Fetch Miss Ann. I ain't tellin' ye again."

Ann Pearson knew her herbs, of that much Rye was certain. She had been a calm, sensible presence when Jeanette's health had been imperiled.

"Benny, what's amiss?" Rye asked, trying for a jocular tone. How long had the boy been in this condition, and what the hell was wrong with him?

"Fetch Miss Ann, please." The lad was begging now. "I'm dying, Colonel. You have to fetch Miss Ann."

Rye had half reached for the boy, prepared to extract him from his cocoon of wool and distress, but something stopped him. He'd been through many a battle, and yet, it still took him a moment to realize why he hesitated.

Benny's unwillingness to move, his desperate rudeness to the person who provided him food and shelter, his decision to hide in the place that signified safety to him, all converged to support one conclusion. Benny wasn't having a sulk or enduring a case of too much winter ale. He exuded the same quality of hopeless suffering common to soldiers wounded in battle, half fearing death and half comforted by the possibility. Rye had seen enough battles and their aftermaths to recognize the condition.

Benny was injured.

Seriously injured.

"I'll send for Miss Ann. Don't move, boy. Stay right where you are."

Rye half slid down the ladder, spooked both horses, and bellowed for Louis to attend him immediately.

"THE LAD SAYS he's come from Colonel Orion Goddard," Henry announced. "Says he needs to talk to you, Miss Ann. Won't talk to nobody else."

Henry was cheerful and energetic and subscribed to the universal understanding at the Coventry that footmen were entitled to flirt with maids, customers, char girls, and other footmen. He'd learned—as they all learned—not to waste his time flirting with Ann.

Colonel Goddard's emissary, by contrast, was a spare, lean lad of ten or twelve years. With the poor, guessing an age was chancy. Generations of inadequate nutrition resulted in delayed development and less height.

"Are you hungry, young man?" Ann asked.

The boy shook his head, but peered past her into the vast, bustling kitchen.

"Henry, please have Nancy put together some bread and butter for the lad. What is your name, child?"

"M'name's Louis. The colonel gimme this for ya." A surprisingly clean paw held a folded and sealed note.

Ann knew two things about Colonel Sir Orion Goddard. First, he had come to his sister's side when called. He'd sat with Jeanette, Lady Tavistock, now Jeanette Dorning, for more than an hour while Sycamore Dorning had been unable to guard his lady. The colonel hadn't taken so much as a sip of tea or a crust of bread while on duty at his sister's bedside.

Nor had he lingered when it had become apparent that the lady was on the mend. He'd asked Ann to send word if he was needed again and slipped away without bidding his sibling farewell.

That had been several months ago, and Ann hadn't seen the colonel at the club since.

The other fact she recalled about Colonel Sir Orion Goddard was that he favored good old lavender soap, and plenty of it. He did not merely douse himself with lavender water and pretend that passed for washing. He scrubbed himself thoroughly, the scent emanating from his hair and his clothing, as well as his person.

The soap he used was French rather than English, based on the aroma of the lavender, and hard-milled French soap came dear. Ann did favor a man who took cleanliness seriously enough to pay for good soap.

She slit the seal on the note. In the kitchen, Monsieur Delacourt began yelling about the impossibility of finding fresh leeks—fresh, not three days old!—in the foul blight upon the face of civilization known as London. The sun had barely set, and Monsieur was already in fine form.

Sir Orion had an elegant hand for a soldier: *Young Benny has been hurt and is asking for you. I fear serious injury. Please come with all possible haste, Your Obed Serv, Colonel Orion Goddard.*

Only a very upset man would neglect to refer to his knighthood in his correspondence. Ann untied her apron and slipped it over her head.

"What do you know of this?" she asked the boy.

"Benny went missing yesterday—went missing again. He were out of pocket a few weeks ago too. Tendin' to business, like the colonel says. Colonel says please come double-quick-forced-march-enemy-in-pursuit."

Monsieur would have three apoplexies if Ann abandoned her post this early in the evening. Henry returned and passed the child a sandwich of cheese, butter, and bread with the crusts still on.

"Best get back to the kitchen, miss. Monsieur's in rare form."

Monsieur's rare form made a nigh nightly appearance. The man was incapable of subtle emotion, and every evening's buffet was a performance. Jules Delacourt could be funny, but he could also be savagely critical, and needlessly so.

"Wait for me," Ann told the child.

She gathered up her cloak and waded into the pandemonium of Monsieur's kitchen. He was still ranting about wilted leeks, so she waited patiently until he'd cursed Haymarket, English roads, English farmers, and the English sky, which felt compelled to produce English rain at least every seventy-two hours.

"You are holding your cloak," Monsieur said. "I do not pay you to hold your cloak, Pearson. Somebody must oversee the sauces, and that somebody is you. Do not try my temper this evening, or I shall chop you up and add you to the curry, though there is barely enough of you to make a proper curry."

Monsieur was handsome in the dark-eyed, dark-haired Gallic tradition, and he would age splendidly, for all he'd become tiresome within a week of taking employment at the Coventry. He was a competent chef, and thus his foibles were tolerated.

Were he female, he'd be making one-tenth of his current salary, and he would have been sacked before the first tantrum concluded.

Ann passed him the note. "A child has been injured, and Mrs. Dorning's brother has summoned me."

Monsieur read the missive and handed it back. "Are you a surgeon now, tending to clumsy children?"

Ann merely stared at him. Monsieur well knew Mrs. Dorning's feelings regarding family, and more to the point, he knew Mr. Dorning's devotion to that same family.

"Don't tarry on this errand," Monsieur said with a sigh. "The leeks are atrocious, Pearson. English leeks are a tribulation invented strictly for penitential purposes, and this lot is truly disgraceful."

Monsieur had doubtless chosen *this lot* that very morning after no less than fifteen minutes' deliberation over the entire wagonload.

"Soak them in ice water, and they'll revive after an hour or so,"

Ann said. "Works for celery as well, if that diatribe is on your program tonight."

Monsieur smiled—or bared his teeth. "How you wound a sensitive soul who has never wished you anything but good. Be off with you, I must save the buffet from a fate worse than Scottish porridge."

The child who'd brought the note stood in the doorway to the back hall, watching Ann solemnly. The boy was not impressed with a busy kitchen and was not angling for more food. He was silently begging Ann to hurry.

She settled her cloak about her shoulders, snatched up a straw hat, and retrieved a basket of medicinals from a cupboard. Then she followed the lad into the gathering gloom of the evening and started praying.

CHAPTER TWO

"She's here!" Louis's shout nearly startled Rye out of his boots. "I brung the lady!"

"Good work," Rye said, going to the top of the ladder and peering down into the shadowed stable. "Miss Pearson, if you could join us up here? Louis, fetch the lantern and then see to your supper."

The stable had grown dark while Orion had waited, and memories had crowded in. How many hours had he spent in the infirmary tents, listening to a dying man's final ramblings or writing out the last letter the fellow would send home? How many times had he refused a fallen soldier's entreaty for a single, quick bullet?

"Colonel," Miss Pearson said, arriving at the top of the ladder. "Good evening."

Orion took the basket from her and waited while the lady dealt with her skirts and climbed from the ladder into the hayloft. Louis passed up the lantern and tried for a gawk. He climbed back down when Orion aimed a glower at him.

Benny clearly did not want an audience.

"Miss Ann has come," Orion said. "You will do as she says, Benny, and if she says to send for the surgeon, we send for the surgeon." No soldier ever wanted to fall into the surgeon's hands, much less commend another to that torment.

"I ain't 'avin' no bloody sawbones," Benny muttered. "Go away, Colonel."

"You're insubordinate," Orion said, brushing a hand over the boy's brow. "Mind Miss Ann, or you'll be scrubbing pots for a week, lad."

Miss Pearson watched this exchange with an air of puzzlement. "Where is the injury?"

"He won't tell me," Orion said, straightening. "Won't let me move him, won't stir from his nest, but there is a wound."

"If you will give us some privacy, I'll see what I can do."

Orion regarded the miserable child curled in the hay. "This boy is dear to me. Please spare no effort to bring him right." He would not embarrass Benny with a closer approximation of the truth: Loss of the child would unman him and send the other five boys howling with grief.

"We need privacy, Colonel."

"I won't go far." Rye *could* not go far, could not leave a man downed on the battlefield. "Holler if you need anything, and I do mean anything."

"I understand." She made a gesture in the direction of the ladder, her gaze calm and direct. *Be off with you. I have the situation in hand.*

He'd forgotten how petite she was, how serenity wafted about her like a fragrance. "Benny was right to send for you, and thank you for coming."

"I will render a full report as soon as I've examined the patient, but I cannot do that until you remove yourself from the immediate surrounds."

Orion made himself descend the ladder and busied himself tidying up the horses' stalls while soft voices drifted down from the hayloft. Benny was holding a conversation, not merely moaning out orders, an encouraging sign.

Night finished overtaking day while Rye worked. Summer had

departed and autumn had arrived. Rye's hip told him as much on the chilly evenings and chillier mornings. Miss Pearson remained in the hayloft, speaking quietly. Benny responded, and the cadence was that of a normal chat, though Orion could not make out the words.

"Colonel?"

"Here." Orion left off scratching Scipio's neck and returned to the foot of the ladder.

"The patient will make a full recovery, but I need a set of clean clothes, warm water, and some rags. Also a sewing kit if you have one."

"Stitches?" *The poor lad.* "I have some laudanum if that will help."

"Let's start with the clean clothes."

"But that—" *Made no sense.* Orion's protest died aborning as Miss Pearson's skirts appeared at the edge of the hayloft, followed by her person climbing onto the ladder.

A gentleman did not watch a lady descend a ladder, even in the near darkness of a stable in the evening. Miss Pearson wasn't strictly a lady—she labored hard for her bread—but Orion had at one time considered himself a gentleman.

He turned his back until Miss Pearson was standing before him in the gloom of the barn aisle. She'd taken off her straw hat, and her cuffs were turned back. She smelled good—flowery and fresh—a contrast to the earthy scents of the stable.

"Benny will be well," she said with calm conviction. "Clean clothes are the first priority. Bone broth, chamomile tea, light activity, and the malady will ease its grip in a few days."

"You're sure?" Orion said, peering down at her. "You aren't a physician, and the boy was clearly in misery." *Showed evidence of serious injury.*

"I am as certain of my diagnosis as I am of my name, Colonel. Fetch the patient some clean clothes, and you and I will talk."

Orion's relief was unseemly. He'd worried for Jeanette when food poisoning had brought her low, but Jeanette was an adult, and she'd clearly had Sycamore Dorning to fret for her too. These boys had nobody and nothing, and life had already been brutally unkind to them.

"Thank you," he said, taking the lady's hand and bowing. "Thank you from the bottom of my heart."

Miss Pearson ambushed him with a hug—a swift squeeze, followed by a pat to his shoulder. For a small woman, she hugged fiercely. The embrace was over before Orion could fathom that he was being hugged, and that was fortunate.

He'd sooner have taken another bullet than endure Ann Pearson's affection.

"The child is lucky to have you," she said, stepping back. "I gather Benny is one of several children in your care."

"They are hardly children anymore. They eat like dragoons and grow out of clothing almost before it's paid for." Orion cupped his hand to his mouth. "Watch the lantern, Benny. I'm off to find you clean togs and scare up the tisanes Miss Pearson has prescribed."

Benny's head appeared over the top of the ladder, bits of hay cascading down. "You won't tell the others?"

Tell them what?

"You are suffering a brief indisposition," Miss Pearson replied. "Perhaps something you ate disagreed with you. The colonel and I will discuss what's to be done."

Some silent communication passed between Miss Pearson and the patient. Benny shrugged and withdrew from sight.

"No more piking off," Rye called up to the loft. "I don't care if you have consumption, the Covent Garden flu, and sooty warts. You don't desert the regiment just because you feel poorly."

"Yes, sir." The resentment Benny packed into the two mumbled syllables was reassuring.

"Come, Colonel." Miss Pearson gathered up her basket and marched down the barn aisle. "I daresay Benny could use some sustenance, and I want a look at your medicinals."

Orion followed reluctantly. "You're sure the lad will come right?"

"Benny will be fine. Have you eaten supper?"

"No, and now that I know we won't be measuring Benny for a shroud, I admit I am famished. The cook/housekeeper usually leaves me a tray on the hob before she departs for the night. You're welcome to share."

"Your help doesn't live in?"

Rye crossed the alley and escorted Miss Pearson into the garden, where crickets sang a slow lament to winter's approach. A cat skittered up over the garden wall, and fatigue pressed down on Rye like the darkness itself.

"My housekeeper lives around the corner with her daughter and son-in-law. I believe Mrs. Murphy has a follower and would rather see him on her own turf. My maid-of-all-work and man-of-all-work are a married couple—he also serves as my coachman—and they dwell over the carriage house."

Miss Pearson moved through the night with the same easy assurance Orion associated with her in other contexts. She'd been comfortable in Jeanette's sick room. In the Coventry's kitchens, she'd been thoroughly at home.

"You have married servants, Colonel?"

"My former batman and his wife. I value loyalty over convention."

"I suspect you value loyalty over almost every other consideration. My gracious, your roses are lovely." Miss Pearson made her way down the cobbled path to the overgrown roses along the stone wall. "These are not damasks, and yet..." She sniffed. "They are marvelous."

"Careful," Orion said, pausing on the path. "That one is French and has serious thorns. A gardener at the Château de Neuilly traded me a pair of bushes for a few bottles of wine. Said that rose originated on the *Île Bourbon*."

"Perfumiers would pay you a fortune for these roses." She bent closer and took another whiff of pink blooms.

"I traded champagne fit for a king for that specimen. I was trying to sneak my best vintage into the cellars of the Duke of Orléans, but I suspect my wine never went beyond the servants' hall."

Miss Pearson made a pretty picture, sniffing the roses by the light of a gibbous moon. Something of poignancy tried to gild the moment, with the crickets offering their slow song and the thorny roses perfuming the night air.

She'd hugged him, was the problem. Nobody hugged Orion Goddard, and he liked it that way. Needed it that way.

"Your champagne was well spent," she said, straightening. "Do your boys maintain this garden?"

His boys. They were his, though he didn't dare think of them in those terms. "They do, with some guidance from me. Shall we go in?"

"I suppose we ought to. Benny can't spend the night in that stable."

"I'm sure he has on many an occasion. Benny's my best sentry. Likes his privacy and thinks deeply as a matter of habit. The other fellows don't quite know what to make of him, but they worried at his absence."

"You worried at his absence," Miss Pearson replied as Orion ushered her into the hallway that led to the pantries and kitchen.

"Nearly panicked," Orion said. "The lads have eaten, so if you're hungry, we'll have to forage. Drew!"

Drew trotted across the corridor from the servants' hall. "Sir? How's our Benny?"

"He ate something that disagreed with him and needs a clean set of togs brought over to the hayloft. A basin of warm water and some rags wouldn't go amiss either, though he'll want privacy if he has to clean up. See to it, please."

"Aye, sir." Drew bowed to Miss Pearson—where had the lad picked up that nicety?—and scampered up the steps.

Miss Pearson began opening the kitchen's cupboards and drawers. She was on reconnaissance, clearly, and because Orion knew only the basics of survival when it came to the kitchen—bread, butter, jam, cheese, that sort of thing—he let her explore.

The tray on the hob held a bowl of lukewarm soup, as well as bread and butter. Many a night, Orion had subsisted on the same, but he was truly hungry and for once wanted something more substantial.

"The chophouse will be open for another hour," he said, "or we can manage sandwiches if that will suffice."

Miss Pearson left off pillaging and gave him the oddest look. "Sandwiches will do, and we begin by washing our hands. What is Benny's full name?'

"Benjamin," Rye scrubbed up at the wet sink and moved aside so Miss Pearson could do likewise. "The boys all choose their names when they come to live here. Drew, for example, is Andrew Marvell Goddard. Drew was smitten with the poet's epitaph 'the ornament and example of his age, beloved by good men, feared by bad, admired by all, though imitated by few; and scarce paralleled by any,' or something like that. That Marvell talked the crown out of hanging Milton impressed Drew as well."

Miss Pearson rummaged in her basket and set a tin on the worktable. "And you gave the boys your family name?"

"Goddard is the only name I have to give them." The only name Orion had to defend, and he'd made a bad job of that mission thus far. With Jeanette safely married and another good harvest all but complete, he'd see his name properly cleared.

"And the rest of Benny's name?"

"Benjamin Hannibal Goddard, his middle name chosen for the famed Carthaginian of old. Why?"

Miss Pearson swung the kettle over the coals on the raised hearth that took up half of the kitchen's outside wall. She'd made a pretty picture in the garden, and she made a different sort of pretty picture in the kitchen.

Rye should have tarried longer in France, where a call upon a certain good-humored and friendly widow in Reims could have figured on his itinerary.

"You had no idea, then?" Miss Pearson asked as she withdrew a loaf from the breadbox and took a knife from a drawer.

"No idea of what?"

She wielded the knife with a mesmerizing sort of competence, the slices perfectly even. "Not Benjamin Hannibal, Colonel. The child's name is Benevolence Hannah."

Orion was hungry enough to risk snitching a slice of bread. He tore a crust off and stuck it in his mouth. Reasonably fresh, probably made that morning.

"Strange names for a lad."

Miss Pearson paused in her artistry and slanted him a look.

The bread abruptly got stuck in Orion's throat.

Benny's indisposition that had visited last month and was back again a few weeks later. The use of grime as camouflage for cheeks that would never grow a beard. The reticence around the other boys, the knit cap worn in all weather.

"Rubbishing hell."

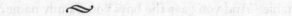

CAVALRYMEN HAD a reputation for rash behavior, though after offering his brief profanity, Colonel Goddard merely stared at the kettle steaming over the coals.

"*Benevolence Hannah*? And his—her—ailment is of the female sort?"

"You are not to blame Benny for her subterfuge, Colonel."

A muscle flexed along his jaw, and a good square jaw it was, too, shadowed with a day's growth of dark beard. Like the typical cavalryman, Colonel Goddard was big and lean—he wanted for some decent meals, in Ann's professional opinion—though he moved quietly despite his size. He had something in common with Monsieur Delacourt, too, in that both claimed the slightly Romanesque features of the handsome Gaul.

Monsieur, though, had learned to use a winsome smile on occasion. Ann could not recall seeing Colonel Goddard smile, ever.

"The blame is mine," the colonel replied, stalking away from the hearth. "I am the commanding officer in this household, and Benny is my responsibility."

"You cannot command her to be other than she is."

"Why not? The army does that all the time. Commands a weaver's fifth son to become a sharpshooter, turns a seamstress's pride and joy into a sapper."

What had the colonel been, before the army had turned him into a saturnine officer sporting a piratical eye patch and a slightly uneven gait?

"Benny is female, sir, and she cannot change that. She said you don't take in girls, but once you take a lad on, you never throw him back. You cannot abandon her now."

The colonel rummaged in the window box and produced a tub of butter. "Can you tolerate crusts on your bread?"

"Of course, besides, you cut the crusts off last thing so the bread is less likely to fall apart as you spread the butter and mustard and so forth."

"If there's mustard to be had, I would not know where to find it."

Ann went to the pantry, found the mustard by scent, and set it at the colonel's elbow. "You truly had no idea Benny was female?"

"None. I'm hoping the lads knew and helped her perpetrate her subterfuge. *Her*. Benny is a her. Of all the perishing... What else have I missed, and am I the only one she hoodwinked?"

"How old is Benny?"

"I have no idea. She's been here for about two years."

"Then she was at a dangerous age to be on the streets. This is mustard *à la dijonnaise*."

"There is no safe age to be on the streets, Miss Pearson. You can detect the wine?"

That he knew how Dijon mustard was made surprised her. "The

verjus, which gives it that pungent, slightly grape-y nose. The wine reinforces the same impression on the tongue."

He began applying mustard to bread in even, careful swipes of his butter knife. "I did not know mustard had a nose."

"Everything has a nose to some of us." Ann took up the cheese knife and wrestled a half wheel of cheddar from the window box. "What will you do about the girl?"

The colonel helped himself to the first slice of cheese Ann cut. "Nothing, for now. I will consider options, discuss them with the affected parties, and present Benny with some choices. I know little of females beyond the obvious, but I do know ordering them about generally produces poor results."

The cheese was a pale cheddar, an unreliable sort of cheese in Ann's opinion. The flavor changed with location, age, packaging, and storage conditions. This wheel was in the palatable phase between little flavor at all and the nearly acrid qualities of a cheese aged too long.

Rather like the colonel—mature, a bit sharp, not yet bitter? "What do you consider obvious about females, Colonel?"

He paused with the butter knife in one hand and cocked his head to the side, raising one brow. He did not smile, but by the light of the hearth, Ann saw merriment in his gaze.

"Probably the same qualities you consider obvious about the male?" he replied, collecting slices of cheese.

"The male? You mean the gender that assumes a tiny set of peculiar appendages renders them the lords of creation, superior in intellect, wit, strength, and all worthy measures?"

"You disagree?"

"Superior in stupidity and arrogance, perhaps. What are you doing?"

"In my stupid, arrogant way, I'm trying to make sandwiches and stave off starvation. The cheese goes between the slices of bread, as best I recall."

Was he teasing her? About *food?* "If we are to enjoy the bread, butter, and cheese, then the sandwiches are better served toasted, and that means the spices must be dusted over the cheese before we melt —" She reached over to remove the top bread slices from the sandwiches he'd proposed to ruin. The colonel did not budge, which meant she nudged up against his arm.

"You barely come to my shoulder," he muttered, "and yet, you scold me."

"I scold you in the kitchen because I am a professional cook. You might scold me in the stable because your expertise lies there. You will talk to Benny before you do anything?"

The colonel jammed the cork lid onto the crock of mustard and tamped it down with one large fist.

"The difficulty," he said, "isn't Benny. The difficulty is what to tell the other lads. If they don't know Benny is female, then they have exhibited all manner of vulgar and unseemly behaviors around her. The lads will be mortified, and Benny will lose her friends, while I will be branded a traitor because I knew and didn't warn the boys. Morale will suffer. Regimental politics are more complicated than waging war."

Something wistful in his tone caught Ann's ear. "Do you miss the military?"

"Not in the least. You mentioned spices?"

"Tarragon, thyme, a dash of dried onion if you have it."

He waved a hand toward the pantry. "Explore to your heart's content, but mind you, I am truly hungry, and all of your subtle art will be lost on me."

"It won't be lost on me." Ann soon had toasted cheese sandwiches cut into triangles. She served that fare with a plate of peach slices and tankards of summer ale. Peaches were still a rarity in most households and not a fruit Ann had worked with in a professional sense.

Perhaps... but no. If an idea originated anywhere but in Monsieur's handsome head, the idea was not worth pursuing.

"Best eaten hot," Ann said, taking a seat at the worn table near the hearth. To her surprise, the colonel held her chair. "Thank you."

He took the place across from her and bowed his head. "For what we are about to receive, we are pathetically grateful, and that includes gratitude for the company as well. Amen."

They ate with their hands, the colonel exhibiting the sort of focused enthusiasm for the food that would gratify any cook. He left not a crumb on the plate, but partook only sparingly of the peaches.

"Finish the fruit," he said. "You enjoy it."

"I do," Ann said, picking up another succulent slice. "The peach would go well with cinnamon, nutmeg, cloves, perhaps a dash of vanilla, though the fruit flavor is subtle, and thus the spices must be understated as well. This is a fruit that would make excellent dessert sauces, and a peach compote has possibilities as well."

He took a considering sip of his ale. "You are passionate about cooking."

The colonel offered a mere observation, but Ann's guard went up from long habit. "Every creature must eat, and preparation of safe and nutritious fare ought to be of central importance to any society."

He regarded her in the flickering light cast by the hearth fire. "The kitchen is more than that for you. It's a calling. You put up with the tyrant in the Coventry's kitchen because you learn from him, though flattering his vanity grates on your soul."

Ann took the last peach slice, wanting to savor it. "Has your soul been grated?"

"Like a hard cheese upon the reality of military life. I'll walk you back to the Coventry when you're finished eating."

A mental portcullis had just been dropped. "I've no need of an escort, Colonel. I am not your sister, a fine lady who marries into titled families."

He gave her an appraising look. If Ann had been one of his subordinates, that look would have inspired her to part with her innermost secrets and most desperate dreams. She'd cast them before him like a child emptying her pockets to exonerate her from a crime that had yet to be named.

The crime of independent dreams, in her case.

"Mrs. Dorning cannot be blamed for her first marriage," the colonel said, rising. "Her second marriage was apparently a love match."

"You don't believe in marrying for love?"

He took the empty plate to the dry sink. "I don't believe in marrying at all, for the present. What others do is no concern of mine, but if Dorning makes Jeanette miserable, he won't live to regret it for long. What sort of supplies will Benny need?"

Ann explained the mechanics of sewing linen around a wad of sponge and affixing a string. She left the details of using the resulting profoundly intimate article to the colonel's imagination, though he showed no embarrassment with the topic.

"What of bandages?" he asked. "As I recall, the ladies in camp requisitioned a portion of our old linen sheets and had special... They laundered them separately for reuse."

"Have a word with your housekeeper," Ann suggested. "She and her daughter regularly face the same inconvenience, and they will grasp the situation readily enough."

"Not a conversation I look forward to." He collected Ann's cloak from the peg she'd hung it on. The garment was warm from the fire's heat, and he did her the courtesy of holding it for her.

"We should tidy up," Ann said, though, in truth, she simply wanted an excuse to tarry. The kitchen and pantries needed a thorough scrubbing if the spices weren't to take on the scent of dust and the cheese the odor of coal.

"We should get you back to the Coventry. Dorning will note your absence, and I will be interrogated. Concocting a credible tale to offer him will take some delicacy."

Ann donned her straw hat. "Why not tell your sister the truth?" And why not marry? The colonel was attractive in a severe way, he was fastidious, he cared for children, and he owned a profitable champagne vineyard, among other holdings.

An eye patch and a taciturn disposition were easily overlooked if a man was sober, solvent, and reasonable.

"Because," the colonel said, bowing Ann through the back door, "to explain the situation to Jeanette, I'd have to call on her, and this I am loath to do. She has acquired nieces, nephews, and in-laws by the platoon, to say nothing of a shamelessly attentive spouse, and I am *de trop*."

He offered Ann his arm, another courtesy she hadn't anticipated. She took it, expecting to be half marched along the street, but the colonel's pace was moderate and matched to hers.

"What bothers you most about Benny's situation?" she asked, when it became apparent that the colonel had no conversational pleasantries to offer.

He was silent for some dozen yards. Around them, London was shifting into its nocturnal rhythms, with fancy coaches replacing mounted traffic and linkboys hustling off to await custom outside the larger gatherings. Near the theaters and in the parks, a different sort of commerce would be getting under way. Might the colonel detour on his route home to sample those wares?

Ann hoped not, for his sake. He was too grand a man to expire of the diseases that went with casual evening encounters on London's streets.

"What bothers me about Benny's situation," he said, "once I get past the mortification of not having seen it for myself, is that we must let her go. She cannot remain in the boys' dormitory, I have no lady of the house to provide proper supervision to her, and yet, Benny is one of ours. She belongs with us, and we must let her go."

They approached the back entrance to the Coventry, which was illuminated with several lanterns. The sadness in the colonel's voice was all the more apparent for being quietly offered. He passed Ann her basket, bowed, and would have marched off into the night without another parting word.

Through the Coventry's open windows, Ann could smell roasted beef, baked potatoes, fresh bread, and sweat—the kitchen was hot and noisy, and for once, she would rather not join the culinary affray.

"Nobody fretted over letting me go," she said. "I wasn't much older than your Benny, and I promise you, Colonel, it will matter to her that you and the boys will miss her. I will call upon you later this week, and we can discuss Benny's situation at greater length."

She hugged him again, because he worried for a girl, because he kept his distance from a sister awash in wedded bliss, because he knew women should not be ordered about.

"I am in your debt," he said, his arms closing around her tentatively. "You need not trouble yourself further on Benny's behalf."

Or his. The words went without saying. Ann stepped back after indulging in a good whiff of bracing lavender.

"I will call on you Wednesday nonetheless. Even undercooks have a half day."

No emotion registered on his lean countenance, not relief, resentment, nothing. "Until Wednesday, then." He bowed again, but waited at the foot of the back steps when Ann expected him to stalk away.

More courtesy, more gentlemanly consideration. His polite gestures wrapped her in warmth as substantial as any hug.

"Good night, Colonel."

"Good night, Miss Pearson, and thank you."

He would wait in the night air until Domesday, a conscientious sentry, so Ann slipped into the Coventry and traded her cloak for an apron. She had the oddest sense that the colonel had been thanking her for attending the girl and also for feeding him, sharing a meal with him, and perhaps—maybe—for hugging him.

CHAPTER THREE

The Aurora Club was not in St. James's proper, nor was it in the first stare of fashion. Members joined for the decent cooking, the quiet ambience, and the company of men who were honorable, but not too virtuous. Not all were former military. A few were younger sons seeking respite from the more fashionable venues patronized by older siblings and papas.

Rye was joined at table by two men he would cheerfully have taken a bullet for—his cousins, and much more than mere cousins—though explaining Benny's situation even to them had to wait until the brandy was making the rounds.

"Bit of a contretemps on the domestic front," Rye said, offering the decanter to his companions.

"Putting your handsome foot in parson's mousetrap, are you?" Captain Dylan Powell asked, shaking his head at the proffered libation.

Powell was the sweetest of men, his voice imbued with the musical signature of the native Welshman. He was above medium height, blessed with rakish dark hair and a dimple, and could flash a smile to melt the reserve of the sternest dowager.

Powell was a dissenting preacher's son sent to the army to sow his wild oats, and he often made the sentimental declarations other men didn't dare even think. He was easy to like, but his temper—slow to ignite, terrible to behold—made him not as easy to befriend.

When he got to muttering in his native tongue, prudent men located the nearest exit.

His friends at the Aurora were not particularly prudent.

"I'll have a nip," Major Alasdhair MacKay said. "Or more than a nip. The English weather makes a man old before his time." MacKay was what the regimental ladies had called a braw, bonnie laddie, with dark chestnut hair and Viking-blue eyes. As a younger man, he'd been a dedicated flirt, and like Powell, he had a temper. Unlike Powell, MacKay's wrath was often a function of nothing more serious than an empty belly.

Drunk or sober, wielding a Baker rifle, MacKay could also hit the epaulette on a galloping cuirassier from three hundred yards.

A desultory rain had begun as Rye had made his way to the club, just enough wet to turn the cobbled streets slick, not enough to deter him from the prospect of an excellent beef steak. Sandwiches with Miss Pearson had made a fine appetizer—exceptionally fine—but only that.

Rye passed the brandy to MacKay, who took only enough to be polite.

"The Scottish winters make a man dead before his time," Powell observed. "If you want well-behaved rain, come to Wales. You can't see it coming down, it's so gentle, and the rainbows are magnificent."

"And you can't keep the Welsh rain from soaking your entire kit," MacKay replied, swirling his brandy. "You getting hitched, Goddard?"

The question was casually put—both times—but an unspoken tension had arisen at the table. To break ranks was bad form, while to lead a charge showed memorable courage. The first of Rye's circle to marry would do a little of both.

"Who would have me?" Rye asked. "My problem is Benny."

"The nipper who wears the cap?" MacKay asked. "Delicate lad. Is it his lungs?"

Rye rose, drink in hand. "Let's take this to the reading room."

The reading room was predictably deserted, also poorly named. Little reading happened here, but for the occasional newspaper perused of a morning. The Aurora's members more often read their papers in the dining room, each man for the most part at a solitary table. An occasional comment would be offered to the room at large about the latest scandal or feat of government stupidity, but the object of the exercise was to be alone together.

The reading room was for drinking not-alone together.

"Has the lad run off?" Powell asked. "Boys and mischief can't seem to resist each other."

Rye took the wing chair closest to the hearth. MacKay took another, while Powell wandered the room.

"The lad is a girl," Rye said, small words to describe a large problem. He took off his eye patch, stuffed it into a pocket, and scrubbed his brow.

"And how," MacKay said carefully, "did you stumble upon that revelation?"

A slight menace underlay the question. MacKay was nothing if not protective of the ladies. Rye suspected a matter of the heart drew MacKay to London as winter approached, for clearly, the man was homesick for his chilly Highlands.

"The female indisposition befell Benny," Rye said, "and I gather she had no idea what was amiss. Poor lad—nipper, *girl*—thought she was dying."

Powell said something in his native Welsh.

"I heard that," MacKay replied, tacking on something unintelligible in the Highland tongue. They could mostly understand each other, which was fortunate when Powell's temper flared. MacKay would offer some terse guidance in Gaelic, and Powell would regain his composure—sometimes.

"Helluva thing," Powell said, "to find a female lurking undetected among the infantry."

"But it happens," Rye replied. Sometimes the ladies joined up to avoid starvation, sometimes they took the king's shilling to pursue the man who'd stranded them at the altar, but it did happen, and became the stuff of late-night camp stories. "Benny was miserable."

"'Tisn't fair, what the ladies endure," Powell observed. "Eve offered Adam the apple, and so every woman is relegated to suffering. If Adam had been a better husband, he'd have told her, 'Evie, me love, I'd rather have your kisses than that stupid apple.' He'd have chucked the fruit and kept paradise for us all. But no, he was useless to her when she needed him to show some sense, and what was he thinking, allowing her to wander off on her own in Eden?"

"Dissenters," MacKay muttered. "Goddard has a problem, so please don't start spouting Scripture."

"My problem," Rye said, "is complicated. If the other boys know Benny is of the female persuasion, then I can intimate that I knew, too, and was waiting for Benny to say something. If they didn't know, I have to extricate Benny from the household without anybody's feelings being hurt or secrets being betrayed."

"I care naught for secrets," MacKay said. "But you can't blame the wee lassie. London is—"

"Hell's privy, for an orphaned female," Powell finished for him. "We know, MacKay." He took the chair between Rye's and MacKay's. "What does young Benny have to say for herself?"

"I'm giving her time to sort that out."

Powell shoved Rye's shoulder and sank into a reading chair between Rye and MacKay. "You're at a complete loss and stalling your arse off."

"That too. She was uncomfortable. Physically uncomfortable."

"Cordial with a tot of the poppy," Powell said. "My sisters, who know everything, swear by it."

"If you were my brother, I'd take to tippling too," MacKay

replied. "You need a woman, Goddard, to speak to the lass. To explain the things men don't know."

"What don't we know?" Powell retorted, crossing his arms and putting his booted feet up on a hassock. "If that girl spent any time on the streets, she knows where babies come from. Live demonstrations take place nightly mere steps from the theaters."

"There's more to it than that," MacKay said. "Mess and pain, calendars and tisanes. Mysterious female whatnot. What will you do, Goddard?"

"I thought I'd consult men with more experience than I have." The sight in Rye's left eye was improving, at least under low light. Compared to the months immediately following his injury, when he'd dared not open his bad eye in full sunlight, he'd come far.

"Consult your sister," Powell said, closing his eyes. "Sisters know everything. They are born knowing everything. Witness, my sister Bronwen suggested I join up. Wellington would still be toiling his way across Spain if I hadn't lent him a hand."

MacKay smacked Powell's arm. "Wellington was dead stuck until I arrived, and you know it."

Rye had been dead stuck until these two had shown up in the officers' mess. He'd been close to them in his youth, and they'd brought with them memories both happy and embarrassing.

Only Rye had been saddled with a knighthood, but for each man, peacetime posed a special kind of problem.

"The way I see it," Powell said, "Benny is still one of your lads. You put the situation to her same as you would any difficult mission. There's an objective, terrain, enemy lookouts, the usual hazards. What is the objective, by the way?"

To keep the girl safe. The objective was always to keep the rank and file safe from avoidable perils. "That's part of the challenge. Benny has some say in what the objective is, doesn't she?"

"Nothing for it," MacKay said, leaning past Powell to appropriate a sip from Rye's glass. "You must talk to the girl. Have a straight-up, man-to-man, er... well, an honest talk with her."

"Good luck." Powell's words held not a hint of teasing.

"You two have been no help whatsoever," Rye replied, getting to tired feet. "I believe I'll frolic in the rain rather than waste any more of my time here." The temptation to fall asleep in the exquisitely comfortable chairs by the roaring fire in the company of good friends was nigh overwhelming.

But Rye avoided leaving the children without an adult in the house overnight, and MacKay was right: An honest conversation with Benny was unavoidable.

"You've made out your will, right?" Powell said as Rye stretched in the fire's heat. "I get the horses."

"MacKay gets Scipio, you get Agricola, but you have to agree to take some of the lads too."

"I'll send them to my sisters," Powell said. "Look how well I turned out, after all."

MacKay didn't dignify that with a riposte.

"Thank you, gentlemen," Rye said, "for a pleasant meal."

"Let us know how it goes." MacKay saluted with Rye's drink. "Women are complicated, and they develop that quality earlier in life than is convenient, to my way of thinking."

"I wouldn't know." On that statement of lowering fact, Rye left his friends to their brandy. They were conversing softly in what passed for their common language as he closed the door to the reading room.

Did he and Benny still have a common language? He pondered that question all the way home, but still had no satisfactory answer when he summoned her for an audience in the morning.

THE PAIN HAD EASED, as Miss Ann had said it would. The awkwardness of facing the colonel was growing by the moment.

Benny stood at attention before the great desk, while Colonel Goddard flicked beads on an abacus before her. They were never to call their commanding officer Sir Orion, though he'd been knighted along with hundreds of other brave soldiers.

Once upon a time, Benny had wanted to be a knight.

"So how did you make Miss Pearson's acquaintance?" the colonel asked, putting down his pencil.

"You had us watching the marchioness last spring, and I... the scents from the Coventry's kitchen are ever so lovely. I took to biding in the maple tree in the garden there, and Miss Ann smelled me."

The colonel regarded her with that slightly raised eyebrow the boys dreaded. He wore his eye patch today, doubtless to hide the scars, but all that patch did was make him look more fierce.

"Gracious, child, is bathing really all that distasteful?"

Benny shook her head.

"Ah," the colonel said, coming around the desk and propping a hip on one corner. "You wore camouflage. Soot on the cheeks, dirt on your elbows. Clever of you."

Benny flicked a confused gaze at him. "I deceived you, sir."

"Have a seat."

Benny would rather have leaped out the window, but Miss Ann had said *the business* would result in others viewing Benny differently. The colonel had never invited Benny to have a seat before, for example. *The business* was awkward, but also grown up. That wasn't all bad, was it?

Benny sank into a chair and nearly did bolt out the window when the colonel took the chair beside hers.

"I never did inquire whether you were a boy or a girl, did I?" he mused. "You did not deceive me, so much as I deceived myself. Do the boys know?"

This conversation was extraordinary because it *was* a conversation, a discussion rather than an interrogation or handing down of orders.

"I 'spect Otter does. He kept mum, though."

"Otter excels at keeping mum. How are you feeling?"

Benny had the oddest sense the colonel was stalling. "Fidgety.

Miss Ann said there's no reason to give my courses more than a passing thought, and soon I will pay no more attention to them than I do a monthly bout of hay fever. I do not care for the bellyache part."

"What lady would? But that's the problem, Benny, you are a lady, a female, and this is a bachelor household. You cannot continue to bide here unless I find a housekeeper to live in, and even then..."

Benny nodded. She'd had two good years with the colonel. Plenty to eat, a safe place to sleep. A roaring hearth in winter, books to puzzle over, and mates, even if the boys weren't exactly her friends. She had learned to read properly, made a start on French—she could speak it passably already—and learned some ciphering.

"I'll go, sir. I can apply to the agencies for a maid's post, and I'm a hard worker."

A silence stretched, and the ache in Benny's throat eclipsed yesterday's tearing pain in her vitals. She had hoped for the impossible and put off the inevitable as long as she could.

"Who are your people, Benny? You speak well enough when you want to, and you're taller than the average urchin. You were given a name worthy of a preacher's daughter, and—"

"I won't go back there. I'll pike off, in truth, sir, and not even the lads will be able to find me. I have me wages." Ire made Benny less careful with her diction, but especially now, she must not return to the place she'd once called home.

"Benny, I forbid you to take to the stews. You can still impersonate a boy for some time, but boys on the streets aren't much safer than girls. Eventually, somebody will uncover the truth of your situation."

The colonel's order came as pathetic relief, for Benny would never disobey a direct command. "I don't want to go, sir. This is me home."

"All children leave home eventually, Benny, though if it were up to me, I'm not ready to part with you either. Is there a profession you'd like to pursue? A trade or calling?"

"I want to read better. Miss Ann shows me words when we sit in the garden together. And she knows French and German and Eye-talian. I sometimes help out at the Coventry when my chores are done here."

The colonel shook the abacus so all the beads slid to one side. "The Coventry is a glorified gaming hell, Benny. Not a place I'd like to see you employed."

"Meaning no disrespect, but it's a supper club, sir, and the dishes Miss Ann makes... She says spices are the secret, but she knows about more than spices. She gave me a crepe once, with cream and blueber-ries... all hot and buttery. I dream about the crepe."

"You smile when you describe it."

Was smiling a bad thing? The colonel never smiled, and he certainly wasn't smiling now, so perhaps it was. "You'd smile, too, sir, if ever you did eat one of Miss Ann's crepes."

"I daresay I would. We should move you out of the dormitory, Benny."

"Then they'll all know."

"A lady is entitled to some privacy."

"I ain't... I am not a lady."

The colonel rose, and because he'd not given Benny leave to stand, she remained in her chair, and that made the colonel very tall indeed. Benny had never been afraid of the colonel, but she respected him rather a lot.

"That's the thing, young Benevolence Hannah," colonel said, resuming his perch against the desk. "You are a lady, maybe not in the sense of a fancy lord's daughter is, but in the sense that you are owed respect and protection. You are a lady, and you must never forget that."

Benny had deceived this man for years, and she would not deceive him now. "Me mam weren't a lady."

"She is deceased?"

"Dunno. Don't care." Had stopped caring the moment Mama had kissed Benny's cheek, told her to be good for *Madame*, and stepped into her fancy lord's coach.

"My father nearly died a bankrupt, Benny. Only my sister's timely marriage cleared my family's debts and let me buy my colors. Papa could well have expired in debtors' prison, in which case I would have been making my way on the streets as you did. You are not your mother, and the great lot of people who matter in this life won't know or care about your origins."

Benny wasn't sure what that speech was about, but the idea that the colonel could have ended up on the streets fascinated her.

"Miss Ann said I wasn't to worry. That you wouldn't toss me out."

"But you did worry, and I'm sorry for that. Miss Ann will call here later this week, and she might have some ideas where you're concerned. You cannot sleep in the dormitory again, Benny. Wouldn't be decent."

"I'll sleep in the stable, sir. Otter's farts are prodigious ripe. He favors the cabbage, he does. Eats it *on purpose* and then abuses us all night with the stink."

"Boys can be awful," the colonel said, gaze on the abacus. "You mustn't tell them I said that, and you will not sleep in the stable. I've asked the housekeeper if you can bide with her and her daughter at night if we can't find some other arrangement for you."

Mrs. Murphy was a good soul. She did not care for mud, and she was always blessing everybody's heart, but she laughed a lot and never begrudged a boy—a child—a slice of buttered bread.

Benny stood. "I'm not to be tossed out, then?"

"Never. You belong with us, Benny. You might take a position as a cook's apprentice if Miss Ann can find you one, you might go to work for a baker or as an under-nurserymaid, but we are your family, and you will always have a home with us."

"I'll have to start wearing girl clothes." This, along with regular applications of soap and water, was not an entirely unwelcome prospect.

"We all don the uniform of the regiment we're assigned to, Benny. You will face many adjustments, but you've already shown me that you are resilient, clever, and determined. Think of Miss Ann's crepes, and do what you must to learn how to make them for yourself."

"Make crepes, sir?" That possibility intrigued as a wildest dream intrigued. "You think I could?"

"In time, if you apply yourself, but I cannot speak for Miss Ann's willingness to teach you. Mrs. Murphy will take you 'round the shops this morning and find you some appropriate clothing, but, Benny, how does this situation sit with the boys?"

"Ask Otter. He mighta told 'em all without lettin' on. I should do my chores now, sir."

In the stable, Benny could rejoice in the knowledge that she wasn't to be cast back into the streets. In the stable, she could be relieved and happy and tell the horses and cats her good fortune.

"Do your chores today, but we'll have to reconsider assignments once you start wearing skirts. Mrs. Murphy can doubtless use more help in the kitchen for the nonce."

"I still want to rake the barn aisle morning and night, sir."

"You want to feed the damned cats."

"Aye, sir."

The colonel pushed to his feet, his countenance going quite stern. "You may be excused, but, Benny, I meant what I said."

"Sir?"

"This is your home, we are your regiment. If you take a mad fit and commit regicide, the first place you turn for help is here. If you gamble away the crown jewels, you come here to lament your folly. Do we have an understanding?"

Not exactly. Benny wasn't sure what committing regi-whatever meant, but she grasped that the colonel was saying something man-fashion that had to do with belonging and safety.

With caring.

She darted across the room before her courage deserted her, seized the colonel in a hug, which was like hugging one of the oak beams that held up the barn roof, and then scampered for the door.

She wasn't to be sent away, and someday, she might learn to make blueberry crepes.

As she pulled the door closed behind her, Benny made a mental note to ask Miss Ann what *resilient* meant. The colonel had said the word as if it were a good thing, so Benny wanted to know what it signified.

"SIX COURSES," Ann said, quite firmly. "The traditional progression plus cordials after the dessert."

"No extra removes?" Aunt Melisande asked. "At Helene Craighead's last formal dinner, she had extra removes and another cold dish after the entrées. People talked about her extravagance for a week."

"You want them talking about the menu," Ann replied. "The exquisite pairing of the wines and course selections, the beautiful presentation, the faultless service, and the gracious conversation. Guests stop tasting what you put in front of them when the menu is too lavish."

A truth too many hostesses never grasped.

"You are certain?" Aunt set aside the menu Ann had spent hours researching and testing. "The brigadier gives me great latitude with my entertainments. He expects food worthy of our standing."

When had a lot of retired generals and their wives and daughters become more finicky than a pack of dowager duchesses?

"I am absolutely certain, Aunt. You could feed your guests buttered bread and mulled cider, and if you made them feel welcome, provided interesting conversation, and sent them away full, they'd enjoy the evening."

"You have little grasp of polite society if you believe that."

When Aunt frowned, she conjured up both the spoiled young woman she'd been prior to marrying Uncle and the settled matron she was becoming. She was still beautiful—a wife nearly twenty years younger than her husband was well advised to remain beautiful as long as she could—but Melisande was perpetually discontent, and that showed.

"I feed polite society every evening, Aunt. I see what disappears from the buffet a quarter hour after it's served, what remains unfinished at the end of the evening. I know which dishes are all clever presentation—popular the first time we set it out, not of much interest thereafter—and which are constant favorites. At the Coventry, I can experiment without anybody the wiser, and I take advantage of that privilege."

Aunt poured herself another cup of tea, a stout black that had beery notes on the tongue. "You should not be working in that place, Ann. If anybody learned that my niece…. Suffice it to say, the brigadier is not happy with the situation either."

Ann had been hearing this refrain for three years. "I am well compensated for my time. I get to cook to my heart's content, and I am learning much." A small falsehood. Jules had stopped presenting new recipes less than a year after he'd taken over as chef. "Have you had a chance to pass my menu suggestions to Mrs. Bainbridge?"

"Yesterday. She was intrigued. An apple cider glaze for scallops would certainly be novel."

The glaze was delicious. "That recipe is also simple to prepare, which matters, and can be made with ingredients common to any country kitchen." Honey, dark vinegar, pepper, spinach, bacon… nothing fancy, though the results were impressive.

Impressive mattered to a London hostess more than flavorful, nutritious, or cheap to prepare, while for Ann, expense would always be a consideration.

The Pearsons were gentry, but Grandpapa had been wealthy enough to afford London seasons for his daughters. Mama had married a solicitor, and there had been ample funds to send Ann to various schools and academies, each more pretentious than the last. She had run away for the final time at age fourteen, and by then, Mama and Papa had succumbed to influenza, Grandpapa had been

ailing, and Aunt had been following the drum in Spain as the dutiful
wife of the brigadier.

Ann tried a bite of shortbread and wished she hadn't. "You can
tell Mrs. Bainbridge I am available to discuss the menus at her
convenience."

Aunt set down her tea cup. "No, I cannot. As far as Emily Bainbridge is concerned, you bide in genteel obscurity down at the family
seat in Sussex. You send me recipes by post, and that's the extent of
your culinary eccentricity.

"You insist on disgracing your upbringing," Melisande went on,
"by laboring like some scullery maid. If that became common knowledge, Emily Bainbridge would be serving up the gossip for the next
five years. You know you are welcome to bide here as my companion,
and despite your age, I live in hope that your selfish flight will end in
matrimony. That can't happen unless you put aside your foolish
attachment to cooking, of course, because no man wants to take in
hand a headstrong, unnatural female."

Ann needed Melisande's connections, needed her entrée into
polite society's dining rooms and buffets. She chose her words carefully as a result.

"If I used my inheritance to open a school, would that be less of
an embarrassment?"

"A *cooking* school?" Melisande's tone conveyed both disdain and
amusement, as if cooking weren't a necessary daily undertaking in
most households. "Were you a French chef of considerable renown,
then such an enterprise would be bearable, but you are not, and you
never will be."

"French chefs can be more trouble than they're worth. Let me
know what Mrs. Bainbridge says, and please tell her I have more
recipes if these won't suit."

"Your mother would die a thousand deaths to know what's
become of you."

Your cook is cheating on the shortbread with lard. Your devoted brigadier has been seen at the Coventry with Emily Bainbridge clinging to his arm.

"I am content, Aunt." A trifle lonely, truth be told, and utterly sick of Monsieur's drama in the kitchen, but happy too. That Mama might well have been mortified by Ann's vocation barely signified.

"You think you are content," Melisande said, offering a plate of petits fours, "and I know what it is to be young and in thrall to silly dreams, so I turn a blind eye to your stubbornness for now. Promise me the Coventry's guests never see you, Ann. You owe the brigadier and me, as well as your future expectations, that degree of discretion."

"Our chef isn't about to allow the guests to see the army of minions who turn his ideas into delicious reality." Ann managed a sip of her tea. "The Marchioness of Tavistock has consulted me for menus."

"She's Mrs. Dorning now, unless somebody wants to show her undue courtesy. Her husband is your employer. Of course she consults you."

The marchioness did not consult Monsieur, and that drove him to sniffing and pouting as badly as if his soufflé had fallen.

The point of the call had been achieved. Ann had made certain Mrs. Bainbridge had her menu and turned over another list of suggestions for Aunt Melisande's upcoming officers' dinner.

"If your cook has questions," Ann said, rising, "please let me know. Some of the recipes are complicated, and she should practice them before serving them to your guests."

"She has enough experience with your *suggestions* by now to know that, though I must say, the results are delicious and present well."

"Is that a compliment, Aunt?"

Melisande rose gracefully, her airs still those of the regimental darling. "I do not doubt your talent, Ann, merely your good sense. You could have married a wealthy cit and put on all the lavish dinners you pleased, but you insist on squandering your good name on sculpted potatoes. I worry about you."

On the quiet nights, when Monsieur retired early and left the kitchen entirely in Ann's hands, she worried too. The Coventry could be closed down with a single raid, or Monsieur could have her fired on a whim. The Dornings might sell the club, and the new owner could see the kitchen staff replaced.

Ann's inheritance was safely invested, but Melisande was right: The post of undercook was not a certain path to fame and acclaim.

"You worry for nothing," Ann said as Melisande escorted her to the front door. "I am happy, and my employers value me."

The hour was too early for the butler to be manning the door in anticipation of morning callers, so Melisande herself passed Ann her cloak.

"Your mother was headstrong," Melisande said. "Papa wanted a minor title for her, a younger son at least, even a barrister might have served, but she had to have her solicitor."

Aunt and Mama had been fifteen years apart in age and thus hadn't known each other well. "Mama and Papa were devoted, as you and Uncle are."

Melisande's expression turned wistful. "I was headstrong once too, Ann. Nothing good comes of women who want more than their due. I wish you would remember that. Only the brigadier's vast patience with a younger wife saved me from making a complete cake of myself."

The brigadier had made a cake of himself at the faro table not a week past.

"You don't often speak of the early years of your marriage," Ann said, pulling on her gloves. "Following the drum sounds patriotic and glamorous, but I imagine it was trying as well."

Melisande rearranged the folds of a man's greatcoat hanging on a peg. The scents of tobacco and beeswax clung to the wool, which was excellent quality. The brigadier came from old money—old, modest money. He was a distant, if polite, uncle and, according to Aunt Meli, much respected at Horse Guards.

"I was not suited to many aspects of being an officer's wife," Melisande said. "I suspect few young women are. I will see you next Wednesday, weather permitting."

She pulled Ann in for a hug, a surprisingly affectionate gesture, and Ann hugged her back. Melisande meant well, and maybe someday, the menus Ann passed to her would have their intended effect.

"Where are you off to now?" Melisande asked, stepping back.

"I must call upon Colonel Sir Orion Goddard," Ann said. "We have a mutual project to discuss."

The warmth in Melisande's eyes evaporated. "He's a single gentleman of dubious repute, Ann. Your good name will be tarnished past all bearing if you make a habit of such company and such behavior."

"The colonel's sister is married to my employer, and he has been all that is gentlemanly in my presence. I am not a brigadier's pretty wife, Aunt. I am an undercook by choice. If the colonel wants to discuss a menu with me, I cannot receive him at the club, can I?"

Not that he'd set foot there, and not that the colonel looked to be anything more than a beefsteak-and-ale man.

"Be exceedingly careful," Aunt said. "Your uncle is notably reticent on the subject of the colonel's military record. Goddard does not merit a place at the brigadier's military dinners."

"Fortunately," Ann said, gathering up her parasol, "the war is over." Some wars were over. "I bid you good day, Aunt, and will see you next week."

Ann left, relieved as always to be free from the gently relentless censure of her only living relative. Melisande was gaining a reputation as a hostess of some renown, no little thanks to Ann's menus. Her *suggestions* extended to centerpieces, table linen, wine and spirits, and even the tea tray following the meal.

Ann loved to create not merely a meal, but an occasion at supper.

Aunt scolded her consistently for that ambition, and just as consistently requested Ann's aid.

"I should be used to her hypocrisy by now," Ann muttered, declining to open her parasol. The sharp autumn sunshine felt good on her face, though the lingering taste of lard marred an otherwise beautiful morning. Aunt's cook was probably selling the extra butter out the back door, as many a cook did with her employer none the wiser. Lard could lighten the texture of a piecrust, to be sure, but in shortbread it wasn't to be borne.

Ann turned her steps in the direction of Colonel Sir Orion's abode, her mind consumed with two puzzles. First, Aunt was drinking more, probably gin in her morning tea. Not genteel, but a soldier's wife brushed up against the ungenteel occasionally, and gin was a discreet drink. Most people would have been unable to detect evidence of its consumption.

Second, if Colonel Goddard's military record was so dubious, why had he attained the rank of colonel and then been knighted? That made no sense. None at all.

CHAPTER FOUR

"Benny has developed a routine," Rye said, realizing in the same moment that he should have rung for a tea tray. Ann Pearson wasn't a fancy lady, but Rye needed a substantial favor from her, and she was a lady of the un-fancy sort. "Forgive me, I am out of the habit of entertaining guests. Shall I ring for tea?"

Mrs. Murphy might well be off at market, in which case Rye would look like a fool for offering courtesies he could not produce.

"No, thank you," Miss Pearson replied. "I have already enjoyed my morning tea. Tell me of Benny's routine."

God be thanked for a woman who didn't fuss. "Benny has taken a room upstairs—the governess's room, I suppose. The lads helped her kit it out and scrub it down. She rises, attires herself as a boy, and joins the others for breakfast. Her day begins with chores in the stable, and when those are complete, she changes into a dress. She assists Mrs. Murphy for the balance of the day and makes another pass through the stable after supper."

Miss Pearson had the gift of sitting quietly. She did not fluff her skirts, twiddle her lace collar, or toy with a bracelet intended to call attention to her graceful hands. She perched on the sofa, perfectly at home in Rye's guest parlor, which he'd asked Mrs. Murphy to dust and air in anticipation of this call.

Rye had no use for this room whatsoever. He managed his affairs from his office and retired to his personal sitting room when he was done with the business of the day.

"Despite this routine, Colonel, you worry for the girl."

Rye cast himself onto the sofa beside his guest, then realized he ought to have taken a wing chair, and *then* realized he ought to have asked her permission to sit.

He rose. "I beg your pardon. I did not mean to presume." Though he was about to presume mightily. For Benny's sake, he must.

Miss Pearson patted the sofa cushion. "Please do join me, Colonel. I am frequently a puzzle to my betters. My speech is that of a finishing school graduate, and my antecedents are genteel enough, but to the consternation of all, I delight in beating egg whites into meringue. Experimenting with spices is my guilty pleasure."

Rye sank into a wing chair. "I do not number among your betters."

"A lady refrains from arguing with a gentleman, else I should correct you, *Sir Orion*."

She looked so prim and serene in his parlor, and yet, he'd seen her scamper up a barn ladder while holding a basket. She'd known his kitchen at sight better than he knew it, and she wasn't too proud to look in on Benny.

"What makes you think I'm a gentleman?"

"You care for Benny and the lads. You came at once when your sister was in peril. You labor mightily to retrieve your family holdings from the brink of ruin. You receive me here—a room recently treated to a thorough dose of beeswax and lemon oil, unlike the rest of your abode—rather than in your office."

Rye seized on the least bothersome observation. "You noticed the scents of beeswax and lemon oil?" He certainly hadn't.

Miss Pearson tapped her nose, which shaded a trifle on the bold side. "A competent cook pays attention to the senses of taste and smell."

Ann Pearson paid attention to much more than that. Her perspicacity was at once troublesome and reassuring. Benny would thrive under her tutelage, if Rye could persuade the woman to take on that challenge.

"You are more than a competent cook," he said. "You are second-in-command to one of the foremost chefs in London. That a woman holds that post is most unusual."

"Unusual, but neither illegal nor unheard of. Most cooks are women."

"I was trying to pay you a compliment, not incite a skirmish. Will you take Benny on as an apprentice? I have racked my brains for a subtle approach to that request, but subtlety has ever eluded me. Besides, you strike me as a woman inured to plain speaking."

Though not quite that plain. Truly, Rye had been away from polite society, and from ladies of any sort, for too long.

Miss Pearson's brows rose, then drew down. "You flatter me, Colonel, and Benny would doubtless make an apt pupil, but I cannot take on the responsibility for an apprentice. I haven't the authority, and the introduction of an assistant to the undercook without prior permission from the chef would be akin to petit treason."

Well, damn. Protocol had been the very devil in the army. "Benny cannot stay here much longer, and she cannot be cast upon the charity of the employment agencies. As soon as her gender becomes apparent, the talk will start."

Miss Pearson rummaged in her reticule and produced a small tin with flowers etched on the lid. "Would you care for a pastille, Colonel? I make them myself."

Rye avoided sweets, but all this infernal talking had left him parched. He took two. The flavor was a smooth peppermint, refreshing without bitterness. Miss Pearson took two as well.

"Could Benny not simply remain here as a maid-of-all-work, Colonel? This is her home, after all."

Precisely what Rye had told the girl, more fool he. "First, my housekeeper does not prefer to bide here overnight, but is doing so only as a temporary favor to me. She has a follower and will not be denied his company indefinitely. Second, a maid-of-all-work holds a precarious and grueling post. If Benny must labor for eighteen hours a day, then she should at least have a trade or profession to show for her efforts. Third, Benny adores your blueberry crepes."

Miss Pearson's smile was unexpected and luminous. "She does?" That smile would inspire new recruits to babbling and seasoned officers to gawking and flattery. Such a smile held secrets and wishes come true and dreams brought to life.

When Miss Pearson smiled like that, she wasn't merely pretty, she was *alluring*.

Rye crunched his mints and mentally kicked himself. "Benny is a notably reticent creature, but about your blueberry crepes, she becomes as voluble as Otter discussing the finer points of mud larking. Benny dreams of those crepes."

"I fed her one just as the crop was ripening—weeks and weeks ago. I was experimenting with spices. Everybody assumes blueberries should be consigned to the same old cinnamon and nutmeg routine, or perhaps—for the adventurous—a dash of lemon zest. But I thought basil deserved a try, and lavender adds unexpected complexity. It's a pairing that makes people stop and wonder what exactly that little extra something is. Benny didn't gobble hers up either, but rather, savored every bite. I am babbling. I do apologize, but fruit flavors want a careful touch."

"You are passionate about your profession." At one time, Rye had been passionate about the profession of soldiering. Now he was passionate about his vineyards. Though, when had passion become dogged determination?

"You have the right of it, Colonel. I am passionate about cooking. I am supposed to want nothing more than a spouse and babies, my own household, and a domestic table to set every evening. Alas, I am more interested in *pièces montées* and sauces."

Rye liked Miss Pearson's honesty, though he saw little point in spun-sugar castles. "Wait until a spouse and babies are beyond your reach, Miss Pearson, and you might revise your assessment of their worth."

She glanced around the room, which had been well appointed by somebody. The wallpaper was flocked, the draperies lace, the andirons adorned with brass lions sejant.

"Your means do not limit your marital prospects, Colonel."

Perhaps her honesty had its drawbacks. "My past limits my marital prospects. My former commanding officer is no longer at home when I call. I make a tidy income, God be thanked, but rumors of misconduct from my army days haunt me and limit my business prospects. Now that my sister is comfortably remarried, I am free to rehabilitate my reputation." Perhaps then, Rye might find a woman equal to the task of turning a field command center into a home.

Miss Pearson produced her flowered tin again. "Have another mint."

They were good, as mints went. Pleasant. "You can see how Benny's situation becomes complicated."

Miss Pearson did not take a mint for herself. "Complicated, how?"

"If word gets out that I house a very young female without proper chaperonage, the worst conclusions will be drawn, about Benny and about me. For my sake as well as hers, I must find another solution." And *soon*. Talk spread through polite society faster than flame burned down a dry fuse.

"Surely you exaggerate, Colonel? Benny should be beneath the notice of the gossips."

"Benny's antecedents are not..." How to put it? "Benny is apparently not legitimate, and I gather her mother's profession..."

"Oh dear. That is unfortunate."

Silence crept into the conversation—embarrassed perhaps on Miss Pearson's part, thoughtful on Rye's. Miss Pearson held an unusual position, and she was ambitious too. That's what all that lemon zest and basil was about—ambition, a thirst for recognition, a desire to excel.

"What could I offer you, Miss Pearson, that would tempt you to take Benny on in your kitchen?"

She rose and pretended to study the cutwork yellowing behind glass near the window. "It's not my kitchen and will never be. The Coventry needs the cachet of a French chef."

"What do you need?" Rye grasped strategy, and he'd been an adequate officer as a result, though nobody would believe that now. He knew how to motivate his subordinates and how to brangle with his superiors such that they weren't offended, and all the bright ideas ended up being theirs.

Miss Pearson slanted a glance at him over her shoulder. She was petite but well formed, and her garb was fancier than that of a cook on her half day. Who were her people, and how had she come to be the Coventry's undercook?

"I need nothing, Colonel, but what I want is hard to explain."

"Try."

This time when she sat, she took the second wing chair, next to his, and perched on the edge of the cushions.

"I want menus, Colonel. I want to plan the most talked about, impressive, enjoyable formal dinners. I want to be the genius behind the buffet that is too pretty to eat, but too delicious to resist. I want my Venetian breakfasts to be the delight of all who attend because they are *breakfasts*, not mere excuses to flirt away the afternoon in Godmama's conservatory."

She spoke with the fervor of British officers who'd contemplated the conquest of France. Neither mountains, nor blizzards, nor bad rations, nor disease had been allowed to stand in their way, and Rye had shared that ambition.

Now rumor, the most insidious force of all, thwarted his plans.

"And if I could give you menus to plan?" he asked. "Would you take on Benny then?"

Miss Pearson swiveled her gaze to Rye. "I would if the decision were mine, but I would still lack the authority to hire her, sir. I am an employee at the Coventry, an underling. I have no more authority to hire staff there than a footman has authority to hire the boot-boy. You, however, are a family connection to one of the Coventry's owners."

Rye was brother to an owner's wife. "I do not expect my sister to publicly acknowledge me." In fact, Jeanette's former in-laws had done their part to cast aspersion on Rye's good name. The offending parties had left London several months ago, and yet, Rye was still the object of nasty rumors.

"You came when your sister was suffering with food poisoning," Miss Pearson said. "Dropped everything and would not leave until you knew she was safe. Will you not allow the marchioness to exert a small degree of influence to aid Benny? The kitchen needs more hands, Colonel, and the club can well afford another apprentice on its books."

Asking Jeanette for a favor was... Rye would sooner campaign across the whole of Spain in his bare feet.

"Crepes are simple to make," Miss Pearson went on. "Start with five basic ingredients, always sift the flour twice, and allow the batter to rest before cooking. That's important, the sifting and the resting."

She sounded like Rye on the topic of Burgundian grapes. "I have no idea what you're talking about."

"I'm talking about a young girl embarking on a profession that will support her well for the rest of her life and also make her happy. A word in your sister's ear, and Benny can have her dream."

Phrased like that, Rye could humble himself to make this request of Jeanette. A commanding officer put the welfare of his troops first. If the officer's pride suffered, that was of no moment.

"I'll see what I can do."

Miss Pearson rose. "What's the real reason you are reluctant to see Benny hired at the Coventry?"

Rye stood as well, as manners required. He'd secured Miss Pearson's support for the plan, which had been the objective of the interview. That was progress.

"I have asked you to take her on," he said, as they made their way from the parlor. "What makes you think I'm reluctant?"

"You are. I will keep her safe, Colonel. The Dornings do not tolerate bad behavior toward or among the staff. Monsieur will berate Benny regularly and perhaps reduce her to tears on occasion, but he will not strike her, and the footmen and waiters will not interfere with her."

"Did Monsieur make you cry?"

Miss Pearson paused at the front door. "He did, and that was foolishness on my part. No man's vanity is worth my tears. I would like to see Benny before I take my leave."

Some man's vanity had vexed Ann Pearson exceedingly. Whoever he was, Rye wished him to perdition.

"Benny is still in the stable," he said, draping Miss Pearson's cloak about her shoulders. "Why don't I leave you ladies to have a private chat, and then I will walk you back to the Coventry?"

Miss Pearson took her hat from him, but didn't put it on. "You need not provide me with an escort, Colonel. I am an undercook, not a grand lady."

She had made the point before. Rye took her hat and set it gently on her head. "Nonetheless, I have it on the best authority that I am a gentleman, so I will meet you in the stable in a quarter hour. The back terrace is this way. Do come along."

He strode down the corridor toward the library, and much to his surprise, Miss Pearson followed him without arguing.

"YOU HAD the lavender soap put in Benny's room, didn't you?" Ann asked as the colonel ambled at her side along the walkway. He apparently did not expect her to hang on his arm like some mincing ninnyhammer, but he did keep a pace Ann could easily match.

"What makes you think that?"

He tended to answer questions with questions, a sign of inherent caution. He would never get eggshells into his batter, but always crack his eggs over another bowl. Would he experiment with the recipes printed in the cookbooks, or keep strictly to the directions and ingredients listed?

What sort of lover would he be?

Ann tossed that thought into her mental midden, though she knew it would visit her again.

"Your housekeeper, Mrs. Murphy, favors chamomile soap, and that's what Otter uses as well. You, however, prefer French lavender, and now Benny washes with it too."

"You've met Otter."

Apparently not a cause for rejoicing. "He is a perfectly delightful boy, Colonel. How is it the children speak French?"

"My mother was French. I grew up speaking both English and French, and that ability served me well in the military, for the most part. The properties I hold in Champagne are through Mama's side of the family, though my paternal grandmother was also French. Through her, I claim rural land in Provence."

Hence the luscious soap. "And yet, with all that familial loyalty to France, you joined the British military."

His steps slowed as they approached a wider thoroughfare. "The English have no idea the trouble they cause when they go a-plundering. From Scotland to India and over to America, families have dealt with the British menace by assigning one son to each side of any conflict that involves Merry Olde England. Whichever son is on the winning side can salvage the family fortunes when the hostilities cease."

And alas for the other son. A military man would notice this aspect of history. "Is that how you ended up with your French holdings?"

He came to a halt, waiting for traffic on the street to clear. "Some of my maternal family made it to England when Napoleon routed the British forces at the siege of Toulon. Some remained behind, professing loyalty to France. None of those who survived in either land had an easy time of it, but knowing two languages improved their chances."

"Is everything with you a matter of survival, Colonel?" A coach and four thundered past, and Ann stepped off the walkway. Before her second foot could follow the first, she was snatched back onto the walkway and plastered against a hard male chest.

A curricle barreled along perilously close to the rear of the coach.

"Steady," the colonel growled. "Damned fool toffs drive like a trip to the tailor's is a race to Brighton."

Ann could not have moved if she'd wanted to, he held her that snugly, but then, if not for the colonel's support, her knees might have given out.

"He almost hit... I almost..." The curricle rattled around the corner, not a backward glance from the driver.

"You're safe. A near miss only. Breathe."

Ann breathed in lavender and warmth, a hint of saddle leather—the colonel apparently hacked out of a morning—and the soft wool of his coat. She breathed in composure and the steady calm of a man born to command.

But no, that wasn't quite right. Not command. In any case, she could not stand in the middle of the walkway parsing the colonel's scent while half of London gawked at the spectacle she made.

Ann stepped back. "Thank you. I should be more careful."

"Yonder driver should have been more careful." The colonel did offer his arm, and Ann allowed herself to grasp it. "Let's take the alley, shall we?"

He apparently knew where he was going, for by turns and shady backstreets, he brought her to the Coventry's garden gate.

"Do you often navigate by the alleys?" Ann asked.

"Yes. I don't often recount my French heritage, though it's common knowledge."

"*Je dois beaucoup à la langue Française, Colonel.*"

"And why do you owe much to the French language?"

The Coventry's garden walls were high—better than six feet—so nobody at the club would see Ann tarrying with her escort. She was peculiarly unwilling to part from him, too, and not simply because he had the reflexes of a cat.

"I had excellent French teachers at school," Ann said, "and when I sought a post as a cook's apprentice, I was hired because the Englishwoman I worked for could not read French. She needed my French, and I needed her instruction. I taught her what I could, because you are correct: A facility with both languages is never a hindrance and often a help."

Ann was fairly certain that smiling wasn't in the colonel's vocabulary, regardless of language, but his gaze did acquire a hint of humor.

"You are pragmatic," he said. "A fine quality in any officer."

"I am a cook, and if I want to read Carême's menus or his articles and recipes, I must know my French. Then too, our chef at the Coventry frequently lapses into French, and one wants to understand his mutterings. Thank you for your escort, sir."

The colonel flicked a glance at the closed garden gate. "This is your half day. Why come to your place of work?"

"I'll pop in and make sure the kitchen starts its day on sound footing. Our chef arrives in the early evening and remains until past midnight." Though Monsieur was arriving later and later and in an increasingly unreliable state of sobriety.

"That's not the whole reason." The colonel stepped a few paces away, pivoted, and returned. "Do you fear that if I know where you dwell, I'll trespass on the knowledge? Dump Benny on your doorstep like a foundling?"

Ann patted his lapel. She would not normally be so forward, but she wanted to rattle him a little—to see if he *could be* rattled—and she liked touching him.

"The habit of suspicion has too firm a grip on you, Colonel. I use my afternoons to experiment in the kitchen. Only junior staff is on hand, and my time is my own."

"Target practice and drills," he said, scowling down at her. "Does Sycamore Dorning appreciate what a treasure he has in you?"

Oh, probably not. Ann was neither French nor male nor—she hoped—a martinet. "I am well compensated for my labors."

"Not what I asked. My thanks for looking in on Benny, and I will have a word on her behalf with your employers."

Ann anticipated a salute and a dismissive *carry on, Pearson.* Instead, the colonel bowed.

"*Au revoir, mademoiselle.*" He straightened and would have marched off to instruct his urchins on the art of the siege or something had Ann not put a hand on his sleeve.

She had to go up on her toes to kiss his cheek. "Until next we meet, Colonel. I live in the boardinghouse beside the bakery around the corner. The door is blue." If he took a good whiff of her cloak, he might divine where she lived. "Thank you for your escort and for preventing me from injury or worse."

She lingered near enough to inhale the sunny essence of Provence one more time, then eased back.

The colonel's expression gave away nothing. Not dismay at her forwardness, not pleasure at her friendliness. If he was pleased, offended, bemused, or annoyed, she'd never know that from his gaze.

He touched her cheek with a gentle brush of his fingers. "Dorning and his club don't deserve you."

Then he stalked away.

All manner of odd feelings did battle inside Ann as she watched Colonel Sir Orion Goddard march off to his next battle. The emotional melee followed her inside as she divested herself of cloak and bonnet and washed her hands.

The season had passed for blueberries, but the pear harvest had been good, so she set out the ingredients for a batch of crepes and sorted through her impressions of the colonel. His manners wanted polish, he lacked any semblance of good cheer, and his own commanding officer would apparently not receive him.

But the colonel saw clearly what Ann herself hadn't wanted to admit: She was pulling more than her share of the load at the Coventry and getting far less than her share of the credit.

She admitted something else too: As a lover, Orion Goddard would be tender, tireless, and passionate. So very, very passionate.

RYE TOOK himself around to the main thoroughfare and paused for a moment of reconnaissance. The Coventry enjoyed a fashionable address, and the street was thus busy. A crossing sweeper dodged between vehicles to retrieve steaming treasure from the cobbles, narrowly avoiding the wheels of a barouche. The lad was tired or drunk, gin being cheaper than bread and more readily available to such as he.

"Is Dorning home?" Rye asked, flipping the child a coin.

"Aye, Colonel. So's his missus. The 'ousekeeper went to market at first light and came back midmorning. A pair of grooms is down the pub 'aving a pint."

"And you've been here since dawn?"

The boy nodded. "Small pickin's, Colonel. The ponies ain't poopin' on my watch. The Quality has gone off to the grouse moors and 'ouse parties."

Rye passed him two more coins. "The ponies will trample you if you don't get some rest." Rye put his fingers to his lips and let out a sharp whistle. "Louis will spell you while I call on my in-laws. How are things at home?"

The boy, whose somewhat humorous *nom de guerre* was Vulture, sported more than the usual number of bruises beneath his grime.

"Pa got slapped into the sponging 'ouse. Ma took the weans to her brother's, and Uncle don't like me much. I'm on me own for a time." This recitation was made with the perfect indifference of a scout who'd seen the entire French host approaching, arms at the ready.

The boy wasn't twelve years old, if that.

"You leave your barrow and shovel in the Coventry's stables of a night and come around to my house to bed down and take your meals. If you don't want to come inside, you can take the night watch in my stable. Louis will tell you we're a man down, though don't press him for details."

Vulture peered up at Rye with the combination of banked hope and bravado that betrayed a child on his last prayer.

"I don't care for baths, Colonel."

"Then take night watch in the stable,"—where the boy would find adequate warmth and safety and an abundance of blankets—"but you will wash your hands before eating, or Mrs. Murphy will report you for breach of manners."

A fortnight around the other boys, another two weeks of increasingly cold nights, and Vulture would submit to regular bathing. With any luck, he'd soon join the boys at their afternoon lessons, and they'd feel Benny's impending absence less keenly.

Louis trotted up from the discreet distance he'd maintained on the trek from Rye's house. "Vulture."

"Fat Louie."

They grinned at each other, clearly prepared to engage in a battle of insults, which would probably escalate to shoving, profanity, and fisticuffs, though Rye hadn't the time to indulge their good spirits.

"Vulture is late for his nooning, Louis. You will please take over for him while I call on my in-laws. Vulture might well be biding with us for a time, in which case I will need another sentry to keep watch from this post. I leave you gentlemen to discuss suitable resources for that office."

Vulture shot Louis a puzzled glance.

"He means you have to pick a lad to take over watching and sweeping for when you aren't here," Louis said. "A reliable lad with sharp eyes."

"Get something to eat," Rye said. "And I do mean food, Vulture, not just drink, or you'll end up in the sponging house, or worse."

The boy trotted off, while Louis surveyed the street. "His pa isn't in the sponging house, Colonel. His uncle set the watch on his pa for cursing the king. Half the Cock and Hen heard him."

And taverns, being full of the crown's spies, were stupid places to express honest sentiments regarding the monarchy's excesses.

"Vulture can bide with us for now. Please explain the rules to him, and he'll need a name once he starts sleeping in the house."

"Aye. His name's Victor. He don't use it much."

"Doesn't. Set a good example for him, Louis. I shouldn't be long."

Even if Rye spent only fifteen minutes in his sister's household, the time would be long. He crossed the street and rapped the knocker stoutly anyway. To his eternal frustration, Jeanette's husband opened the door—Sycamore Dorning's grasp of protocol was sadly lacking—and Rye thus found himself behind enemy lines without allies.

A daunting if familiar place to be.

"Colonel, good day." Dorning's tone was anything but welcoming. "Jeanette is napping, and not even for you will I wake her. She will interrogate me regarding the purpose of your call, so prepare to endure my company, and do not think to blow retreat. We are family now, and Jeanette will expect us to act like it."

He grabbed Rye by the sleeve and yanked him into the house.

CHAPTER FIVE

"Ann came around again?" The brigadier posed the question mildly over his luncheon soup, but then, his manner with Meli was invariably courteous.

"Ann makes her weekly call early enough in the day to not be seen," Meli replied. "Does this bisque need salt?" Of course it did not. Ann's recipes were, without exception, delicious. She quantified every ingredient, in so far as one could, and left no steps to the cook's imagination.

"The soup is fine. My compliments to the kitchen." The brigadier patted his lips with his table napkin and put his empty bowl aside. "You always set such a fine table, my love, and I hesitate to broach any topic that implies remote criticism of your choices, but is it necessary to see Ann so frequently?"

Well, yes, it was, if Meli was to continue collecting the recipes that gained her increasing cachet in all the right circles.

"I am her only relation, my dear. She is young and without guidance."

The brigadier flicked a glance at the footman collecting the soup bowls. Thomas bowed and withdrew, closing the parlor door behind him. Meli's husband would always have the subtle air of command, a trait she'd found dashing as a new bride. Now, Horace seemed a trifle rigid to her and in need of obedience in even small matters. The staff respected him. Meli was fairly certain they did not like him.

The brigadier's hair was increasingly gray, and he kept threatening to grow a beard, which would be entirely gray.

"Ann is no longer a reckless, bereaved child," he said, "intent on daring all for a London post. I indulged her in that regard because she presented us with a fait accompli, and war is uncertain. If anything had happened to me, Ann would have been at the mercy of courts and solicitors. A cook has a respectable trade, but I never envisioned..." He gazed down the length of the table at Meli.

"You never envisioned her serving out her apprenticeship and actually plying her trade." Meli picked up her glass of wine and moved to the place at Horace's right hand. "Neither did I, but she enjoys what she does, and she is of age." Ann also had a modest fortune, which was hers to manage now that she had reached the antediluvian milestone of five-and-twenty.

"Can't you find her a husband, Melisande? Sooner or later, somebody will learn that she spends her days chopping cabbage and plucking geese in a gaming hell. I dread the explanations we'll have to make."

Meli dreaded those explanations too. "What few people I mention Ann to believe her to be my retiring, rustic niece cantering toward spinsterdom at the family seat. You need not worry." Meli patted his sleeve. "I have sent out the invitations to your autumn supper."

"Have you now?"

Horace's quarterly officers' dinners were the high point of his social calendar, bringing together the best and brightest of his former comrades and direct reports. Wellington held such dinners, and Meli had had the inspired idea of taking up the tradition.

Though actually, Ann might have mentioned the notion to her first.

"I anticipate every single invitation will be accepted. Nothing save ill health or recent bereavement stops your men from paying their respects."

Horace caught her hand. "They all long for another chance to flirt with you, my love." He kissed her knuckles, exactly the sort of gallantry that had first brought him to Ann's notice. "Do you ever miss being on campaign?"

Well, no. Not ever. Only a daft woman would miss death, dismemberment, camp rations, unrelenting illness, intrigues, constant fear for her husband... the whole business. Horace, in his delicate way, was asking about Philippe, a topic never raised between husband and wife overtly.

"A warrior is bored by peace," Meli said. "A warrior's wife thanks God nightly for the cessation of hostilities. You always made such a dashing figure riding before the troops, but I tell you honestly, Husband, I hated seeing you off to battle. The thought of losing you..." At her worst and most foolish, Meli had never wished anything but a contented old age for her spouse, which he—oddly—might find more trying than a battlefield death.

Horace studied her, her hand still in his. "I believe you mean that."

"I most assuredly do. I am proud to be your wife, and that has always been true."

Horace stroked his thumb over the back of her hand. He was a considerate and undemanding lover and only affectionate when private. Meli esteemed him for those courtesies, even if they did bore her a bit.

"Philippe is in London, Melisande. I thought you should know."

Meli endured the inevitable welter of feelings that came with thoughts of a man she'd once regarded as the love of her life. Shame was predictable, for with Philippe, Meli had disgraced her marital vows. A current of longing nonetheless accompanied her guilt. If only there hadn't been a war, a husband, a passel of generals intent on slaughter and spying...

Wistfulness inevitably rose as well. She had loved Philippe. She had known passion with him, desperate, glorious, wild passion, such as only young people in the throes of their first love affair can know.

"Philippe who?" Meli said, raising her chin. "My recollection of the various Frenchmen we encountered grows increasingly vague. I trust his path and mine will not cross, and I would appreciate it if you would aid me in that objective."

Horace half rose to kiss her cheek. "No more need be said. Why don't you bring your place setting down to my end of the table, and you can tell me all the latest gossip. I heard Mrs. Bainbridge played a little too deeply at faro last week."

Meli complied, relieved to have the subject of Philippe closed. What was he doing in London, and how should she react if she did see him? London had only so many parks, and Philippe loved to be out of doors. He was from quite good family and would likely be socializing beyond the émigré community.

She collected her cutlery and joined Horace at the sunnier end of the table, keeping the conversation to tattle and household matters. Daniella's progress with her letters and the head maid's chronic sore knee. Horace reciprocated with the gossip from Horse Guards, and another meal passed without incident.

Horace rose to take his leave with another kiss to Meli's cheek. "I'm off to lecture the solicitors. The investments aren't performing quite to standards, and the lawyers need to know that I'm well aware of the problem."

"You are ambushing them?"

"A surprise inspection. Have no fear, though. Unless you take to gambling in Emily Bainbridge's fashion, we are still quite comfortably well fixed and can afford every indulgence where the regimental dinners are concerned."

Horace was a good husband and a good provider. Meli truly did esteem him and always had. "Would it be too great an imposition to ask for more of your company, Horace? I grow a bit lonely late in the evening."

He smiled, exhibiting a soupçon of the old dash. "Never let it be said I allowed my lady wife to languish for lack of my attentions. You will have my company tonight, if that suits."

"That suits wonderfully."

He bowed and withdrew, leaving Meli to pour herself another glass of wine and wonder how exactly Horace had heard of Emily Bainbridge's gambling problem.

SYCAMORE DORNING VALUED family above all else, but precisely *how* to value Orion Goddard, reluctant brother-in-law and grouch at large, remained a mystery. Even Jeanette was short on ideas when it came to coaxing Goddard closer to the familial hearth.

"I'm having lunch sent over from the club," Sycamore said. "You will join me, or good food will go to waste."

"No," Goddard replied, passing along his hat, gloves, and walking stick, "it will not. Your kitchen staff will ensure the food is consumed, and I'd like to discuss that staff with you."

"I am in great good health, thank you, and yourself?" Sycamore led his guest to the family parlor. One of Jeanette's embroidery projects lay on a sofa cushion, a pair of new throwing knives graced a side table, and a pile of smutty political prints Sycamore was sorting for a bound volume sat on the low table.

The humble side of domestic bliss was on display, and Sycamore hoped Goddard would perceive it as such.

"Apologies for my lack of small talk," Goddard said, pausing on the threshold of the parlor and glancing around the room. "My sister thrives?" His tone suggested only an affirmative answer would spare Sycamore a slow, painful death.

"We thrive in each other's care. With the right woman, marriage is a consummation devoutly to be wished. You might consider it. Please do have a seat, and tell me what about my kitchen staff interests you."

Goddard chose the wing chair facing the door, while Sycamore took up one of the throwing knives.

"I have a problem," the colonel said, "in the person of one Benevolence Hannah Goddard. She is of an age to apprentice to a cook, and Miss Ann Pearson has agreed to see to her instruction, if you allow it."

Sycamore tossed the knife at the cork target situated between framed prints of nightshade and jasmine. The blade obligingly struck in the center, but then, the distance—unlike present company— was no challenge at all.

"Is your problem child an illegitimate daughter?" Jeanette would have something to say about a niece toiling away in the club's kitchens.

"Hannah is no blood relation to me, but she is my responsibility. She will work hard, she already gets on well with Miss Pearson, and she cannot bide under my roof much longer."

Not a by-blow, then. "An émigré's offspring?"

Goddard took up the second knife and balanced it across his index finger. "Hannah's antecedents are humble and, as far as I know, thoroughly English. Miss Pearson is willing to take her on, but you must approve the arrangement lest your fancy chef cause difficulties."

Monsieur Jules Delacourt was largely responsible for the renown attached to The Coventry Club's kitchens, and Sycamore avoided crossing him.

"You and Miss Pearson have discussed the matter?" As far as Sycamore knew, Ann Pearson and Orion Goddard had met only the once, and in passing, months ago. And yet, here was Goddard all but insisting that Miss Pearson be assigned an assistant.

Miss Pearson, not the renowned Jules Delacourt.

"Your undercook and I have discussed the particulars. You need not part with any coin, but I want signed articles of apprenticeship for Benny's... for Hannah's sake."

A rap on the door heralded the arrival of lunch, which was fortunate, because Sycamore honestly did not know how to react to this request—demand?—from Goddard.

The footmen set two trays on small folding tables, bowed, and withdrew. The aroma of good, hot food reminded Sycamore that he was hungry. He took the second wing chair and prepared to tuck in.

"Might we wash our hands?" Goddard asked.

Well, yes, of course. "There's soap and water in the breakfast parlor," Sycamore said. "Shall we take our trays in there?"

Goddard picked up his tray and gestured toward the door, as if Sycamore were the guest and Goddard the host.

They tended to their ablutions, Goddard doing a thorough job, and then settled at the table. When Sycamore would have reached for his tankard of cider, Goddard bowed his head. Some muttering in French ensued while Sycamore's stomach growled.

"Amen," Sycamore said, flapping his table napkin over his lap. "I didn't know the army put such fine manners on a fellow."

"It doesn't." Goddard lifted the cloth covering his dish and sniffed. "How soon can Hannah take up her post?"

The kitchen had created magnificent hot sandwiches, piles of thinly sliced smoked ham with slabs of melted cheddar between toasted bread. Cold cider was the perfect beverage to wash down such fare, and bowls of hot apple compote awaited he whom the sandwiches had not entirely satisfied.

"I haven't said Hannah can take up a post," Sycamore countered. "I know many families embark on shared business ventures, but an apprenticeship can quickly become problematic."

Goddard ate with peculiar delicacy, the crumbs all falling onto his tray, his pace deliberate. "Hence the need for written articles" he said. "I want Hannah to have genuine credentials when her term of service is up. These sandwiches were not made according to any recipe devised by Ann Pearson."

"There are recipes for sandwiches?"

"Nor was the apple compote."

"How can you tell?"

"The sandwiches have not even a hint of mustard, no dried onion, not so much as a pinch of basil. Miss Pearson is a firm believer in spices."

Sycamore took another bite. "How would you know what my undercook believes in?"

"She told me so. What must I do to get you to provide Hannah a job with Miss Pearson?"

Sycamore munched for a moment. "Why not apprentice her to Delacourt? He's the outstanding talent in my kitchen. The whole staff considers themselves lucky to work with him."

Goddard slanted a look at Sycamore, and exactly how did a man's gaze manage to be pitying when that man gazed out of only a single eye?

"Delacourt will take offense at your hiring him an apprentice he hasn't chosen for himself—a female, no less—and Hannah honestly knows little of what goes on in a kitchen. She will need a patient instructor, not a half-drunk, self-adoring drill sergeant. Decide what the price for this favor will be, and I will gladly pay it."

Sycamore took a considering sip of his cider and wished Jeannette were on hand. The price should be regular calls on Jeanette, but she would not want her brother coerced into socializing with her. Sycamore did not need coin—which Goddard well knew—but Goddard had to have something useful to offer.

Something Goddard would value. Something Sycamore valued as well, lest the exchange be insulting to Goddard.

"How is it Hannah is among your dependents, Colonel? Is she the by-blow of a fellow officer?"

"Most of my fellow officers will have nothing to do with me. Hannah, Benny to her familiars, is among the infantry I employ in furtherance of my business interests."

"She is one of your urchins." London was awash in urchins. The newspapers perennially lamented that state of affairs, and periodic collections were taken up, but nothing stemmed the tide of feral children littering the streets in the jewel of civilization's crown. That many of those children were female was a doubly uncomfortable thought.

"Hannah numbered among my general factotums. I would not send her to you did she not have letters, manners, and regular exposure to what passes for religion among the English."

"You are English."

"I am half French, which limits my influence far more than you might think. That Hannah was foisted off on you by a family connection who bears the cross of French blood will spare her the worst of your chef's posturing."

Goddard spoke as if Delacourt's little tantrums were more than passing displays. "Delacourt will have no excuse for pique, provided the child is as quick-witted and well mannered as you say she is."

Goddard's silence spoke volumes. How did he do that? How did he imply that Sycamore lacked an accurate grasp of the politics of his own kitchen?

"Has Miss Pearson been telling tales out of school, Goddard?"

"When you have the privacy to do so, ask her how the kitchen is managing, and then *listen* to what she says and what she doesn't say. My concern is Benny."

Sycamore took a spoonful of compote, which was rich and sweet, if somewhat uninspired. "I will take on your erstwhile urchin, but I have conditions."

Goddard waved a hand. He did not touch his compote.

"First, we will begin with a trial period of three months, during which Miss Hannah can withdraw from her post without repercussions, provided she gives notice, or Miss Pearson can decide the child is not suited to the job, again with notice."

"Reasonable. What else?"

Sycamore ran a gaming hell, but he was not a born gambler. He put his next condition before his guest, hoping it wasn't a significant blunder.

"You will guarantee me a supply of champagne during those three months, at the same prices you offer to your best customers. My current supplier, a Frenchman, has grown greedy, despite the volumes of custom I offer him. I want to remind him that business is undertaken for our mutual benefit, not his unilateral enrichment."

Goddard toyed with his spoon, the gesture having something of annoyance about it. "How many cases will you need?"

Sycamore named a quantity that should make any humble, half-French vintner pause. The Coventry offered free champagne after midnight, and the guests invariably indulged a tearing thirst at the tables. The free champagne had gone from a courtesy to an amenity to a signature of the club's fine hospitality, while Sycamore's supplier had become an arrogant pain in the arse.

"You will take delivery at the dock," Goddard said. "I see no point inventorying that much wine in my cellars when the bottles are bound for consumption at your tables."

"Reasonable," Sycamore said, saluting with his spoon.

Something flitted over Goddard's countenance. Not humor, exactly, but a leavening of his features. Once upon a time, Orion Goddard had probably been handsome, back before he'd donned an eye patch and forgotten how to smile.

Did Miss Pearson make him smile? Jeanette might know.

"One other condition," Goddard said, rising.

"You aren't having any compote?"

"The sweet doesn't tempt me. Help yourself to mine."

Sycamore would, once he'd seen Goddard out the door. "What's your other condition?" he asked, getting to his feet.

"As your waiters serve the champagne, their trays will contain not only the filled glasses, but also the bottle from which the glasses were poured. You will also display the bottles at the bar, and if anybody asks—which they will, for my wines are superior to the pedestrian product you're serving now—you will reply that, as a favor between family members, I have generously allowed you temporary access to some of my humbler stores."

Admiration for Goddard's strategy warred with surprise at his *coup d'audace.* "You have?"

"I am not in the habit of dissembling, Dorning. I will take it upon myself to acquaint Miss Pearson with the terms of our agreement. Hannah can start at the first of the week, and I expect you to provide her lodging, as you would any other apprentice."

Goddard swiped two sandwiches from the tray, wrapped them in a plain handkerchief, and slipped them into a coat pocket. "I can see myself out."

"Why do I feel," Sycamore asked as he accompanied his guest to the door, "as if my superior officer has just come through on inspection?"

"Because he has. Please give Jeanette my most sincere regards. I'll await your articles of apprenticeship for Hannah." Goddard slapped his hat onto his head and gathered up his walking stick and gloves. "Jeanette is truly faring well?"

"She's blooming. My family adores her. She already has favorite-auntie status with my oldest niece, and we are looking for a property of our own in Surrey. You need not worry for her, Goddard. She made a splendid match."

Goddard merely glowered, which he did quite well, and slipped out the door. For a big man, he moved quietly, and for a man with a hitch in his gait, he moved with dispatch.

Sycamore returned to the breakfast parlor, there to finish up the leftovers. Jeanette found him polishing off Goddard's apple treat ten minutes later.

"Did I, or did I not, hear my brother's voice as I was getting dressed?" she asked, allowing herself to be pulled into Sycamore's lap.

Sycamore hoped, ages and ages hence, that he and Jeanette were still on pulling-her-into-his-lap terms. Jeanette was striking rather than pretty, with strong features and red hair, but what Sycamore loved most about her was her ferocious heart and loyalty.

She was devoted to her idiot brother, more's the pity, though in his way, Goddard was equally loyal to Jeanette.

Sycamore offered Jeanette his cider. "Goddard was asking that we take on a female apprentice in the Coventry's kitchens. I agreed. Have some compote."

Jeanette allowed him to feed her a bite. "Orion asked a favor of you?"

Sycamore thought back over the conversation. "I am nearly sure he did, but then, I ended up placing an enormous order for champagne with him and agreeing to advertise his vintages at the club, in addition to providing employment for one of his pickpockets."

Sycamore was not entirely certain how all that had transpired under the guise of a favor between family members, but he had the niggling suspicion that the outcome, from free meal to free advertising to free transportation of the bottles, had gone exactly according to Goddard's plans.

"This is progress, Sycamore," Jeanette said. "That Orion would ask this of us is progress." Jeanette offered Sycamore an apple-flavored kiss, and all thoughts of Rye Goddard's schemes and skills went straight out of Sycamore's head.

YESTERDAY'S MEETING with Sycamore Dorning had gone well, though Rye had been disappointed to catch not even a glimpse of Jeanette. He needed to see her blooming, needed direct evidence that her second marriage was an improvement over the first.

Perhaps soon...

He rapped on the blue door of the house next to the bakery that rendered the entire neighborhood redolent of fresh bread and cinnamon. No wonder Ann Pearson had chosen to bide here. The location was not only close to her place of employment, but her delicate nose would enjoy the ambient scents.

"Good day, sir." A small, elderly woman in an enormous muslin mobcap peered up at him through a half-open door. "Deliveries at the rear, and we're all Church of England here."

"Colonel Orion Goddard, at your service. I have come to call on

Miss Ann Pearson." That Rye would *come to call* on a young lady was a peculiar notion, but he had a debt to repay.

The door swung open. "Have you now? Have you indeed? Well, stop dawdling on the stoop like a contrary cat, Colonel. Miss Ann never said anything about expecting a caller, but then, my hearing isn't what it used to be."

"I hazard your hearing is quite sharp, ma'am, and your eyesight keen as well."

The old dear cackled merrily and made no move to take Rye's hat or walking stick. "You hazard correctly. You may pace in the parlor for the nonce, looking earnest and gallant, and what shall we do with your pretty basket?"

"I will guard it myself until such time as Miss Pearson can join me, assuming she's at home."

Faded blue eyes perused Rye from head to foot. "If she's not at home, my lad, I certainly am, and my sister will be as well. That is a basket from Gunter's, unless I am much mistaken."

Rye leaned close enough to lower his voice. "You have not been mistaken on any matter of serious import since old George first went mad."

"Miss Ann has attracted the notice of a man of discernment. Don't expect me to put in a good word for you, Colonel. If Miss Ann is to start having gentlemen callers, they must stand or fall on their own merits." She tossed off a spry curtsey and left Rye alone to study the parlor.

He did not pace, he inspected. The parlor bore the scent of rose potpourri, and nary a cobweb or fleck of coal dust was to be seen. The furniture was sturdy and comfortably faded—no spindly chairs or fussy hearth screens for the ladies—and the rugs a little worn, though freshly beaten.

A genteel boarding house, then, and Miss Pearson had a pair of sentries guarding her citadel. If Rye had ever needed to take the measure of morale in camp or winter quarters, he consulted the older women, and their intelligence had never failed him.

"Colonel Goddard." Ann Pearson paused in the doorway to curtsey. "This is a pleasure."

She was balm to a soldier's eye, all tidy and spruce in an ensemble of chocolate brown. Dark hair tucked into a perfect bun, skirts freshly pressed, hems spotless. Her shawl was crocheted of hunter green wool. Her eyes—a few shades lighter than the shawl—conveyed welcome.

Her greeting was apparently genuine.

"Miss Pearson, good day." Rye swept off his hat, bowed, and mentally scrambled for further pleasantries. *I have missed you* would probably send the lady pelting for the stairs. *You have been much on my mind*, while true, was unthinkably bold.

"I brought food," he said, hefting the basket unnecessarily. "Coals to Newcastle, I suppose, to bring food to a cook, but I wanted you to have a bottle of my champagne, and good wine should not be consumed on an empty stomach."

She advanced into the room, leaving the door open, of course. "You brought me a basket from Gunter's?"

"Presuming of me, wasn't it? Mostly, I am delivering a bottle of wine because I am in your debt." And because he had wanted to see her, to be with her, to have conversation with a woman of sense and good cheer.

She grasped his elbow. "Let's repair to the garden, Colonel. Miss Julia and Miss Diana will enjoy spying on us, and we aren't likely to be blessed with many more such fine days. We can make a picnic of our noon meal."

"That isn't... I hadn't intended..." He hadn't dreamed he'd be invited to picnic with her. "If you insist."

"I do. Part of the magic of good food is that it can bring us together with good company. I detect apple tarts, mild brie, butter biscuits..."

"You can tell all that simply by scent?"

"I can. The linen has been pressed with only a hint of starch and dried in a baker's kitchen overnight, would be my guess."

She led him to a back hallway that opened onto a small flagstone terrace. Grass tried to wedge its way between the stones, but somebody had waged the battle to contain such intrusions. The garden itself consisted of a white birch sapling in one corner, a few square yards of grass, a birdbath—unoccupied at present—and some potted pansies along the brick walkway.

Rows of what Rye presumed were spices grew up along the stone walls, and a tall wooden gate led into the alley. A grouping of wrought-iron furniture occupied the center of the terrace, four chairs and a table. The flagstones were dotted with dead leaves, though Rye would have bet Agricola's new bridle that the whole terrace was thoroughly swept each day.

"The ladies like to read out here," Miss Pearson said, leading him to the table and chairs. "Natural light is easier on the eyes, and fresh air is good for us."

"To the extent London *has* any fresh air." What this little garden did have was privacy. No tall trees bordered the garden, meaning no enterprising spy in the alley could peer down onto the terrace. The wings of the house sheltered the grouping, such that Miss Julia and Miss Diana might keep watch from an upstairs sitting room, but no neighbors would learn that Miss Pearson had picnicked with a caller.

Better that way for all. Rye held the lady's chair, a courtesy with which he was out of practice, but managed adequately. He put his hat and walking stick in an empty chair and set the basket on the table.

"We get a good breeze off the river for much of the year," Miss Pearson said, "but I agree. On a bad day, a rainy day, a cold day, London is a tribulation for the olfactory—oh look. The apple tarts are still warm." She unwrapped the red-checked cloth. "If I am not mistaken, a bit of anise has crept in beneath the cinnamon, clove, and nutmeg."

She sniffed the tart the way some women might have sniffed a bouquet of roses. She sniffed everything, in fact, from the roast fowl to the herbed butter, to the linen-wrapped bread. Rye took the chair at her right elbow and enjoyed her enjoying the food.

"You will think me odd," she said, setting aside the apple tarts. "I am odd. I didn't realize other people ignored scents more effectively than I do until my father referred to me as his little hound puppy. He joked about housing me in the kennel."

Rye did not find the joke humorous, but then, he was famous at the Aurora Club for his lack of levity.

"Perhaps other people don't ignore scents so much as we are scent-blind or scent-deaf," he said. "I could not have told you what was in the basket beyond a suspicion that it held something freshly baked. May I open the wine? I have an ulterior motive for bringing it by."

Miss Pearson looked up from unpacking her treasures. "You announce this ulterior motive before the bottle is opened?"

"Subterfuge is not my gift. I want your professional opinion of my champagne."

Before leaving his house, Rye had debated whether to pluck the last blooms from the rosebush in his garden. His French roses were bedraggled this late in the season, but Miss Pearson had remarked their scent. He'd not brought the roses—bad enough he'd brought the picnic basket—but apparently, asking Ann Pearson to taste his wine was a finer gift even than exotic roses.

"You want *me* to taste your wine?"

"I very much do. Your palate is refined, your knowledge of cuisine sophisticated. I am but a soldier who happened to inherit vineyards and farms. I made changes to my cousins' wineries, and one wants... That is... I think I have made improvements, but my opinion is hardly expert."

"Open the bottle," Miss Pearson replied, her smile fading. "I promise you honesty, Colonel, but if a tasting is your ulterior motive, what was your main objective?"

Rye's folding knife included a corkscrew. He extracted the knife from his boot and tended to the wine.

"You come armed to a picnic," Miss Pearson said.

"I come armed nearly everywhere. I have enemies, Miss Pearson. Their preferred weapon lately is gossip and tattle, but they might tire of wounding with a thousand whispers and resort to more expeditious means of seeing to my ruin."

Miss Pearson set about arranging their feast, and she had a knack for the task. The cloths used to wrap the biscuits and tarts became table linen, the plates and cutlery a still life. When a shower of golden birch leaves drifted onto the table, the effect was perfection.

"Shall I pour?" Rye asked. "I brought the basket as a thanks for your willingness to take on Hannah's education. The primary reason for my call is to inform you that Sycamore Dorning has agreed that the girl will be answerable to you, starting Monday. She's to be properly articled, though we'll start with a three-month trial period."

"Was that your condition?"

"Dorning's. Either you or Hannah can decide you don't suit and abandon the arrangement without penalty."

Miss Pearson brushed at the fallen leaves. "Monsieur won't like it."

"Does Monsieur ever like anything?"

She made up a plate for Rye of two tarts and a butter biscuit with a generous portion of cheese on the edge of the plate. Her hands were competent, the nails blunt and clean, a pink, irregular scar across the back of one thumb. A burn, doubtless, a hazard of her profession.

"Monsieur likes his brandy and his fits of pique," she said. "I should taste your wine before I eat."

Rye poured out, passed her a serving, and touched his glass to hers. "To new ventures."

She sniffed the wine before sampling, her expression intent, as if listening to far away music. Rye ought not to stare at her as she rolled the wine on her tongue, but she was so focused on her investigation, he doubted she noticed his rudeness.

"Lovely texture," she said. "Light, just the right effervescence. The nose has a hint of toast with butter and honey. The palate is orange with overtones of almonds." She took another taste. "Maybe an insinuation of vanilla or orange pastry crust. I'd have to think about it."

"Do you *like* it?"

She set down her glass. "I do, Colonel, and I would not offer you anything but the truth when it comes to food and wine. That is top-quality champagne, far above the insipid pinkish business served at the Coventry. Mr. Dorning should exert himself to acquire as much of your inventory as he can, for it would make an excellent comple-ment to our private dinners."

Rye wanted to toss his eye patch in the air and whoop with glee. "You truly like it?"

"You neglect your own glass, Colonel, and yes, I truly like it."

He took a sip, not because of the fruity, toasty, vanilla whatever, but because he and Ann Pearson were in accord, and *she liked his champagne.*

"I have no sophistication in polite matters," he said, "but my champagne fortifies me. To me, it captures all the sunshine and vigor of the French countryside, the tradition and abiding resilience of my mother's people. Joy and elegance, determination and humor. I taste that."

"Well said," Miss Pearson replied, lifting her glass a few inches. "You bring poetry to your picnics along with your other weapons, Colonel."

She smiled, and for no earthly reason Rye could articulate, he chose that moment to taste *her.* He kissed her on the lips, a presump-tion and an act of hope. France and England had both survived the wars, so had Rye.

When he was with this woman, he was glad of his victory. Battles remained to fight, but what was a soldier if not a fighter? Perhaps for a moment, he could be a little bit of a lover as well, or an affectionate friend.

Something sweet and fine.

Ann's lips were soft and yielding, though Rye could taste surprise in her response. When he would have desisted, she cupped his cheek, her palm and fingers callused and warm.

"Whenever I sample this fine vintage," she said, "I will recall the man who introduced me to it, and I will smile at the memory." She caressed his cheek and brushed his hair back from his brow, then sat back.

Rye wished he'd brought a second bottle. As Ann turned the discussion to the curriculum Benny would pursue, he wished he could lay his entire champagne inventory—and his heart—at Ann Pearson's feet.

Perhaps someday, but today was not that day.

CHAPTER SIX

Aunt Melisande's letters to Ann from Spain and Portugal had always painted a gay and adventurous picture of life following the drum. The scenery was dramatic, the regimental entertainments frequent and merry. The battles were passingly vexatious but exciting.

Melisande had clearly been a regimental favorite, much doted upon by her husband and his fellow officers.

Even as Ann had pored over recipe books, pestered the cooks at her boarding schools, and dreamed of spun-sugar castles, she'd envied Melisande. All those gallant soldiers, all those new sights and valorous deeds...

As Ann had matured, she'd realized how little of wartime reality Melisande had conveyed in her letters. Unless Uncle Horace had been very protective, Aunt had seen death and horror, injustice and tragedy. The scent of a battlefield had to have been a nightmare.

And yet, as the leaves scraped across the sunny flagstones, and Orion Goddard refilled Ann's champagne glass, she had reason to envy Melisande her years with the army. The colonel had *listened* to Ann's prattling regarding Hannah's education. He'd held Ann's chair for her.

He'd kissed her, and when she'd kissed him back, he'd accepted her overtures with a sweet, easy confidence that put her in mind of his French antecedents and his champagne. Heady and light, delicious and fine.

"How soon will you know if Benny has a cook's vocation?" the colonel asked, dabbing cheese on an apple tart and setting it on Ann's plate.

"You are eating only the one?" she asked.

"I suspect Miss Julia and Miss Diana will see to the leftovers."

"They can afford to order their own baskets from Gunter's, but they prefer my cooking most of the time. On occasion, my experiments are fit only for the slop pail."

"I cannot believe that." The colonel swiped a finger through the drizzle of apple filling crossing his plate. "Perhaps when you were less experienced, you had the rare unexpected result, but by now, you know the terrain blindfolded."

Ann knew sauces, she was making good inroads on desserts and side dishes, but Jules jealously guarded his dominion over the roasts and entrées. Ann did not want to spend this impromptu picnic boring the colonel with a recitation of kitchen skirmishes.

He eyed his hat, as if he were thinking of making an escape.

"Tell me about your eye patch, Colonel Goddard. I suspect you don't wear it merely to appear dashing." Ann took a bite of tart to cover her mortification. She should never have pried like that, never have been so blunt. Fine white lines radiated from the colonel's eye, scars so delicate they would be invisible by candlelight.

"Nobody asks," he said, considering his wine, "but everybody stares. The tale is simple: Early in Napoleon's military career, while he was tossing the Austrians out of Italy, his artillerymen had a few lucky shots, managing to land a mortar directly upon the wagon holding his opponent's powder magazine. In addition to creating one hell of an explosion, he depleted the other side's store of ammunition and raised morale on the French side. This became something of a sport among French artillerymen thereafter, to blow up powder magazines."

"A deadly sport."

"Warhorses become inured to much, and the mules favored by the artillerymen are even more stoic, but that much noise and mayhem... The disruption is as bad as the actual injury and destruction. I happened to witness a lucky French volley at too-close range. I raised my arm to shield my face, but was only half successful. For days, I had little hearing. For weeks, I was blindfolded."

"Your hearing came back?"

"For the most part."

Ann waited, hoping he'd tell her the rest of it, because clearly the tale was unfinished. She had missed the empty pleasures of a young woman of means—a London Season, flirtations, pretty dresses—and those had been easy to pass up.

But toiling away in a hot, busy kitchen night after night, Ann also missed any hope of conversations like this, personal and genuine, with a man of substance. She in fact had no real female friends either, outside of Miss Julia and Miss Diana, and suspected her weekly calls on Melisande were as much about disseminating menus and recipes as they were about maintaining a family tie.

"When a storm approaches, I have headaches on this side," the colonel said, tapping his left temple. "I am grateful to see and hear as well as I do, because for far too long…. The wounds were slow to heal, and the surgeons kept me in the dark. The blast had knocked me off my feet, and I was nursing broken ribs and a very sore hip as well."

Ann did not like to think of this hale, fit man condemned to a cot in some stinking infirmary tent. "How did you remain sane?"

"The army teaches a man patience, perhaps too much patience. After following all manner of daft orders for a few years, if a soldier is told to remain abed and wear a blindfold, he remains abed and wears the blindfold. I thought about my family's process for making champagne, the grapes we use, the method of aging in the bottle. The medical officer was French-born, oddly enough, and he promised me even the damaged eye would have some sight if I behaved, and he was right."

Ann suspected Orion Goddard had not told this tale to anybody, not even his sister. "For you, it would have been worse to lie obediently on that cot in the dark than to take on the French army with nothing but your sword."

The colonel poured her more wine. "I am not a hero, Miss Pearson. I was simply one of many soldiers and luckier than most. The incident earned me a promotion I have never felt I deserved and might have also figured in the knighthood that even my commanding officer begrudges me."

The second glass of champagne was as good as the first and held up easily to the food it accompanied. Some champagnes were like afternoon dresses—pretty enough, but not adequate for evening occasions. The colonel's vintage was equal to any hour, a light midday repast or full banquet honors.

Like the man himself.

"You begrudge yourself that knighthood," Ann said.

The colonel sat back and crossed an ankle over the opposite knee, a relaxed, informal pose that showed off his physique to excellent advantage. He would age well and soundly, for all his early years had been spent in battle.

"I don't understand why my name was included on the honors list at all," he said. "I am in disgrace with my regiment, though I have never been able to ascertain exactly why. The trouble started before the Hundred Days, when we all thought the last shot had been fired, and Bonaparte was buttoned up on Elba."

Bonaparte had become unbuttoned, as it were, escaping from his island after less than a year of exile, mustering the French army to his cause, and re-entering Paris in a matter of weeks. That entire unexpected coda to years of war had lasted little more than three months and culminated in the great slaughter at Waterloo.

The great victory, rather. "Did you serve during the Hundred Days?"

"I was considered unfit for duty, and as depleted as Wellington's forces were after nearly a year of peace, I took that to mean I was undesirable rather than unfit. Just when I think the rumors about me are beginning to subside, they start up again."

Ann took the butter biscuit from his plate and held it out to him. "Gunter's butter biscuits are not to be missed. I would give much for the recipe. I can come close, but I cannot re-create them exactly."

He broke the biscuit in half and took a bite. "I generally avoid sweets."

"Why?"

"I am less apt to miss them, and if I expect my boys to learn some self-restraint, then I must practice limiting my pleasures, too, mustn't I?"

He passed Ann half of his biscuit, and she was not about to refuse such a treat. "Tell me of the rumors, Colonel. We hear everything at the Coventry, sooner or later. The military contingent doesn't frequent our tables in great numbers, but we get enough retired officers among our customers to hear what's making the rounds at Horse Guards."

He put the uneaten portion of his biscuit back on his plate. "The telling makes for poor conversation, Miss Pearson, and I have taken up enough of your time. My thanks again for being willing to oversee Benny's apprenticeship." He rose, the chair scraping discordantly against the flagstones.

Ann rose as well, though she didn't want him to leave. She liked him, liked his honesty, liked his concern for Benny, liked that he'd share his past with her.

Liked that he'd ask her opinion of his champagne and liked—very much—that he would kiss her.

"I'll send one of the boys around to take the basket back to Gunter's," the colonel said, gathering up his hat and walking stick. "My regards to Miss Julia and Miss Diana."

He hesitated before descending the garden steps, and Ann spoke rather than hear him apologize for kissing her.

"You should not tie it so tightly," she said, moving to his side and reaching behind his head to undo the string holding his eye patch in place. "We wear caps and aprons in the kitchen all day, and you would be surprised what a difference a loose bow can make."

Before he could protest, she had the tie undone and his eye patch off. A pink crease crossed his forehead where the leather had bitten into his flesh. Ann rubbed her thumb along that small discomfort, knowing that she was presuming terribly, but also knowing she was right.

A small, relentless hurt could eventually cause considerable pain.

"The scars hardly show," she said, winnowing her fingers through his hair. "Do you truly need the eye patch, Colonel?"

He was regarding her out of two clear blue eyes, and he was not smiling. "On bright days, I need the patch to avoid headaches, but I must tell you, Miss Pearson, the sight of you on this pretty autumn afternoon is enough to make me rejoice that I have any ability to see at all. Before I make a complete fool of myself with further excesses of sentiment, I will take my leave of you."

He didn't bother to retie his eye patch, but instead stuffed it into his pocket, bowed without taking Ann's hand, and marched down the steps onto the brick walkway.

"You'll call again?" Ann asked, wishing she could command him to pay her another visit. "I enjoyed your visit very much, Colonel."

He paused halfway to the gate. "I ought not."

He was trying to be polite, drat him. "Limiting your sweets again, Colonel Goddard?"

His smile was subtle, mostly in his eyes, only a touch of humor about that tender, wry mouth. "Exactly so, Miss Pearson. Removing myself from some of the most alluring temptation I can recall in ages." He saluted with his walking stick and let himself out the back gate.

Ann watched him carefully close the gate behind himself, while she refused to entertain the notion that perhaps Melisande had a point. Perhaps the company of a good man, a family household, and the prospect of friendships outside the kitchen might have something to recommend it.

Ann resumed her place at the table and took up the colonel's uneaten half biscuit.

Whatever rumors plagued him, they must be very bad. Eventually, they would find their way to the Coventry, and when they did, Ann would be listening for them.

"I FOUND a place for the girl. She'll be apprenticed to a cook." Rye made this announcement while settling between his friends in the Aurora Club's reading room. The fire was throwing out good heat, Rye's belly was full, and Benny was soon to be settled in a new post.

All was right with the entire dratted, bedamned world.

"Cooking is a respectable profession," Dylan Powell said, slouching low in his chair. "I'm fond of good victuals myself."

"You're worse than a biblical plague," Alasdhair MacKay muttered, propping his foot on a hassock. "Seven years is a long time to be apprenticed. Is the girl in London, or did you send her off to the provinces?"

"I sent her to the Coventry, as it happens. A few streets away from home." And yet, Alasdhair was right. Seven years, the length of most enlistments, could be an eternity. Benny hadn't gone off to war, exactly, but she'd be going off alone.

Worse, when she left on Monday morning, she'd be leaving for good. Going out into the world, never to return if matters went well. And Rye had ingratiated himself with no less person than Sycamore Dorning to bring about Benny's departure.

What the hell was I thinking? "She'll learn more at the Coventry than she would in just any old household kitchen. She'll get to use her French."

"The Coventry has a fancy chef." Dylan's observation was ever so casual. "A Frenchman."

Jules Delacourt. Rye had made inquiries among his émigré connections and heard nothing untoward so far. A bit of a temper, a tendency to drink, the usual shortcomings for a talented chef.

"Benny will be apprenticed to the undercook," Rye said, "an Englishwoman of irreproachable antecedents." Though, in point of fact, Rye knew little of Ann Pearson's family. She dwelled in a respectable boardinghouse, had ambitions worthy of her talent, and had been educated beyond her trade. She'd learned French, for example—and how to kiss.

Rye mentally slapped himself for that observation, but when Ann Pearson had kissed him back, he'd become like a glass of good champagne, imbued with effervescence of the animal spirits and of the heart. Fortified and—had he run mad?—sparkling.

Something about the way Alasdhair crossed his feet on the hassock struck Rye as restless. Then too, his cousins weren't bickering.

"How's business?" Dylan asked.

Jeanette had forbidden Rye to bequeath the vineyards to her, claiming no interest in the vintner's trade. Alasdhair and Dylan were thus Rye's heirs, and their interest in the business was thus justified.

"Managing," Rye said. "I've agreed to supply the Coventry over the winter, and as it happens, I have the product on hand to manage that easily." In a fit of optimism, he'd sent off instructions to have yet more inventory brought into the country. His entire market-ready stores were never kept at one location, because warehouses could burn, and a merchant's life savings would perish with them.

"You have the inventory because the English aren't buying your champagne," Alasdhair said. "When was the last time you found a new customer, Goddard?"

"The Coventry is a new customer."

"Dorning is family now," Alasdhair rejoined, taking a sip of his brandy. "The Coventry relied on Fournier for their champagne until you came along."

And why the hell would Alasdhair have bothered to learn that?

"Fournier raised his prices, and on a customer who bought increasingly large quantities. Because the Coventry relies on champagne as part of its *métier*, diversifying the supply is only prudent. Besides, our champagne is better than Fournier's."

"Your champagne is cheaper than Fournier's, lately," Alasdhair retorted. "Did Lady Meecham renew her order?"

"No." And she had made it plain that Rye had only received her custom because a hostess who risked running out of champagne punch at her annual ball would never live down the disgrace.

"What about the cloth merchants' guild?" Dylan asked. "Did they ask you to save them enough crates for next year's banquet?"

"No." Rye had snabbled that order because the ship ferrying Fournier's bottles across the Channel had been blown back to Calais by foul weather and then had to wait nine days for favorable winds. "I'm starting on my rounds for the spring orders. Everything slows down as winter sets in."

"Try the brothels," Dylan muttered, crossing his arms and closing his eyes. "A damned lot of libation is consumed in those establishments, and they have the money to pay for it."

"I am not selling my grandmother's champagne in furtherance of lechery."

"Now you take up against lechery," Dylan said. "I despair of you."

That wasn't quite right. Rye's friends were *worried* for him. Nothing less than genuine concern would have them posing such pointed questions about the business.

"What aren't you two saying?" he asked, feeling as if he were prying a confession from Otter or Louis. "Out with it. Is there some bill floating through Parliament to raise the excise taxes again?" Taxes were a fact of life, unless a man chose to do business with the gangs running the coastal trade, in which case extortionate schemes took the place of the crown's levies.

Alasdhair rose to refresh his drink. "We're hearing rumors."

"London is perennially full of rumors."

"Worse than usual," Dylan said, eyes still closed. "About you. Mutterings that you were promoted because your incompetence in the field was getting good men killed."

"I went out of my way to keep my men as safe as they could be under the circumstances. I followed orders, and you two know it." Rye had *always* followed orders.

Alasdhair resumed his seat. "The gossip also bends in that direction—you dodged orders to avoid engaging the enemy."

"Who didn't? Every commanding officer was criticized for every order he gave, failed to give, followed, failed to follow, failed to follow quickly enough, or didn't follow carefully enough. The men talked more than they marched." Though these rumors were doubtless circulating in the officers' ranks, if Dylan and Alasdhair had heard them. "Where are you coming across this gossip?"

Dylan yawned. "Here and there."

"Over cards," Alasdhair added. "Over a pint, along a bridle path, while indulging in my usual penchant for lechery."

Since mustering out, Alasdhair had been a veritable monk. "If you are hearing the talk in all those places, and it's reaching both of you, then somebody wants me to know I'm being slandered."

And that, apparently, was the warning Rye's friends were trying to convey. Fournier might resent Rye's contract with the Coventry, but Fournier would also respect that Rye had a family connection to the Dornings. Fournier had gambled with the Coventry and lost—this round.

"I haven't stepped on any particular toes lately," Rye murmured, "so I am left to wonder why the rumors are gathering force again now, as well as who is behind them. What has changed?" If anything, banishing Jeanette's in-laws from London in spring should have quieted the talk, not given it fresh life.

The silence that spread was broken by a burst of laughter from the dining room down the corridor. Elsewhere, life was rollicking along, nary a care in the world beyond whether to keep tomorrow's appointment with the tailor or nip down to Brighton before winter descended in earnest.

"Might be time for you to check on your vineyards," Dylan said quietly.

"I already checked on my vineyards." Had escorted a pair of Jeanette's younger family connections to France to learn the art of making champagne. Lord Tavistock and his cousin reported to Rye regularly by letter.

"Then check on your farms in Provence," Alasdhair said. "The talk circulating now is the kind that can provoke a man to call out the fools spreading the gossip."

"Move to France for a while." Dylan opened his eyes and sat up. "Leave your horses and your pickpockets with us, and let the talk die down."

Rye had tried letting the talk die down. Years after the cannon had ceased their volleys on the battlefields, he was still skirmishing with an unseen enemy. One who apparently wanted him either dead on the dueling green or permanently disgraced.

"I am done with killing," he said. "If I know nothing else about myself, I know that." Rye also knew he would not willingly abandon his boys, not as they were embarking upon the difficult years of adolescence.

They each needed to find a place in the world, and that journey was much easier when a lad had a home to navigate from. Then too, Benny might need a place to come back to, and a half-dozen émigré households relied on Rye's support.

"Killing might not be done with you," Alasdhair said, downing his drink and getting to his feet. "Powell and I will walk you home."

"That's not necessary."

"They are *children*," Dylan spat, rising. "Those little thieves and rogues you employ as your eyes and ears. They could summon the watch or land a few blows, but against a pair of toughs with knives, those boys would be powerless or, worse, distract you in a fight. We'll walk you home, and we will take the streets, not the alleys you favor."

Alasdhair rose as well, and while Rye could have held his own against either man in a fair fight, he could not best them both at the same time.

"I accept your friendly offer of an escort," Rye said, standing. "This once." They couldn't nanny him at every hour, but that was not the point. The point was that a pair of generally sensible men who well knew Rye's abilities with his fists and firearms were worried for him.

He ambled along through London's noisome darkness, ignoring the invitations of numerous prostitutes, half of whom knew Alasdhair by name. While Alasdhair stopped to exchange a few words with one of them—quiet words Rye and Dylan weren't meant to overhear— Dylan pretended to study the sulfurous illumination of the nearest streetlight.

"You really ought to spend some time in France, Rye."

"That won't solve anything."

"It will keep you alive, which solves rather a large problem for those you'd leave behind. There's something else you should know."

In Rye's late-night imaginings, where he relived old battles and prognosticated about new ones, he speculated that Dylan and Alasdhair were planning to leave England. The New World held vast opportunities for men who could work hard and plan carefully. He'd hate to see them go.

Hate it, but wish them well. "Whatever it is, just tell me."

"Deschamps is back in London."

Philippe Deschamps, former officer in the French army, charmer at large, and opportunist without limit.

"We are no longer at war with France, Dylan, and I, for one, am pleased to keep it so."

"He's a dead shot, Rye."

"So am I. Shall we be going? It appears our dear Alasdhair has been taken captive."

"Dare!" Dylan called. "Leave the lady in peace, or pay her for her time."

Alasdhair glowered at him. "A moment." He passed something to the woman—a flash of metal gleamed in the lamplight—and jogged to Rye's side. "What is the bloody hurry?"

Dylan resumed walking. "We're out after dark on London's streets. It's cold, dark, and miserable, not to mention dangerous."

"*She's* out in the same weather," Alasdhair said. "Hasn't eaten for two days."

She'd eat well within the next hour, would be Rye's guess, which turned his thoughts in the direction of Miss Ann Pearson, who could rhapsodize about anise hiding beneath other spices, or butter biscuits she could not exactly replicate.

Would Ann Pearson miss him if he moved to France? The question was academic—he was not about to scurry away merely because gossip was once again turning against him—but if he should find himself dwelling in France, he would certainly miss her.

Miss her a lot.

And her kisses.

~

"BY THE END of the first day of my apprenticeship," Ann said, "I thought my arms would fall off."

Henry had taken Benny to the staff hall, where she would choose a hook for her cloak, find clean aprons and caps, and sample the lemonade, ale, and bread and butter that were available to the staff at all hours.

"Your employer was determined to exhaust you?" Colonel Goddard asked.

His patch was firmly back in place, his gaze still on the doorway through which Benny had disappeared. Ann should not be so glad to see him, so willing to offer him her hand to bow over.

But she was.

"The work *is* exhausting," she said. "I was given simple tasks, such as churning butter and beating eggs, so I might be useful while watching how the kitchen went on. I was also given tasks that allowed me to sit, which was a mercy when a cook has to be on her feet for as much as eighteen hours at a stretch. But my manners are remiss. May I offer you tea, Colonel?"

Monday morning had dawned windy, wet, and raw, and yet, Colonel Goddard had brought Benny to the club himself. He held his hat in his hands, and he'd gone so far as to unbutton his greatcoat, though he made no move to take it off. Even bareheaded, even under the kitchen's fifteen-foot ceilings, he was an imposing presence.

"I would not want to put you to any trouble. I should be going, but I'd like to take a proper leave of Benny."

Other than Henry and one potboy the worse for drink, the kitchen at this hour was deserted. The kitchen staff would wander in at mid-day, the waiters not until late afternoon. Ann had wanted Benny to start when she and the girl could make a thorough tour of the kitchen without an audience.

"I thought Benny and I would begin with a batch of crepes," Ann said. "She would enjoy sharing them with you, Colonel."

Ann would enjoy sharing another meal with him.

He circled his hat in his hands. "I thought you said the batter had to rest."

And he had recalled her words. "I made the batter last night. Benny can learn to cook them this morning and to clean up the mess as well. She can watch me making a pear filling while she beats the heavy cream, and her first lesson as a cook's apprentice will be delicious and in good company."

Benny scampered into the kitchen, her apron rolled up at the waist to prevent her hems from dragging, a puffy white cap hiding her braids. The girl was neat as a pin and bore the scents of starch and lavender soap.

"Reporting for duty, Miss Ann." She snapped off a curtsey and offered a tentative smile.

"First rule," Ann said, "no running, ever, just like in the stables you love so well. You don't want to accidently jostle the *rôtisseur* when he's carving his roasts. We might walk swiftly, but we do not run."

Benny nodded solemnly. "Yes, Miss Ann."

That was the proper response. Had Benny made an excuse or offered a denial, Ann would have delivered a stern lecture, regardless of the colonel's presence.

"Hands," Ann said.

Benny obligingly held out two pale paws.

"Wash them again," Ann said. "Washing your hands marks the beginning of your every task as a cook. Normally, I would have you read the whole recipe and ask me any questions before we begin, but we aren't cooking from a recipe this morning."

"No recipe?" the colonel asked.

"I will rely on memory and inspiration," Ann said as Benny walked *quite* quickly to the wet sink under the windows. "May I take your hat and coat, Colonel?"

He passed her his hat and turned his back, and Ann lifted his greatcoat away as he shrugged loose of it. The wool was heavy and soft, first quality, and redolent of cedar. She indulged in a sniff before he faced her again. Cedar and leather, London's smoky rain, and that underlying hint of Provence he carried with him everywhere.

"My hands are clean," Benny announced. "Do we get to eat the crepes?"

"We will share them with Colonel Goddard, assuming our efforts are successful." Ann started Benny on the arduous business of whipping air into cold, heavy cream.

"And what might I do to be of use?" the colonel asked, slipping his sleeve buttons into a pocket and turning back his cuffs. "I'll have you know I've peeled potatoes and apples by the hour, though army cooks are inclined to leave the skin on to save time."

"You keep me company," Ann said, nodding to a stool beside the cook stove, "while I create the pear sauce. When the sauce comes to a rolling boil, I will start on the crepes, and you can continue stirring."

And exactly when had the sight of a man's wrists become so distracting?

"I'm not to wash my hands before I start?" he asked, settling onto the stool.

"You used your lavender soap thoroughly this morning, and you are not embarking on a career as a cook."

"Alas for me. Does champagne go well with pears?"

While Ann mashed some of her pears and sliced the rest, and debated whether to include a dash of rose water, a dollop of honey, or the zest of a lemon, the colonel lounged on his stool and discussed wine pairings and winemaking with her.

At some point, he slipped into French, as did Ann, and all the while, Benny toiled away at her whipped cream.

"You are happy," the colonel said when the sauce was burbling gently. "You look happy, you sound happy. Stirring up that pot of gold, you radiate contentment. Your French is also impressively facile."

Ann *was* happy. Taking on an apprentice had first struck her as a recipe for complications and years of thankless work, but seeing Benny eager to learn, watching her go at her assignment with gleeful enthusiasm, Ann allowed that an apprentice was a step toward opening a cooking school. Not entirely a bad thing.

And yet, that wasn't the whole motivation for the good cheer Colonel Goddard noted.

"Thank you," she said. "With Monsieur Delacourt regularly trying to confound us all in his native tongue, one wants to keep the vocabulary fresh. When are you happy, Colonel?"

He watched Benny, his expression wistful. "I was happy showing a pair of striplings around my vineyards. They will try to outdo each other learning the business, they will bumble and occasionally fail, but I realized that I am no longer a stripling myself, haven't been for years, and there's peace and satisfaction in knowing that leg of life's journey has been completed."

He did not recount a particularly stirring battle or close-run horse race against his fellow officers.

"I want to open a school for cooks," Ann said, though she hadn't planned that admission. She took up a pinch of ground ginger and sprinkled it into her pear sauce. "A daft notion, but why teach only one apprentice when half a dozen could be learning at the same time? The school could serve as a kitchen for charities, or offer hot meals to the working folk who have only chophouse fare to sustain them."

"What's stopping you from opening this school?"

Ann added a dram of rose water. The resulting aroma as steam rose from the pot was lush and sweet. "I hesitate for want of courage, I suppose. My aunt and uncle would be scandalized. Bad enough I am a cook, but at least nobody ever sees me toiling away."

She added a pinch of cinnamon. "The irony is, I became a cook in part because I used to have my father's company only at meals. He was always out and about, riding his acres, meeting with tenants. Had I been a boy, I could have spent much more time with him. But even Papa grew hungry, and my grandmother insisted he be punctual for meals. He saw me at table, though I was all but invisible to him everywhere else."

The colonel passed her half a lemon. "I can offer only one man's humble opinion, Miss Pearson. I am exceedingly glad you number among the female of the species."

At that precise moment, Ann was also glad to be female and, more than that, to be feminine. She hadn't flirted with a man since the sous-chef at her last post had coaxed her beyond the limits of good sense.

With the colonel, Ann wanted to transgress yet further.

"It's getting thick," Benny hollered.

"Scrape the sides of the bowl frequently," Ann replied. She stirred her pear sauce down, then took up the half lemon. "You removed the seeds."

"The task wanted doing, and you are busy."

Ann considered the lemon, the tartness it would add, the hint of substance on the tongue the texture of the sauce would acquire by association.

"When you kissed me, I was happy then too, Colonel." She squirted lemon juice into the pot, inspiring another shift in the fragrance rising from the sauce. Five minutes more on the fire, and she'd have the result she wanted.

"Shall I take over stirring?" he asked, rising from his stool.

Heaven preserve her, she liked even standing next to him. Liked the sense that they were both enveloped in the heat from the stove and the scents from her concoction.

"Please, and I will inspect Benny's progress." Her hand brushed his as he took up the wooden spoon, and the contact reverberated through her imagination. She mentally poured a helping of his champagne into the saucepot, an experiment to try some other day, when she wasn't tempted to moon over a man to whom a passing kiss had doubtless meant little.

Benny had done a magnificent job with the cream, and she paid rapt attention as Ann demonstrated how to cook a crepe. By the time Benny had tried flipping the last few herself—and done a reasonable job—the sauce was ready.

They ate their crepes at the wooden counter beneath the window, the wind and rain lashing what leaves remained on the oak tree in the garden, while the kitchen was warm at their backs.

"These are good," Benny said. "As good as the blueberry crepes, but different."

"When we make crepes again," Ann said, "I will show you how to mix up the batter. We will find you a journal, Benny, so you can keep notes of your own and have a record of your progress as a cook."

Benny sat a little taller on her stool. "I am going to be a cook, and everybody will say my crepes are the best in London."

"See that they do," the colonel said, crossing his knife and fork over his empty plate. "And more to the point, see that you make the regiment proud, Benny. Or do we call you Hannah now?" He rose and took his plate to the wet sink, while Benny stared hard at the two remaining crepes on the warming dish.

"I would like to be Hannah," she said. "Benevolence Hannah Goddard. You'll tell the boys, sir?"

The colonel's expression was utterly solemn. "I will tell the boys." He took his coat down from the drying peg before the open hearth and retrieved his hat from the mantel. "Miss Pearson, thank you for a delightful meal. I know Hannah is in good hands, and that means the world to me."

He was saying good-bye in a way the girl herself could not fathom. This parting would change the course of her life, and the course of the colonel's too.

"I will take the best care of Hannah, Colonel. She will want for nothing."

Benny helped herself to a plain crepe, rolling it up and swiping it through the pear sauce on her plate. "'Bye, sir. I get to mix up the batter next time."

"I am dismissed," the colonel said softly. He tapped his hat onto his head and donned his coat. "Miss Pearson, good day and good luck."

Another good-bye. Ann had served him her best pear sauce, and he was walking away. "I'll see you out."

"That's not..." He fell silent. "Very well." He gave Benny a quick, tight, one-armed hug while she munched her crepe, then followed Ann down the passage and up the short flight of steps that led to the garden terrace. "You will notify me if Benny needs anything?"

"Of course. A journal would make a nice gift from you. Pencils are better than pens for jotting down kitchen notes."

"I will see to it." He paused at the door, the wind whipping through the garden audible proof that his journey home would be cold and unpleasant. "Do you know when else I was happy, Miss Pearson?"

"Ann. We've cooked together. Please call me Ann." *And please don't go.* How many times was she destined to have that useless thought where he was concerned?

"Do you know when else I was happy, Ann?"

"Tell me."

"When I was watching you stir that pot, when I was kissing you, when I was listening to you prattle on about when an apprentice is ready to take on desserts and meat dishes. I was happy watching you arrange an impromptu picnic on your terrace, and I will be happy when I recall all of those moments on the dark and chilly nights to come."

He sent one last glance in the direction of the kitchen. "I will miss her terribly."

His hand was on the latch. Ann caught him by the arm, though, of course, this man would come and go as he pleased.

"May I bring Hannah to call on you and the boys on our half day?"

Broad shoulders relaxed, military posture eased. "You wouldn't mind?"

"Not in the least."

"The boys and I would be in your debt." He did not kiss her, but he did smile, a purely charming, delighted smile that banished the wind, rain, and cold as effectively as did the roaring fire in the kitchen's open hearth.

"Until Wednesday, Colonel."

He bowed politely and slipped through the door.

Ann watched his progress across the dank and chilly garden. She was halfway through her lecture to Hannah about cleaning every utensil and bowl thoroughly after each use when she realized that, for a man who claimed to avoid sweets, Colonel Goddard had certainly made short work of a plate full of crepes.

CHAPTER SEVEN

"Cousin!" The child hurled herself at Orion, and he had no choice
but to catch her up in his arms.

"Nettie, mon agneau chéri. Qu'est-ce tu dessines?" His lamb had
left behind the toddler's solid physique for the more coltish dimensions of girlhood. When had that happened?

"She is drawing battles, of course," Tante Lucille said, motioning
Rye into the parlor. "You bring the cold and damp with you, and why
did not that useless Marie hang up your coat?"

"Marie took a little package for me to the kitchen." A sizable
package bearing tea, spices, honey, white flour, a half wheel of cheese,
and a few other comestibles. "Show me your great battle, Nettie."

She scrambled out of his embrace. *"Devez-vous parler anglaise,
Colonel?"*

"We must both speak English, child, until you can think as easily
in one language as the other." Though it was never quite that simple.
Rye dreamed in French, the language of his mother's lullabies, while
English was the natural choice for cursing.

"I am drawing the great Bonaparte," Nettie said, retrieving a
square of paper from the table by the window. "He was victorious

everywhere save Waterloo, and then he was defeated by the treacherous mud."

The great Bonaparte had erred beyond redemption by trying to best a Russian winter, and he'd made tactical blunders approaching his final battle too—thank the heavenly hosts. Rye shrugged out of his coat and hung it on the back of a chair facing the hearth. The fire was giving off adequate heat, but no more than adequate.

"You have drawn the emperor on a fine steed," Rye said, bending to kiss Tante Lucille's smooth cheek and taking a seat at the table. "He looks quite handsome." Nettie had drawn Bonaparte brandishing his sword. In battle, the man had been brave to a fault.

"Madame Martin comes by," Tante Lucille said. "She shows Nettie a few little things to improve her drawing."

Thus did the émigré community sustain itself. Madame, whose late husband had once owned thousands of acres, would not take money for instructing Nettie, but she would enjoy a cup of tea and some sandwiches during the lesson, and Lucille would press the leftovers on Madame when she left, *lest they go stale*.

Lucille, despite her advanced years, watched other people's children most days. The fiction that the children gathered in Lucille's parlor merely to play preserved parents from parting with coin. More than once, Rye had stopped by of an evening and found Lucille reading to a half-dozen children whose mothers were apparently employed in evening work.

If there was any justice, Bonaparte would have been made to apologize to his countrymen and countrywomen for what his ambitions had cost them.

"Nettie," Rye said, "might you see if Marie can use assistance in the kitchen? I did bring a few little treats with me, and they will need to be put away."

Nettie was out the door in the next instant, Bonaparte clearly forgotten.

"You spoil her," Lucille said. "Little girls should be spoiled from time to time. Little boys too. We heard you took some business from Fournier. Well done."

Rye had come here specifically to catch up on the gossip, but Lucille's blunt change of subject rankled. "How did you hear that?"

"Fournier grumbled, *naturellement*, and because he grumbled to his valet, his clerks, his mistress, his groom, and his dog, one could not help but hear. Our champagne is far superior to the pig swill he peddles, and he knows it."

Fournier served a decent, irreproachable champagne. His fault lay in what he charged for his product. "Dorning has allowed me a foot in the door at The Coventry Club, and Fournier will respect the family connection, but somebody has taken it into his head to breathe new life into the old rumors about me."

Lucille twitched at her shawl—only the one today, an exquisite creation of crocheted wool. The colors were an autumnal blend of gold, copper, olive, and slate blue and the weave loose. In her youth, Lucille wouldn't have been caught even at home in such a pedestrian garment, but for the next six months, she would likely wear it daily.

"Fournier is a businessman," Lucille said. "He would not dredge up military gossip to use against you. He would malign your grapes, your bottles, your prices, but not *you*."

"How do you know the gossip is military, Tante?"

Her dark brown eyes went to the scene beyond the window, a modest street of shops that might have been busier, but for the inclement weather. Few trees would sport many leaves after today's foul weather, and the sun would reach more of the pavement, when the sun deigned to appear at all.

"With you," she said, "the worst gossip is military. They cannot forget, these English, and they do not forgive. They want French lady's maids and French chefs. French valets, French tutors, and French fencing masters. They neglect to recall that we French have ears and long memories of our own."

"What have you heard?"

She waved a delicate hand sporting a fingerless, crocheted glove.

"You were a bumbler as an officer. You made foolish decisions. Your men suffered needlessly."

Mere grumbling. Persistent grumbling. Like every officer, Rye had made mistakes. Understandable, well-intentioned mistakes. Blunders even, or he'd followed stupid orders.

"Nothing more than that?"

Tante was spared a reply by Marie arriving with the tea tray, Nettie gamboling at her side. The maid set the tray down carefully, curtsied and left, while Nettie eyed the tea cakes. The service was Sèvres, and Lucille had famously secreted it in the trunks of her negligees and stockings when she'd fled to London. She'd been smart enough to bring fancy snuffboxes, vanity sets, and jewels as well, and her foresight had saved lives.

Her wealth had long since been dissipated when Rye had found her dwelling among London's émigrés. Lucille had allowed Rye to compensate her for Nettie's upbringing—and house her and a half dozen of her aging friends—in exchange for that assistance.

He sipped a cup of tea to be polite and ate a small slice of the *tarte aux pommes* he'd brought from Tante's preferred French bakery.

"The tart wants something," he said, dusting his hands over his plate. "It's good, but too well behaved."

"Calvados," Tante replied, sipping her tea. "In the cream, in the filling. A touch only. Monsieur Roberts would not waste his stores of good brandy on everyday preparations, but still, the tart is good."

The tart was French, and that sufficed for Lucille, despite its prosaic flavor.

"The tart is very good," Nettie declared. "May I have more?"

Tante went off into a scold entirely in French.

"You may be excused," Rye said, untucking the table napkin from beneath Nettie's chin. "I want to hear an English poem from memory the next time I visit, Nettie."

Nettie scrambled out of her chair. "I will find something from Mr. Wordsworth. He likes France."

Nowhere near as much now as he had earlier in his career. The Terror and ensuing wars had cost France many of her English admirers.

"You choose the poem," Rye said, "and it must be English."

She made a face and trotted off without sparing him a curtsey.

"There is time to make her into the perfect English schoolgirl, Orion. Have another slice of tart."

Had Ann made that tart, she would have known exactly how much calvados to add, when to add it, and how to flavor the cream.

"Tell me more about these rumors, Aunt, and please don't prevaricate."

She sniffed, she adjusted her shawl, she generally exercised an old woman's right to make company wait upon her pronouncements.

"They say you sold secrets to the French. That you did so in exchange for promises that the retreating French army would not loot your farms in Provence."

"The fighting remained west of Provence."

"The looting went on all over France, my boy. The Grande Armée made off with our sons and husbands, then it made off with our livestock, and eventually, our very buildings were ripped down to feed its campfires. Thank the merciful God I was not in France to see that."

The émigrés endured a torn existence, longing for home, mistrusted in England, bitter toward France's democratic violence, and unimpressed with the recently restored monarchy.

"Who says I sold secrets to the French?"

Lucille gave him an imperious stare.

"I know Deschamps is back in London, Lucille. He has reason to dislike me, and I most assuredly do not like him."

Lucille glowered down an aquiline nose. "If we slandered all whom we dislike, we would have no time for laughter. Besides, what Frenchman would boast of having relied upon a spy? Dirty business, spying. War is at least honorable, no sneaking about involved."

Many a Frenchman would boast about having compromised an

English officer's honor. "Very well, I will confront Deschamps myself."

"Vous avez l'intelligence d'un mulet."

"The stubbornness of a mule, perhaps. Mules are actually quite smart." Rye rose and gathered up his coat. "Wordsworth wrote a lovely little verse about a rainbow. Nettie might consider starting there. It's only eight or nine lines." *The child is father of the man...*

That sentiment put him in mind of Ann, longing for her father's notice, looking forward to each meal in hopes she might gain a moment of his attention.

"You must not confront Deschamps," Lucille said, rising. "He is no fool."

"Somebody is interfering with my business, attacking my good name, and going to great lengths to do it. Selling secrets to an enemy is treason, Aunt, and a hanging felony. If I could in any way see how the charges might be justified, I'd withdraw quietly to France and ponder how to atone for my error, but I cannot."

Rye had had opportunity after opportunity to betray his command—officers on all sides of the conflict faced such temptations—but he'd made his choice for England and kept his word.

"If you are determined to die of male stupidity, you should first bring your sister around to meet Nettie. They are family."

"Jeanette doesn't even know Nettie exists..." Well, that might not be true. Sycamore Dorning had chanced upon Nettie and her nurse paying a call upon Rye's household. Dorning was entirely in Jeanette's confidence.

"Jeanette should know of Nettie's existence, Orion, because you are soon to be spitted upon Deschamps's sword, and I will not live forever."

"I fence well enough."

"Deschamps is a former French officer. He will fillet you *comme un maquereau*."

Like a mackerel. "I merely want to talk with him, Aunt."

She snorted as only a disgusted elderly Frenchwoman could

snort, and she had a point. Jeanette and Nettie were related, and keeping Nettie's existence secret served no one. Rye had promised his sister he would make an effort to socialize with her, but the rumors—the intensifying rumors—bothered him sorely.

Jeanette, and even Sycamore Dorning—damn it all to hell—were owed an explanation.

"I will take my leave of you, and you have my ongoing thanks for all you do for Nettie. I will call again next week and expect to hear my poem."

Aunt made no move to accompany him into the chilly hallway. "If you are alive next week. Do you dislike the French countryside so much, Orion? You could take Nettie to live with you in Champagne or Provence, and she would have no need of silly English poems."

Wordsworth was sentimental, not silly. "I delight in the French countryside, but the market for my wine is here." His boys were here, Jeanette was here. His parents were buried in England on the Surrey property where he'd been raised.

"Deschamps is biding with his cousin, Mullineau," Tante Lucille said, "the cloth merchant. Deschamps rides out on fine mornings and frequents La Retraite of an evening. You will be careful, Orion. If you can be neither intelligent nor sensible, you will at least be careful."

"I am always careful." He took his leave, using the walk home to mentally rehearse his discussion with Jeanette. How to explain Nettie, and more to the point, how to explain his failure to mention her to Jeanette previously?

Upon arriving home, Rye took up his daily battle with the ledgers in his study, the fire's feeble efforts to dispel the chill abetted by a decent glass of brandy. Rather than pour another, Rye bestirred himself to build up the fire.

He'd added half a bucket of coal, poked some air into the flames, and was replacing the hearth screen before he noticed that his cavalry sword no longer hung in its assigned place over the mantel.

No matter. He kept the thing on display as a reproach and a warning, not because he cherished it as a memento. He'd killed with that sword and intended to finish out his days without ever killing again. If Mrs. Murphy had taken it down to give it a dusting, she'd soon have it back up again.

He resumed his tallying and came to the same conclusion he usually did: Without substantial new custom, his best vintages were destined to spend the next several years gathering dust at his expense.

"ANOTHER INVITATION?" Horace asked.

Meli would reproach the butler later for bringing the note to her at the breakfast table. "Ann's duties do not permit her to call on me this morning."

Ann further promised to send along the menu and recipes for Deidre Walters's buffet by the end of the day—and that assurance was none of Horace's concern. Deidre's youngest was enthralled with the harp, and nothing would do but half of Mayfair must delight in the girl's talent while her mama cooed and clapped after each piece.

And because Miss Walters's talent wasn't likely to impress the audience all that much, Deidre wanted stellar offerings on the buffet at the interlude.

"I thought Wednesday was Ann's half day," Horace said, pouring himself another cup of coffee. "Half days are for walking in the park and calling upon acquaintances. Shopping for bonnets and gloves. What at the Coventry could possibly come between a young lady and her opportunities to shop?"

Why would Horace recall Ann's half day? But then, his mind worked like that. He had the memory of a homely spinster keeping track of social slights, a talent that had served him well when negotiating myriad military procedures and rules.

"You are correct," Meli replied. "Today is Ann's half day, but she has taken on an apprentice, a girl from Colonel Orion Goddard's household. Ann has some errands to run with her new protégé. Will you attend the Walters's musicale with me?"

Horace paused with his coffee cup halfway to his mouth. "Goddard's household hasn't any females, other than a daily housekeeper and a maid-of-all-work. Perhaps he's taken to foisting his émigré connections off on his in-laws. Who is this protégé?"

And this was the inconvenient side of marriage to a man who recalled details and expected his every question to be respectfully answered.

But then, familiarity with the exact make-up of a former direct report's household went beyond recalling a stray detail.

"I hardly know who she is." Meli used the honey whisk to trail a skein of sweetness into her tea, though what she truly longed for was a slosh of brandy to settle her nerves. "The Walters's musicale is next Thursday, and while I understand that you are no great fan of the harp, you do have a good opinion of Captain Walters. His baby sister will entertain us."

"Walters married the Glenville girl." Horace refolded his newspaper and pressed it flat beside his plate. "Flighty thing, but she bore up cheerfully enough on campaign."

Horace slurped his coffee, a habit that increasingly grated on Meli's nerves. Horace had always slurped his coffee and his tea, but since settling into London life, that singularly ungenteel noise struck Meli as proof of his increasing years.

"Who else will be there?" he asked, perusing his newspaper.

Melisande rattled off a guest list rife with military acquaintances, a few bachelors to make up the numbers, and the usual sprinkling of wallflowers to swell the audience ranks.

"I suppose we must show the colors," Horace said, taking another slurp. "Truly, my dear, I do not fathom how your niece can prefer the drudgery of a cook's life to genteel entertainments and your own company. Ann isn't bad looking, and she has some means. She would make you a perfect companion. Is there some reason she disdains to join our household?"

"Stubbornness, I suppose." Though Meli almost—almost—understood the allure of having a skill for which a woman would be paid a decent wage. If that woman was unmarried and of age, she also had the legal standing to keep her wages for her own use.

No hoping her husband had instructed the solicitors on the matter of her monthly pin money. No economizing on candles to replace a pair of slippers that had become unfashionable in a single Season.

Still, to work all day, dealing with animal carcasses, coarse company, and manual labor... That was much too high a price to pay for a loss of standing in genteel society.

"You can be stubborn too," Horace said, "and I must tell you honestly, Melisande, I do not care for any association between my family and Orion Goddard. I stood by him through all the rumors and even the official inquiry, but that there *was* an inquiry was most unfortunate."

The military was always convening boards of inquiry. As best Meli recalled, Horace himself had requested that Goddard's situation be investigated, claiming that was the only way to clear the colonel's name.

Goddard had been knighted, suggesting somebody had been convinced of his worth. To observe as much would doubtless send Horace off onto one of his diatribes about military justice, appearances, the honor of the regiment, and necessary compromises for the greater good. As a younger wife, Meli had heard that speech more often than any other in Horace's substantial repertoire.

"I can hardly persuade Ann to give up her cooking if she's no longer permitted to call on me, sir."

Horace set down his coffee cup and folded his paper up. It never occurred to him that when he marched off to his club every morning, he might leave the Society pages for his wife to read. Meli was reduced to paying for a second subscription that was sent to her sitting room at noon, after the maids had had a chance to iron the pages.

That precaution was necessary, because Horace would notice

ink-stained fingers and doubtless inquire as to how Meli had acquired them.

"Ann is family," Horace said. "We would never turn her away, but neither should you ignore the risks she runs to her good name and to your own by association. You might remind her that Goddard is not well regarded among his fellow officers, and perhaps she will choose her next apprentice with more care."

Actually, Orion Goddard had been well liked by his peers and respected by his subordinates. He'd been mentioned in the occasional dispatch—a high honor—and there was that knighthood.

"I don't think Ann had any choice about taking the girl on," Meli said. "Goddard is Sycamore Dorning's brother by marriage, and the Dornings are notoriously loyal to family. If Dorning told Ann to take on an apprentice, Ann could not have refused that direct order." Then too, the Dornings boasted an earldom among the family treasures, and Sycamore Dorning's wife was the widow of a marquess.

That Horace, who well knew the value of influence and social standing, would eschew Goddard's company when the colonel could claim such connections was a puzzle.

And a worry.

Horace rose and tucked the newspaper under his arm. "Enough about Ann and her misguided notions. I'm off to hear all the news at the club, my dear." He came down to Meli's end of the table and bussed her cheek. "What have you planned for today?"

"I must begin the preparations for our officers' dinner in earnest. Choose the flowers, inventory the linen, ensure the Portuguese silver is polished. The staff looks forward to those dinners, as do I."

She didn't, actually—the same stories, the same jokes, the same sly winks—but Horace did, so Meli would make the effort.

Horace caught her hand and bowed over it. "Truly, I am well blessed in my wife, Melisande. I will happily escort you to the Walters do, and I am sure you will be the prettiest lady of the whole gathering."

He smiled, kissed her knuckles, and took his leave of her, ever the gallant officer, though Meli was no longer the blushing young wife who thrived on flummery and flirtation. Philippe Deschamps had disabused her of much silliness, then war, polite society, and the passing years had done the rest.

Meli waited until she heard the front door close before she slipped her flask from her skirt pocket and tipped a quarter of the contents into her tea. She had downed a fortifying swallow of Dutch courage when the footman returned to clear away the empty place at the head of the table.

She'd meant to use Ann's weekly call to ask her to finalize a menu for the officers' dinner. The task could not wait another week, so Meli would have to send a note around to Ann's lodgings. How to do that without Horace getting wind of it was yet another puzzle.

A commanding officer's wife had to be good at solving puzzles and intrigues. Meli would solve this one too.

~

"ORION, DO COME IN." Jeanette's smile was hesitant, and that alone shamed Rye. He'd kept his distance from his only sibling, hoping that his troubles would not become her troubles. Thus Rye had been nowhere nearby when Jeanette had acquired troubles of her own, and Sycamore Dorning had charged into the breach.

"Jeanette." Rye bowed, an awkward courtesy between brother and sister, but with Dorning hovering at Jeanette's elbow, courtesy was the safer alternative. "You look well."

"I enjoy great good health, thank you. Won't you have a seat?"

And that was another courtesy, to treat her own brother to the manners due a caller. Rye took the wing chair facing the parlor door, which seemed to amuse Dorning.

"Shall I ring for a tray?" Jeanette asked, resuming her place on the sofa. Dorning, of course, took the place beside her and possessed himself of her hand, as if Rye might presume so far as to ask his sister to stroll with him in the garden.

"A tray won't be necessary. I don't want to take up much of your time, but I did want to thank both you and Dorning for your kindness toward Hannah."

Dorning left off stroking Jeanette's wrist. "Miss Pearson's apprentice has been entered on the wage books as Hannah Goddard. Jeanette saw no reason to keep the girl's family connection quiet."

This was not good, and a problem Rye should have foreseen. "As I have never married, and Hannah bears my name, the inferences might redound to Hannah's discredit."

Dorning linked his fingers with Jeanette's. "Not in the kitchen, they won't. In the kitchen, an association by marriage with the Dorning family will keep my chef from being unduly stupid where the girl is concerned."

Now was not the time to inform Dorning that Rye's reputation was undergoing one of its periodic whippings at the figurative cart's tail, but that discussion would have to take place soon.

"I see your point," Rye said, "though allowing Hannah to claim that connection might also make her more resented."

"Stop it." Jeanette shook her hand free from her husband's grasp. "Both of you stop circling each other like tomcats in the stable yard. I have asked Miss Pearson to keep me apprised of Hannah's progress and spoken to Jules Delacourt myself regarding my interest in this particular apprentice. He has assured me that he will do all in his power to see the girl well educated."

And Jeanette, having little acquaintance with a Frenchman in a temper, would have been satisfied with those reassurances.

"In any case," Rye said, "you extended a kindness to a member of my household, and I am grateful to you both."

"You're welcome," Dorning said, the words anything but gracious. "Will you blow retreat now that you've done your duty? Scamper off to your club for recluses and reappear seven years hence to thank us again when Hannah's apprenticeship is complete?"

"I have promised Jeanette I will not play least in sight again,

Dorning, and I keep my word. To that end, I wanted to acquaint my sister with a family matter that might one day concern her."

Jeanette passed her husband a knife that had been sitting atop a bound volume on the low table. The blade was designed for throwing, a single dark curve of metal that ended in a lethal point.

"Rye, are you well?"

"I am, actually." Impending cold weather had caused his hip to stiffen up of a morning, but other than that, the headaches were infrequent, and he was sleeping reasonably well. "I haven't anything truly serious to impart, but I thought you should know that our cousin Jacques's daughter is here in London, a child of about five. I've placed her in the keeping of Lucille Roberts, whose family owned land near Grand-mère's farms."

Jeanette and her husband exchanged some sort of look. "The Roberts family owned quite a lot of land, didn't they?" Jeanette asked. "They raised the traditional herbs, thyme, basil, rosemary... I forget what else. Mama corresponded with them."

Ann Pearson would know each of the traditional herbs of Provence and have her own recipe for blending them.

"Jacques married one of the Roberts ladies," Rye replied. "He managed to send the child here before Wellington made it into France. She was an infant at the time and recalls nothing of the journey." *Thank God.*

"I have a cousin in London?"

"A small cousin at some remove, and like you, she is named for Grand-mère. Nettie looks a little like you."

Jeanette's husband watched her and said nothing. Dorning had come upon little Nettie in Rye's back garden just the once, months ago, and apparently had said nothing about the encounter.

"I would like to meet her," Jeanette said. "Nettie is family."

That was the response Rye had been hoping for, and yet, to share Nettie with Jeanette also meant a loss. The upbringing of a girl child would more naturally fall to Jeanette, and Rye would no longer be the only cousin visiting Nettie's household.

"I will happily introduce you to her."

"Introduce *us*," Dorning said, casually hurling the knife in the direction of a cork target on the opposite wall. "I am well versed in the art of doting upon younger female relations, and this Nettie person will benefit from my expertise. She can laugh at my French, and I will let her dance upon my toes."

Rye would be doubly displaced then, because a married couple would have more to offer an orphaned child than a military bachelor did.

"She is bilingual, though French is still her preferred tongue. I don't want her to lose the French, but neither do I..."

"You don't want her to suffer for her heritage," Jeanette said. "I understand. Are there other relatives lurking on your coattails, Rye?"

"She is not on my coattails. I have inherited more of the family's French holdings than is my due, and any number of Frenchmen regard that as a gross injustice. Perhaps one day, some of those holdings can be Nettie's."

"I have a platoon of siblings," Dorning remarked, "and yet, they collectively do not haul about half of the complications and secrets that Jeanette's one brother seems to have acquired. When can we meet the girl?"

That Rye's visit had achieved its objective should not leave him feeling so empty. "I'll send a note around to Tante Lucille and see if Friday suits. Please do not think to pluck Nettie away from all that is familiar. She is dear to Lucille and has a circle of little friends among the émigré community."

Dorning retrieved the knife from the center of the target. If Ann Pearson ever watched Rye the way Jeanette watched her husband merely stroll across the room, Rye dearly hoped that he and the lady were behind a locked door on that happy occasion. Dorning was somehow preening for his wife's delectation, even in the way he walked, even in the way he stroked the point of the blade with his fingertip.

"The situation is more complicated than simply a child fond of her playmates, isn't it?" Jeanette asked. "You support Lucille Roberts. She probably supports others with your largesse, or aids them. Removing Nettie to dwell with me here would be like pulling a loose thread that unravels half a garment."

Rye had forgotten what a noticing sort of female Jeanette was. In a little sister, that trait had been inconvenient.

"Precisely," he said. "Lucille does not hire a drawing instructor for Nettie, but a neighbor drops by regularly and provides that service over a full tea tray. Nettie's clothes are stitched up by another neighbor, because Lucille's eyesight—which misses nothing—is too dim to manage the chore. The nursemaid sends half her pay back to France and so forth. These people cannot go home, so they make a home here as best they can."

Dorning laid the knife on the low table, which was proof positive this household was not ready to receive a child. That thought begged the question of whether the boys had taken a notion to inspect Rye's sword without permission, for the damned thing still hadn't been returned to its proper place.

"We will merely call upon little Nettie," Jeanette said. "Introduce ourselves. Would she like a new doll?"

Rye studied the botanical print of some seven-petaled white flowers blooming amid dark green foliage. "She has a half-dozen dolls."

"A stuffed pony?" Dorning suggested. "Some mighty steeds for the dolls to charge about on?"

"She has several of those."

"A little tea set?" Jeanette asked. "A hobby horse?"

Rye shook his head, feeling abruptly very foolish. "She needs books in English, the sort of books girls might like to read."

Jeanette acquired a determined expression that Rye recalled from her earliest youth, one that accentuated her resemblance to Nettie. "I will consult my sisters-in-law, and we will make a list."

"The child will need a library to house the results," Dorning said. "Trust me on this, Goddard. I notice you did not answer Jeanette's question about other French relatives hiding in the hedges. Have we only the one small cousin to spoil?"

"Yes." Jacques hadn't been able to get any of his older children to safety, and his wife had refused to abandon them. "Nettie has siblings in Provence, and they are well provided for."

"No parents?" Dorning asked quietly.

Rye shook his head. "Nor grandparents. I'll take my leave and send around the direction if Lucille is willing to receive us on Friday."

"If not Friday," Jeanette said, taking up the knife Dorning had put on the table, "you ask her when, Rye. Nettie has lost much, but she has us."

Jeanette threw the knife with as much force as Dorning had, and her throw landed closer to the center of the target than his.

"Please do not think to furnish the child with weapons," Rye said. "She's five, as best I can figure."

"No knives," Dorning said, "yet. I will see you out."

The moment turned awkward, for how did a brother take leave of the sister whom he'd all but scorned for several years?

Rye took the six steps necessary to reach for Jeanette's hand, but she rose and wrapped him in a hug instead.

"I have missed you, Rye. Missed you sorely and worried over you. I never wanted you to go to war, and I wish..."

He gave her a gentle squeeze, and it hit him with a hard pang of the heart that she was not the seventeen-year-old girl who'd seen him off to Spain. He and Jeanette had missed much, while he'd been soldiering and she'd been enduring a difficult marriage. They had missed much since he'd come home as well, and that was also his fault.

"I wish too, Jeanette. But we have today." A refrain among the refugees who gathered around Lucille's pretty tea service.

"We also have business to discuss," Dorning said when Rye stepped back. "Come along, Goddard, and tell me when I might have my champagne."

Rye had already sent Dorning a specific date by letter, and Dorning had provided a deposit as a show of good faith by return post. Dorning kept silent until Rye was at the front door, coat buttoned, walking stick in hand, and the butler had withdrawn belowstairs.

"You did not tell Jeanette you'd come upon Nettie in my garden months ago," Rye said. "I appreciate your discretion."

"The encounter slipped my mind until recently," Dorning replied. "I have been preoccupied with getting off on a sound marital foot with my wife. Which I am, by the way. A splendidly sound marital foot."

Rye peered through a spotless window to study the traffic passing on the street beyond. "Your foot has nothing to do with Jeanette's air of contentment, Dorning."

"Noticed that, did you? Jeanette does seem to be truly content. She's learning the bookkeeping for the club from my brother Ash, she's a dab hand at correspondence, and she talks recipes with Miss Pearson. Even Delacourt seems to like Jeanette. They speak French so quickly I cannot tell if they are arguing or teasing, but Jeanette says I need not worry, so I don't."

"You worry," Rye said, finding a backward humor in the realization. "You worry like a commanding officer worries for his recruits and a mama bear worries for her cubs."

Dorning smiled, all charm and self-satisfaction. "A papa bear, please. Shall Jeanette and I take little Nettie driving in the park if the weather's fine?"

"No, you shall not."

Dorning's smile became a smirk. "Don't be peevish, Goddard. You have neglected to show the little dear the wonders of London, but Jeanette and I can correct your oversight and take her for a treat or two at Gunter's. The menagerie would doubtless delight a child of such tender years, and one must not neglect to feed—"

"*Pour l'amour de Dieu, chut.*"

Dorning looked Rye up and down. "And why should I hush?"

"Because a discreet call upon the girl is one thing, but now is not the time to announce that Jeanette has established ties with a long-lost French cousin."

Dorning glanced back in the direction of the parlor and heaved a put-upon sigh. "This is complicated?"

"The matter requires discretion."

"Shall I call on you this afternoon?"

Nothing and nobody—least of all Sycamore Perishing Dorning—would come between Rye and the afternoon's call from Ann Pearson.

"Join me at the Aurora for dinner. We can dine early in deference to your responsibilities at the Coventry."

"We will dine at the usual hour, lest Jeanette fret because you and I are off in the corner being *discreet*. I have no secrets from my wife, Goddard."

A state of affairs about which Dorning was inordinately proud. "Nor would I ask you to keep any, but you do apparently claim a modicum of discretion, despite all press to the contrary. I will see you tonight."

Dorning held the door for him. Rye checked the street to ensure Louis was in sight, then trotted down the steps and made for home.

CHAPTER EIGHT

"We are *de trop*, Colonel." Ann tugged gently on Orion Goddard's arm. "Leave the infantry unsupervised for a moment."

He tarried in the doorway to the servants' hall, his gaze on the children clustered at the end of the table nearest the hearth.

"She looks happy," he said, gaze on Hannah and the boys enjoying the butter biscuits Ann and Hannah had brought from the Coventry's kitchens. "She looks rosy and proud and happy. Thank you."

"She was even happier to make her first batch of butter biscuits this morning," Ann said. "The cinnamon aroma in the kitchen, the taste of the first batch warm from the bake oven, the longing glances from the waiters and footmen... She reveled in all of it. Hannah will make an excellent cook, if early days tell the tale."

Though they often did not. The absconding apprentice was a caricature in British humor, but all too often a reality as well.

"I am in your debt," Goddard said, "and you are correct. My hovering presence isn't necessary. I would invite you up to the guest parlor there to lament the weather with me, except I forgot to light the fire until you were on my doorstep, and the room is quite chilly. My office is warmer, if you can bear the slight to good manners."

"I am too pragmatic to value manners over comfort, Colonel, and I did not surrender all of the biscuits to the children." Then too, Ann wanted to see his office, a space where he would not normally welcome a social caller.

He'd seen her kitchen, after all.

"Cider and biscuits?" he asked, detouring into the kitchen. "Or could I tempt you to try my hot buttered rum, in deference to the weather?"

"Is the recipe yours?"

"My grandfather's, then my father's, and now mine."

Ann was torn between the notion that a lady did not take strong spirits and a burning curiosity to know his recipe.

The colonel leaned closer, as if the children laughing and carrying on in the hall might overhear him. "I'd take it as a kindness if you'd say yes. My hip is predicting colder weather, and a medicinal tot would enliven my afternoon considerably."

"In the interests of facilitating your good health, I will accept a small serving of your hot buttered rum."

The ingredients were few and readily at hand: dark rum, butter, brown sugar, water, spices, and—Ann would not have thought to add this—a precious dash of vanilla.

"You don't measure the spices?" she asked, itching to take notes regarding the order in which the nutmeg, cinnamon, cloves, and allspice went into the mix. No ginger, which was sensible. Ginger had a pungent quality the other warm spices lacked.

"A pinch per serving," he said, giving his melted butter-and-spice mixture a stir. "The real question is how much hot water to add, and that's a matter of personal taste. Shall we take our drinks to my office, where we can enjoy them without the sound of pitched battle from across the corridor?"

"A happy battle," Ann said, taking the steaming teakettle off the hearth swing. "I'd like my drink to resemble yours as nearly as possible."

He poured off his mixture into two sizable, plain mugs. "I prefer mine at what we used to call marching strength."

"If I'm to learn to make this concoction to serve at the Coventry, then I must acquaint myself with the version that will appeal to a robustly healthy male in his prime."

"About as much water as rum," he said, stepping back. "And I will cheerfully carry you home if the dose is too extreme for the patient."

He could do it too. Toss her over his shoulder and march back to her house, there to delight Miss Julia and Miss Dianna with his manly vigor.

Ann poured the hot water into the mugs, creating the most delicious scent imaginable. Buttery heaven, redolent of exotic spices and a rich, rummy undernote.

"I will carry the drinks," the colonel said, "and you will leave the mess for Mrs. Murphy to tidy up."

"If Mrs. Murphy is smart," Ann replied, leading the way to the steps, "she'll pour a dollop of rum into the dregs of the butter mixture and make herself a midafternoon treat."

"Mrs. Murphy is smitten." Colonel Goddard collected the mugs and followed in Ann's wake. "She has a swain of recent acquaintance, and I fear she will soon trade the glory of keeping my house for the joys of holy matrimony."

"Don't you mean the bonds of holy matrimony?"

"Left at the head of the stairs," the colonel said. "Bonds are not always a bad thing, Miss Pearson. Soldiers who've bonded with their comrades will fight more fiercely than those who do battle simply to earn the king's shilling. You are employed by a pair of siblings, and if I were to offend one Dorning brother, I have no doubt the remaining six would see me taken to task. That door," he said, nodding. "You are sworn to secrecy regarding unpaid bills and personal correspondence."

Colonel Goddard's office was, like the man himself, tidy and unassuming. The scent was leather, books, ink, and a hint of pipe tobacco. A manly space, and—as promised—well heated.

"You spend a lot of time in here," Ann said, inspecting the artwork. No military portraits or battle scenes. Instead, a landscape hung over the mantel, pastures and tilled fields under a pretty summer sky, a Tudor manor off to the side with red roses climbing halfway up one wall.

Opposite the windows hung a pair of portraits, the first of an older gentleman in the finery of the previous century. The second portrait was of two children, a boy and girl, the boy several years older than the girl. She had russet braids and a serious gaze that put Ann in mind of Jeanette Dorning. The dark-haired boy, who stood with a hand on the girl's shoulder, bristled with mischief and high spirits.

"You were a rascal." Ann set her reticule on the desk that faced the hearth. Two wing chairs stood between the desk and the fireplace, a hassock before one of them. "That has to be you and Mrs. Dorning."

"Guilty as charged. My childhood was mostly happy, though I cannot say Jeanette's early years were as sanguine as my own. I was the indulged only son, the apple of my papa's eye. We lost our mother too soon, though that took a harder toll on Jeanette than on me. You must not let your drink get cold. I believe you promised me biscuits, Miss Pearson."

"And I always keep my word." Ann wanted to make a circuit of the study, to handle the three little netsukes on the mantel—an elephant, a tiger, a horse—and to open the delicate cloisonné box on the windowsill to see if it held snuff, mints, or nothing at all.

The usual office accoutrements were in plain sight—abacus, paper, wax jack, pen tray, ink, quill pens, blotter, pounce pot, correspondence—but the small touches made the room as much a haven as a place of business.

The colonel brought her drink to her. "What does that look portend? Does the sight of my slippers offend?"

"Not at all." His scuffed slippers were tidily placed before the hearth, where they would stay warm until he had need of them. "I'm asking myself why the Coventry's kitchen has no small touches. Why not display a pretty painted tray on the deal table, or bring in the occasional flower from the garden?" Ann's own kitchen wasn't any more welcoming than her place of business.

The colonel touched his mug to hers. "To your health, Miss Pearson."

"And yours." Ann cradled the warm mug in her hands, a pleasure in itself, as was the spicy scent. She tried a cautious sip. "That is a powerful brew, Colonel."

"I'll fetch the teakettle if you'd like to add some water to yours."

Ann took another sip. "Warms the innards, which I believe was the point." The toddy also delighted the tongue with its smooth texture and spicy flavor.

"My grandmother liked hers with a dash of raspberry liqueur and fewer spices," the colonel said. "Shall we be seated?"

"My imagination will gallop away with that idea—raspberry liqueur and rum—and you will make a sot of me as I concoct my recipes."

The colonel took one of the chairs before the fire, Ann took the other.

"Raspberry liqueur makes a nice addition to champagne, according to some," he said. "Others like to blend the juice of oranges with a humble champagne, or even lemonade. I can't see it myself."

Ann could taste these ideas and smell them and see the pretty results. "You mentioned cold weather earlier. Can you truly predict the weather with your old injury?"

"Yes. Bad weather bothers both my hip and my head. Do you mind if I remove my eye patch? The day is gloomy enough that I need not fret over the light."

"Don't stand on ceremony on my account, Colonel. Tell me

about that manor house. The landscape looks like Surrey to me, or possibly Kent."

"The ancestral home," Colonel Goddard replied. "I let it out, but the lease is coming up for renewal, and I'm considering selling the place."

"It's not entailed?"

"My father broke the entail—with my consent as the heir—because we were in dire financial straits, and Papa was considering liquidating. Then Jeanette bagged her marquess, and disaster was averted for Papa and me, not so for Jeanette."

The fire blazed merrily, but the dreary weather—a brooding, leaden overcast chased by a chill wind—made the room dark.

"Forgive me," the colonel went on, stripping off his eye patch and tucking it into a pocket. "I ought not to burden you with ancient history."

"Your sister's first marriage was unhappy?"

"Utterly miserable, though I did not know that until I could do nothing for her. Papa bought me a commission with a portion of the largesse Jeanette had earned us, and off I went to play soldier. When I came home on my first winter leave, I realized I had made a serious mistake, but by then, the senior officers had decided my French antecedents were useful. Mustering out was not possible."

Ann tried another sip of her drink, this taste going down more easily, as did the next and the next. Her immediate superior was overly fond of spirits, and had Ann limitless access to the colonel's toddies, she might engage in the same folly.

Somebody had, in fact, nearly drained her glass.

"My aunt plagues me," she said, apropos of nothing. "Wants me to become her companion, to take my place in polite society. She fails to realize that I've seen much of that society at the Coventry, many of them not at their best. I like what I do, I make a difference to those who work with me."

The colonel set aside his drink. "No question of mustering out? Aren't you ever lonely, Ann?"

"All the time."

Had the colonel not used her name, she might have scrounged up a reply with pretensions to wit or charm. He'd spoken softly, though, and in his question lurked an admission that *he* was lonely, and had been for some time.

"I was an only child," Ann went on, because with Orion Goddard, she saw no point in dissembling. "I did not realize that most children have playmates, siblings, schoolmates... until I was nine years old, and my grandmother took me to some village celebration. She told me to go play with a group of children kicking a ball around, but I could not ask them for permission to join the game because I knew none of them by name. They knew each other's names, but I knew no other child in the whole shire by name. Watching them play, I realized my situation wasn't normal."

Colonel Goddard rose and took Ann's mug from her hand. She had no idea what he was about, but when he scooped her into his arms and settled back into his wing chair, she did not protest.

"Go on," he said, as if Ann weren't curled against his chest like an oversized feline. "You were sent away to school, and surely you learned some names there."

"How did you know?" And how did one conduct a conversation when cuddled up against so much male muscle and warmth?

"Settle, Ann. I harbor no untoward designs on your person."

"And if I have designs on yours, *Orion*?"

"With a horde of banshees ready to interrupt at any moment, your designs are doomed to failure, alas for me. My friends call me Rye. Tell me about school."

They were to be friends, then? Cuddling friends? Ann would ponder that mystery later, when she wasn't so comfortably ensconced in such a sweet embrace.

"My grandmother died. I was dispatched to the Midlands, where all good girls go to learn how to gossip, flirt, and tipple. The other students were busy making sheep's eyes at the drawing master, while I spent my free time in the kitchen. My classmates thought me odd, I thought them tedious, and if there's one thing young ladies do not tolerate, it's being considered tedious. You will put me to sleep if you keep that up, Colonel."

He was rubbing her back in slow circles that spread a warmth as insidious as that offered by the toddy.

"Call me Rye. That's a direct order. We're drinking companions now, and we've made pear sauce together. How did you come to be apprenticed?"

"My father died. My aunt—the only person who might have dissuaded me—had married and was no longer in England. I wrote a letter purporting to be from her informing Headmaster I was to spend the summer with her friends in London. I had enough samples of her penmanship to copy her hand. I applied to every agency that placed apprentices until a situation arose that suited me. By the time my aunt's next letter reached the headmaster months later, I had signed my articles and was delighting in my new profession."

The colonel's caresses moved to Ann's neck and shoulders, the pleasure of his touch exquisite. "You had made your bed, and you were determined to lie in it as only the young and foolish can be determined."

"That too. Aunt was a new wife. She and my uncle protested by letter, but they weren't in a position to undo the damage, and besides, I was happy, after a fashion."

"Pleased with yourself, you mean. Close your eyes, Ann. Rest. I'll keep you safe from invading forces."

He would keep her safe from designs on her person, too, drat the luck.

Ann could feel the colonel's heartbeat beneath her cheek, while the fire was a steady warmth at her back. She could not in seven eternities have predicted that her call upon Orion Goddard would end up in this cozy embrace by the hearth, nor would she have said she was particularly fatigued if asked.

And yet, she was so very tired, now that he held her like this. As her eyes drifted closed and her breathing slowed, she gave in to an exhaustion of more than the body, and to the very great comfort to be had in Orion Goddard's arms.

"SO THIS IS the most notoriously unassuming club in all of London?" Sycamore Dorning asked, glancing about at the Aurora's wainscoted foyer. "Nobody even knows who the members are."

"To learn who the members are," Rye replied, "you'd merely have to lurk across the street and watch who comes and goes. Secret entrances are for those with something to hide."

Dorning passed his greatcoat to the footman. "You doubtless did not join this august establishment until your scouts had monitored the comings and goings long enough that you knew the company to be had here."

"My scouts are good," Rye said, "but they don't move in exalted circles freely enough to know a viscount from a vintner. I simply asked for a list of the members and gave my word the information would go no further. Here at least, my word is still good. Table for two, Tims, where we won't be overheard."

"Very good, Colonel. I'll tell Lavellais, and he will find you in the lounge. Welcome to the Aurora, Mr. Dorning."

Tims glided off, moving soundlessly across the parquet marble floor.

"He knew who I was," Dorning said, frowning. "I like to think I enjoy a certain cachet, but he's a footman, and I'm nearly certain he's never seen me before."

"Why would you think that? You swan about at the Coventry like the king at a royal levee, you bear a resemblance to no less than eight siblings, one of them titled, and you are a stranger to any form of subtlety. Then too, you hold the vowels of half of polite society, and until recently, you also had a bachelor's welcome."

Rye led his guest to the Aurora's lounge, which could have served as the library of any Mayfair town house, right down to the bookshelves along the inside wall and a scattering of the week's newspapers on end tables and sideboards.

"You make me sound like a cross between a communicable disease and a meddling auntie," Dorning muttered. "Your dear sister finds me charming."

So did Rye, in the odd moment. "Jeanette has always enjoyed a challenge. She set out to dam up a stream once, and half the shire was soon complaining of the terrible drought. My father's steward didn't want to get her in trouble, so I had to help him unbuild what Jeanette had spent a week constructing."

"She simply built it up again?"

"I explained the problem to her—sheep will turn up thirsty under all that wool—and she settled for re-creating the Pool of London. She was six years old and intent on joining the Royal Navy."

Dorning scowled at one of Rye's fondest recollections. "I don't like that you know things about my wife that I don't know."

Rye had the same curiosity where Ann Pearson was concerned. How long was her hair? Who was her favorite poet? If she could be served any meal in the world, what would the menu be and with whom would she share it?

He'd learned one thing about her: She wasn't a sot. Her toddy had hit her like a mortar blast, knocking her literally off her feet.

Well, no. Not exactly. Rye had *swept* her off her feet—a first for him—and she had cuddled up like a weary kitten. She was small, nicely curved, and sturdy, and holding her had been balm to Rye's heart.

Also damned distracting. "Your siblings know things about you that Jeanette will never know," Rye said, choosing a pair of wing chairs in a corner of the room. "In your case, that is doubtless a mercy. I haven't the luxury of keeping you in ignorance about my own circumstances."

Dorning settled into a chair and crossed his legs at the knee, dandy-fashion. "This is where you explain why flowers wilt when you pass and songbirds are struck mute?"

"To the extent I can explain. Some of it is mysterious even to me." Before the lounge acquired any more occupants, Rye took a seat and sketched the particulars.

At his father's urging, he'd bought his colors. His knowledge of French language and military history had marked him for attention from the generals. His career had advanced rapidly, until the final push into France.

At that point, his commanding officer had tasked him with occasional casual reconnaissance, and nothing had felt right since.

"What does that mean?" Dorning asked. "Nothing has felt right?"

"I was told from time to time go have a look around beyond the camp, to assay the mood of the countryside, to mingle with the locals and hear what I could hear. My Spanish is not as good as my French, but by then, it was certainly serviceable."

Dorning withdrew a knife from his boot. "But wasn't an officer out of uniform—?"

"Considered a spy if captured, and thus subject to torture. I was careful, my French was that of a native. I could spy with much less risk than most, but it struck me as odd that I was an ineffective spy."

"Ineffective. Is that how you admit you made a poor job of listening at keyholes?"

Explaining the situation to another officer would have been difficult enough, but Dorning lacked military experience. He had no frame of reference for the story Rye was trying to relate.

"We all listened at keyholes as boys," Rye said, "but spying for military purposes is a different matter. You note the condition of pastureland—has a large herd of hoofed stock recently grazed down and trampled what should be a hayfield ready for scything? Is the tavern out of summer ale well before harvest? Are the women particularly nervous, and have the children all been confined indoors?"

Dorning flipped the knife from hand to hand. "I do not think I'd enjoy the business of war."

"We all half hope and half fear we're ill-suited to it, but then you survive a battle or two, and it's like a drug. Nothing makes you feel as alive, and nothing corrodes your soul as effectively. I reported back to my superior officer after every excursion, never having seen anything of any great value. The war was going well for us by then, and everybody—including the Spanish locals —knew it."

"But the war did not go well for you?"

The war was still not going well for Rye. "Talk started in camp, probably from the pickets who saw me leaving after dark in civilian attire, then returning hours later. I was not a womanizer of any repute, my facility with languages was common knowledge, and my orders were to be kept secret."

"With the entire camp ringed by sentries, whose sole purpose is to keep watch?"

"Precisely, and when the French began to have better luck ambushing our patrols and supply wagons, my name was brought up in a very unflattering context. To protect me, my commanding officer convened a board of inquiry. French desperation was blamed for our misfortunes, but the cloud over my reputation never entirely dissipated."

Dorning slipped the knife back into his boot. "Is the crown in the habit of knighting spies?"

"I attributed that mishap to some general or other hoping to reward me for service that could not be acknowledged. After the board of inquiry, I was tasked mostly with interviewing prisoners and managing supplies, which is exactly where you'd billet a man whose loyalty was suspect. I offered to resume active duty during the Hundred Days and was politely told to go to hell."

"Your name was not, then, cleared by the board of inquiry."

"Far from it. Any measure taken to exonerate me—the board of inquiry, the promotion to colonel, the knighthood—has only made me look more guilty. My commanding officer has insisted that ignoring the whole problem and going quietly about my business is the only prudent course, but the scandal could well ruin my business. I am nearly certain I know the French side of this equation, but who the British traitor was, I cannot say."

The *maître de maison* appeared in the doorway, a slim, immaculately groomed man of indeterminate years and African descent.

"Lavellais summons us," Rye said, rising. "There's more to the tale, but it can wait until we've eaten."

"Colonel, Mr. Dorning." Lavellais bowed, exuding the dignified good cheer of a duke. "Your table is ready, though, Colonel, you should know that Major MacKay and Captain Powell have just arrived. If you'd rather remove to a private dining room, I can take you through the cardroom."

Dorning was family, Dylan and Alasdhair were more than family. The notion of serving as a social nexus for unrelated parties was novel for Rye, but probably a bit like translating between languages.

"If Powell and MacKay are amenable," Rye said, "my cousins can dine with us."

"Cousins," Dorning said as Lavellais led them down the corridor. "My wife has grown, male cousins in Town at this unfashionable season, and this is the first I'm hearing of it. Should Jeanette plan to receive these cousins?"

"Dylan and Alasdhair only bide in London for part of the year. They ask after Jeanette, but until recently, she was a titled widow with a limited social calendar."

"Widows need family more than most, Goddard. I begin to think you were raised by wolves or, more likely, by some sort of reptile that lays its eggs in the sand and then crawls off to devour feckless rabbits."

Papa had spent hours tramping about the hedges in search of feckless rabbits. "From what Jeanette tells me, your titled father disappeared for weeks at a time to commune with ferns and orchids. Do not attempt to annoy my cousins for your amusement, Dorning. They are former military, and their patience, compared to my own vast stores, is limited."

Rye managed the introductions, knowing full well that both Dylan and Alasdhair were keeping questions about Dorning behind their teeth for now. While the meal was served, the talk remained general—who had taken a bad fall following the hounds, who was hiding from creditors.

Dorning listened more than he spoke, did justice to the steak, and kept his throwing knife out of sight. While Rye let Dylan and Alasdhair carry the conversation, he wondered if Ann would have enjoyed the *haricots vert amandine* and if she had a favorite recipe for steak gravy.

Would she ever again doze off in Rye's lap, and did she feel the same yearning that he did to share impossible pleasures?

When drinks had been carried to the reading room and the door firmly closed, Dorning took up a pose leaning on the mantel.

"Do I assume your cousins are in your confidence, Goddard?"

"You had better," Dylan replied amiably. "We are his *cousins*."

"Forgive Dorning," Rye said. "He is so mobbed with siblings he has little experience of relatives beyond immediate family. Dylan and Alasdhair served with me. They know my circumstances."

"We also know," Alasdhair said, sinking into a reading chair, "that Deschamps is underfoot in London, and if anybody is responsible for bringing misery upon your good name, it is he."

"Philippe Deschamps?" Dorning asked.

"You know him?"

"He's stopped by the club a time or two. Gambles prudently, flirts outrageously. Did not care for Fournier's champagne. Good-looking devil."

"Emphasis on the devil," Dylan muttered.

"You're jealous because you're dog-ugly," Alasdhair replied, though without heat or humor.

"Your cousins are like brothers," Dorning said, as if considering a fact that contradicted a pet hypothesis. "Or maybe like sisters."

"Returning to the matter at hand," Rye said, "Philippe

Deschamps was the aide-de-camp charged with carrying messages between the French camp and our own."

"What sort of messages?" Dorning asked.

"Prisoner lists, prisoner casualty lists," Dylan said. "We'd spend all day Monday trying to kill each other and the rest of the week being exquisitely civilized about the aftermath. The French military is fanatical about organization, and they wanted to know who of their number had fallen in battle, who had deserted, who was waiting for death in our infirmary, who was likely to recover and be sent to a parole village in Sussex."

"We fudged a bit regarding the deserters," Alasdhair said. "So did the French."

"Deschamps was doubtless keeping his eyes and ears open when he enjoyed a polite dinner with the commanding officer," Rye said, "but that sort of white-flag reconnaissance was expected. We'd send him off with a fine bottle of port, he'd gift the commanding officer with some decent brandy, and hostilities resumed the next morning."

Dorning looked fascinated. "And this sort of thing went on throughout the war?"

Dylan added a square of peat to the fire. "I was once tasked with negotiating access to a village whorehouse with my French counterpart. The French took Monday, Wednesday, and Friday. We got Tuesday, Thursday, and Saturday. The ladies had Sunday off to go to Mass, the whorehouse being Spanish."

"And you think Deschamps was your spy's point of contact among the enemy?" Dorning asked.

"We're almost sure of it," Rye replied, "but we cannot be nearly as certain who Deschamps's source of information was on our side."

Dorning finished his drink and set the glass on the sideboard. "But somebody has found it excessively convenient to pin that dishonor on you, Goddard. We need only determine who and decide whether or not to kill him. Are we agreed?"

"No," Rye said, wishing—of all things—that he could discuss this whole mess with Ann. "We are not agreed, Dorning. Not at all."

~

"I DO NOT WANT to go to the Coventry today," Ann informed an enormous fluffy gray cat. "This is a first for me." A somewhat disconcerting first for a woman who'd risen each morning, year after year, with cooking on her mind.

Boreas squinted at her from the side of the desk and went on rumbling like the autumn storms he was named for. Miss Diana and Miss Julia spoke to him freely and even invented replies from him. Ann was not quite that far gone.

Yet.

The day was brisk, the sky overcast, with no shift in light to delineate morning from afternoon. The colonel's hip had portended cold weather, though the day wasn't quite bitter. Worse, though, the weather was windy, giving the sullen air a bite that whistled beneath doors and rattled windowpanes.

"This should be a perfect day to spend in the kitchen," she said as the cat began licking his luxurious fur. "I don't want to go near the kitchen."

Aunt Melisande's note sat on the blotter, in this, the family parlor, not that Ann's only family would ever think to call on her here. Aunt inquired rather directly as to when Ann would provide the next menu, and could Ann please offer *a few suggestions* for the brigadier's quarterly officers' dinner as well?

"Time is of the essence," Ann quoted softly. Why did that one line from Melisande's little epistle rankle exceedingly? Not as much as the closing, though: *You have your orders, my dear. Please do march out smartly! M.*

A single consonant, as if such correspondence would somehow damn any who knew the author's identity.

"As if I am the poor relation," Ann said, running a hand over Boreas's soft fur.

The cat looked up sharply when a solid triple thump came from the direction of the front door.

"Not Mrs. Becker," Ann muttered. "Please not Mrs. Becker and her ailments." Mrs. B was a widow, and she came around regularly to lord her bereaved status over Miss Julia and Miss Diana, who, in their own words, had been too sensible to get caught in parson's mousetrap.

Ann took up a thick wool shawl and made her way to the door, dredging up a smile of welcome.

"Colonel Goddard." Her smile became genuine. "What a lovely surprise. Do come in."

"Miss Pearson, I hope I am not presuming. The hour is early for a call, but I know your afternoons are spoken for."

He made no move to enter the house, and the sight of him—eye patch securely in place, bearing erect, breeze whipping his dark hair —was rendered even more dear by the fact that he held a half-dozen pinkish roses in a small bouquet. His free hand sheltered the flowers from the wind, but their perfume came to Ann nonetheless.

"From your walled garden?"

"The very last of the stragglers," he said, still making no move to enter the house. "I thought you should have them. Their fragrance speaks more for them than does their appearance, and tonight would see them nipped, I'm sure."

"Please come in, Colonel. The day is too brisk to chat away the morning on the doorstep."

Humor lit his gaze, as if he knew that pragmatic speech for the sop to Ann's dignity that it was. The scent of the flowers was luscious, even if they weren't awash in glossy foliage, and that the colonel would bring them to her...

"I'm supposed to declare that you shouldn't have troubled to bring me flowers," Ann said, taking the bouquet from him, "and pretend eight more such offerings are already wilting in my conservatory, but this was very sweet of you, Colonel."

"I have an ulterior motive." He peered around, ever the reconnaissance officer, though Miss Julia's and Miss Diana's housekeeping exceeded even military standards.

"Which you make it a point to once again announce. You have little talent for subterfuge. Come to the parlor with me, and we'll find a vase for these blooms."

He accompanied her to the parlor, and Ann was glad that the older ladies were fanatical about the domestic arts. The room was warm, tidy, and as well lit as a parlor could be on such a dreary day. Though with Colonel Goddard on hand, the space seemed smaller, the ceiling lower.

"You trimmed the thorns," she said, filling a vase half full of water and setting the flowers on the windowsill. "Considerate of you."

He stroked the cat, who rose to encourage more such cosseting. "Who is this grand fellow?"

"Boreas, named for the Greek deity who brought the autumn storms. He offers us an expired rodent just often enough to maintain his credentials as a mouser. Shall I take your coat, Colonel?"

He passed Ann a gray wool scarf of exceptional softness, then set about undoing his buttons. "My grandmother knitted that scarf. The wool is from Ouessant—Ushant, to the English. A delightful little breed of sheep has called that island home since antiquity. When I was in Spain, I might have misplaced my telescope or my flask, but I would never misplace that scarf."

Ann took a whiff, finding his signature lavender scent beneath the predictable aroma of wool. "And is your grandmother still knitting you scarves, Colonel?"

"She went to her reward before the Hundred Days, and I considered that a mercy. Most of my French relatives were enthusiastic supporters of Bonaparte, until his mad venture to Moscow. Half a million soldiers killed in a single campaign rather put a damper on the populace's interest in further warfare. Unlike the English army, which maintains itself mostly through recruitment, the Continental forces practice conscription, which has drawbacks."

Ann took his coat and arranged it over the back of the chair at the desk, inside out, the better to absorb the fire's warmth.

"Your hair," she said, winnowing her fingers through his locks.

"The wind has disarranged you." That, and she wanted any excuse to touch him. Such a longing was novel and not entirely welcome—she had menus to plan—but she suspected her preoccupation with the colonel would not fade anytime soon either.

The memory of a short nap cradled in his arms plagued her. He'd spoken honestly about having no untoward designs on her person, but when his affection was so generously given, he didn't *need* untoward designs to put her into a complete muddle.

Aren't you ever lonely, Ann?

All the time.

Her admission had left her restless and discontent, also resentful of Aunt's demand for menus. "Shall I put together a tea tray?" Ann asked.

"Might we be seated?" came from the colonel in the same instant. "No tea," he said. "You spend all day toiling in a kitchen for others, and I did not come here to add to your work."

She gestured him into one of the two wing chairs by the hearth. The sisters spent many an evening in those chairs, swaddled in shawls, reminiscing. Ann knew that only because one day a week the Coventry was closed, and thus she was free to join her housemates by the fire.

"A tea tray is not work," Ann said.

"It's not a frolic either." Colonel Goddard filled the chair, his long legs reaching nearly to the hearth's fender. "I had supper last night with your employer."

"Was that a frolic?"

Again, the brief humor came and went in his gaze without touching his mouth. "Hardly. How well do you know Mr. Sycamore Dorning?"

"This is your ulterior motive? To quiz me about my employer?" *Drat and perdition.* "I don't tell tales out of school, Colonel."

The cat leaped down from the desk and appropriated a place on the colonel's lap.

"He'll get hair all over you."

"Lending me protection from the elements. Have you ever considered the origin of that phrase, about telling tales out of school? I think of the boy who's bullied, of which there are too many. He's to value the privilege of being abused by his peers above the protection his elders might afford him if he tattled."

"Or he's to refrain from gossip. Mr. Dorning bullies nobody, though he can be both charming and emphatic. Why do you ask?" Very charming and very emphatic, which was fortunate when somebody had to jolly Jules Delacourt out of a surly mood.

"I put a matter to Dorning in confidence, and I am concerned he'll nose about and make a bad situation worse. When I realized that trusting to his discretion might have been ill-advised, my next thought was, I wish I could discuss this matter with Miss Pearson. She is a woman of great good sense, and she will hear things at the Coventry that might bear on my circumstances."

Ann had been valued for her ability to concoct rich sauces, for her subtle use of spices, for her hard work, though not nearly often enough. To be valued for her great good sense called to the girl whose papa hadn't valued her for anything.

"What exactly is your situation, Colonel?"

"Should we have left the parlor door open?"

"Miss Julia and Miss Diana are off on their weekly trip to the lending library. They will stop at a tea shop and, if the weather stays dry, a yarn shop. This is their version of patrolling the perimeter, Colonel, for all the best tattle is to be had over books, tea, and knitting. You need not worry that we'll be interrupted or overheard."

The cat arranged itself in a perfect feline circle of contentment, the tip of his tail resting over his pink nose. The colonel gently stroked the beast's back, and Ann envied the idiot cat those caresses.

Sorely.

"I am not concerned about being overheard," the colonel said. "I was more worried about the proprieties. When last we met, I took liberties with your person. I have been prattling away over here, burdening you with my business, and all the while trying to figure out if an apology is in order."

"The flowers were a peace offering?"

"If a peace offering is needed."

"And if no such offering is required?"

"They are a token of my sincere esteem."

Ann would have bet her best carving knives that Orion Goddard hadn't brought flowers to any other woman, much less taken liberties with her person, for quite some time. That Ann had earned his esteem pleased her and sent all thoughts of menus, sauces, and spices right up the chimney.

"Tell me of your situation," she said, "and I will offer you as much good counsel as I can."

"I was hoping you'd say that."

He launched into a tale of military intrigue, gossip, and commerce that absorbed Ann's full attention as the cat purred, the temperature dropped, and the morning eased its way into early afternoon, and still, Ann spared not a single thought for her duties at the Coventry.

CHAPTER NINE

Rye had missed the company of women, and his decision to bide in England rather than France was partly to blame. At the height of post-revolutionary zeal, the French had flirted with the notion of extending the vote to women, though nothing had come of it.

Still, they had been able to entertain the idea, while even the most radical English reformer could not.

Then the Corsican's nearly two decades of warfare had seen hundreds of thousands of France's adult males sent to their eternal reward, leaving the women to raise the children, farm the land, and run the shops. Between Napoleon's democratizing influence and the realities of life with a deficit of men, French women enjoyed far more freedom and practical authority than did their proper English counterparts.

Ann Pearson trod a curious path between the sheltered ornaments of Mayfair and the more enlightened French exponents of femininity. London was probably full of her ilk—the military had seen its share—but Rye did not meet them in the normal course.

Lately, his normal course had been even more solitary than he preferred, consisting of the company of his minions, his horses, his cousins, and his diminishing list of customers.

Aren't you ever lonely, Ann?

All the time.

"Who benefits from keeping you in disgrace?" she asked when Rye had sketched out his situation for her. "Whose fortunes depend on your banishment from the best clubs, the ballrooms, the hunt meets?"

"I do not engage in blood sport," Rye said, "but your question merits an answer. Anybody selling champagne in London benefits from blotting my escutcheon, anybody seeking to discredit Fat George's knighthoods, anybody who..."

Ann glanced up from some piece of needlework she'd taken out half an hour ago. "Yes?"

She occupied the second wing chair, the firelight creating flickering shadows against the curve of her cheek. One shawl was wrapped about her shoulders, another spread over her knees.

The picture she made was cozy and domestic, and Rye wanted to haul her into his lap again, and this time not so she could doze off like a contented cat.

"I told myself," he said, "that nobody was selling any secrets to the French, that good and bad luck befell both sides, and coincidences are just that. That is precisely what the board of inquiry concluded, and they interviewed half the camp."

"But?"

"But if somebody *was* selling secrets to the French, then pinning the blame for that treason on me makes perfect sense."

"Even now?" she asked. "The war has been over for some time."

"A few years are but a moment when the charge is treason." Rye did not like to think that one of his fellow officers or—more likely— some disgruntled private, an artillery sergeant going deaf, or a laundress with a grudge had turned traitor. But conditions in Spain had been miserable, rations often short, and tensions high.

"I was sent out on clandestine reconnaissance because my commanding officer sensed something was afoot. He had an instinct for such things, for when to observe protocol and when to look the other way. He never imparted the details of his suspicions, but he was worried."

Ann tucked her needle into the corner of her fabric and returned the project to a wicker basket. "Why not confide in you? Why not give you the benefit of his hunches and discuss them with you?"

Rye had pondered that riddle too. "I asked him that, asked him what exactly I was to investigate, what rumors had reached his ears. His reply made sense: to share such information with me would have biased my observations. Out of loyalty to him, I'd see whatever supported his theories and be less likely to notice what refuted them. So I played the role assigned to me. I observed and reported, nothing more."

"And thus you fell under worse suspicion, because you had no real justification for your outings other than a superior officer's hunches and could report nothing but general impressions."

Rye hadn't realized the vulnerability of his position until he'd been under oath, a panel of senior officers regarding him with chilly skepticism.

"The colonel spoke up for me at the board of inquiry, told them he'd ordered me to keep my eyes and ears open."

Ann waved a dismissive hand. "That's like Jules declaring that my best *sauce Hollandaise* is not bad. He gives his judgment with a condescending little sneer, so anybody listening concludes the sauce is nearly pathetic."

"I could have a word with Jules, a quiet word in a dark alley." The cat, who had fallen asleep in Rye's lap, resumed purring, as if he approved of that notion.

"Jules is unhappy," Ann replied. "He's homesick and cooking not at a fancy gentlemen's club or great house, but at a gaming hell. Oh, the ignominy."

"French pride is nearly as formidable as its English counterpart."

Ann smiled at him, a conspiratorial, private smile that made Rye want to... well, cuddling up in her lap wasn't the half of it. An hour chatting before the fire could apparently be a powerful aphrodisiac, and balm to the soul too. Ann had *listened*, encouraging Rye to sort through his situation more thoroughly than he had when reporting the general outlines to Sycamore Dorning the previous evening.

More thoroughly than he had in quite some time.

Who benefits? A question that bore further study.

"You have been very generous with your time," Rye said, "and this cat will soon think he owns me. I really should be going."

"I did not even feed you." Ann folded up the shawl that had been draped across her knees. "Some cook I am."

Rye rose, yielding his place to the cat, and offered the lady his hand. "You do not need to feed me, Ann. I am fortified by your companionship and keen good sense." He kept her hand in his when she'd risen, and she regarded him with a frown.

"I believe you have just pronounced my Hollandaise not bad."

Whatever did she...? "I value you for more than your good sense, but I am trying not to make a habit of presuming on your person."

She ran the fingers of her free hand through his hair, and how he adored when she did that. Felt it right down to his vitals and understood why some bold felines demanded affection from any passing human. Her touch felt that good.

"You are trying to be gentlemanly by limiting your compliments to only my good sense?" she asked, peering up at him.

"I am." By application of great personal discipline, he did not allow his gaze to stray over her physical attributes. "I see you in my dreams, Ann, and they are very pleasant dreams." Also disturbing, for a man who typically dreamed of vineyards, ledgers, and battles.

She leaned into him on a sigh, snuggling close like a cat. "I see you in mine too."

～

ANN FELT the shift in Orion, when inherent military bearing gave way to the posture of a man holding a woman he cares for. His arms enfolded her gently, and he bent near, drawing her into the curve of his taller body.

"I told myself that I would not presume this time," he muttered.

"You aren't presuming. To ignore such an attraction would be folly, Colonel."

"Rye." He nuzzled her temple. "If we are to kiss each other witless, please call me Rye."

His version of witless kissing began with a sweet little buss to her cheek, then another to her brow. The scent of his lavender soap was stronger this close, and the warmth radiating from him was luscious.

Ann wrapped her arms around his neck and sank her fingers into his thick, dark hair. He needed a trim; she needed to kiss him, so she did.

The touch of his mouth to hers was gentle at first, though in no way tentative. He took his time, giving her precious moments to register sensations—his hands low on her back, his shoulders so broad and muscular. His breath a soft heat against her cheek.

She was melting inside, like caramel left near the hearth, going all viscous and warm. When she felt the first touch of his tongue, spices came to mind—cinnamon and nutmeg, a whisper of cayenne.

Orion Goddard was stealthy and subtle about his advances, while Ann wanted to plunder and pillage. She wedged a thigh between his legs to emphasize her demand.

He growled, and the battle was joined. By the time they broke apart several passionate eternities later, Ann's blood was at full boil, and Orion was panting like a spent steeplechaser.

Also smiling, as if he'd just been granted the keys to the celestial kingdom. "My eye patch, please." He held out a hand.

Ann surrendered the requested item. "I want to remove more than that from your person." Much more.

He used the windowpane as his mirror, tying his eye patch back in place. "What I want at this moment shocks me."

That was encouraging. "I am not without experience, Colonel. I assume you aren't either. Nobody need be shocked."

He snapped off a bloom from the bouquet on the windowsill and tucked the stem through his lapel. "The mechanics of intimacy, pleasurable though they are, do not occasion shock, Annie Pearson. It's here,"—he tapped his chest—"where you wreak the worst havoc."

"Do I?" She liked the sound of that very much, and she liked as well the sight of him, tall, weathered, a trifle disheveled, a fading rose on his lapel. "Do I truly?"

"You *listened* to me," he said, bracing his hips against the windowsill. "Let me prattle on like a schoolboy retelling the Battle of Hastings. You ply me with soft cushions, a warm hearth, and a shameless cat. You kiss me as if..."

He rose and turned away—very rude, that—but Ann had the sense he needed the privacy to gather his thoughts.

"As if you are my favorite dessert," Ann said, crossing the room and wrapping her arms around him from behind, "and somebody has finally perfected the recipe." She pressed herself to the hard planes of his back, her embrace a little desperate. Holding Orion felt good and right, but did nothing to stem the tide of desire that threatened to engulf her.

Where had this passion come from, and what was she to *do* about it?

He turned and looped his arms around her shoulders, resting his chin on her crown. "We ought not to be carrying on like this before the window, Annie."

"This is not carrying on. Not nearly."

He took her hand and pressed it to an impressive bulge behind his falls. "*Very* nearly. The sooner I subject myself to the bracing effect of the elements, the more likely I am to survive this ambush without... without behaving rashly."

Ann itched to caress him intimately and learn just how rashly they could enjoy each other.

"I should be getting to the Coventry," she said, giving him a single glancing pat. "Did you want me to listen for any particular sort of gossip?"

He twitched her shawl up around her shoulders. "A fellow named Philippe Deschamps has graced the Coventry's tables a time or two. He might well be spreading talk about me, or his presence might be provoking others to talk. He was the French officer most likely to have met with any spy from my camp."

"The waiters repeat nearly everything they hear at the tables. I'll pay attention to them for a change. I don't want to move."

"Do Miss Julia and Miss Diana make a weekly venture of their library sortie?"

"Without fail."

"Might I call again next week, Annie?"

Annie. She'd never had a nickname before. "If you don't, I will have to call on you."

"We keep the cellar stairs unlocked during daylight hours for the trades." He murmured the words close to her ear, inspiring visions of daylight raids and wild interludes in his study. "I ought not to have said that, because it implies that all I seek from you is... Tell me to hush, Annie. Tell me not to be presumptuous and impulsive."

Ann's grip on him became fierce, because he was right: Physical arousal was a formidable distraction, but the feelings... oh, the feelings.

"We are lonely," she said. "Tired of being lonely, tired of solitude and self-sufficiency, but what draws us together is more than that."

He put a finger to her lips. "Not another word. You are due at the Coventry, and I must resolve once and for all the small matter of somebody trying to destroy my reputation and my business. I will call on you again next week, if you'll allow it."

"I will allow it." Ann would be counting the hours, which bothered her. On the one hand, she never wanted to turn loose of Orion Goddard. On the other, she had toiled for years to achieve professional standing one step shy of the foremost honors to be had in a kitchen.

She desired Orion Goddard, respected him, liked him, and was even a little besotted with him, but he was right: Indulging her impulses with him could come at a price much higher than she was prepared to pay.

Ann pondered that lowering thought while Orion escorted her the short distance to the Coventry's back gate and then right up to the back door.

"Until next week," he said, bowing correctly over her hand. "I will see you in my sweetest dreams."

She curtseyed. "Until next week." She slipped through the door lest she make free with his person on the very doorstep, but hadn't so much as unbuttoned her cloak before Jules, looking irascible and smelling strongly of overindulgence, blocked the hallway to the kitchen.

"Pearson, you are late, and that is no sort of example to set for your new apprentice."

Ann looked him up and down, in no mood for his tantrums. "While you are for once on time. Would you also like to choose tonight's menu for a change, or shall I just go ahead and do that, the same as I have for the past fortnight?"

She brushed past him, knowing she ought not to provoke him, but no longer willing to pretend he was the kitchen's indispensable talent.

Because he wasn't and never had been, and that he'd ruin her great good spirits with his petty tyranny vexed her exceedingly.

AGRICOLA HAD NOT INITIALLY SHARED Rye's enthusiasm for some exercise on a cold, still morning, but as they'd approached the park, the gelding had caught sight of open expanses of grass covered in sparkling hoar frost. He'd gone so far as to give a ponderous buck and shimmy and to whinny to his kin on the bridle paths.

"That's my boy," Rye said, patting Agricola's muscular neck. "Let's have a gallop, shall we?"

They had more of a canter, albeit a brisk canter. Agricola was winded and had broken a light sweat by the time Rye brought him down to the walk.

Rye turned his horse up a quiet bridle path, because ambling a few streets in the morning air would not be enough to cool out his mount. Then too, Rye wanted to linger in the quiet of the park the better to savor memories of his latest encounter with Ann Pearson.

Beneath her tidy, sensible mien beat the heart of a passionate woman. And Ann wasn't merely sensible, she was smart. Observant, as a good scout ought to be, and logical.

Who benefits from keeping you in disgrace?

Years ago, any other officer might have enjoyed seeing Rye fall from favor. He wasn't from a military family, he was half French, he had no great wealth. He'd had no chance of ever becoming one of Wellington's direct reports, because he wasn't one of the bluebloods who could trace their lineage back to the Domesday Book.

Rye wasn't from the enlisted ranks either, but he'd tramped across Spain right alongside the men who'd served under him. He'd been neither a harsh disciplinarian nor one to shirk battlefield duty. Rye could not see the rank and file bearing him any serious grudges, or having the social standing to put him in disgrace.

Something more than a grudge was at work.

Agricola whuffled as Rye steered him around a bend in the bridle path. They were working their way to the northeast corner of the park, putting off a return to London's busy streets as long as possible.

A horse and rider came toward them at the trot, and Agricola sidled off the path in a creaky semblance of good spirits. The other horse—a chestnut with a graying muzzle—whinnied in response.

The rider looked to have every intention of trotting on past, but the horses had other ideas. The chestnut stopped and craned its neck, and Agricola did likewise. Nostrils flared, ears pricked.

Rye sat calmly through this reacquainting ritual, while Brigadier Horace Upchurch hauled hard on his horse's reins.

"Stop that, Egret. Behave yourself at once."

Egret stood a good eighteen hands, and his great size had been much envied by junior cavalry officers. A horse that tall—six feet at the withers—put his rider literally above the affray of battle, and galloped into any conflict with nearly a ton of momentum. Egret had enough draft horse in him to add muscle to that momentum and enough of the riding stock to be nimble as well.

Though even the brigadier's mount was showing signs of age. His muzzle was gray, and he'd apparently developed a stubborn streak. All the brigadier's blustering did not deter Egret from properly greeting his old friend.

"They don't forget," Rye said when the mutual sniffing concluded. "How are you, sir?"

"I am well, Goddard. And you?" Upchurch was very much on his dignity, as usual. He'd fallen into the stern-but-fair category of senior officer, and Rye had respected him for that.

"Managing. Might I ride with you for a bit?"

Upchurch glanced around. "If you must. One doesn't like to encourage bad behavior in one's mount, and Egret has forgotten his manners."

"You don't want to be seen with me." The conclusion should not have hurt, but it did. Upchurch had quarterly officers' dinners, rotating the invitations through all of his former direct reports and many of his peers. Rye had never received an invitation.

He'd attributed that slight to an oversight, to his frequent travel on the Continent, to Melisande Upchurch's sense of who would socialize well with whom, to his lack of participation in the Hundred Days...

Never to his own commanding officer's distaste for him.

"You've heard the talk," Rye said. "What exactly is being said?"

Upchurch turned Egret in the opposite direction Rye sought to travel. "If you must know, the whispers are that you kept your vineyards and farms because you betrayed your country. That your father's business was failing until you bought your colors, and within a year of you reporting for duty in Spain, those fortunes began to improve. That you yet prosper because the French recall how useful you were to them."

"My father lost those vineyards and farms," Rye said, "and they came to me only after the peace, when it became apparent no French heirs had survived to claim them."

"I know that," Upchurch said, "and you know that, but circumstances conspire to put you in a bad light, Goddard."

A bad light? A *bad light*? "The talk has worsened lately. Any idea who might be behind it?"

Upchurch fussed with his horse's mane. "Who knows? The longer we're at peace, the more adept the typical officer becomes at gaming, wenching, and gossip."

Was that how Upchurch spent his time? "My sister's dowry brought my family's finances right and bought my commission," Rye said, though he ought not have to remind Upchurch of those facts. "But for Jeanette's marriage to the marquess, my father might well have died in debtors' prison."

Upchurch peered about as if he'd not been hacking out in Hyde Park on sunny mornings for years. "Melisande mentioned as much."

So Upchurch had discussed the situation with his wife. The fair Melisande had chafed against military life, then settled down to become the consummate officer's helpmeet. She'd enjoyed the attentions of all the gallant young officers, but the marching, mud, and battle hadn't appealed to her at all.

"Would Melisande consider buying her champagne from me?" Rye asked, half ashamed of himself for the question. "My business does not, alas, prosper. I bottle the finest champagne to be had in London, and increasingly, nobody wants it at any price."

Upchurch looked at him for the first time in the entire exchange. "Your business is suffering?"

"I am not French enough for the customers who want the cachet of a French merchant for their fine wines, and I'm not a loyal enough British subject for those whose snobbery runs in a different direction."

"You were always loyal." Upchurch made the words a grudging admission rather than a ringing endorsement.

"I remain loyal."

"Perhaps that's the problem." Upchurch gathered up his reins. "Have you considered a remove to France, at least until the talk dies down? Retreat can be the wisest course, Goddard. Live to fight another day."

"As far as I know, nobody's trying to kill me." Kill his reputation, his business, his ability to support his dependents, and—worst of all? —his chances of more than a passing liaison with Ann Pearson.

"Nobody is trying to kill you yet," Upchurch said, "but if some hotheaded lieutenant gets to drinking and misremembering, or some old general who sat upon the board of inquiry takes to spreading gossip in the wrong places, you might well find yourself challenged."

Had Upchurch heard something Rye had not? "Challenged over what?"

Upchurch glanced around, though this corner of the park was deserted by all save the birds and squirrels. "You recall the ambush of that patrol scouting along the Bidasoa river?"

"Of course." Every single soldier had been taken prisoner. The war had ended within a year, and all of them had made it home—Rye had made sure of that.

"They were your men, Colonel. Scouting parties explore the terrain assigned to them."

"They were ambushed attempting to cross the river. That's a notoriously exposed moment in any mission." And Rye hadn't told them to cross the river, only to locate places where it might be safely forded by mounted forces.

"Every man on that patrol fell into French hands, and most of them yet live to tell about it. Perhaps they are the source of your troubles."

Rye instinctively rejected that theory, though he'd have to examine it in detail later. "You could put a stop to the speculation, if that's the case."

"No, Goddard, I cannot. If I protest too loudly in your defense, you will only look that much more guilty. I cannot abide that a loyal officer is being subjected to slander, but trust me, towering indifference is your best weapon against this foe. That, or a timely remove to your French holdings."

Agricola stamped a hoof, apparently ready to return to his stall and the pile of hay awaiting him there.

"If I abandon London now, I lose what custom I have remaining and gain no orders for next year's Season. Autumn and winter are when I most need to be tending to business, or by summer, I will be in dire straits."

"Conduct your business by correspondence."

Rye had tried that. His letters generally went unanswered or merited only a pro forma response doubtless drafted by a clerk.

"If I knew why I am the object of such aspersion, I might more readily stop it."

Upchurch nudged his horse a few steps away. "Goddard, you were a fine officer, so perhaps you can consider this by way of a direct order: Give it up. Somebody has nothing better to do than fan the flames of gossip where you are concerned. Don't dignify that campaign with return fire. March right past and continue on to France."

"If I do that," Rye said slowly, "I confirm my guilt. I abandon the land of my birth and appear to seek safety in the society of my vanquished enemy." Would the boys adjust happily to France, the boys born and left to make shift on London's streets? Would they abandon Hannah, so new to her apprenticeship, to ramble around the French countryside?

Rye did not want to abandon Hannah, did not want to abandon Jeanette when he and she were so new to their rapprochement, and most assuredly did not want to abandon his prospects with Ann Pearson.

"You won't leave England, even for a time?" Upchurch asked.

"I cannot. I am only recently returned from a prolonged visit to France."

"Then I will continue to do my duty by you, Colonel, discreetly of course, and Melisande will add her quiet word or two in your favor. I wish you a pleasant day and every success with your vineyards." He touched his hat brim and spurred his horse into a brisk trot up the path.

Agricola swung his nose around to sniff at the toe of Rye's boot.

"I'm as puzzled as you are," Rye said, giving the horse leave to walk on. "Upchurch makes sense—he's always made sense—but he also knows more than he's saying." And Upchurch had ever been one to ignore troublesome realities—men brawling outside the mess tent, a lack of adequate grazing where he'd chosen to make camp, Melisande's more determined admirers...

Rye was pondering the whole exchange as Agricola paused in his progress to leave a steaming pile of manure on the path. Had the horse not stopped, Rye might have missed the horseman half hidden along a row of plane trees.

"Deschamps, good day."

The Frenchman rode forth on an elegant bay. "*Goddard, bonjour. Comment allez-vous?*"

"I am well enough, but when in England, I speak English." Mostly. He'd probably slipped into French when kissing Ann.

"Very well, then we speak English. How was your chat with yon brigadier?"

"Pleasant. Were you eavesdropping?" Deschamps was dressed in the first stare of London fashion, but he was no longer the charming young aid-de-camp. His eyes held a coldness, and the left side of his riding jacket lay slightly askew at the waist.

He was armed, when merely hacking out in a public park in broad daylight.

"I was trying to avoid an encounter with Upchurch, if you must know. He has aged, and old soldiers are prone to tiresome reminiscences. I hear you peddle champagne these days."

In a former life, Rye had known exactly how to deal with Deschamps. The Frenchman had been the open spy, the delegate given safe passage into the enemy camp by the exigencies of war. Rye himself had performed that office on occasion, though infrequently.

In that former life, Rye could commiserate with a French counterpart about the horrors of war without in any way compromising either party's determination to win that war. But this version of Deschamps was a puzzle. He had no charm, no warmth, no sense of toiling along parallel paths that were likely to intersect mostly on a battlefield, to the manly regret of all concerned.

His dark good looks were turning sharp-edged, his gaze bitter.

"What brings you to London, Deschamps?"

Deschamps cocked his head, a ghost of his old insouciance in the gesture. "The fine weather. The excellent company. The magnificent entertainments."

Rye glanced up at the sunny sky. "You have a knife in each of your boots, a pistol at your side, and a pocket full of sand, the better to blind footpads who think to take you unaware. That horse is blood stock, fast enough to outdistance any who give pursuit. You have enemies in London and would not come here but for dire necessity."

Deschamps urged his gelding forward, so Rye allowed Agricola to toddle on as well.

"This is why I lost my enthusiasm for warfare," Deschamps said. "The generals can hold all the peace conferences they like, but that doesn't create peace. It only creates terms of surrender and a means of enforcing an armistice. Your champagne is quite good, I'm told."

"The best to leave France." What game was Deschamps playing?

"Then I wish you every success in that venture, Colonel, and in all of your endeavors. Our paths had best diverge before we break from the trees, *non*? London has eyes and ears, and not all of them are loyal to you. Some of them quite the opposite, I believe. But then, you know that and know to be careful as you navigate the streets of this fair city." He tipped his hat and turned his horse down a smaller path leading off to the left.

What in blazing hell was that about? Rye turned Agricola for home and wished that he'd spent his morning sipping coffee in his office rather than let himself be lured into the park on a promise of sunshine and fresh air.

~

JULES HAD GONE QUIET, and the whole kitchen felt the tension. For the third day in a row, he was at his post shortly after noon, sending Ann—and Hannah—the sort of brooding looks that boded ill.

"Pardon me, ladies," Henry said. "Mrs. Dorning is asking for a word with you, Miss Pearson." Hannah looked up from the bushel of peas she'd be expected to shell before sunset. The object of the exercise was not only to prepare a sufficient quantity for the evening buffet, but also to give Hannah so much practice at a simple chore that she became efficient at it.

Already, her nimble fingers had the pattern down: twist off one end of the pod, twist off the other, split, run a thumb down the middle to dislodge the peas, discard the husk into a slop bucket.

"I won't be gone long," Ann said, untying her apron. "When the bushel is done, you will have some bread and butter, Hannah."

"Yes, ma'am."

"I can help for a bit, shall I?" Henry offered.

"Wash your hands before you touch one of my peas, Henry Boardman," Hannah replied, "and you're to help, not shirk your own duties while you gabble my ear off."

How well Hannah knew the adolescent male. Henry saluted with mock seriousness and marched over to the sink.

"Mrs. Dorning is the colonel's sister, isn't she?" Hannah said.

"She is."

"He worries about her."

Very likely, Orion worried equally about Hannah. "You can visit the colonel and the boys again on our next half-day afternoon, Hannah. Or you could write a note, and I'm sure Henry would be happy to deliver it for you." Henry was all of sixteen to Hannah's thirteen or fourteen. The exercise would do him and his esteem in Hannah's eyes good.

"I could send them a recipe for Mrs. Murphy," Hannah said. "The crepes, maybe?"

"The boys would love your crepes. Perhaps you could make them a batch when next you visit, but ask Mrs. Murphy to help you with the pear compote."

Ann hung her apron on a peg in the hallway, grabbed her cloak, and descended the steps that led to the tunnel passing between the Coventry and the Dorning dwelling on the opposite side of the street. The wine cellar and pantries ran most of the length of the street, and during the day, the passage was kept unlocked for Mr. Dorning's convenience.

"Thinking to introduce your protégé to a fine claret?" Jules emerged from the shadows between two rows of wine bottles.

"I'm thinking to heed a summons from Mrs. Dorning. Perhaps you're the one introducing himself to the claret."

With Jules, to show weakness was to invite constant harassment. Ann had taken nearly a year to figure that out. He wanted only the ruthlessly focused in his kitchen, and he wore down the rest or taught them to keep their distance. Ann understood his methods, though she neither liked nor respected him for using them.

Perhaps the military was like that, harsh by design because the stakes were so much higher than a successful torte or roast. Ann would have to ask Orion when next they met.

"I'm making room for the next shipment of champagne," Jules said, sauntering forth. "The footmen lose and break too many bottles, or claim to."

Jules helped himself to the cellar's inventory without limit and occasionally ordered some bottles opened for the rest of the kitchen staff. The footmen, dealers, and waiters never imbibed during working hours, because the customers came in close proximity to them.

Jules's sporadic largesse was part of any tyrant's strategy for maintaining control. Bread and circuses between battles and tantrums. When the wine did flow in the kitchen, Ann abstained. A mug of porter with the midday meal was fine, but to add alcohol to a long evening of work around knives, flames, and boiling saucepots was asking for trouble.

One of the first lessons any apprentice learned.

"I have never quite satisfied myself as to what sort of wine you would be, Pearson." Jules prowled from between the racks, gazing down at Ann as if she were a plucked pullet that had yet to be consigned to a particular recipe.

"I am not a wine, I am a busy undercook, and Mrs. Dorning has requested a moment of my time. I'll bid you good day."

"It is a good day," Jules said, taking up a lean against the wine rack. "My new *sous-chef de cuisine* starts this evening. Pierre comes very highly recommended."

The wiser course would have been to bustle away, to pretend to have not heard that comment. "Your new assistant?"

"My new *sous-chef*." Jules smiled as if he spoke about his first-born son. "Pierre DeGussie has worked in Paris. He's very ambitious, very competent. He claims to have more recipes in his head than Carême could dream of, each one more delicious and beautiful than the next. You might have to help him with his English cookery books."

"A man with that many brilliant ideas will hardly need to read the humble recipes we publish here in London. Are we so short-handed that you need another assistant?" And a sous-chef, not an undercook. How much was the talented Pierre to be paid, and was his lodging included in his remuneration?

Jules gave Ann a look designed to infuriate her—pitying, patient, a little sad. "You have been with me for more than two years, Pearson. I have seen your recipes, tried your wine pairings. You work hard, but the Coventry's kitchen requires the sort of sophistication only a true chef can bring to the job. It's as well you have an apprentice to train, for I've no doubt you will leave us soon enough for the joys of motherhood and domesticity."

He waggled a bottle of wine. "That is always the way with *les femmes*. A few good years in the kitchen, then your true nature must have its due. There is no shame in this. No less authority than the good God Himself has ordained that it must be so."

Jules turning up pious was absolute proof that he was scheming, if ambushing Ann with news of a new assistant chef hadn't all but declared his intentions.

"I will look forward to meeting Monsieur DeGussie later today," Ann said. "And if he needs any help with his English, I will instruct Hannah to provide it. She's quite literate, and her French is good." Hannah had those skills thanks to her own hard work and Orion Goddard's ability to see the day when France and England were neighbors instead of former enemies.

Jules saluted with his bottle. "Ever gracious of you, as always, Pearson. Please give my regards to Mrs. Dorning."

Ann dipped a curtsey and left, though even that minor display of manners sat ill with her. She did not work for Jules, she worked for the Coventry. Jules had not hired her, the previous owner had, and Ann hoped only the current owner could fire her.

Not a theory she wanted to test. She mentally left the exchange with Jules in the cellars, where it belonged, and presented a cheerful greeting to Mrs. Dorning.

CHAPTER TEN

"Goddard." Xavier Fournier rose from a wing chair before a blazing hearth, his hand outstretched. "This is an honor and a surprise. You must sit and join me for a cup of tea. Or would brandy suit? One knows not whether to approach you from your English side or your French side."

Fournier treated Rye to a charming grin and a crushing handshake. He was a dark-haired bear of a man who had taken to English fashions like a recruit to his grog. Fournier wore three watch chains across an exquisitely embroidered waistcoat. The fabric was maroon satin, the stitching blue, green, purple, and gold in a fantastic array of birds and flowers.

The pin in his cravat was gold tipped with nacre, which strictly speaking was allowable for daytime, though unusual. Rye felt about as well turned out by comparison as a raven would next to a peacock.

"I won't take up much of your time," he said, "and you need not trouble with the hospitable displays. I come on a matter of business."

Fournier's smile dimmed. "You want to buy my champagne. You have your foot in the door at the Coventry, but lack the inventory to meet the demand. I congratulate you on your good fortune, but that is no reason to neglect the civilities."

"Brandy, then." The day was chilly and gray, as the next five months were likely to be chilly and gray.

"Brandy is the French choice. One applauds." Fournier poured from cut crystal decanters on a rose marble-topped sideboard. The scrollwork and ornate brass fittings proclaimed the piece an example of Louis XIV cabinetry.

The rest of Fournier's office was furnished with a similar blend of tastefully displayed wealth and understated style. His carpet was Savonnerie, his curtains delicate Brussels lace. His andirons were topped with brass fleur-de-lis polished to a high shine.

Ann would notice the scent, though all Rye could detect was a faint fragrance of sandalwood that probably emanated from his host.

"To a world that adores our champagne," Fournier said, touching his glass to Rye's, "and pays a good price for it. I hope Dorning is not getting too much of a family discount from you?"

The brandy was excellent, mellow and fiery, complex and satisfying. Ann would enjoy it for the nose alone. She might also enjoy Fournier's gracious good cheer, though Rye found his host's expansive charm unsettling.

"Dorning isn't getting any family discount, not that my arrangement with him is your business."

"Good for you," Fournier said, sipping his drink. "And Dorning pays on time and doesn't play games about broken bottles or mislaid cases. I was never successful getting Jules Delacourt to develop recipes to flatter my champagne, but then, Jules is a cook, not a sommelier. Shall we pace around one another hissing and spitting like lovesick tomcats, or sit before the fire like gentlemen?"

Rye took a seat before the fire, for good brandy ought to be savored. "My errand is actually somewhat insulting—to you."

"Not very English of you, to offer insults to my face. The Scots will insult a man openly, but so cleverly he doesn't notice until the whole room silently mocks him. The Irish speak eloquently with their fists, but the English murmur in their gilded tents."

A biblical allusion, and apt. "Somebody is murmuring about me and my past, Fournier. Is that somebody you?"

Fournier took the opposite wing chair and crossed his legs at the knee, like the Continental dandy he pretended to be.

"*Non*. You do not deserve ill treatment from me, and—*quel dommage*—your champagne doesn't either. I serve a good wine, you serve a fine wine. The question is, can the English tell the difference, and are they willing to pay for quality when they bother to notice it? You hope yes, I hope no."

That query was, in fact, the pivotal point upon which Rye's business would prosper or flounder. Would the English pay more for higher quality? The temptation to explore the topic further with Fournier was distracting.

"You aren't putting it about that I sold out to the French while yet wearing a British uniform?"

Fournier's dark gaze lost any hint of jovial bonhomie. "You famously did not sell out, which is why you now support half the old women among the émigrés. This is common knowledge in certain quarters."

"I do not support half the old women among the émigrés."

Fournier held up his glass, the amber liquid reflecting the flames dancing on the hearth. "Lucille Roberts, as is known to all the world, presides over a henhouse full of elderly ladies and their various impecunious nephews and un-dowered nieces. The grannies would canonize you if they could, and because you look after them, their families are in your debt. The most common reason to curry favor among people who have neither wealth nor influence is guilt, though the English call this *charité*. Ergo, you remained loyal to the English half of your heritage, and you are atoning to the French half with your generosity."

The brandy made a good first impression and improved upon that with further acquaintance. "You don't consider basic decency a reason to look after the elderly?"

"Basic decency is fine for one's immediate family and donations to the poor box, but it does not sell many cases of champagne. Tell me of the slander, Goddard. I like to think of you suffering, for God has surely blessed your vineyards to an unfair degree. I prefer that you suffer for some heroic fault—vanity, perhaps—which does not appear to afflict you, if your tailoring is any indication. Maybe stubbornness will be your downfall. I can but hope, *non*?"

"Must I have a downfall?"

Another smile, more piratical. "Frankly, no. The English became fond of champagne before we French saw it as anything other than a failure of proper winemaking, but then, the English had sturdier bottles than we did, thanks to their endless supply of coal-fired furnaces. If enough Englishmen become enamored of effervescent wine, then London will soon be flooded with others like us, peddling their French vintages. France can make a fortune off the Englishman's thirst. I like this plan very much."

"Sparkling wine strikes me as a libation that ladies should enjoy," Rye said, though what had that to do with anything?

"Everybody should enjoy champagne," Fournier said, finishing his brandy. "*L'empereur* had the right of it in this as in so many things: 'Champagne! In victory one deserves it, in defeat one needs it.' Napoleon's dictum applies to life, does it not, for what is life but a series of victories and defeats?"

Rye did not want to like Fournier, did not want to find him charming and shrewd, and yet, he was both. "For some, there's apparently time in life to spread treasonous rumors about me. If I went back to France with my tail between my legs, you could make your fortune that much faster."

Fournier took his empty glass to the sideboard and resumed his seat before the fire. "You are still at war, Goddard. You suspect ambushes behind every stirring of amorous hedgehogs in the English undergrowth. The London market has room for us both, and for others besides, but we must each find our place in that market. My tenure at the Coventry was limited by the size of Dorning's demand. His club prospers, his orders for champagne grew quickly, and now lesser venues are copying his signature gesture of hospitality. Unlike Dorning, those lesser venues do not cater to discerning palates."

"You can charge them more for a humbler product."

"Precisely, and there are more of them, so I need not rely on the whim of a single customer to whom all my best inventory is promised. I will part from Dorning without rancor, because he has you to meet his demand at prices he can afford to pay. All is well, the customers are happily swilling champagne, and I need not worry that you will accost me in some dark alley with revenge on your mind because I have put you out of business. Am I not a genius among men?"

"And so humble, Fournier. I do not take revenge in dark alleys."

"Neither do I, and if I did manage to destroy your business, I would court the scorn of an army of old Frenchwomen. My grandmother would haunt me, and this is not a fate I would wish on any man."

Rye took a final sip of his brandy, not sure what to make of the conversation. "Somebody wants me utterly disgraced."

"I am not that somebody, though it strikes me that you should tell your old women of your concerns."

They are not my old women. "Why involve them in what could quickly become a matter of honor?"

"*Une affaire d'honneur.* Bah. This is how Englishmen attempt to make their drunken stupidity appear brave. The old ladies have granddaughters and goddaughters in service, working as lady's maids and companions. They hear everything. The nephews and grandsons are fencing masters, dancing masters, and drawing masters in the best English households, and they hear even more. Whoever speaks against you does not want to confront you over pistols or swords, so perhaps your foe is a woman."

Not a cheerful thought, but worth pondering. Rye had accomplished what he'd come to do, so he rose and set his glass on the sideboard. "I have been notably careful not to give offense to any ladies."

"You are a monk," Fournier said, getting to his feet. "This is not good for the animal spirits. The French and English parts of you would agree on that. Might your French half do me a favor, Goddard?"

"If I cannot meet demand at the Coventry, I will tell Dorning to maintain an overflow contract with you." Rye could make that offer because he knew damned well he could meet the Coventry's demand, easily.

"Most generous of you, but that is not the favor I seek. Would you put in a word for me at the Aurora Club?"

"Is that request an ambush, Fournier?" Though the Aurora already had several Frenchmen on its rolls, as well as the occasional German professor and at least one American whose fortune had origins in trade.

"I merely make a polite request, Goddard. I must ingratiate myself with the club set if I want such organizations to purchase my champagne. I cannot aspire to the more exalted institutions in St. James's, but one must make a start. My sons, should I be so blessed, can build on the foundation I lay, but not if I neglect to purchase the bricks."

Every Frenchman was a philosopher at heart, according to Tante Lucille. "I will vouch for your business integrity and gentlemanly demeanor. I will not criticize your champagne."

Fournier clapped him on the back. "You will damn with faint praise, eh? I will not attempt to sell my wine to the Aurora, you understand, but I will learn of the house parties, who has a daughter making a come out, and so forth. Then I send a short letter humbly offering my wares, and business does not intrude on a social venue. The English must have their crotchets, *non?*"

Much business transpired in the clubs, which Fournier would soon realize. Rye suspected, however, that Fournier's motivation was subtler than mere mercantile ambition. He would offer his wares, but he would also inch closer to acceptance in the middling level of English society where much of the work was done, and increasingly, much wealth also accumulated.

"I will walk out with you," Fournier said, escorting Rye to the front door and passing him his greatcoat. "I have an appointment at Angelo's. Do you fence, Goddard?"

"I do not." Rye did not have time, and—might as well be honest— he had no taste for turning a lethal pursuit into mere sport, nor any longing for the company of those who did.

"So *sérieux*, Goddard." Fournier donned a flowing black cape and tapped a top hat onto his head, which made his height even more formidable. He tilted the hat at a jaunty angle and wrapped a maroon silk scarf about his neck. The embroidery on the scarf echoed the pattern of his waistcoat, a detail few Englishmen would have aspired to.

His finishing touch was a cherrywood walking stick with a dark red gemstone set into the top.

"Garnet," Fournier said, winking. "I cannot afford rubies, but the garnet is said to bring peace, health, and prosperity to the home. Perhaps if I acquire those blessings, a wife won't be far behind."

He led the way out into the dreary day, tipping his hat to passing ladies and generously rewarding the crossing sweepers. Rye stalked along at Fournier's side, wondering why an exponent of a foreign and defeated nation should strut around London as if he'd been given the freedom of the city, while a knighted soldier endured slander and falsehoods.

"You don't miss France?" Rye asked as they waited for a phaeton to rattle past.

"I miss France every day, but I thank the good God that I have a livelihood and my health. Too many men brood for too long, Goddard, and that is not my nature. I go to fence with Philippe Deschamps, a former officer in the Grande Armée. Perhaps you know him? He was once a charming young rascal, and now he's all sour and silent. Woman trouble, one supposes, along with a surfeit of bitter regrets. He should drink more champagne."

"Is that your solution to all woes?"

"You have a better one?"

A quiet hour with Ann Pearson had done much to restore Rye's sense of pleasure in life. "Not at the moment. Give Deschamps my regards."

"I will do that, and, Goddard?" Fournier stepped close. "The bottling technique of Madame Clicquot, with turning the bottles and the ice?"

"Icy brine. What of it?"

"You do this with your champagne?"

Champagne had fizz, but it also tended to muddiness, due to the dead yeast that remained after the first fermentation. Madame Clicquot's technique, turning the bottles upside down to allow the sediment to settle in the neck, where it was more easily removed, was only a few years old.

"We use her technique," Rye said, "and see much less waste as a result. We immerse the neck of the upside-down bottle in freezing brine. The frozen lees are disgorged naturally before the sugar is added for the next phase."

Fournier was listening intently, also—for once—scowling. "This undertaking is complicated."

This undertaking, and the desire to learn the details of the new process, were also at least half the reason for Fournier's jovial welcome. To have that motive in plain sight was something of a relief.

"I will send you a letter of introduction, Fournier, so your winemakers can pay a call on my own and discuss the innovations in detail. Turning the bottles and so forth is tedious, but the results are worth it."

Fournier took his hand. "My grandmother would have liked you. Good day, Goddard, and thank you."

He sauntered away, exuding great good cheer, while Rye turned his steps for home and pondered the encounter. Ann might be able to make sense of it, while Rye was puzzled. Fournier had presented himself as more of an ally than a competitor, and yet, he was off to frolic with Deschamps. Was that a casual connection? A warning?

Could a woman be behind Rye's troubles?

Rye was arguing with Otter over the need to learn Latin—the boys, with the exception of Victor, were already fluent in French—when another aspect of the meeting with Fournier dawned upon him.

Fournier had not once referred to Rye as either Colonel or Sir Orion. The entire conversation had been conducted with last names only, and Rye had been comfortable with that.

He'd been simply Goddard to Fournier, no rank, no title, and he'd preferred to do without them—a realization he would also discuss with Ann when next he called upon her.

~

"I DID NOT KNOW if offering a tea tray would be coals to Newcastle for a professional cook," Mrs. Dorning said, smiling serenely from her corner of the sofa, "but you must enjoy the occasional cup."

For Ann to take tea with Mrs. Dorning would be to cross a social boundary, though not one of unprecedented dimensions. In modest homes, the lady of the house might enjoy a cup of tea with her housekeeper or cook while considering menus or reviewing ledgers. In modest homes, the lady of the house was not the widow of a marquess or married to an earl's brother.

"I enjoy any chance to get off my feet, ma'am," Ann said, scooting forward a little on the chair cushions, "and a cup of tea is always welcome."

Her ladyship—Society would probably afford Jeannette Dorning that courtesy, though she was strictly speaking no longer entitled to it—poured from an exquisitely decorative Sèvres service, all gilt and pink and blue flowers.

"I was hoping you might bring Hannah with you, but then, I did not make that apparent, did I?"

"Shall I fetch her?" The tea was fragrant and piping hot, with a rich reddish hue. Hannah would have enjoyed a cup, though Ann suspected she'd enjoy more catching up on Henry's endless store of gossip.

"How is Hannah adjusting to her new station?" Mrs. Dorning asked when Ann had been offered good shortbread—her own recipe —and finished her first cup of tea.

Ann knew the civilities expected over tea in part because she'd gone to a proper girls' school, but also because Grandmama had insisted. Gentry could be higher sticklers than the nobs, or so Papa had often grumbled.

Ann was gentry, landed gentry as it happened. How easy it was to forget that, after two years of Jules's carping about everything from how thickly Ann sliced a ham to how long she left her croissants to bake.

"Hannah is taking to the kitchen with cautious enthusiasm," Ann said. "She's a hard worker, pays attention, and wants to excel. Barring a mishap, she ought to make an excellent cook someday." Not a chef, of course. Women could not be chefs. They fed the vast majority of George's loyal subjects, and had from time immemorial, but they could not be chefs.

No matter how competent such a woman might be with both French and English cuisine, no matter that she'd read every word Carême had written, and tried many of his published recipes too.

"Are more apprentices needed?" Mrs. Dorning asked. "I don't mean to pry, but Mr. Dorning's approach to the Coventry is to hire good people to manage the various domains and to stand back unless asked to intervene. He focuses on the patrons because that is a host's singular duty."

Ann nibbled her shortbread and pondered the possibility that Mrs. Dorning was attempting to spy on her husband's business operations. That made no sense, when husband and wife were reported to be very much in each other's pockets.

"The kitchen is always busy," Ann said, "but your question would be better directed to Jules Delacourt, ma'am. He oversees the whole kitchen."

Mrs. Dorning made the sort of face that Ann reserved for sour milk. "Monsieur Delacourt has an entire arsenal of flattery to aim at me, but when I want an honest answer, he turns up vague and philosophical. 'Who can say what is enough, madame?'" She'd taken on Jules's accent and deepened her voice to mimic him.

"You have him to the life."

"You should hear Mr. Dorning's impression," Mrs. Dorning replied. "As a boy, Mr. Dorning excelled at aping his older brothers. May I tell you something in confidence, Miss Pearson?"

Ann wanted to sprint for the door rather than find herself caught up in a marital intrigue. "Of course, though you must know my first loyalty is to the club."

"My second loyalty might well be to the club, given what it means to my husband," Mrs. Dorning replied. "Jules has asked that another undercook be hired, a Frenchman, and they do not come cheaply. Mr. Dorning assented on a trial basis, because he felt that sop to Jules's dignity necessary after taking on Hannah at my brother's request. My question relates to the boys in my brother's household. Has Hannah said anything about them?"

What manner of intrigue was this? "She mentions them by name from time to time. Theodoric—she calls him Otter—likes buttered turnips. Bertie forgets to wash his hands." John knew all manner of filthy songs. Louis was their scout. A new boy, Victor, seemed to have Debrett's off by heart as a result of watching from his street corner and memorizing the crests of passing coaches.

"Would they make passable clerks?"

"Mrs. Dorning, I hardly know. Hannah describes the boys as lively. Colonel Goddard has them attend to various chores and activities in the morning because they can't sit still for lessons in the afternoon otherwise. They are not scholars by nature, to hear her tell it."

Mrs. Dorning rose and went to the window, which overlooked the street running between her home and her husband's place of business.

"I want to lighten my brother's load, Miss Pearson. Orion would never confide in me, never hint that I might be of use to him, but I hear things."

Orion Goddard confided in Ann, some. She hoped as time went on, he'd confide in her more, but then what? He had domesticity written all over him, while Ann's ambition was to run the Coventry's kitchen some fine day. Passion was lovely for an interlude or an affair, but where did Ann see her dealings with Orion Goddard ending?

"What have you heard, Mrs. Dorning?"

She twitched at the curtain sashes, though the two sides of the drapery hung in perfect symmetry. "I haven't been Jeanette Goddard for ten years. Ladies new to Town know me only as the Marquess of Tavistock's widow, recently married to the youngest Dorning brother."

And thus they did not know of her connection to the colonel. "Somebody cast aspersion on Colonel Goddard within your hearing?"

Mrs. Dorning left off fussing the curtains and faced Ann. "Somebody referred to him as the disgraced colonel, which occasioned knowing glances and a slight shake of the speaker's head, as if to say, 'What a pity, about poor Goddard.' Minerva Dennis has no business spreading talk like that, but everybody else in the group appeared to know what and whom she alluded to."

"Minerva Dennis has been pretending to know all the latest talk since she first flirted with the drawing master at finishing school. She comes around the Coventry with her brother and claims her papa doesn't mind in the least." Jules would say such a woman needed marrying, but from Ann's perspective, Minerva would have been better served with a cauldron and some otherworldly familiars.

"Miss Pearson, how do you know her?"

"We are to trade confidences, then?"

Mrs. Dorning nodded once.

"I attended two years of finishing school with her. She is a cat, and she likely knows nothing about the colonel save some snippet she overheard her brother repeat. Dexter Dennis was in the military, as were many of his friends." Dennis came to the Coventry to lose money, in the opinion of the waiters, for he was more skilled at draining the champagne glasses and decimating the buffet than placing his bets.

"You took Hannah to call upon Colonel Goddard's household last week," Mrs. Dorning said. "Have you any idea what disgrace Miss Dennis might have referred to?"

The colonel himself did not know, but it wasn't Ann's place to reveal that. "You should ask your brother, ma'am. In my experience, he is both honest and honorable."

Mrs. Dorning returned to the sofa. "He is also my brother and unfailingly careful with me. Rye blames himself for my first marriage, but Rye had nothing to do with it. Papa wanted his darling daughter to have a title, and I wanted to make my papa proud of me. If I'd known my vows would result in my brother spending years at war..."

What was wrong with English fathers that their daughters longed so desperately for paternal approval?

"The colonel was a good soldier, ma'am. I believe he regards his years of service with pride."

"Then why is somebody implying that he blundered, Miss Pearson? My own in-laws were guilty of spreading unkind talk regarding my brother, but now I find others are doing worse than that. Why is Minerva Dennis, who has nothing better to do than experiment with new coiffures, slandering Orion over her glass of punch?"

"Perhaps you should ask her." Somebody should. For military men to mutter and murmur among themselves was one thing, but for the talk to spread to female ears was another and an altogether worse development.

"I am tempted to. I am tempted to call upon her with Mr. Dorning at my side. Sycamore has a way of charming and threatening at the same time, and he takes any slight to family seriously."

Ann had heard Mr. Dorning and his brother Ash going at each other with raised voices on any number of occasions. Ash Dorning was far less in evidence at the Coventry since he'd married, while Sycamore Dorning's marriage had resulted in his greater involvement at the club.

"Might you not first call upon the colonel?" Ann asked. "My guess is he'd rather you confront him than resort to stratagems involving Mr. Dorning."

"Orion is aware of the talk, then?" Mrs. Dorning sprung that trap as she casually topped up Ann's tea cup.

"You'd have to ask him, ma'am."

Ann's hostess set down the teapot and sat back. "He already has your loyalty, doesn't he? He does that. Rye has the gift of commanding respect, which makes this slight from Minerva Dennis all the more alarming."

"You really ought to talk to your brother, ma'am."

"Mr. Dorning says the same thing, and he has long practice dealing with family in difficult situations. Sycamore will find positions for Rye's household infantry, but Sycamore will not offer that help until it's clearly needed."

That help was needed. If Ann knew anything about Orion Goddard, besides that he was a highly skilled kisser, she knew he worried over those boys, even more than he worried for his own standing.

"Call on him, ma'am. He won't ask for help. That he asked me to take on Hannah was a matter of dire necessity and because Hannah herself had him send for me."

Mrs. Dorning turned a curious gaze on Ann. "Did she? Did she really? Have another piece of shortbread, Miss Pearson. This recipe is my favorite, and I am something of a connoisseur of shortbread."

It's my recipe. Ann took a bite rather than make that announcement. "Will you call on your brother, Mrs. Dorning?"

"I don't want to offend him, but Sycamore has heard that Orion's champagne is not much in demand, despite its superb quality. I suspect Rye might have to remove to France purely for the sake of economy, and six growing boys must be a drain on his exchequer."

Remove to France? Well, that made sense, and yet... Ann did not want Rye Goddard removing to France. Not yet, not when she'd only recently stumbled upon him. His kisses were delightful, but she thought, too, of how he'd tried to shelter his fading roses from the harsh wind, of his distress at Hannah's discomfort, of his unwillingness to put Ann to the trouble of a tea tray.

He was a good, dear man, and he should not have to leave behind all he valued because of some mean-spirited military prattling.

"Six growing boys are likely a drain on the colonel's patience as much as they are on his exchequer. What specifically do you like about this shortbread?"

Mrs. Dorning considered the two pieces remaining on the plate. "Other than the flavor being a perfect balance between short and sweet, the texture is superior. Shortbread can quickly become as hard as a clay brick, suitable only for dipping, but this shortbread stays light and delectable."

Precisely. "The secret is to cut the biscuits out and set them on a sheet to bake, but to let them sit for a time first. The dough dries out so the baked shortbread is lighter, and the sweetness concentrates. I also use brown sugar instead of white, and you mustn't forget a dash of salt."

The variations from that point were endless—vanilla, lavender, cinnamon, orange, lemon... Rather like Orion Goddard's kisses, each one unique and more delectable than the last.

"It's your recipe, isn't it, Miss Pearson?"

"Yes."

"What should I do about my brother?"

Why ask me? Except Ann suspected she knew why: Mrs.

Dorning hadn't any other siblings of her own to consult, and Rye had prevailed on Ann to solve Hannah's situation. That he would ask Ann for that consideration had been extraordinary.

"What would your husband tell you to do, ma'am?"

"He'd tell me to risk offending Rye by offering support before it's needed, except if I do offend my brother, he will never ask for my help. I am not Sycamore, to take six rejections as evidence that I must apply myself harder on my seventh try."

"Then don't offer your help," Ann said, rising. "Apologize for being the reason he was sent to war. He won't see that coming."

"I *was* the reason he was sent to war."

"Tell him that, and go from there. I must return to my duties at the Coventry, but thank you for the tea."

Mrs. Dorning rose, her smile slight but mischievous. "And for the shortbread?"

"Especially for the shortbread. Good day, ma'am."

They exchanged curtseys, which felt curiously appropriate, and Ann returned to the kitchen just in time to see Jules bump into Hannah's bucket of pea pod shells. The mess went everywhere, Jules went off into a flight of French insults, and Henry's gaze became a careful blank.

"No matter," Ann said, sailing forth before she'd even removed her cloak. "Your clumsiness is easily remedied, Monsieur, and we will have the mess you've created cleaned up in a moment. These little blunders are nothing to be upset about."

Henry blinked, Jules fell silent mid-curse, and Hannah scurried off for a dustpan and broom. Ann set the bowl of shelled peas on the counter—Jules had doubtless been aiming to spill those too—and knew that war had been declared in the kitchen.

And if he hadn't been before, Jules was surely her enemy now.

CHAPTER ELEVEN

Orion Goddard showed up on Ann's doorstep on her half day exactly as he'd promised, and she nearly sent him away.

"Something has vexed you," he said as Ann closed the door behind him. "Tell me."

He made no move to take off his greatcoat, but stood in her foyer, hat in hand, gazing down at her. He looked as if he'd wait until spring, did she ask it of him.

"I fear I will be poor company today, Colonel."

"Rye. The war is over, I'm told. I will leave you in peace if that's what you want, but allow me to pass this along first." He withdrew a bottle from one inside pocket and a paper-wrapped parcel from another. "A token of my esteem and a snack."

"Brandy?" Excellent brandy, judging by the label, the kind Mr. Dorning kept in his office rather than behind the bar. "And gingerbread, still warm." The aroma alone gave away the nature of the snack.

"The weather turns disagreeable, and you have a professional's interest in fine spirits. I thought Miss Julia and Miss Diana might appreciate the occasional nip as well. The gingerbread is because I found the scent enticing on such a chilly day."

"The ladies do have a medicinal dram," Ann said. "Nightly, when Miss Julia's rheumatism is acting up. Thank you." The cordiality of the gestures—brandy *and* warm gingerbread—interrupted the rhythm of Ann's bad mood, as did the colonel—Orion's —delicacy.

He had the gifts of silence and patience.

"I am at peril for losing my post," Ann said, taking Orion's hat from him and hanging it on a hook. "I have failed to be meek and submissive, failed to treat the addition of one needed apprentice as the great imposition on Jules Delacourt's generosity that it isn't. Your coat, please."

"Just because I am here doesn't mean you have to receive me, Ann. For the past two years, my own commanding officer has been out when I call upon him. This is your home, not Delacourt's kitchen."

And that was why she wanted Orion Goddard to stay, because she needed a reminder that life wasn't all about Jules's moods and tantrums, because she needed fresh gingerbread she hadn't had to make herself.

"Surrender your coat, sir. I have looked forward to your visit, and you are right: This is my home, and here at least I should be safe from the drama at the Coventry."

He passed over his coat, so much heavier than the cloaks Ann and her housemates wore. She took a whiff and smiled. Lavender, gingerbread, horse.

"How is our Hannah?" Orion asked when Ann had shown him into the parlor. "And no, you need not get out the tea tray. The gingerbread is for you and the ladies. I'll pick up another loaf for the boys on my way home. Greetings, your highness." He offered Boreas a friendly scratch on the shoulders and left the cat purring on the desk blotter.

"Our Hannah is a hard worker," Ann said, setting the brandy

bottle and gingerbread on the mantel. "She takes direction well, doesn't complain or chatter, and is already making friends with the underfootmen."

Orion went to the window, taking a sniff of the last bud to bloom from his bouquet. Ann had saved the roses that had faded, though the scent of dried petals wasn't nearly as vivid as that of a fresh flower.

"What sort of friends are these underfootmen?"

"The kind who know I will take it very much amiss if they presume on Hannah's innocence."

"Hannah will take it very much amiss, as will I. She can give a good account of herself in a fair fight. Shall we sit?"

Ann took a wing chair, though she wanted to pace. She wanted, actually, to cook something complicated. Double consommé, perhaps. Time consuming, with lots of heat and loud chopping.

Orion took the other chair and passed Ann the shawl that had been draped over its back. "For your knees."

"I'm not..." Except she was a little chilled. "Thank you." The shawl was a soft merino and warm from having been near the hearth. "Jules was in rare form last night, and when I ought to have been sleeping, I was instead thinking of all the things I should have said or done differently. He is angry with me, and I must be made to suffer."

"You doubtless threaten him. Reliving battles is a soldier's particular burden. Is Hannah the problem?"

What exactly was the problem? For all her lost sleep, Ann hadn't put that question to herself. "The conflict has been brewing since the day Jules arrived. Jules demands competent assistants, but only if they lack ambition. He wants the blind respect due a despot, and like a despot, he rules with a combination of charm and cruelty."

"The army had officers like him. They sometimes met with accidents."

"Accidents?"

"A gun misfiring, a girth breaking in the heat of battle, tainted meat."

"A war within a war?" Ann had never considered that military life and a London club kitchen might have some similarities.

"Justice, of a variety enlisted men understood well and officers learned to respect. The average recruit went to war because he had few other options, or in some cases, he was choosing between transportation and war. The army expected foot soldiers to cover thirty miles in a day, carrying up to sixty pounds of gear. The average soldier became as tough as old shoe leather, and such men can be pushed only so far."

"How did you deal with them?"

The cat rose from the blotter, stretched luxuriously, and leaped onto the arm of Orion's chair.

"Permission granted," Orion said as the wretched beast took up a place on his lap. "My mode of command was to keep the men focused on fighting the enemies rather than among ourselves."

"Enemies?"

"The opposing army, of course, but also cold, disease, bad rations, mud, rain, heat... Moving an army across Spain was a challenge in itself, much less with the occasional siege, battle, or ambush thrown in. Wellington understood that and was fanatic about supply lines, and about commending every possible soldier who deserved notice in the dispatches."

Ann toed off her slippers and curled up in her chair. "Jules seldom praises anybody. His words of thanks or encouragement are more precious than rubies."

"Then he's an idiot. Praise should be given honestly and often. What happens if you lose your post?"

Another question Ann hadn't managed to face. "I am in disgrace. Jules can see to it that I never again ply my trade this side of Hadrian's Wall."

"You've tried to make peace with him?"

A pragmatic solution. "I've been making peace with him for more than two years, Orion. Last night, he tripped me when I was carrying a full platter of sliced meat. The platter broke, the meat was ruined, the whole kitchen heard the noise and saw me fall..." That was the part that had cost Ann the most sleep.

"Go on."

"There I was, on my knees on the tiled floor, and nobody would help me up. Those tiles are hard, the floor was slippery, and my knee hurt. Jules stood by, barking at the footmen to clean up after me, at the scullery maid to see to the mess I'd made, and at me to get back to work slicing more meat. My knee needed ice, my apron was a mess, and yet, I knew—I *knew*—that if I so much as put on a clean apron, he'd trip me again, and the next time, I might be carrying a pot of boiling water."

For a moment, the only sound was the cat's purring and the soft crackling of the fire. Contented, peaceful sounds. Ann was far from at peace, but this conversation was helping to organize her thoughts.

"What does Jules want from you, Ann?"

"He might simply want me to leave, a vanquished foe who will never trouble another chef with her upstart ambitions. He might also want me to admit defeat, to apologize for my clumsiness, my incompetence, and my stupidity. To meekly accept all the deductions he makes from my pay as a result of my many shortcomings..."

Orion petted the cat, who squinted serenely at Ann. "And if you left, where would you go?"

And therein lay the real problem. "To my aunt. I am not yet of an age to credibly claim spinsterdom. I have some property from my father, but I cannot bide there on my own. Not yet. I'd have to hire a companion, and my aunt's feelings would be hurt, and she is all the family I have."

Then too, Melisande was an ally of sorts, disseminating Ann's recipes and menus in a strata of society Ann had eschewed.

"It seems to me," Orion said, "that you face two bad options: You can fight on and hope that the next skirmish doesn't involve a lethal or disfiguring mishap. You can quit and go to your auntie, all your years of hard work, your considerable expertise, for naught. What about going up the chain of command?"

"Jules is my commanding officer."

"And Dorning is the general in charge of the whole army. Can you go to him?"

That course of action had not occurred to Ann. "Go to him and ask him to fire one of the most renowned French chefs in London? The customers adore Jules, and he makes certain to keep the kitchen drama out of Mr. Dorning's sight."

"Are you sure of that? Dorning regularly grouses about the chronic uproar in the Coventry's kitchen. He intrudes on Jules's domain from time to time, according to Hannah, and sees the pandemonium first hand. My guess is, if Dorning had to choose between injury to you or turning a blind eye to Jules's tactics, Jules would be the one looking for work."

"That is your guess. In your own situation, has going up the chain of command served you well?"

The question earned her half a smile. "Not exactly, but then, if my immediate superior won't receive me, that leaves only Wellington himself as a court of appeal. His Grace and I have not been introduced. A mere knighthood wasn't sufficient to effect that miracle."

And yet, there Orion sat, the picture of calm. "You don't care?"

"Why should I? I have champagne to make, boys to keep out of trouble, and a lovely woman haunting my dreams." The half smile became something softer and sweeter. An invitation, perhaps, or a memory of simmering desire.

"You raise an interesting point. I had not considered taking my situation to Mr. Dorning." That would require assembling witnesses and proving that accidents had instead been ambushes. Not an easy case to make.

"Consider it, and be careful, Annie. If anything were to happen to you..."

"Yes?"

"I would take it very much amiss, and with your permission, I will convey that sentiment to Monsieur Delacourt." The threat was all the more reassuring for being conveyed softly, between one languid stroke over Boreas's fur and the next.

"Please don't antagonize Jules on my behalf," Ann said. "Not yet. Do you truly dream of me?"

Orion gently deposited the cat on the hassock nearer the fire, took Ann's hand, and pressed a kiss to her wrist. "*Je te désire.*"

Not quite *I want you.* Closer to, *I yearn for you.* "I should lock the door."

"No, you should not."

~

THAT ANN WAS ALSO FACING a campaign of undeserved ill will drove Rye nearly to shouting, except that if he marched over to the Coventry and beat some respect into Delacourt, the result would be more danger and hardship for Ann.

Rye might consult Jeanette, however, or even have a word with Sycamore Dorning. At present, considering strategy that far ahead was beyond him. Ann had removed her slippers and drawn her feet up under her shawl. He adored that she'd be so informal with him, but the sight of her stocking-clad toes peeking out from beneath the fringe of her shawl stole his wits.

Now she offered to lock the door, and Rye had to think.

"This is a parlor, Annie, and while I will cheerfully enjoy whatever liberties you grant me wherever you grant them, might another location serve us better?" He ran his thumb over the smooth skin of her wrist, feeling the pulsebeat of her life's blood.

He could pleasure her on the sofa, in a chair, or against the damned wall, but if it was pleasure she wanted from him, then a bed would be ideal. Besides, he wanted to see her bedroom, to know the scent of the sachets she hung from her bedposts, to learn what tales she read before bed.

Tales of Hollandaise sauce and *bœuf à la Bourguignonne,*

perhaps, or maybe she treated herself to novels of adventure and far-off lands.

"You want to come upstairs with me?"

"I most assuredly do, but only if you want that too." How shy they had both become. Rye marshalled his courage and laced his fingers with hers. "I want to take you to bed, Annie, to make sweet, passionate love with you, to lie spent, amazed, and grateful in your arms. I think of you when I ought to be attending to my ledgers and correspondence. I lie awake..."

She was watching his mouth, and that threatened Rye's dwindling store of self-restraint.

She rose and settled in his lap. "You lie awake?"

How good and right she felt in his arms, how precious. "I lie awake, and I *ache*, Annie Pearson. I ache and enjoy the ache, which is surely the sign of a man who has lost his wits if not his heart."

Ann sighed, her breath a soft breeze against his cheek. "My bedroom is to the left at the top of the stairs."

Rye let the joy of that announcement sink in, then rose with Ann in his arms. "Top of the stairs, to the left," he muttered.

She looped an arm around his neck and managed the door latches. As Rye traversed the house, he wondered if this was how a bridegroom felt, carrying his true love across symbolic and literal thresholds.

Hopeful, nervous, proud, and *aroused*.

He sat Ann on a comfy four-poster bed and stood before her, pleased to find the room warm. "You kept the fire going?"

She leaned her forehead against his middle. "I hoped you would call."

If she'd kept her bedroom warm, she'd hoped he'd do more than call. She'd hoped for more than a quick tup in the parlor, too, and she deserved more than that. Rye's nervousness abated, replaced by a sense that he was exactly where he was meant to be and exactly who Ann wanted to be with.

"Will you valet me?" he asked, though he hadn't needed

assistance undressing since he'd been breeched. He made the request because he suspected Ann would be less nervous if her hands were occupied.

She hopped off the bed. "Of course. Your eye patch first. You have lovely eyes, and I want to see them both."

He passed her his eye patch, feeling oddly exposed by that simple gesture. She'd seen him without it before, but this was different.

"I need a moment to adjust after I've taken it off," he said. "What next?"

By slow degrees, she peeled him out of his clothing, sniffing each garment before folding it neatly. "You greeted your horse this morning."

"Our new lad, Victor, has taken over the stable duties, and the work wants regular inspection. I also like to look in on my mounts. The older of the two was with me on campaign. He likes apples."

Inane thing to say in the midst of a seduction, but Rye was down to his boots and breeches, and Ann was studying his arm.

"You described your injury as being mostly to your hip and ribs, with some damage to the eye and your hearing. You suffered more than that, Orion." She ran her fingers over the scars on his arm, then over the scars on his ribs.

"My uniform caught fire when I raised my arm to shield my face." Thank God that MacKay had been on hand to put it out almost immediately. "The scars on my ribs were from some other battle."

She wrapped him in an embrace. "There were so many, you forget?"

"Right now, all I can think about is getting you out of that dress and into bed." He fell silent, lest he babble in two languages at once.

"You'd best deal with my hooks, then." She presented him with her back, and Rye did as she commanded, freeing her from a legion of hooks, each one tinier than the one before. He untied her stays while he was in the neighborhood and stole a few kisses to her nape.

"Lilacs," he said when her dress and stays had been draped over a chair. "You must wash your hair with lilac soap. Shall I take down your hair?"

"Take out the pins and leave the braid."

"Up on the bed with you, then."

She slanted a dubious glance at him, but complied. Rye pulled off his boots and sat cross-legged behind her. She wore her chemise, he kept his breeches on, the better to comport himself with the restraint the situation called for.

He searched her hair for pins and mentally cast about for next steps. "What sort of loving do you enjoy most?" She had experience. She'd been at pains to assure him of that, but what sort of experience?

"Not hurried," she said, "not furtive. What of you?"

How modest were her sexual ambitions, and what a poor reflection they were upon her previous lovers.

"I hope the interlude can be joyous," Rye said, "sweet, a little wild, and a lot pleasurable. Leisurely until we're overcome by passion. I want my lover to think of me always with fondness and a smile." With Ann, fondness and a smile would not be enough, but a soldier crossed Spain mile by mile, step by step.

"Tell me about the wild part."

And yet, a man could fall in love between one heartbeat and the next.

He showed her, starting with sweet kisses to her shoulders, then turning her to straddle his lap and adding caresses to her breasts. She liked that apparently, arching into his touch, burying her fingers in his hair, and joining her mouth to his.

"Breeches off, Orion."

"Yes, ma'am." But to remove his breeches, he had to part from her, which was difficult when he craved to touch her and taste her and feel her heart beating against his own.

Ann solved his dilemma by extricating herself from his embrace and scrambling under the covers. "Quickly, please."

Rye left the bed and stepped out of his breeches, tossing them atop her dress. He made a little production out of adding a half scoop of coal on the fire, not only to give Ann a chance to inspect him, but also to give himself a chance to gather his wits.

"Should I remove my chemise?" she asked.

He faced the bed and pretended to ignore the cockstand arrowed up along his belly. "If you have to ask, the answer is not yet. When you cannot bear to have the blasted thing on, when you fling it across the room to land who knows where, then it's time to take it off."

Ann blushed, but she did not look away. "Clearly, it's time you joined me in this bed, Orion Goddard."

"A woman of discernment."

She lay back, and he climbed under the covers and crouched above her, not touching.

"Orion?"

"Tell me what you want, Annie."

"You," she said, reaching for him. "I want you."

"I am yours to command." He resumed the slow, soft kisses she seemed to like and by degrees gave her his weight. The fit was marvelous, and the feel of her legs snug around his flanks a pleasure beyond description.

She'd kept the bedroom warm, she'd told him her troubles. She touched him as if he were every weary soldier ever to come home to loving arms, and kissed him as if he were her favorite treat.

He kissed her back with the same sense of rejoicing, for he was hers to command—and hers to love too.

ORION GODDARD'S loving had a relentless quality, an unwillingness to be either hurried or denied, that drew Ann away from the troubles in the Coventry's kitchen. His touch was slow and cherishing, his kisses entrancing.

He focused on Ann, and her focus shifted to him. He was lean all over, tough muscle, scarred flesh, but warm, too, and comfortable with physical intimacy. He ran his hand over Ann's neck and shoulders, and traced her features with delicate fingers.

"You hide yourself," he whispered. "Hide behind recipes and aprons, busyness and competence. You don't have to hide from me, Annie Pearson. Tell me what you want."

You. Closer. More. The words would not come and barely made sense to Ann anyway. Orion knew what he was about, a far cry from the fumblings Ann had endured in previous encounters. She locked her ankles at the small of his back and pulled him closer.

"You are like the cavalry," he said, tracing her brow with his nose. "All headlong and heedless. Wellington despaired of us. Surrender to pleasure, and I promise you victory."

He touched her everywhere, teasing her breasts, caressing her arms, and nuzzling her palms. He was like an incoming tide, submerging Ann more and more deeply in sensation and yearning. When he had introduced her to the wonder of a man's mouth skillfully applied to a lady's breasts—even when she yet wore her chemise —she rallied her wits to return fire.

She started where he had, tracing his facial features, and she spent extra time brushing her thumbs across his brow. That damned eye patch had to be a nuisance, for he went still under her hand, then sighed.

Ann graduated to the planes and sinews of Orion's back, making so bold as to learn the contours of his muscular bum and to put her own mouth to his flat, male nipple. That foray earned her a soft groan. All the while, she was aware that her lover was in a state of splendid readiness for the act itself.

Orion, however, did not seem aware. He seemed content to let her pet and taste him until spring.

"Up," Ann said, giving his bottom a pat. "Please."

He eased up and sat back, his weight grazing Ann's thighs.

"The chemise has to go," Ann said, pulling the hem free from the covers and half raising herself on her elbows. "Get this damned thing off of me."

"Hold still." He complied without so much as a tug to Ann's braid and pitched the offending linen over his shoulder. "The look of you now will stay with me until I'm a tired old man, past all mischief, save what I've stored in memory."

"Enough looking," Ann said, wrapping him in her arms and urging him down over her. "More loving."

He exhibited more of his infernal patience. "You're sure?"

"Yes, Orion, I am sure." About the larger picture—the situation with Jules, Aunt Melisande's backhanded support, the dreaded prospect of becoming Aunt Meli's companion—Ann was in a welter of bewilderment. But in this bed, in Orion Goddard's arms, she knew exactly who and what she wanted.

"So be it," he said, kissing her forehead with an odd solemnity. "But you tell me if I'm blundering, Annie. You pinch my arse, pull my hair, bite my ear. I can get carried away."

"Your version of lovemaking sounds like a brawl." A glorious brawl. Ann would have elaborated on that point, except that Orion hitched closer.

"Hold me," he whispered, tucking an arm under Ann's neck. He murmured something in French—she caught the verb *rêver*, to dream —and the moment did take on the quality of a reverie. She closed her eyes the better to savor the sensation of Orion easing his way into her body. He stole forward by minute increments, then slipped away, then gently pressed forward again.

"You are driving me mad, Orion."

"Good."

Ann came to appreciate his delicacy, for her body had an adjustment to make. He seemed to sense even that, going still, hilted inside her, while he treated her to wicked, heated kisses. His tongue had skills other than the ability to taste, and so, Ann discovered, did hers.

She was exploring that skill when he resumed a slight rocking of his hips, and something about the angle he'd taken was *different*. More maddening.

"Move with me, Annie. Take what you need."

She never took. Never demanded, never insisted, but her self-restraint deserted her when Orion levered up on his arms and began thrusting in earnest.

"This is the part where you get carried away?" Ann managed.

"This is the part where *we* get carried away."

He knew exactly what he was doing, knew exactly how to ply Ann's body so desire rose to a galloping need, then beyond that, to a transcendent pleasure. She arched up at the same moment he tucked close, and she battered him with the cataclysm storming through her.

He might have laughed softly, the wretch, while Ann pressed her cheek to the rough warmth of his chest and shuddered under an intensity of sensation. She had glimpsed these feelings before, fleetingly, glancingly, but with Orion, she became another creature entirely, luminous with bodily joy.

The magnificence faded like summer thunder, and Orion gathered her close. She needed his embrace to keep her from flying into a million iridescent pieces, and she needed his arms around her because tears threatened.

"Catch your breath," he said, stroking her hair. "I certainly need to catch mine."

How gracious he was, particularly for a man who'd denied himself satisfaction, the better to please his lover.

Ann burrowed closer, a greater act of surrender than even what had passed before. "I am all in a muddle." Scattered to the four winds and keenly dreading what a reassembling of wits and dignity would entail. *I need this. I need this man.*

But she did not need the complications that came with such an admission.

"Let's undo you a little more." Orion eased back, and Ann nearly shrieked at him not to leave her yet. She should have trusted him, for he surged forward again, setting up a steady rhythm. "This is not like tea biscuits, Annie, where you must be careful not to overindulge in company. Gobble me up, devour me, and with a little time and inspiration, you can have me all over again."

She had no breath with which to argue, because when she'd hiked her knees the better to wiggle closer to him, he'd taken hold of her foot, his grasp warm and firm. As the abyss of satisfaction loomed before her again, he pressed his thumb into her arch, and several forms of pleasure coalesced.

She *relaxed* into completion, let it wash through her rather than struggling to endure it, and the result was a relief so profound as to defy words. She was satisfied, whole, at peace.

Spent and amazed, to use Orion's words.

"I have been selfish," she said before sleep could drag her under.

"You have been magnificent, but now I must be selfish. Kiss me farewell."

She kissed him, languid heat threatening to flare into another bonfire, even as he slid from her body. He pressed near, rocking against her slowly.

"Someday..." He drifted into French again, the words too soft for Ann to translate. His pleasure came quietly while she hugged him close, grateful that she'd been spared his more tender sentiments.

Ann didn't have a lot of experience, but she had enough to know that Orion Goddard was special. For the closeness he offered her, for the spectacular pleasure, and the simple consideration of a shawl draped over her knees, she would give up much.

Not everything, but much. Much indeed, and that was a problem.

A FIRST ENCOUNTER with a new lover was supposed to be a little awkward, a little sweet, and something to be got through as pleasurably as possible. The true indulgence came later, when habits and needs were familiar, and the lovemaking could be adventurous or comforting at the whim of the lovers.

Not so, making love with Ann Pearson.

She held nothing back, not her kisses, not her passion, not her affection. Rye had withdrawn, of course, and she'd clung to him through the inevitable mess and lassitude. Her hands were marvelous —both callused and tender, a novel sensation—and she was comfortable with silence. She'd pulled the covers up over his shoulders, stroked his hair, even let him doze off.

When had he ever, ever, *ever* fallen asleep in a lover's arms? The words sounded romantic, the reality was fifteen stone of weary lout snoring away atop his lady. Rye had awoken to the feel of Ann's hands moving on his back, the fragrance of lilacs teasing his nose.

In addition to the lovely sense of repletion, he'd also felt—the word both fascinated and unnerved him—*safe*. With Ann, he felt safe. Safe enough to doze off, safe enough to linger.

Safe from what or whom? He pondered that question while wrapped around Ann spoon-fashion, inordinately pleased that he wasn't the only one who'd needed a nap.

He was dreaming of gingerbread when Ann stirred in his embrace, faced him, and tucked a leg over his hip. "You are so warm and lavender-y. I dreamed of Provence, and I have never been there."

I'll take you. She would delight in the herbs, the sunshine, and garden-scented breezes.

"Would you like to go?" A wedding journey came to mind, more evidence that Rye had lost his wits. One tumble, however glorious, did not a betrothal make when a man's business was faltering and his enemies massing their forces.

"My home is in England. A cook cannot gallivant about the Continent on a whim, and who would look after Hannah in my absence?"

"I did not mean leave this minute, I meant..." A long courtship, perhaps? Hannah would be apprenticed for the next seven years.

Ann regarded him in the dim light of the bedroom. "I know what you meant. It's a sweet thought. I think of taking you to see my little manor. Papa left me land in Surrey, and he was wise enough not to sell off all of our trees. We have a proper wood, where I fought every battle in history and lived out every fairy tale ever told by old women to fractious grandchildren."

"You own property?" Perhaps it was the context—naked, under the covers, replete with spent passion—but Ann's admission had the quality of a confidence.

"I lease it out, or my solicitors do. The proceeds go into the cent-per-cents."

She fell silent as if expecting Rye to leave the bed in a fit of male insecurity because she wasn't penniless.

"My family seat is let out as well," he said. "I did not see how I could manage my English acres in addition to farms in Provence, vineyards in Champagne, and a London business. Not without hiring a parcel of expensive stewards or factors. Something had to go, and letting out the country house was the logical choice. Do you miss your home?"

"That's complicated." She rolled to her back, and Rye wanted to pull her close again. "For more than half my life, I haven't lived there, and nobody I love is there anymore. It's a place full of memories."

"Spain is a place full of memories for me, and I assure you, I have no wish to return there ever, and yet, neither of us has sold our family homes, have we?"

His question provoked a frown. "I have my old age to consider. A cook's post is physically demanding and more than a little dangerous. At some point, I will be venerable enough to maintain my own household without causing a scandal. I will have earned my spinster honors and the freedom that go with them. What of you?"

What of him? Rye racketed from London to France and back, tried to keep an eye on Jeanette without intruding, managed the boys, peddled his wares...

"Like you, I envision a time later in life when I am not so caught up in plying my trade, in getting and spending and laying waste my powers, to quote Wordsworth. My childhood was happy, and if I ever have children, I want the same for them. Fresh air, a wood to play in, summer afternoons spent reading tales of heroic nonsense."

And for the first time, he could envision such a life with a specific woman, the one sharing the bed with him. Why her?

Because Ann worked hard for the sheer satisfaction of accomplishing something meaningful. Because she'd turned her back on an easy road and pursued a dream instead. Because she had taken Hannah on despite the resulting inconvenience.

Because she made love like she meant it.

And yet, Ann had put in her years as an apprentice and earned her way to a prestigious post as a cook. Was she to give that up for the privilege of risking her life in childbed every two years?

"You are silent," Ann said. "I treasure that about you. You don't maunder on to hear your own voice, and you notice what's around you. I don't want to leave this bed."

Neither did Rye, but a gentleman—especially one without his clothes—did not presume. "Shall I love you again?"

"We will love each other." She straddled him, bringing the covers up over her shoulders and then tucking close.

Rye reveled in caresses to her back, arms, and—when she gave him the room—her breasts, and in delicate explorations of her feminine flesh. She allowed that and reciprocated with cautious attention to his stones and cock. A trickle of desire became a stream and then a river in full spate.

And yet, he waited, until Ann was undulating slick flesh along the length of his rigid arousal.

"Must I send an engraved invitation, Annie?"

"Yes. I haven't much experience with men who take their time. Send an invitation or give the command, and please do it soon."

"Do you cook your best dishes in a hurry?"

She went still. "Rushing a recipe is a sure means of ruining the result."

"Precisely." Rye shaped her hips, loving the feel of her. "Some meals can be thrown together without much effort, and they nourish adequately. Others must be prepared carefully, and they deserve to be savored. Take your time with me, Annie. You can always try a different approach next week."

Her smile was complicated. Clearly, she was pleased with the notion of taking charge of their lovemaking, but sadness lurked in her gaze as well. A next encounter was possible—she had a half day each week—but then what? What of next month or next year?

Rye could not offer her declarations of undying devotion, but he could offer her pleasure and affection, and so he did. When, after three eternities of fiddling about, she took him in hand and fitted their bodies together, he left the decision of how fast and how deeply to complete the joining to her.

When she sought his kisses, he gave them to her.

When satisfaction overtook her, he abetted her pleasure so vigorously she moaned against his chest and clutched his hand for dear life.

And when she subsided into his arms, panting and flushed, he held her as if he would never let her go.

Though, of course, he must. He wouldn't want to, but when the time came, he must let her go nonetheless.

CHAPTER TWELVE

Ann had never known exactly how to handle what came after a tryst. The problem had usually been solved by the threat of discovery, which necessitated a hasty return to normal duties. That same haste meant she'd never been so thoroughly satisfied as she was drowsing in Orion Goddard's arms.

Or so bewildered.

She'd lost count of the times he'd sent her spinning off into bliss, sometimes on a gale-force wind, sometimes on a gentle breeze. And always, always, he'd been there to hold her and soothe her when passion eased its grip.

Orion Goddard was a lavishly considerate lover, tender, skilled, affectionate, and so... so at ease with the whole business.

No, that wasn't quite right. He was at ease *with himself*. His day could not be ruined by an insinuation that he'd used too much flour in his béchamel sauce. He could admit errors and fears, and he wasn't shocked that Ann had chosen a career in the kitchen over rural domesticity.

But then, rural domesticity *with Orion* hadn't been among the options she'd considered. Was it an option now? Did she want it to be?

"Buttered gingerbread," he said, stroking Ann's bum with a warm hand. "With mulled cider if you have it, a restorative after our exertions."

His touch was like buttered gingerbread, just as rich, delectable, and smooth. Ann peered down at him, for she was still sprawled on his chest. "You are hungry?"

"My appetite for certain pleasures in present company knows no limit, but a shared snack would be a paltry consolation for having to leave this bed."

So that's what came next. He offered his flattery with a brisk little pat on her backside, and still, Ann did not want to give up the warmth of his embrace.

"I have misplaced my self-discipline," she said, forcing herself to sit up, which put her nether parts in contact with his breeding organs. Rye brushed her braid back over her shoulder, as casually as if ladies perched naked upon him regularly.

Ann doubted that was the case. His intimate company was skilled, but Orion would never be profligate with his affections.

"What?" he asked, leaning up to wrap his arms around her. "Do you need to hear that this was special, Annie? That you have forever altered my definition of lovemaking?"

He was special. She was too much of a coward to say that. "You make me feel special."

"Because you are, and if a lover can't remind a lady that she's precious and dear, he has no business putting himself on offer to her. If he can provide her such assurances, she might like the fellow, but only a little and only in the privacy of her thoughts."

"You are awful."

He kissed her nose. "Shall I give the command to charge, Annie?"

"Please."

He spoke close to her ear, not quite a whisper. "I like to think the lovemaking doesn't end when we leave the bed, just as it didn't end when we slept side by side. Passion ebbed, temporarily satisfied, but the closeness and warm regard lingered. I want to see your kitchen, Annie Pearson, the kitchen where you make your first pot of tea each morning, where you rummage for bread and butter on Sunday evenings."

She held him tightly while another bout of tears threatened. "I'll show you my kitchen, but I fear somebody must rebraid my hair before I can venture from this room."

"You are in luck, for braiding is among my meager store of skills."

He had many skills, not least among them the knack of assisting a lady into her clothes while he grumbled about the new boy—Victor—who refused to attend lessons. He chattered about Mrs. Murphy's follower and about his old cavalry sword having mysteriously gone missing, not that he much cared for the sword itself, but the boys had no need of it, and the damned thing was sharp.

Ann did not allow him to replace his eye patch—the house wasn't brightly lit—but she did hand it back to him before they left the bedroom.

"Not so fast," Rye said when she would have opened the door. "First, a hug for courage and a kiss for luck."

The lucky kiss turned into a sweet, hot, tender reprise of the kisses they'd shared in bed, and the hug for courage was fortifying but inadequate.

To withstand Jules's latest fit of pique in the kitchen would take determination and guile, but Ann was completely without weapons when it came to withstanding the greater threat to her peace that Orion Goddard posed with his tenderness and passion.

She was still puzzling over that conundrum when Rye sat with her at the kitchen table enjoying fresh, buttered gingerbread and mugs of steaming mulled cider.

"You've been working on menus," he said, eyeing the ingredient lists and scribblings Ann had spread out on the table the previous evening.

He leafed through the pages, one by one, studying her recipes. "You are very thorough, but then, I knew that."

"I made my usual early call on my aunt this morning. She's planning a formal dinner for thirty, and everything must be perfect. I provide the menus, and she crows about her talented niece to any who will listen." Or that was the plan. Ann was no longer confident that a lot of officers and their wives were much interested in fancy dishes and pretty centerpieces, for none of them had ever asked to consult with her following one of Aunt's dinners.

They mentioned their menus to Melisande, who conveyed requests to Ann only indirectly.

Orion perused the nearest recipe. "No fricassee of gryphon wings or chimera tails in aspic?"

"The guests will be mostly former military. Beef will figure prominently on the menu, as will fowl, and all manner of fancy potatoes. Aunt Melisande's cook is a good soul, but somewhat lacking in imagination."

Orion licked butter off his thumb. "Melisande? That's an unusual name."

"She and Uncle Horace, along with their young daughter, are my only family. If Aunt had made a great enough fuss when I started my apprenticeship, I would have been bundled back to school for more deportment, drawing, and drivel. Aunt and Uncle were in Spain at the time and left me in peace, but for the occasional epistolary sermon. In their absence, the solicitors kept an eye on me."

Orion put down the rest of his slice of gingerbread. "Melisande is married to Horace, and he's former military? Would this be Brigadier Horace Upchurch, by any chance?"

Gingerbread and cider were a good combination, but Ann would not have wanted to consume her portion without butter. Butter smoothed out the spices, curbed the sweetness, and made a little meal where a snack might have been.

"The very one. Uncle Horace was in Spain for the whole Peninsular campaign," she said, "and Melisande followed the drum. She's quite a bit younger than Horace, but they seem devoted. Do you know him?"

Rye took another bite of gingerbread and chased it with a sip of cider. "Our paths crossed. I can taste the cinnamon in the cider, but what other spices do you use? The combination is delectable."

Ann prattled on, pleased that he would ask. He took his leave fifteen minutes later on a spicy kiss and another fortifying hug, as well as a request for permission to call again next week.

Permission she had granted. While all might not have been precisely right with Ann's world, she dreaded her return to the Coventry's kitchen far less than she had before Orion Goddard's call.

She was precious and dear, and so was Orion Goddard, and for now, that was enough.

HORACE BEDAMNED HELLISHING Upchurch was Ann's uncle.

Well, blast. Blast and damnation. Rye had nearly choked on his gingerbread, so shocked had he been. He ducked into the bakery to pick up a second loaf, and the baker's assistant had to ask him twice what he'd come to purchase.

Rye bought the gingerbread and left the change on the counter.

Would Dear Uncle Horace put in a good word for him with Ann, or warn Ann off a former soldier of dubious repute? Why hadn't Rye admitted his connection to the brigadier on the spot? But then, why had Horace taken to denying the connection generally?

"I coulda nicked that loaf right outta your hands," Otter said, falling in step beside Rye. "Or your pocket."

"I told you to stay home, Theodoric."

"You tell me a lot of things, but don't worry. I keep my mouth shut. I could carry the gingerbread for you."

"So generous of you, but then half the loaf would disappear between here and Mrs. Murphy's pantry."

Otter grinned as they waited on the street corner for a pause in traffic. "Only half. I'm not greedy."

No, but the boy was insubordinate, also loyal. A complicated puzzle. Rye flipped a coin to the crossing sweeper, who looked to be no more than eight years old.

"The next time I tell you to stay home, you will follow orders, Otter."

"Like hell I will. Your sword has gone missing. We've a sneak thief in the camp, and you're too busy making sheep's eyes at Miss Ann."

Rye had done far more than make sheep's eyes at the woman, but Otter was being delicate. "It might have escaped your notice, but I am of age and have independent means. Calling on the occasional lady should be part of the blessings attendant thereto."

"You're sweet on her," Otter said, dancing ahead on the walkway. "We all are. You could marry her, and we'd be fat as lords in a month. Something is off about the warehouse inventory."

Marry her. Rye hadn't stumbled across those words in his mental peregrinations, and they were fine words in the right circumstances. Ann deserved commitment and devotion, despite her fierce independence. Becoming her ally, much less her spouse, would be a challenge.

She loved her cookery, had fought hard for it, and shouldn't have to give it up. But marriage generally meant babies, and...

Rye's steps slowed, though he wasn't approaching any street corners.

Babies, *with Ann.* He'd been dutiful toward his various properties and toward the business he'd inherited, but to have a family with Ann... to build something for that family...

"We going to the warehouse?" Otter asked, shoving his hair out of his eyes.

"Why would we do that?"

"Because the tally is off by four hundred cases."

"*What?*"

"The tally is off by four hundred cases, guv, as in cases missing. Somebody helped themselves to half your goods."

Not half of Rye's goods, not even half the goods he had on hand in London, but certainly a good portion of his profit. "Did Dorning take his order from the warehouse rather than the dock?"

"Bertie says not. He kept an eye on the unloading, lest somebody get light-fingered between the dock and the wagon."

Bertie had doubtless kept an eye from some rooftop when he should have been practicing his penmanship.

"Why did Bertie take it upon himself to oversee the transfer of goods?"

Otter glanced about, and it occurred to Rye that the boy had purposely raised this topic on the street, away from home, and *away from the others*.

"Somebody has it in for you, guv. We all know that. Dorning seems like a good 'un, but we hear things."

Rye resumed walking. "What things?"

"Whispers. The Coventry has its problems."

Ann worked at the Coventry, and thus Rye knew some of those problems. "The chef is an idiot. What else?"

"How did you know that?"

"You aren't the only person with eyes and ears, Otter. Jules Delacourt is probably skimming from the pantries, if not the pantries and the wine cellar." Would he steal from Rye in an attempt to protect Fournier's interests? *Vive la France* and all that?

Somebody had certainly stolen from Rye. The warehouse, usually stacked to the ceiling with cases of champagne and other wines, showed a gaping emptiness near the sliding doors that opened into the yard.

"The thieves weren't subtle," Rye said. "They didn't even try to hide what they'd done." Warehouses were all too easy to steal from, and artfully rearranging the contents could hide the theft for a considerable period. These thieves had wanted Rye to notice the missing inventory immediately.

"Only the champagne was stolen?" he asked.

"Aye." Otter ambled off between rows of wooden cases, his voice floating through the gloom. "The other vintages weren't touched. Louis and I checked twice."

"When did you check?" The warehouse was a cavernous structure, the better to keep the inventory cool. Rye had chosen a building distant from the wharves because wine preferred dry air and because the risk of theft was less.

Or should have been.

"We came here at first light, and no, your watchman didn't see us. He were fast asleep, and anybody with a decent set of picks could have got past the lock on your barn door."

"Fast asleep?"

"He's old," Otter said. "Older than you."

Nicolas was one of Lucille's many relatives and connections. His instructions were to sound an alarm if he detected intruders, not to put himself at risk over a few bottles of champagne.

"Fetch Dorning to me," Rye said. "And fetch him now."

Otter emerged from between stacked cases halfway down the row, something in his hands. "Found your sword, guv. Was lying atop a case of the merlot. Scabbard and all."

Rye unsheathed the sword far enough to see the Goddard family motto. *Cervus non servus*, which translated to something like *a stag forever free*.

Unease uncurled in Rye's belly as he set the sword against the remaining cases of champagne. "I did not steal my own inventory."

"I know that," Otter said, "but somebody made off with a powerful lot of your good wine, and that same somebody was in your study. The lads won't like this."

Rye loathed the idea that his citadel had been breached. Children slept in his house, for God's sake. "Do you trust Victor?"

Otter surveyed the warehouse, his gaze unnervingly adult. "You recruited him. He didn't come begging to us. He has nobody else, and he's not stupid."

"That's not a yes, Otter."

"I don't trust nobody. I could do with a slice of that gingerbread if I'm to hare after Sycamore Dorning."

Rye unwrapped the loaf, used a folding knife to cut off a thick serving, and passed it to Otter. "Tell Dorning there's a problem at the warehouse, and mind Mrs. Dorning doesn't overhear you. I'll wait here."

"Wait carefully, guv. Whoever did this knows you'll be poking about looking for answers."

"Go," Rye said, "and then find Nicolas, wake him up, and send him here as well."

Otter scampered off, gingerbread in hand, while Rye made a circuit of the entire warehouse, counting cases and mentally consulting a map of goods in his head. The thieves had taken the good wine, but unbeknownst to them, the very best of the champagne, the vintage Rye would have proudly served to the monarch himself, sat in a dim corner stacked in unremarkable crates.

Rye opened a case in an abundance of caution and reassured himself the bottles were undisturbed. When he'd counted each case and opened several more, he restored the corner to order and went to the door to wait for Dorning.

Try though he might to assemble only the facts, he could not stop thinking of a new boy who refused to sleep in the house and who frequently skipped lessons.

SYCAMORE DORNING KEPT his peace when he wanted instead to shout and curse.

"You were drugged, Nicolas," Goddard said to the aging Frenchman pacing before the warehouse door. "Somebody stood you to a pint or a dram down at the Coq et Poule and slipped something into your drink. Half an hour later, you're dozing at your post."

Goddard was patient with the old fellow, offering sweet reason instead of profanity.

"Easy enough to do," Sycamore observed. "Most émigrés favor a few specific pubs, and you apparently prefer the Coq et Poule. If the Coq has recently switched to winter ale, then a little bitterness in your pint wouldn't be noticeable."

Nicolas, who had the dimensions of a wizened jockey, shook his head. "Not a pint. I drink the brandy before I come to work, to keep away the cold."

"Brandy is even easier to doctor," Sycamore said. "My sister-in-law is something of an expert on medicinal herbs. She could mix up a brew that would knock you flat before you could say *vive l'empereur*."

The little man still looked unconvinced, while Sycamore could not read any reaction at all from Goddard. The colonel's calm was unnerving, though Jeannette had that same vast composure in the face of monumental provocation.

"To unload four hundred cases of champagne," Goddard said, "even with a half-dozen men on the job, would take time, Nicolas. You might doze off for a few minutes or even half an hour, but not for half the night."

"I do not doze off, Monsieur Goddard. You pay me to keep the wine safe, and I am awake at all times."

"What of the lock?" Sycamore asked, rather than allow Gallic pride to continue denying the obvious.

"Picked," Goddard replied, "though not very competently. The tumblers were damaged. Nicolas, you are excused, and because the job has become more dangerous, I will find somebody to watch through the night with you."

"I have a cousin," Nicolas began. "Very trustworthy, very—"

Goddard waved a hand in a gesture that managed to look French. "I'm sure he is, but if you work with somebody you don't know well, you will be more wary than if I employ your trustworthy cousin. This was not a casual purloining of a few bottles, my friend. This theft was carefully planned and executed mischief."

Nicolas rubbed his chin, peered around the warehouse, and took a muttering, shuffling leave of his employer.

"That was brilliant," Sycamore said, "that bit about being more wary. Spared everybody's pride. I do hope the next warehouseman you hire won't be on nodding terms with Methuselah."

Goddard retrieved a cavalry sword from atop some crates and headed for the door. "I'm cold, furious, and hungry. Come along."

And yet, he'd been the soul of civility and patience with the old watchman. "Where are we going?"

"To my house, where Jeanette will not see me in a temper and hear me using profanity."

Sycamore had seen the inside of Rye Goddard's house exactly once, and then only a foyer, hallway, and back garden.

"Jeanette hears me using profanity regularly. She even—I tell you this in familial confidence—occasionally uses a discreet *damn* herself."

Goddard stopped outside the warehouse to pull the door closed. "Do you drive her to it?"

"Oh, sometimes. She has her hands full with me and seems to enjoy the challenge. Are we to parade through town with your sword on display?"

"No." Goddard shoved the sword at him. "Conceal it under your cloak."

Sycamore did as directed, because twitting Goddard in his present mood was ill-advised. "That champagne had to be worth a pretty penny."

"It was, and had I not lost customers steadily over the past few months, and had I not had your order sent over from Calais directly, I'd be without goods to sell until I could replace what was stolen."

Goddard set a brisk pace, for all his gait was slightly uneven.

"But as it happens, the loss of inventory, while inconvenient, will not cripple you?"

"I doubt crippling me outright was the point. That very sword was taken from my office, Dorning. Stolen from my home and left at the scene of the crime. It's engraved with my family motto, and I know my own weaponry when I see it."

The sword was surprisingly heavy, but then, it was a lethal weapon, not a fashion accessory. "Diabolical," Sycamore said, understating the case by miles. "To take something so personal and use it to emphasize a second, larger theft."

"What has been stolen is my patience. I'd suspect Fournier, but he has an entirely different and more credible scheme in train."

"We're not taking the alleys?" Sycamore asked. "On every other occasion when I have been honored to perambulate in your company, we've kept to the alleys."

"That was for the sake of my boys, to make their job easier. The streets are crowded and escort duty more difficult. Then too..."

"Yes?"

"The alleys are quieter, and I do prefer quiet. I don't hear as well as I ought, and quiet eases that burden."

Goddard didn't hear as well as he ought, he nearly limped, and he wore an eye patch. That a man already beleaguered by wounds and woes was also the victim of thieves bothered Sycamore. What bothered him more was the challenge of how to relay events to Jeanette honestly without upsetting her.

"Then you might not hear a thief thumping around in your study when you slept on the next floor up?"

"I might not, but I know how the thief gained access to my home."

They turned down another street. Goddard slipped the crossing sweeper a coin and muttered a few words in French. The boy grinned and nodded, and the coin disappeared into his pocket.

"How did the thief gain access?"

"Mrs. Murphy leaves the door unlatched throughout the day for deliveries and also for her admirer. I suspect she has taken to leaving the door unlatched at night for Victor, our new boy. He doesn't care to bathe and sleeps in the stable. If the night is bitter—and the nights are getting colder—an unlatched door means he can sneak into the kitchen in the small hours and, come morning, pretend he's simply showing up early for breakfast."

"You run a charitable establishment while pretending to sell champagne. Does Jeanette know the extent of your eleemosynary activities?"

"The boys all earn their keep, besides,"—Goddard turned up his own front walkway—"but for Jeanette's sacrifice, I could easily have been on the streets myself or, worse, locked up with my father in debtors' prison. She spared us that. These boys have no sister willing to endure a purgatory of a marriage so they can amount to something."

Jeanette's first marriage had indeed been a purgatory. "You and Jeanette are overdue for an embarrassingly frank discussion of the past, and then I do hope you both set it aside once and for all. She is now married to a man who adores her without limit, and dwelling on what has gone before serves no purpose."

Goddard opened the door and waved Sycamore into the house. "The sword, if you please."

Sycamore handed it over. "You don't set much store by the weapon itself, do you?"

Goddard hung it on a coatrack as if it were one of a half-dozen umbrellas or an everyday walking stick.

"I keep that thing as a warning to myself, as a reminder that I have taken lives and bear the weight of that violence on my conscience. I was lucky. I lived to see another day, but fighting like that—to the death, for some fat king or aging emperor—took a toll I refuse to pay again."

"So you will seethe and fume and hire more watchmen, but you won't fight whoever has done this to you? Isn't it possible that the same people who whisper against you in the clubs are now escalating their attacks and inflicting material damage to go with the harm to your reputation?"

Goddard wrested Sycamore's cloak from him and set his hat on the sideboard. "It's entirely possible. Somebody wants me out of

England, but what I cannot fathom is why. Come along. We'll eat in the kitchen like farmers, and you will give me the benefit of your thinking regarding my various suspects. Fournier is among them, as is that fellow Deschamps, but I cannot rule out a disgruntled Englishman who resents the fact that I've been knighted."

Sycamore followed, more curious than hungry, but also a little dismayed. Jeanette needed to know her brother was safe, and better still if Sir Orion allowed a smidgen of contentment into his life. If the list of suspects included every soldier who'd ever borne a grudge against a commanding officer, then Goddard's potential detractors were legion.

"Tell me more about Deschamps."

"He's a former French officer, devilishly handsome, and a known spy." Goddard took off down the steps leading into the bowels of the house. "If he's still frequenting your club, then your job is to find out what the hell he's doing in London."

Sycamore followed, though he'd been hoping to see the house's public rooms. "I have a *job*?"

Goddard paused at the bottom of the steps. "I realize even that limited brief exceeds your meager capabilities, but somebody has declared war on me, and needs must. If I approach Deschamps directly, he'll simply prevaricate."

"So approach him indirectly."

"I tried that. How is Jeanette?"

Worried about you. "Thriving in my loving care and happily taking an interest in activities at the club. We're buying a property out at Richmond and hope to use it for our market garden."

"My boys could help with that undertaking. They are honest and hardworking, and for all I know, I'll soon have to flee to France one step ahead of the watch."

They are not your boys. "You'd flee to France?"

Goddard looked around the kitchen, which was tidy, warm, and dimly lit. "I don't know. I don't want to, but... I don't know. How hard can it be to find bread and cheese?"

"Well, there's the breadbox, and the cheese might be in the window box this time of year. Swing the kettle over the fire, and we'll manage."

Goddard produced a half loaf of bread wrapped in linen. "If I must retreat to France, will you do something for me?"

"I will hire those hooligans of yours, if that's what you're asking." The cheese was not too sharp, not too mild. Sycamore set it on the wooden counter along with a tub of butter, cheese toast being among the delicacies he'd learned to prepare during his limited banishment to university.

"My hooligans will be a credit to any organization that employs them, and their spoken French is better than yours. Are we having tea, ale, or cider?"

"Cider."

Goddard smiled, a surprising, wistful expression suggesting that, in the right light, he might have a certain roguish appeal.

"Look after Annie Pearson. She puts up with more than you know from that fop Jules Delacourt, and he's not half as talented as you think he is."

"More to the point," Sycamore said, "he's not half as talented as *he* thinks he is, but he brings a certain cachet that the club needs." Sycamore busied himself slicing cheese, though he'd figured out exactly how he'd start in his recounting of the day's events to Jeanette.

Orion Goddard referred to the estimable Miss Pearson as *Annie* now, and when faced with the prospect of a retreat to France, all Goddard asked was that Sycamore look after her.

Not look after the business, the boys, the real estate, or even Jeanette, but look after *Annie* Pearson. *Well, well, well.*

"Don't cut the bread too thickly," Sycamore said, "and Miss Pearson looks after herself."

Goddard tested the blade of the bread knife against his thumb. "I know. Damn it all to hell and back, that much I do know."

ANN GAINED new respect for soldiers at war, for the Coventry's kitchen became a battle zone.

The spices were tampered with, such that the jar labeled tarragon contained nutmeg, and the one that should have held nutmeg instead held ginger. Ann only discovered the problem when she'd dusted nutmeg onto a spinach quiche that had to be consigned to the staff hall.

The footmen gobbled up the entire quiche, oblivious to the blunder.

Emptying each jar, washing it thoroughly, and refilling it with the proper contents took most of an afternoon, but Ann used the exercise to teach Hannah about the uses of different flavorings.

The next day, somebody soured the heavy cream, which became apparent as soon as Ann added a dollop to her white sauce and watched an hour's worth of work curdle.

"I don't understand," Hannah said softly as she set a fresh bottle of cream on the counter. "Why would a chef do mischief in his own kitchen?"

"We don't know that Jules is doing this," Ann replied, though Jules had his own spice cabinet separate from that of the rest of the kitchen, and Jules did not typically use much cream in the main dishes.

"He's doing it," Hannah said. "I forgot my journal last night, so I came back down here after the club had closed, and he was wandering around, drinking from a bottle and looking mean."

"He's homesick," Ann said, sniffing the new bottle of cream and finding only a fresh dairy scent. "Taste this." She poured a small portion into a glass.

"It's fine," Hannah said, after taking a sip and swiping her tongue over her top lip. "Will we make the pear compote for the buffet tonight?"

"That is a good suggestion. If you were to make our recipe better, what would you add?"

Hannah's brows knit. "Chopped walnuts?"

Ann wanted to hug the girl. "Walnuts are a fine idea, though I suspect almonds would do as well. Look in the pantry to see which we have more of."

Hannah had learned not to scamper, but young Henry Boardman had just arrived—twenty minutes late—and was dashing past the mullioned window that looked out on the garden. One moment, Henry was pelting for the staff hall, the next he'd gone sprawling and brought a tray of wineglasses down with him.

"Sodding, almighty, bloody..." Henry sprang to his feet and marched up to Jules, who was lounging against the deal table. "Why the hell did you do that?"

One of Henry's hands was bloody, and shards of glass adorned his sleeve.

"You tripped," Jules said, smiling faintly. "You hurry because you are late again, and you do not watch where you go."

"I am not late. I fetched fresh flowers for the bar like Mrs. Dorning told me to, which meant I started my shift *early*. I watch where I go, and you tripped me."

Jules glanced up at the kitchen's high ceiling. "So dramatic, you English, and so proud. One stumbles occasionally, and this is no shame. I will dock your wages only half the cost of the wineglasses, because—"

"You should pay for the damned glasses yourself," Henry retorted. "For interfering with me when I'm attending to my duties and then blaming me, just as you would have blamed Hannah for spilling the peas."

Jules met Ann's gaze. "The girl was clumsy, as young girls often are. Right, Pearson?"

The club would open in an hour, and thus the kitchen was at its busiest. Pierre, the new sous-chef, was by the enormous open hearth, a carving knife in his hand as hams and beef roasts turned slowly on the spit.

Jules had timed this latest stunt for the moment with the biggest audience and the greatest disruption to the kitchen's smooth functioning. The three scullery maids were at the wet sink, gawking over their shoulders, while various assistants at their stations were pretending to chop or stir or slice. Hannah stood in the doorway to the pantry, looking ready to make a bad situation awful.

"Pearson," Jules said, prowling around the broken glasses, "do you now ignore your superior when he addresses you directly?"

Glass crunched under Jules's boots, expensive glass that Henry could not afford to replace. "Hannah was not clumsy," Ann said, "and neither was Henry."

"We have a difference of opinion." Jules smiled pleasantly. "Step into my office, Pearson, and we will resolve our differences."

"Nan, please fetch the broom and dustpan," Ann said. "When the floor has been thoroughly swept, take a damp mop to it. Only damp. We don't want anybody slipping and falling *by accident*."

"Yes, Miss Pearson."

"Henry, your hand is cut, and your coat needs to be brushed off. Hannah, see to his hand, and wrap the cut in a honey poultice for at least twenty minutes."

Hannah curtseyed, while Henry glared daggers. The footmen did not in theory work for the kitchen, so Henry wasn't at risk for losing his post, but he was clearly at risk for losing his temper.

Ann followed Jules up the steps and along the corridor to a cozy office that faced the stable. A fire burned in the grate. The shelves behind Jules's desk were stocked with cookery books in French, Italian, German, and English, as well as unbound treatises on cooking.

The room smelled faintly as if somebody had spilled brandy on the carpet sometime in the past week.

Jules took the seat behind the desk, and produced a bottle from a drawer and two glasses. "Do not glower at me like that, Pearson. You will have wrinkles. Wrinkles become nobody. Care for a drink?"

"No, thank you." Ann did take a seat, because she refused to stand about like a naughty schoolgirl waiting for Headmaster's tongue-lashing. "You owe Henry an apology." Every person in the kitchen, save perhaps Pierre, was owed an apology for some display of arrogance or meanness by Jules, and Pierre's turn would come.

"I don't owe anybody anything," Jules said, pouring himself a measure of young calvados, based on the apple and pear aroma. "I work for my wages, and Mr. Dorning is happy with the result. You are not happy."

Ann was furious, and thus her tongue ran away with her good sense. "I am happy with my post. I am not happy with you."

Jules held his glass up at eye level, and Ann wanted to dash the drink in his handsome face. "Pearson, you are ambitious, which is an unbecoming quality in a woman who also lacks great beauty. I grant you that some of your sauces are quite passable, but the Coventry's kitchens do not have room for your ambition and my talent."

Ann thought back over the past fortnight, trying to put her finger on what had brought Jules to the point of making ultimatums and tripping footmen.

"You are jealous of a simple pear compote," Ann said. "The customers raved about it, as they do not rave about your roasts."

Jules set the glass on the blotter, rose, and leaned across the desk. "A few women nattering on about a sweet is nothing to trouble myself about. Out in the kitchen just now, you contradicted me before the whole staff."

"I corrected you because you were in error and directly asked for my opinion." He'd been lying, though Ann had enough restraint not to make that accusation.

"You were disrespectful, Pearson, and that I cannot have."

"Then leave your post in high dudgeon," Ann retorted, getting to her feet as well. "Tell Mr. Dorning the staff has fallen below the standards you need to adequately display your talent."

Beneath the scent of his shaving soap, Jules bore the vinegary air of a man who habitually over-imbibed. His eyes were bloodshot, his complexion was becoming ruddy, and when he'd held his glass up, his hand had shaken slightly.

"*Non, ma petit dragon.* I will not hand you a kitchen where I have spent two years attempting to cater to English palates and humoring the incompetence of English staff." He sat back down and picked up his drink. "I am prepared to be reasonable, for a time. Give your notice in the next fortnight, and I will allow the girl to stay."

Ann had known this was coming, and yet, the blow still hurt unbearably. "Give my notice? When I have worked for better than ten years to attain the rank of assistant? When I have been at the Coventry longer than you have? I'm to walk away from all of that because you are jealous of a dessert?"

Jules sipped his brandy, watching her over the rim of his glass. He still commanded brooding good looks to go with his arrogance, but his eyes held a reptilian chill.

"Please put from your limited female mind the notion that I in any way care about a few compliments tossed in the direction of your humble mashed pears. You have airs above your station, Pearson. You encourage disrespect in the staff and disrupt my kitchen. To use the English term, you and I simply do not get along. As it is *my* kitchen, you are the one who must go. You either give your notice in the next fortnight—and make that a convincingly sensible decision— or who knows how many more glasses young Henry will have to pay for?"

In this much at least, Jules was right: Ann *did not* get along with him, did not, in fact, respect him or trust him, and that wouldn't change no matter how hard she worked or how humbly she behaved.

She was tired of the battle, one she would lose eventually anyway. Jules had stamina for the fight, better weapons, and dirtier tactics. If Ann continued to thwart him, he could well see her injured or maimed. Then too, Henry had four younger brothers, and his wages were probably supporting them all. Hannah had nobody save the colonel, and he was already providing for too many people.

Orion's question, about going up the chain of command, came to mind, but Ann had little direct interaction with Mr. Dorning, while Jules's rapport with the owners was well established.

"I must think about this," Ann said. "I'll want a glowing character from you, and I might need more than two weeks to find a suitable post."

Jules saluted her with his drink. "You can be sensible. I had hoped that was the case. I will write a character so laudatory that heaven itself would employ you. The gentlemen's clubs often hire women in their kitchens, I'm told."

Oh joy. A post in the clubs—venerable institutions that served little other than steak and potatoes with the occasional cherry tart or barley soup.

"I have not made my decision," Ann said, "and I have food to prepare. Please stop endangering the staff with your displays of pique, Jules."

"They are my staff," he said, topping up his drink, "and you are no longer welcome to number among them. Back to your post, Pearson, and think about what I've said."

Ann was only too glad to get back to the kitchen, but she had just negotiated the terms of her surrender, and she and Jules both knew it.

CHAPTER THIRTEEN

Hannah wrapped the poultice around Henry's hand, then held up his glove. "I can make you a fresh poultice later. The honey keeps the wound from festering."

"And what will keep my temper from festering?" Henry retorted, wiggling his fingers into the glove. "Damned frog martinet. I've a mind to have a word with Mr. Dorning."

"And who will Mr. Dorning believe? The damned frog martinet, or the underfootman who fell on his arse and broke a dozen fancy glasses?" She and Henry were at the long table in the staff hall and had the room to themselves.

The pantry doorway had afforded a clear view of the whole incident in the kitchen, and as sure as Otter's cabbage farts stank, Jules had tripped Henry. Jules had lounged by the window, seen Henry hustling in from the garden, then waited until Henry had been barreling across the kitchen to stick a foot out at the worst moment.

"I fell on me hands and knees, not me arse," Henry said. "Though what did I ever do to Jules that he'd take out after me like that?"

"You liked Miss Ann's compote," Hannah said. "We all did, and so did the customers. You proposed to marry Miss Ann for her compote." The colonel would marry Miss Ann even without tasting her compote, of that Hannah was certain.

"I'll have to cut this glove off," Henry said, working the kid over his bandage. "Damned Jules will dock my pay for that too."

"If it hurts, let me know, and we'll take the bandage off until you're done for the night."

Henry rose. "Best get back to work, Han. No telling how long Jules will keep Miss Ann from her post, but the customers show up hungry just the same."

"Don't turn your back on Jules," Hannah said, collecting her journal to add the correct measure of walnuts to her pear recipe, once Miss Ann told her what the correct measure was.

"What's that?" Henry asked, pulling on his second glove. "A ledger?"

"In a manner of speaking. The colonel gave it to me." The journal was handsomely bound, the pages smooth and already cut. "Henry, if I asked you to take a note a couple of streets over for me after you finish tonight, could you do that?"

Henry flexed the fingers of his injured hand. "I'm usually working until the wee hours, Han."

"Doesn't matter. I want you to deliver the note to a boy who sleeps in a stable. Has to be in the night, or he's not alone to receive it."

Henry slanted her a look. "You sweet on this boy?"

"I am not. He smells like horse poop and skips his lessons." Though Victor could get a message to Otter, and that mattered.

"As long as he's not trying to turn your head. I saw you first."

"Away with you, Henry Boardman, and I will give you the note when I take my evening break."

Henry grinned, made her a pretty bow, and marched off.

Hannah remained at the table, took out her pencil, and carefully tore a sheet of paper free from her journal. The colonel had said to send to home if she ever needed help, and right now, Hannah needed help.

~

"THAT WAS the best recitation of a poem ever in the history of verse," Rye said. "I am impressed."

Nettie curtseyed before the hearth. "Thank you, *monsieur*. Tante says I am very clever. I will make the poem into French, and you will like it better."

"You can translate the poem if you wish, but I will want another by heart in English next week," Rye replied. He would also make sure Tante Lucille's coal supply had been replenished by next week. "The first half of a Shakespeare sonnet, if the whole thing is too much at once."

"Might I have a tea cake, Tante?"

"You are too forward, Nettie." Tante passed over a tea cake nonetheless. She still wore only the one shawl, but she'd also draped a robe across her lap. "Back to the nursery with you, and take a tea cake for Nurse too." The second tea cake she wrapped in a table napkin.

"Nurse will be proud of me for the rainbow poem." Nettie hugged Rye about the neck and skipped from the room, waving her tea cake.

Tante took a placid sip of her tea. "The child will fall and choke. She will leave crumbs on my carpets. She will gobble both cakes, and Nurse will never be the wiser."

"She will arrive at the nursery in great good spirits," Rye said, trying to find a way to sit in the venerable wing chair that didn't annoy his hip, "share her booty with Nurse, and know an entire sonnet from memory by this time tomorrow." Nettie would be proud of herself, too, and to a child, that mattered.

To anybody.

"Why are you sad, Orion?" Tante asked, setting her cup and saucer on the tray. "You watch Nettie like a man going off to war watches the children playing in the churchyard."

Tante had seen too many men go off to war. French and English, and both nationalities had doubtless watched the children playing in the churchyards with the same wistful heartache.

"You have suggested I could take Nettie back to France, but I don't want to uproot her."

"Children adjust. I will not live forever."

Rye told himself that Nettie and her playmates kept Lucille young. Tante had left her homeland more than a quarter century ago, though, and the intervening years had been difficult. This refrain—*I will not live forever*—had become more frequent of late.

"Are you well, Tante?"

"I am tired, Orion. The English weather ages a woman." Had this pronouncement been accompanied with sighs, pleas sent heavenward, or other dramatics, Rye could have dismissed it as commonplace histrionics.

But English winters *were* miserable to old bones, and to not-so-old bones.

Poverty was a weight no woman should have to bear, much less in her later years.

And homesickness tore at the heart, regardless of age.

"I might well be returning to France for a time, Tante. Would you like to accompany me?"

Lucille considered him. "To Provence?"

"I can escort you there if you'd like to return. Nettie's siblings are there."

"First, you say your customers are here, then you say you can return with me to Provence. Not long ago, you were tarrying in Champagne with Jeanette's young relatives. What is afoot, Orion?"

Why did he prefer the women who dealt in honesty to the pretty flatterers? "The business with Deschamps has escalated. Somebody has stolen a substantial amount of champagne from my warehouse, and that same somebody took my cavalry sword from my very home."

Tante sliced into the apple tart Orion had brought from Roberts's bakery. "You had Monsieur add the calvados. I can already smell the fragrance."

"He offered me a choice of *pommeau* or calvados. You had specified calvados." The cost of the tart had been outrageous, but Roberts would put the rest of the bottle to good use, and Tante would invite her friends over to sample the sweet.

"A good, robust calvados too," she said, cutting a small serving. "You must try it."

"Another time, when I haven't overindulged in tea cakes."

Tante's look said she could count to two in several languages, thank you very much. "Tell me of Deschamps."

A goddamned snowflake wafted past the window, a warning shot fired by the approaching winter. The air wasn't cold enough that the snow would accumulate, but the weather had turned, and Channel crossings henceforth would be rough.

"I'm not sure Deschamps has anything to do with my situation, but I've noticed a pattern. When he's in London, the rumors start up again. This has been going on for more than five years. I looked back over my journals, and the connection is plain."

"Or the coincidence. Have you spoken with him?"

"He denies the charges, though I sensed he was lurking in the park for the express purpose of accosting me."

Tante closed her eyes as she ate a morsel of the tart. "Most men lurk in the park to meet the ladies. You might consider doing that yourself, Orion. Take a wife and forget about the rumors. We can find you a nice French girl when we are in Provence. Monsieur Roberts has outdone himself."

She did homage to the tart while Rye admitted to himself that no nice French girl stood a prayer of catching his eye.

"Does somebody wish for you to shoot Deschamps, perhaps?" Tante asked. "They instigate mischief against you, hoping you will call out Deschamps?"

An interesting theory. "Not a reliable or efficient plan, is it? As you say, Deschamps is quite skilled with both pistols and swords, while I am impaired by poor hearing, bad eyesight, and an unreliable hip." None of which affected Rye's aim with a pistol, but all of which impaired his fencing.

"You are even more impaired by a soft heart. You are done with the killing. Hence, you retreat to the land of your mother's people."

The longer Orion discussed the situation with Lucille, the more heavily the choice weighed on his heart.

Who benefits? Ann's question came back to him, but as usual, no answer accompanied it. "You mentioned that Deschamps had woman trouble. Can you give me any details?"

"I am speculating. He is handsome, angry, and subjecting himself to the society of his enemies. London is not a cheap place for a foreigner to visit, nor particularly welcoming. But he is here again, is he not? Lurking in the park, brooding at his club. Just as you wonder why somebody would steal your champagne and your sword, I wonder why he's underfoot when he could be tucked up in his mama's chateau, flirting with the maids and reliving the glories of fighting for *l'empereur*."

She took another tiny bite of her tart, no doubt tasting the days of her own glory.

"I've met somebody." Rye hadn't planned that admission, but Tante was wise and kind, and he needed her counsel. "A woman. She cooks."

And Annie Pearson kissed and made love and had her very own pair of fierce old godmothers.

"How did you meet this woman?"

"Through Jeanette, indirectly."

"That is the best way, through family and friends. She is English, this woman who cooks?"

She was marvelous. "Yes."

"And her people are here, her kitchen is here. Would she go with you to France?"

Rye shook his head. He would ask, or he hoped he would, but Ann ought not to go with him. That would mean marriage, and he was a man somewhat the worse for past battles. His business prospects were floundering, enemies lurked on the edge of his camp, and all manner of obligations beset him.

Ann ought to stay in England, making her kitchen magic, and Rye ought to leave for France on the next packet.

"How did you do it, Tante? How did you turn your back on everything and everyone you knew and loved, put your whole life into a few trunks, and leap into a foreign land that would never be your home?"

She took a third nibble of her tart and set the plate aside. "One grew tired of the savagery, Orion. The Terror spread its tentacles out from Paris, and nobody was safe. Women, children, the infirm... The bloodlust spared nobody, and we could see no end to it. We had murdered our king, a reasonable man who loved his country, and we dispatched his wife and children as well."

She sighed softly, her gaze on the past. "There is no justification among decent people for murdering and mistreating children. Then we turned on one another. The Austrians were encroaching, England has never been our friend for long, the Prussians weren't to be trusted, and I was exhausted. I made the right choice to come to this island. A time arrives when bravery is foolishness. If now is that time, then live to regret your decision, but don't be so brave you end up needlessly dead."

"You counsel retreat."

"If you die with a sword to the heart, nobody will be left to spoil me and bring me tarts, *non?*"

Ann could make that tart and would enjoy experimenting with its variations. She had, in fact, battled long and hard for the privilege of making tarts and wasn't likely to walk away from her victories for the sake of marriage to him.

"Has Jeanette brought her husband around?"

"*Oui. Mr. Dorning est trés charmant—et astucieux.* Charming and shrewd, as the English say. He is in love with Jeanette, and she with him. Nettie likes them both."

That was good, and painful. "Jeanette is family to Nettie, and they should know one another." Orion rose, and three more snowflakes drifted past. He felt abruptly old and sad, though he had much to be grateful for. "I will come for my sonnet next week."

"See yourself out," Tante said. "The hallway is cold, and the tea is still warm. If I had to choose between winter in Provence and winter in London, I know which one I would pick, Orion. Which one anybody with sense would pick."

That choice was easy, but for Orion, the choice between winter in Provence and anywhere with Ann Pearson was much more difficult.

～

THE AGENCIES HAD RESPONDED to Ann's inquiries swiftly: Nobody sought to hire a cook.

London was shifting into winter hibernation, when those able to do so left the capital for country abodes, and those who could not socialized much less than in other seasons.

Ann was seeking employment at the worst time of year. And that realization had made the need to review the officers' dinner menu with Melisande all the more pressing. Over a pot of unremarkable China black, Ann presented the dessert options.

"The syllabub is so…" Melisande made a face. "So pedestrian, and cranachan is *Scottish*."

As was some of the best whisky, and Ann doubted very much that the brigadier would quibble over its nationality.

"The pear compote has been very popular at the Coventry," Ann said, "and you could have it brought to the table in a flaming sauce."

"Flaming dishes always create an impression," Melisande said, considering the recipe. She would no more be able to grasp the result of following the instructions than Ann could imagine battle tactics given a map of unknown terrain, and yet, Melisande dithered.

"And tell me, Ann, what of a wine pairing with the pear dish?"

"Champagne would go very nicely and make an unusual choice."

"Emily Bainbridge never serves champagne."

Which had exactly nothing to do with completing a meal on a spectacularly sophisticated and delectable note of sweetness.

"Mrs. Bainbridge certainly avails herself of the free champagne on offer at the Coventry."

Melisande sent Ann a considering glance. "She does?"

"That champagne is a hallmark of the club's late-night hospitality, and Mrs. Bainbridge enjoys a liberal portion."

"I am so glad you won't be working there anymore."

Ann took the pear dessert recipe from Melisande and added it to the stack of recipes brought for Melisande's consideration.

"I have learned what I could at the Coventry, and I will surely find another post come spring." Very likely at a gentleman's club, where Ann would spend her evenings mashing turnips and beating eggs for meringues.

"You should spend the winter with me, Ann."

Ann tucked her recipes away in her reticule. They were more precious than rubies, did Melisande but know it.

"I beg your pardon?"

"Well, if you aren't working," Melisande said, pouring herself another cup of tea, "then you aren't earning any coin, and unless you want to dip into savings—the brigadier disapproves of dipping into savings—then you will be hard put to make ends meet. Stay with me, and you can oversee the preparations for the officers' dinner yourself."

Clearly, Ann was supposed to be delighted at that prospect. "I am not needed in your kitchen, Aunt."

"But you could mess about there, nobody the wiser. If you were on hand, I could be certain this dinner would keep people talking until Yuletide. I would like to see more of your recipes, Ann, truly I would. Speaking of Yuletide, there's always some socializing around the holidays, open houses and at homes, and you could accompany me and see what other hostesses are serving."

Melisande sipped her tea with the satisfied air of a cat who'd just spied an unguarded bowl of cream.

"You want me to plan a menu for your holiday open house?"

"And my at homes. I have them twice a month, and half the regiment shows up, but I'd like to offer more than sandwiches and dry cake."

On the one hand, Ann wanted and needed to cook, and Miss Diana and Miss Julia had no appetite for rich or expensive dishes. On the other hand, Ann was a professional with years of experience, and Melisande expected her to work for free and pretend all that effort and expertise was an indulged peculiarity.

An eccentricity. *Messing about.*

"I will consider your offer," Ann said, "and thank you for your generosity. I have been careful with my wages and need not pinch pennies just yet." Then too, Ann liked her life, but for Jules's petty games.

She liked Miss Diana and Miss Julia, liked being able to trot around London on her own without maids, footmen, or a chaperone. She liked being able to set foot outside her door and, with a single sniff, know what had come from the bakery's ovens that morning.

She liked very, very much being free to spend time with Orion Goddard in private.

"Ann, I know you think my existence frivolous," Melisande said. "I have but the one daughter, and she's too young to need much from me besides kind governesses and the occasional outing to the park. But I do socialize, and I can give you the opportunity to see your cooking from the perspective of those who enjoy a meal."

Vain, self-absorbed, and shallow Melisande might be, but she wasn't stupid. "Go on."

"You spend all this time choosing and testing recipes, then sampling the results," Melisande said. "You are never seated with the guests to see the impression your dishes make when the footmen set them before the host or hostess. You never experience the aromas at the table, all blending as the wine is poured. You never eat the portions the guests are offered, never assess the whole meal as a progression of courses."

Ann wanted to argue—she knew her recipes—but Melisande was right. To cook a meal was like directing a play, a very different exercise from sitting in a theater box with friends and enjoying the performance over the bustle and chatter of the pit and gallery.

Melisande had decided that having a free chef for the winter suited her ambitions, while for Ann...

Orion Goddard had made her no promises, and Ann had been very clear with him that larking off to France did not suit her plans.

She wished now she hadn't been so clear. "I will consider your invitation, Aunt. If you are content with the selections you've made for the menu, I will calculate the portions needed to feed thirty for supper. Your cook will have the recipes by tomorrow."

Melisande's frustration showed in a pinching of her lips. "You are so stubborn, Ann. I despair of you. I offer you an opportunity to frolic to your heart's content in my kitchen, to make connections in polite society, and you turn up difficult. What is so blessed precious about chopping leeks all day that you'd hesitate to join this household?"

My freedom is so precious. The respect of the staff at the Coventry. Access to a kitchen larger than all your public rooms put together. The privilege of enjoying Orion Goddard's intimate attentions without fretting that I'll cause a scandal.

So much that was so dear hinged on remaining independent from Melisande's household. "I will take you up on your offer to attend the dinner, Melisande. Let's start there." Ann rose, lest Melisande wheedle and browbeat her into a greater concession.

Melisande got to her feet as well. "You have suitable attire for a formal dinner?"

"I am your spinster niece who has been rusticating for years, as far as your friends know. I'm sure I can dress myself adequately to uphold that fiction."

"I will have to find another fellow to make up the numbers,"

Melisande said, walking Ann to the door. "The brigadier might know somebody."

"I will bring my own escort," Ann said, "a former military man who has at least a passing acquaintance with Uncle Horace."

"This is an officers' dinner, Ann. Don't show up with some infantryman-turned-groom from the Coventry's stable."

"It might surprise you to know, Aunt, that at the Coventry, we enjoy the custom of the occasional duke and even George himself from time to time. I will bring an officer, you need not worry about that."

Melisande passed Ann her cloak and then her bonnet. "You aren't thinking of bringing Jeanette Dorning's brother, are you?"

Such enthusiasm. "The last time I checked, colonels were included among the officers' ranks, and yes, I might well bring Colonel Sir Orion Goddard as my escort. He is a gentleman and acquainted with Uncle Horace. Perhaps you also knew him in Spain?"

Melisande passed Ann her parasol. "I did. Why he was knighted, I do not know. There was talk and a board of inquiry if I recall correctly."

"That board absolved the colonel of any and all accusations of wrongdoing, and thereafter, he was knighted. Can your other guests claim that honor? I thought not. I must be going."

"I'll find you somebody other than Goddard," Melisande said. "He's not good *ton*, Ann."

He is my friend and my lover and better ton *than you can aspire to be.* "Don't bother. I'm sure the colonel is free to accompany me. If you want me to consider biding with you this winter, Melisande, you will accustom yourself here and now to the notion that I see whom I please and do as I please. I am not a schoolgirl who can be scolded into submission with threats of your disapproval."

Melisande smoothed the drape of Ann's cloak. "Were you ever?"

"Yes." For too long—but thank heavens the lure of the kitchen had been sufficient motivation to put aside that foolishness. "Please give my love to Horace and Daniella."

Melisande kissed Ann's cheek and let her go, then stood at the window and watched her progress down the steps and onto the walkway. She was still watching when Ann offered her a parting wave.

The whole conversation had been uncomfortable, probably for both parties, and a lingering disquiet stayed with Ann as she made her way home. In girlhood, Ann had told herself that school wasn't so bad, that the other students weren't so unbearable, that an occasional afternoon pestering the school's cook was enough indulgence of a little hobby.

Leaving Mayfair for the busier and more commercial neighborhoods abutting it, Ann made up a similar litany about a winter spent in the Upchurch household.

It would be for only a few months.

Melisande meant well.

Not even Carême had the opportunity to partake of the banquets he planned.

And just as when she'd been a girl, Ann's list of considerations felt like so many lies told to pour the sauce of patience on a dish of flaming misery.

ORION WISHED Ann lived several miles more distant from his house, because he needed the walking time to rehearse his confession.

Confessions, plural. Informing Ann that Horace Upchurch had been Rye's commanding officer shouldn't be too awful. She'd wonder why Rye had dissembled, and he could explain: He'd simply been surprised and then uncertain about how to broach a difficult topic.

Explaining to Ann that France was becoming an inevitability was a more delicate discussion. Rye was essentially blowing retreat without sighting the enemy. One name for that behavior was cowardice. That half of London thought him a spy was annoying and unjust. That Ann might think him a coward was unbearable.

To stand and fight was brave, to walk into an ambush—into more ambushes—would be stupid. Rye had considered a retreat to avoid stupidity, and yet, leaving London now felt all wrong. He was knocking on the blue door before he'd reasoned himself into a worse muddle yet, and then there was Ann, looking dear and delicious, as she welcomed him into her home.

"That is an apple tart," she said, taking the parcel from Rye and kissing his cheek. "A French apple tart." She gently peeled away his eye patch and tucked it into a pocket of his cloak.

"I patronize a bakery that my French friends prefer. I had Monsieur Roberts make up a special order for an older lady with whom I've long been acquainted, and I hoped you might enjoy a sample of the same treat."

Ann set the parcel on the sideboard and unwound the scarf from Rye's neck. She sniffed the wool and took his hat next.

"Monsieur Roberts's bakery is gaining quite a reputation," Ann said. "Miss Julia and Miss Diana like to stop there on fine days and treat themselves to his profiteroles. I confess I have a weakness for his eclairs."

I have a weakness for you. Rye was happy just to hear Ann's voice, to see her bustling about her domicile. He wondered if that lifting of the spirits was what a married man experienced when returning home at the end of a workday.

Somebody glad to see him, somebody happy to share the day's events. Somebody to kiss his cheek and assess whether he was full of good news or merely relieved to be home. The cat stropped himself against Rye's boots, adding to the sense of domestic welcome.

"Shall we enjoy the tart with a pot of tea?" Rye asked, unbuttoning his cloak.

Ann's gaze went to the steps. "Later?"

Or maybe married men had other reasons to hurry home of an evening. "Annie Pearson, are you eager to have your way with me?"

"Yes."

"I am flattered." Also torn, because they had things to discuss, difficult things.

"Only flattered? Not eager?" She took his coat and hung it on a peg next to ladies' cloaks and bonnets.

Rye stepped close enough to take Ann in his arms. "When it comes to you, my dearest, most delectable Annie, eager is an understatement. I'm a-boil with longing for you, but a fellow doesn't just take off his hat and unbutton his falls."

She burrowed closer. "Some fellows don't bother taking off their hats."

"Such a fellow would be an idiot, when he could instead spend a moment reveling in the pleasure of your embrace, when he could allow himself the joy of anticipating the coming interlude. Kiss me before I forget what language I'm babbling in."

A smiling kiss was a lovely way to begin a tryst. Rye had made Ann smile, and that made him smile, and the damned cat—winding himself between their feet—was probably smiling too.

"I've missed you," Ann said, subsiding against Rye's chest. "I have things to tell you, but they can wait."

She fit him perfectly, and the feel of her was luscious, all warm, feminine, sweet, and sturdy. "I have things to tell you too," Rye said. "Not particularly cheerful things."

Ann chose then to run her hand over his falls. "My mood is growing more cheerful by the moment, Orion. Will you please take me upstairs?"

He ought to kiss her nose, step back, and tell her he was leaving London for a time—possibly a long time. He really should explain that his situation was growing more difficult by the week, and that his business prospects, never very impressive, were dwindling apace.

Instead, he scooped her into his arms and all but charged up the steps.

"Every lady should be carried off by a dashing swain at least once in her life," Ann said, looping an arm around his neck. "You make me want to cook banquets for you to keep up your strength."

"You make me want to..."

"To be wild?" Ann asked as Rye set her on her feet in her bedroom.

"That too, but also to be close." To have his bum patted in the odd moment when nobody was looking and to be hugged when he walked through the front door. Whatever the opposite of war was, he wanted that with Ann.

To love, to build a shared life both humble and precious.

Ann slipped from his embrace, and his rosy anticipation suffered a chill. What things could she have to tell him? Gossip from the Coventry, perhaps? News of Hannah?

"Ann?"

She shut the door and locked it. "For this one hour, Orion, let's be both close and wild. I have looked forward to your next visit more than you can possibly know."

Her honesty caused more heartache than she could possibly know, for this might well be their last encounter. He would miss her, worse than he'd missed home when he'd gone to war. A soldier knew that some fine day he might return to his loved ones and to the familiar haunts of his peacetime life.

As Rye undid Ann's hooks, tapes, bows, laces, he was hit with the realization that to part from Ann would wound him as no battlefield ever had. He gathered her close so her back was to his chest and buried his face against her shoulder.

"You are precious to me, Annie Pearson."

She turned in his embrace and wrapped her arms around his waist. "And you to me, Orion Goddard. Make love with me."

He gave himself up to making pleasure with her, to cherishing her caress by caress and kiss by kiss. By the time he had her naked on the bed beneath him, her braid was coming undone, and her gaze had taken on a heat that frayed his self-restraint.

"Someday," she muttered, locking her ankles at the small of his back. "Someday I will find the discipline to make you as overwrought and muddled as you make me."

They weren't likely to have that day. Rye shoved that sorrow aside and teased at Ann's sex with his cock.

"You are muddled, Miss Pearson? It seems to me you know exactly what you want."

"I know exactly who I need, Orion, but you are maddeningly—"

He pushed forward. "Yes?"

"Maddeningly delicious," Ann said, closing her eyes. "Why must you feel so wonderful inside me?"

"What comes after wonderful?"

Her breath hitched, telling Rye that he'd found the angle needed to answer his own question.

"I don't..." Ann moved in a luxurious undulation. "Angels defend me. This is better than last time, and I didn't think anything could surpass that pleasure."

Oh Lord, she was too much. Too honest, too enthusiastic, too perfect for him. A skirmish ensued, between Rye's determination to make his lady happy and his body's need to share in the joy. Determination won by a narrow margin as Ann shuddered out her satisfaction while clinging to Rye in a desperate embrace.

He stilled rather than tempt himself beyond reason.

"That was..." Ann sounded dazed and happy. "That was well past wonderful. That was spicy and sweet and rich and hot and... I'd say sinful, except with you, nothing of wrongness applies."

She battered him with dearness, and Rye retaliated by sending her over the edge again, this time in a blaze of passion as explosive as it was intense. When she was drowsing in his arms, he withdrew and spent on her belly, then tucked close and let himself drift.

As she'd said, sweet, rich, hot... all the wondrous qualities of passion made deeper by profound caring.

"I don't want you to go," Ann said when Rye lifted up enough to retrieve the handkerchief from the bedside table. "I don't want to let you out of this bed, much less back into your clothing."

Rye tidied up as best he could and shifted to his side, spooning himself around his lover. "Nobody need go anywhere at the moment. Close your eyes and rest, Annie. I will be here when you awaken."

She took his hand. "I will dream of you."

"And I of you."

Except that he didn't. Rye remained awake, memorizing the rhythm of Ann's breathing and the curve of her cheek. She was the banquet prepared especially for him, and he was nearly certain he'd have to leave her and go off to France where, in all the ways that mattered, he'd soon starve.

ANN LAY in Orion's arms and suffered nightmares of guilt. She should tell him she'd lost her job, tell him she was soon to remove to her aunt's household.

He would be disappointed in her for abandoning Hannah so soon.

He might also wonder why Ann would give up on her dreams without more of a fight, but she wasn't giving up. She was retreating, taking stock, trying on a different perspective—wasn't she?

"You are awake," Orion said, glossing a hand over her hip.

How she loved his touch, and how she would miss it. "Thinking. I am soon to leave the Coventry." That pronouncement was as graceless as overly salted soup, though Ann was relieved to have made it.

Orion shifted to crouch over her, though Ann remained on her side rather than face him. "What happened, Annie? You fought battle after battle to gain your post at a prestigious club, and you are invaluable to the Coventry. Who has done this to you?"

"Jules Delacourt. He has decided that the kitchen isn't big enough for his talent and my ambition, to quote him."

Orion nuzzled her ear. "The boot is on the other foot. The kitchen isn't big enough for Delacourt's arrogance and your ability. Shall I have a word with my dear brother-in-law?"

Sycamore Dorning was first rate at handling the customers, and he kept peace among the waiters, dealers, and footmen. He delegated matters in the kitchen to his chef and would not appreciate Orion's meddling.

"You shall not."

"Because,"—Orion gently rolled Annie to her back—"you do not want to be the cause of acrimony between me and my family. Dorning is a big boy. He's up to a little blunt speech from a concerned brother-in-law."

"Mr. Dorning's entire livelihood depends on his club, Orion. He cannot fire Jules without earning the notice of the gossips. The cachet of having a French chef does much for the Coventry's reputation, which—need I remind you—is that of a *supper* club that offers other amusements."

Orion rolled with Ann so she ended up straddling him. "Illegal amusements. I admit that Dorning has an Achilles' heel, in that a disgruntled chef could inspire the authorities into making a raid, but you don't owe Dorning lifelong fealty, Annie. What has sent you from a post you love?"

This was not where and how Ann had envisioned having this discussion, which showed a poverty of imagination on her part. For Orion Goddard, intimacy was not only of the body, but also of the heart. To deal with difficult matters in bed was of a piece with his notion of an intimate friendship.

I will miss him until I'm too old to boil my own water for tea.

"Jules can ruin my prospects," Ann said, curling down onto Orion's chest. "He can make it so that not even the gentleman's clubs will hire me, and no family of any standing will let me so much as wash their pots. He can do this even if he leaves the Coventry, but he won't leave the Coventry."

"Because you have whipped that regimental kitchen into shape, and it more or less runs itself."

Well, yes. "As much as any kitchen can run itself. I'll give Pierre copies of my more popular recipes before I leave, and Jules has said he'll write me a glowing character."

"But he hasn't yet, has he?" Orion posed the question gently and began stroking Ann's back in slow caresses.

"No, he has not." Ann swallowed past a lump in her throat. To speak of leaving made it more real and made the grief bigger.

Orion muttered something about applying *mes poings* to Jules's arrogant, French *nez* and delivering *un coup de pied rapide* to Jules's presuming arse.

"You will not use your fists on his nose or deliver any swift kicks," Ann said, torn between amusement and despair. "Jules will insult your champagne, and he can make those insults matter."

"I hate this, Annie. Jules is like an officer unfit for command. He turns the unit upside down with his ineptitude and fragile self-regard, takes responsibility for none of the mayhem he causes, and never suffers any consequences. Those who try to correct him are insubordinate, and who should determine their punishment but the very fool whose incompetence necessitated the blunt speech."

This tirade suggested army life had had tribulations both on and off the battlefield. "Jules is a French chef, and a certain high-handedness is expected from him." Nobody ever said why that should be, why arrogance and meanness had any place in an art devoted to nourishing the body and soul.

"To blazes with him, then, and the next kitchen you run will be amazed at their good fortune."

A bedamned tear slipped down Ann's cheek, because Orion's confidence in her ability hurt that much. Nobody else had ever offered her such support, and what might she have done with that kind of encouragement?

"That's the problem," Ann said. "This is the wrong time of year to be looking for work as a cook, and without that character, I will be lucky to find a post at a lowly coaching inn." Though what would be the point of employment in a kitchen that never served anything but dubious soup, bread adulterated into inedibility, and cheap ham?

Orion's hands went still. "Jules needs to meet with an accident."

How I do love you. "He can be a chef without cooking, Orion. He doesn't cook as it is. He prowls around the kitchen, tasting this, sniffing that, and cuffing the unsuspecting potboy between trips to the wine cellar. Jules purposely tripped a footman while I watched and then threatened to make the boy pay for the broken glasses."

"Then you are well away from him. Don't cry, Annie. He's not worth crying over. You will find another post come spring. If it's one thing Mayfair does during the Season, it's consume food."

Jules was not worth crying over, and spring would come around again, both were true, but not much comfort. "I feel like a failure."

And that admission provoked more tears. Orion held her, he used the corner of the sheet to wipe at her cheeks, and he stroked her shoulders and back with exquisite tenderness. Ann did not feel better, exactly, when she regained her composure, but she felt less alone with her misery.

"You are not a failure," Orion said. "You are making a tactical re-evaluation of the terrain. Smart officers always reassess battle plans as the fight progresses, and you are no different. I'll be doing some of that myself over the coming months, which we can discuss later. You can spend the winter cooking for Miss Julia and Miss Diana and impressing all of their friends."

Ann sat up, though she knew her cheeks were splotchy and her hair was a fright. "My aunt has said she will introduce me to her friends, and they are all hostesses of some repute, at least in military circles. I have a silly hope that I can offer the ladies guidance regarding menus and presentation and that they will regard that advice as worth paying for."

Orion brushed her hair back over her shoulder. "If you were a fussy, arrogant Frenchman, they would start catfights over who got to hire you first."

"But I am simply Ann Pearson, spinster at large, and thus I hesitate to join my aunt's household, even temporarily. I fear I will become the dull companion she longs to make me into and never escape that fate. She and her friends will flatter me into giving up my recipes, and I will have nothing to show for years of hard work."

And all over again, Ann would be that schoolgirl longing for escape, longing to read cookbooks by the hour.

Orion levered up to wrap her in a hug. "You are thinking of joining the Upchurch household?"

"For a time, if I must."

His arms tightened around her. "Perhaps that's for the best, but, Annie, that is one place where I could not court you, even if I were to remain in London."

Ann pushed him to his back and pinned his wrists. "Explain yourself."

He kissed her, sweetly and lingeringly, the note of farewell breaking Ann's heart. "Perhaps we'd best get dressed, Annie my love, and fortify ourselves with some apple tart."

Ann climbed off the bed, though for once, the prospect of sampling a delectable treat held no appeal.

CHAPTER FOURTEEN

"Horace, I would never disobey you," Melisande said, trying for a humble note, "but do you think it's easy to come up with different offerings for every dinner?"

The brigadier did not immediately answer her question, but instead gazed upward, as if hoping the heavenly intercessors would fly forth with needed reinforcements bearing wagonloads of marital patience.

When Horace deigned to return to the topic at hand, he spoke in the clipped, quiet tones that he usually reserved for a footman who'd buttoned his coat incorrectly.

"There are cookery books without number, Melisande, and your accomplishments do include literacy." His tone implied that she had few other accomplishments to equal even that humble achievement.

Melisande stared at her husband, who in his own mind was doubtless a warrior aging with dignity. To her eyes, he was becoming a pompous old nincompoop, and if she did not take him to task for his nincompoopery now, she'd spend the rest of her life pretending his insults and arrogance didn't wound her.

"Despite my limited accomplishments," she said, rising and bracing her hands on the desk, "despite my many shortcomings and errors, I have been a *loyal* wife to you, Horace Upchurch."

He looked away, and that small gesture confirmed that Melisande need not be more specific. She could have abandoned him in Spain, deserted the almighty regiment and taken up with a handsome, passionate, French officer. Scandals of that nature had been commonplace, but she'd spared Horace such a resounding defeat.

They'd negotiated a truce only because she had been loyal to her spouse.

"I have been loyal to you as well, Melisande. I don't see what ancient history has to do with you demonstrating unbelievably bad judgment by allowing Orion Goddard onto your guest list."

Horace had been loyal too. In Spain, he had *not* been faithful—his infidelity predating Melisande's, in fact—and thus his righteous ire at her straying had been tempered with reason. He had neglected his wife, leaving her to the flirtations of his junior officers. He'd also left her to suffer all manner of sly looks and unkind talk from the regimental tabbies, and for that, Melisande had been hard put to forgive him.

"Horace, you and Emily Bainbridge have kept company at the Coventry." The shock registering in Horace's eyes was pathetically gratifying. "She chatters, to put matters kindly, and Ann works at the Coventry. Imagine a situation where Ann has to nip out from the kitchen to monitor the state of the buffet, and she sees you and smiles at you."

"Women smile. That signifies nothing."

Good God, when had Horace become such a nitwit? "There are smiles and there are smiles, and believe me, Emily Bainbridge can tell them apart. Ann's smile would be genuine and familiar, and in a moment of surprise, she might greet you with a pleasant, 'Good evening, Brigadier.' If she was harried or exhausted, which I gather she frequently is, she might forget herself so far as to greet you as Uncle Horace."

"She would never."

Melisande wanted to slap her husband. The urge was both tempting and terrifying. "You hang my entire standing and reputation as a hostess on that ill-informed assumption, Horace. Your invitations are universally accepted, but let word get out that some young woman at the Coventry is calling you uncle, and we would become objects of speculation."

"Ann has more sense than to... to... acknowledge me in her place of work."

"Ann," Melisande said, leaning closer, "while still very much a girl, found herself a post as a London apprentice, saved years of quarterly allowances with nobody the wiser, ran off to London from one of the most exclusive boarding schools in the Midlands, and completed a lengthy apprenticeship you were certain she'd abandon in the first three months."

That recitation would be enough to inspire admiration, were Ann not also such a source of vexation.

"She's headstrong. She's not stupid."

"Fine," Melisande said, straightening. "She is not stupid. Her discretion would never falter at the Coventry, though of all the clubs in London, I have no idea why you'd want to frequent that one... Unless the choice of which venue to visit wasn't yours."

Horace was so rarely flustered that to see him at a loss was curious. He cleared his throat, he looked out the window. He reached for his pocket watch, but must have realized that he was betraying guilt.

"Emily Bainbridge gambles," Horace said. "Her husband has asked in confidence that those of us in a position to do so help her moderate her impulses. As his former commanding officer, I felt a duty to..."

Melisande cocked her head.

"There's nothing between me and Emily Bainbridge, Melisande. She's vain and silly, but I came across her on the walkway as I returned home from my club, and she inveigled me into joining her party."

That much was probably true. Emily did not care for Horace's excessive dignity and would have delighted in dragging him into a fashionable gaming hell.

"Back to Ann," Melisande said. "Over the years, between here and Spain, you have asked me to coordinate perhaps forty of these regimental dinners. Assume the average number of courses is eight, though some have ranged as high as twelve, and assume each course requires a wine pairing. That is more than three hundred recipes, Horace, all chosen to create a memorable menu, not simply an edible dish. That is dozens and dozens of wine selections, dozens of different centerpieces and flower selections."

"I know it's not as simple as telling Cook to put on a roast, Melisande."

"You don't know, and I have made it my business to spare you the effort of knowing, Horace. In all the years of our marriage, my pin money has never been increased." To bring this up was very nearly to pick a fight, but when Horace was larking about a gaming hell with one of the biggest gossips in London, some plain speaking was long overdue.

Horace rose, perhaps because a gentleman did when a lady was on her feet, perhaps because he sensed Melisande was circling around to his exposed flank, and he needed to take evasive maneuvers.

"Your pin money was spelled out in the settlements, Melisande, and what this has to do with the great awkwardness of entertaining Orion Goddard under my own roof, I do not know."

Melisande went to the window, rather than allow Horace to appropriate the vantage point. "The settlements, sir, spell out that the quarterly sum will be adjusted annually to allow for increased prices as may be encountered from time to time. Prices have done nothing but increase, even more so since the peace, and you tell me our investments are not performing to standards. And yet, you want these impressive dinners four times a year, parade dress, cannon at the ready."

"Four dinners a year doesn't seem like much, Melisande."

Melisande could not exactly rail against Horace's high-handed-ness when his ignorance of household matters had afforded her much latitude in the domestic domain.

"You insist on maintaining a coach and four when we seldom go any distance," Melisande said. "We keep this grand house, for *three people*, Horace, one of whom is a child. You employ a valet when I am more than capable of looking after you, and... If you think these dinners are a mere incidental expense, I can tell you they easily cost as much as an entire quarter's budget to feed the whole household."

Horace braced a hand on the mantel and stared into the fire. "An entire quarter's budget... for one meal?"

A formal dinner generally contemplated thirty guests. Had Horace thought thirty could dine in style with full regalia as cheaply as one couple, a little girl, and some staff dined on mundane fare?

Apparently, he had. "I will show you my budgets and show you how the expense for one dinner was halved when Ann took a hand in the planning. She knows how to produce impressive results without bankrupting me. She has a sense for wine pairings that impress without emptying the cellar of our best vintages. She plans fewer courses and somehow makes the whole affair more lavish. I don't know how she does it, but your dinners are the envy of our friends because of Ann."

To say that hurt, but then, Ann was involved only because Melisande saw the potential benefit of soliciting her help. Besides, Ann *liked* to cook, liked to fuss with saucepots and spices and so forth. Giving Ann a chance to do what she enjoyed was hardly taking advantage of her.

Far from it.

"An entire quarter's budget..." Horace rubbed his forehead. "I had no idea."

"I should not have troubled you with a matter as trivial as house-hold finances," Melisande said, "but you mentioned the investments. I need Ann to help me maintain standards, Horace, and inviting

Goddard was her one condition for assisting me. If we can endure his company for one evening, I will be in a position to pry Ann loose from the Coventry."

Horace was looking tired and a little bewildered. "How d'you figure that?"

"She went straight from boarding school to kitchen work and has never had an opportunity to live the life of a lady. I will show her what she's missed, introduce her to some of the more gallant bachelors, and prevent her from ever going back to her chopping and peeling. If word gets out that she's a glorified scullery maid, we might eventually recover from the gossip, but Ann will never make the sort of match she deserves."

Horace straightened. "She's a bit more than a scullery maid, if she's been planning the officers' dinners."

"*I* plan those dinners, and I consult Ann on the menu." Also the centerpieces, flowers, music, and presentation of the courses. Truth be told, Ann had even had a few helpful comments on the seating arrangements, her connections at the Coventry having given her a sense of who socialized regularly with whom.

Horace resumed his place at the desk, something about how he lowered himself into the chair suggesting fatigue.

"I thought Ann would give up her harebrained adventures in the kitchen," he muttered, "but she has persisted. The offerings at the Coventry are nothing short of magnificent, particularly lately. It had not occurred to me that Ann had a hand in all that. You are convinced she'll set aside cooking given half a chance?"

Melisande was not sure, but she was hopeful. "Ann comes from gentry, Horace, as I come from gentry. We weren't raised to tolerate the loose morality or wanton excesses of either the lower reaches of society or its most exalted members. We uphold standards, and Ann has allowed youthful rebellion to blossom into a course she cannot quit without appearing to suffer a defeat. She has deviated exceedingly from propriety's dictates. I'll fix that for her, and she will one day thank me."

One day, after Melisande had gathered up all the lovely recipes and all the clever centerpieces, perhaps.

"Then I suppose you must do as you see fit regarding Goddard," Horace said. "I have it on some authority that he's thinking of a remove to France anyway. I was his commanding officer. If I tolerate his presence at my table now, I suppose that will put paid to any notions that I haven't been supportive of him."

"Precisely," Melisande said, tying the window sash back, though a chill came off the panes. "I will put Lieutenant Haines to his left and Mrs. Spievack to his right. Between Haines's chatter and Mrs. Spievack's bad hearing, Goddard will be the first to leave."

"One can hope." Horace pulled a stack of letters to the center of the blotter. "What have you planned for the rest of the day, my dear?"

Next on Melisande's schedule was a cup of tea liberally laced with brandy. She was trying to cut back on her tippling, a slow process.

"I thought I'd take Daniella to the park. Today is sunny, if brisk, and she does enjoy the fresh air."

Horace looked like he had some pontification to offer regarding this mundane outing, but he took spectacles from a drawer and perched them on his nose.

"Children need activity," he said, with the sort of prim condescension that conveyed a world of censure.

Because, of course, if Melisande were to meet Philippe Deschamps anywhere, it would be in the park, where such an encounter could be passed off as a chance mishap.

Truly, Horace tormented himself for nothing. "Would you like to come with us?" Melisande asked. "You and I so seldom spend time together, Horace, and you are my husband."

His smile was inordinately pleased. "Thank you, my dear, but no. The press of business calls me. Perhaps once we have this dinner behind us, we might confer regarding our respective budgets and plan some changes to the household routine."

Horace waving a white flag was a fetching—if slightly disconcerting—prospect. "I'd like that." Melisande would endure that long overdue exercise, in any event, because something had to be done if income was dropping and expenses rising. That Ann had wages to show for her efforts was not lost on Melisande, but what a price to pay for a bit of coin.

Melisande had a hand on the door latch when Horace spoke again.

"I know you think I'm heading rapidly into the terrain of the tiresome old warhorse, Meli, but I do take your happiness seriously. Your loyalty means much to me, and I try in my way to be worthy of it."

Drat and devil take it, there was the gallantry, the gentlemanly decency that Melisande had always found so attractive about her husband.

"Thank you, Horace. Tomorrow, if the weather permits, will you drive out with me?"

He blew her a kiss. "That shall be my pleasure. Enjoy your outing, my dear."

He'd likely forget all about driving Melisande in the park, but the thought was still sweet to contemplate.

What was not so sweet to consider was how Ann could be a guest at the officers' dinner without everybody at the table knowing the recipes, flowers, centerpieces, and even the choice of what roast to bring in on which platter had been Ann's rather than Melisande's.

But no matter. Nobody ever asked about those details anyway, and Ann would know better than to bring them up in company.

"SOMEBODY STOLE four hundred cases of very good champagne from my warehouse," Rye said, watching Ann pour the tea. She was of a piece with the genteel domesticity of this cozy parlor, also of a piece with the Coventry's enormous, bustling kitchen. He liked seeing her both places, and liked seeing her replete with pleasure beside him in bed most of all.

"The thieves plotted this crime carefully," he went on, "drugging an old man, picking the lock, and having enough labor on hand to make off with the goods before anybody was the wiser."

The details made the transgression worse, made it a matter not of spontaneous greed, but of malice aforethought. Malice and determination.

"That's a lot of champagne," Ann said, passing him a steaming cup. "Will insurance cover the loss?"

"No, because I cannot prove the champagne was destroyed, and thus it is regarded as mislaid. I am encouraged by my solicitors to hire runners to track down the stolen cases. I reported the problem to the relevant magistrate's office, and they condoled me on my bad luck."

Ann poured out for herself, but didn't take a sip. She had permitted Orion to arrange her hair in a chignon gathered softly at her nape—not the ruthlessly tidy braids mandated by kitchen work—and the look of her enchanted him.

Enchanted him more than usual.

Whoever had said parting was such sweet sorrow had never contemplated parting from Annie Pearson. Orion's heart was breaking, and after years at war, that should not be possible.

"You don't see such bold larceny as bad luck," Ann said.

"The docks are notoriously riddled with crime, and that's part of the reason my warehouse is well back from the river. Then too, the wine prefers the dryer air, and I want my inventory as close at hand as possible. The neighborhood isn't fashionable, but I thought it safe."

Ann held her tea cup before her, and Rye knew she was having a discreet sniff. To take the olfactory measure of food and drink was second nature with her, and she probably did not realize she did it.

He would miss that, miss how her awareness of any sort of sustenance made him more aware as well.

"No place in London is safe," Ann said, "but something in particular about this theft worries you."

Everything about the theft worried Rye. "I keep my cavalry sword hanging over the fireplace in my office at the house," he said.

"That weapon is a reminder of where fighting leads—to death, dismemberment, and worse, lingering disabilities for men toward whom I bore no personal ill will. When I was assigned the management of mules and prisoners, Ann, I was relieved. The longer I fought, the more the whole undertaking struck me as stupid."

Ann sipped her tea, while the cat was eyeing her lap. Orion scooped the beast up rather than risk hot tea all over Ann's dress.

"Should we have allowed Napoleon to invade England?" she asked.

"Once Nelson scuttled the French fleet at Trafalgar, that was unlikely. Britain started the campaign on the Iberian Peninsula knowing there was little risk of France invading our shores."

"But Bonaparte stopped our trade with the Continent. He forbade even delivery of British mail."

"And this interfered with your correspondence exactly how? We blockaded his ports far more effectively than he stopped us from smuggling our goods into Continental markets. In any case, I kept my sword in plain view to remind me that war for those fighting it isn't about markets, political theories, or the benefits of monarchy over representative governments. It's about killing, violence, and destruction, and I want no more of any of it."

"Thus you take in ragged children and sell your champagne, when nobody is stealing it from you."

"The children just... They come along, and I have more room than I need, and that has nothing to do with anything."

Ann smiled at him, and the idea that he must bid farewell to her, and to those sweet, knowing smiles... He pet the cat, who commenced rumbling.

"What has your sword to do with the stolen goods?"

"My sword was left at the warehouse in place of the purloined champagne. The stolen sword tells me that somebody violated my household, where I billet those self-same children. The watchman who was drugged was old and frail, Ann. He's not fit for anything more vigorous than sounding the alarm, and whoever took the champagne could just as easily have tossed Nicolas into the river. I am being warned, repeatedly, that I and those I care about are in danger."

"And thus you are leaving for France?"

She posed the question calmly, while presiding over her pretty tea service in this genteel parlor full of the contented purring of an overfed feline.

This is what I thought I was fighting for. England's domestic tranquility; the good, dear people at home; the quiet, honorable values that made John Bull the equal of any man the world over.

"In Spain, I gave up my field command without complaint and contented myself with battling reams of paperwork, Ann. When the Hundred Days came, I accepted that I was not welcome to rejoin the fight. As I tried to establish my business here in London, I grasped that doors to certain regimental homes were closed to me. I have accepted my lot and tried to be grateful for it."

"You deserve none of those slights."

"So fierce, and you don't deserve Jules Delacourt's meanness, but you aren't wasting your powers taking him on, are you?"

"I cannot, or somebody wholly innocent of wrongdoing could end up gashed by an accidental knife, burned with a spilled pot of glaze, or out of a job because Jules considers that sort of cruelty an expedient means of punishing me."

"Punishing you for being good at what you do. And I sense that somehow I have stumbled into the same sort of trap, Ann. Horace Upchurch was my commanding officer when that board of inquiry was convened. He did what he could for me, and even he is telling me to leave London."

Ann petted the cat, who'd draped himself across Rye's thighs. "Uncle isn't one to advocate retreat, but he's put distance between you?"

"Yes." Orion watched her hand stroking gently over soft, soft fur.

"You did not want me to know that my own uncle has suggested you leave Town."

"I was surprised to learn that Upchurch was your uncle. I should be grateful he hasn't disparaged me in your hearing." If Ann did not cease petting the damned cat, Orion would have to continue this discussion upstairs.

"This is all so unfair and awkward."

Wasn't it just? "Complicated," Rye said. "I have retreated and retreated, and every wise general knows to be gracious in victory. Somebody is determined to see me not only defeated, but routed and hounded from the field."

Ann lifted the cat onto her own lap, and the beast, after peering about with a disgruntled air, settled in to knead her skirts.

"You fight," Ann said. "You fight for those boys, Orion. You fight for that old lady among the émigrés. You fought for your sister in as much as you could, and you have fought for Hannah. By hiring old Nicolas, you struck a blow against the prejudice he faces in London, and I am certain his wages are generous."

"That's not fighting."

"I fight too," Ann said, stroking the cat, who peered at Orion with feline smugness. "I fight for the scullery maids and footmen, for the idea that a woman's recipes are as valuable as a man's. I fight for my own independence, or I have tried to."

"You have been victorious for ten straight years, Ann. A setback is not a defeat."

"I don't want you to go," Ann said, setting the cat on the floor. "But I know exactly what you are doing, Orion."

"Then please tell me, because my perspective on the whole situation is far from clear."

"You are punishing yourself," Ann said, "because your sister had to marry to get your family out of debt and so your father could afford to buy a commission for you. Now you think that somebody who would drug an old man, commit a hanging felony, and menace children would also come after me. Perhaps these malefactors are already in league with Jules. We don't know."

"Hush," Rye said. "Please hush." She'd named his worst fears and had done so calmly.

"You are leaving England rather than risk embroiling *me* in your troubles, and I could become embroiled all too easily. I am a squire's daughter plying a lowly trade at an arguably improper venue. I have family who would be tainted by any scandal, family you have reason to respect. You leave to protect me and to protect them."

"I have a few allies," Rye said. "My cousins will keep their eyes and ears open, particularly among the former military. I may be able to return in a year or so." By then, Ann might well be cooking for some baron in Derbyshire or a retired general in Somerset.

Ann rose, and thus Rye was on his feet as well. She slipped her arms around his waist. "I esteem you greatly for protecting the whole world, Orion. Me, the children, my family, émigrés, very likely your friends as well. I only wish there was a way I could protect you."

He gathered her close and silently cursed fate in four languages at once. "I can protect myself."

She shifted back enough to look him up and down, her gaze lingering on the scars around his eye.

"I have done something, Orion, and I hope you will not castigate me for it."

"Tell me."

"Before you leave London, there is one more invitation you must accept. I insist upon it, for I would not ride into this battle with anybody else at my side."

"ANN PEARSON HAS GIVEN NOTICE." Sycamore Dorning handed the tidy little missive to his wife, but no matter who read it, it would say the same thing. "I own I am surprised."

"You are horrified." Jeanette glanced at the letter, then set it on the side table. She passed Sycamore one of the throwing knives that adorned their private parlor. "I am none too pleased myself."

Sycamore took the place beside his wife on the sofa. "If Goddard has enticed Miss Pearson into the bonds of holy matrimony, I cannot object to her decision."

"You could ask for Miss Pearson to stay on through winter so you have time to hire and train a replacement."

Sycamore tossed the knife at the cork target across the room, but the throw—smacking the bull's-eye decisively—brought no satisfaction.

"I very much fear she cannot be replaced."

Jeanette picked up the embroidery she'd been working on when Sycamore had interrupted her. "You are only realizing that now?"

"I'm realizing it in a new way now. Miss Pearson is the ballast that allows Jules his dramatics. He is the fire and spice, while she is the…"

Jeanette stabbed at the linen with her needle. "He is the expensive advertisement. She is the hard work, common sense, and actual skill necessary to run a busy kitchen."

Sycamore tucked an arm around Jeanette's shoulders. "What aren't you telling me, darling lady?"

"Much, of course. Jules is a sot."

Sot was a harsh word, and Jeanette was not a harsh woman. Pragmatic of necessity, but not harsh.

"I am aware that he samples the inventory. How could he prepare fancy dinners without knowing wines and spirits?"

"I overhear the footmen and waiters talking, Sycamore. Jules helps himself to anything and everything in the cellars and blames the results on breakage or accounting errors."

Sycamore had wandered home from the club at this daylight hour because Ann Pearson's notice bothered him, and thinking through a bothersome problem was best done with Jeanette's guidance.

"Jules intimates that the footmen and waiters help themselves to the occasional bottle." Jules made those accusations out of the hearing of the staff, of course, and with apparent reluctance.

You must not blame them, Mr. Dorning.

They work hard, Mr. Dorning.

In a private home, Mr. Dorning, the remainder of any opened bottle would be consumed in the kitchen.

"Theft can get a man hanged or transported," Jeanette said. "Rather than bring scandal down on the club by having Jules arrested, you'd let him slip quietly away to France. He knows that."

And therein lay the bothersome problem: scandal and the club, the club and scandal. In a minor way, the Coventry *was* a scandal, being technically illegal as all gaming establishments were illegal. But the Coventry was also entirely different from a dimly lit den of thieves where crooked cards presaged ruin for the unsuspecting.

"I miss Ash," Sycamore said. "He would know to the penny if accounting errors bore any responsibility for an inaccurate tally of our wine and spirits."

"I can do an audit, Sycamore. Winter approaches, and Ash has done much better since spending less time in Town."

Ash, dearest of brothers, suffered periodic, paralyzing bouts of melancholia. "He's done better since taking a wife, as have I. He's after me to finish buying him out."

Jeanette set aside her stitchery. "Tell me the rest of it."

And there was the magic of marriage to Jeanette. Sycamore hadn't known he needed to discuss *the rest of it* until Jeanette had parsed the topic with him.

"Ash would typically take over managing the club in summer, and I'd be free to nip over to Paris, pop in at Dorning Hall, or venture down to Brighton. I did the same for him in winter, and that meant we were both free of the damned club for weeks at a time, confident that all would run smoothly in our absence."

"And now?"

Sycamore took up Jeanette's hoop and traced his fingers over pretty butterflies and blooming buttercups. Winter in London was a dark, noisome prospect compared to the open air and sweeping, snowy vistas of Dorsetshire.

"Now, one person gives notice after years of loyal service, and I face hours of interviews to replace her, the delicate task of finding somebody who can do the job without offending Jules's sense of indispensability, and the inevitable jostling about in the kitchen pecking order when staff changes... Better now than in the spring, but the whole prospect is tiresome. I wanted to spend much of this winter kitting out the house in Richmond."

Also snuggling with his wife, of course.

"Has Miss Pearson said why she's leaving?"

The satin threads were smooth and luminous against the white linen, and Jeanette's skill with the needle exquisite. She was equally adept at picking loose the threads of a problem.

"No, and that bothers me too. Miss Pearson doesn't mention career advancement, matrimonial ambitions, or an aging cousin in the north. She is held in near veneration by the staff, which I'm sure contributes to Jules's sense of discontent in the kitchen, and unless I miss my guess, most of the food we serve is the result of her recipes."

"Nearly all of it."

"Jules says English tastes aren't sophisticated enough for his best creations."

Jeanette took her embroidery from him and stashed it in a wicker workbasket. "Jules talks a lot. How much is he actually cooking?"

Sycamore ventured into the kitchen during working hours only occasionally, and that bothered him as well. He owned the damned club, or owned much of it. Why was he hesitant to roam anywhere on its premises at any hour?

"I love the Coventry," Sycamore said. "I love the complexity of it, the challenge."

"You love being able to show your family that you can make money—something Dornings do not excel at generally—and entertain the highest society night after night. You take pride in that club."

"Well, yes, but I also simply like the work. I like charming the dowagers and consoling the bachelors on their loneliness. I like providing employment for a lot of good folk who seek only a decent wage and the occasional thanks in exchange for hard work. I like how the whole place works together—from the cellars to the buffet to the tables to the staff to the ledgers—to *create* something fine. Nobody needs the Coventry, and yet, London is a little more dashing for featuring such a venue."

Jeanette shifted to straddle Sycamore's lap. "But?"

"But I have proved my point, Jeanette. The Coventry is a business to be proud of, and now I would like to spend more time with you, making the Richmond property into a profitable garden farm. Looking in on the nieces and nephews, taking you to Paris."

"While I would like to take you to bed."

"Bed is a lovely destination, provided you join me there."

She kissed him, which had the delightful effect of putting the whole complication of Miss Pearson's leaving at a slight distance. Married life involved the occasional midafternoon nap with Jeanette, though such naps—while highly restorative—involved little sleeping.

"You should talk to Miss Pearson," Jeanette said when she'd allowed Sycamore to come up for air. "Or I can talk to her."

"I've already told her I will need time to find a replacement. Mrs. Dorning, you aren't wearing stays."

"While you are still in full morning attire."

"I'm sure you will remedy my error. What exactly should I talk to Miss Pearson about?"

"Why is she leaving *now*? Something is brewing in your kitchen, Mr. Dorning."

"Something is brewing in my breeches. Shall we to the bedroom, Jeanette?"

She rose and took him by the hand. "I could do with a nap and a cuddle, now that you mention it."

"When is a nap and a cuddle ever a bad idea?"

A nap and a cuddle with Jeanette was, in fact, a very good idea, leaving Sycamore feeling drowsy, sweet, and in charity with the world, despite the upheaval afoot at the club. As he drifted off in Jeanette's arms, a last thought floated through his mind.

He would try to have a word with Ann Pearson about her sudden desire to quit the Coventry, but he would assuredly have a much more pointed word with Orion Goddard.

CHAPTER FIFTEEN

"Children aren't like foot soldiers," Alasdhair said. "You cannot simply tell them to march this way one day and back the other way the next. They need for life to make sense."

The reading room offered its usual sense of sanctuary, a particularly English sort of haven that came from comfortable chairs arranged around a venerable hearth on a chilly evening. That the brandy was French also somehow made the Aurora Club's ambience more British, and more dear.

"This lot of children has never been the pampered darlings of anybody's nursery," Rye said. "They are tough and resilient."

"They are loyal, Goddard," Dylan said, propping his feet on a hassock. "They won't want to be parted from you or from one another."

Nor I from any of them. "The separation cannot be helped." Ann had seen what Rye had tried to hide from her: For him to remain in Town would endanger innocents—more innocents—and *that* he was unwilling to do.

"How will you choose which children go with you to France and which remain here with us?' Alasdhair asked.

Rye sipped his brandy and pondered that conundrum. His cousin Jacques had faced such a choice under more fraught circumstances and sent his most vulnerable child, the infant Nettie, to safety.

Who among the children was most vulnerable, and should that boy stay in London or go to France?

"Theodoric will want to protect you," Dylan observed. "Choose another boy who gets on well with Theodoric. I'll take the youngest two, and MacKay can take whoever's left over."

"You'll send the youngest two to your sisters," Alasdhair retorted. "You want the easy ones."

"I'll think about who goes and who stays." Rye would probably air his ideas before the boys and see what they had to say. A competent general held a council of war and listened to his subordinates.

And then he alone made the hard decisions.

"What of your émigrés?" Dylan asked, toeing off his boots and crossing his feet at the ankle. "I know of at least a half-dozen old ladies who recall you nightly in their prayers to *le bon Dieu.*"

"There's also Angus and Angie," Alasdhair murmured, getting up to add a half scoop of coal to the fire. "Angus is getting on, and a coachy's hands don't last forever."

Angus had been with Rye in Spain and France, and a tougher, more irascible batman—and kinder, more conscientious horseman— had never cursed the London traffic.

"I'll ask if he and Angie want to go with me." Though neither one spoke even passable French.

The fire leaped up at the addition of fresh fuel, while Rye's spirits were sinking to new depths.

"Are we to start calling on the fair Mrs. Dorning?" Dylan asked. "Comporting ourselves like the doting cousins we've never been? Sending you regular reports?"

"Dropping by the Coventry to swill your champagne for free?" Alasdhair added, settling back into his chair.

Each query was the same question in different words: *Goddard, what the hell are you doing?*

"Fournier and Deschamps both claim innocence," Rye said, finishing his drink. "Jeanette's in-laws once had a hand in spreading gossip about me, but the guilty parties are no longer in London. Somebody with a long memory has decided that I need banishing, but I'm still at a loss to know who or why."

"And if you tarry in Town, the next warning might be to send your warehouse up in flames," Dylan said.

"I can make more champagne. I cannot make more of the people I care for." More cousins, more darling old ladies who tatted the most exquisite lace to edge Rye's fancy cravats, not that he ever wore fancy cravats.

He could not make more dear, courageous boys, who all deserved to have their gifts appreciated and their shortcomings forgiven, even if those shortcomings stank like hell's privy.

Rye could never make more sisters, when only the one had been allotted to him, and he'd bungled being her brother. God help him, he'd probably miss even Sycamore Dorning.

"So why does it feel," Dylan asked, "as if you're choosing the champagne over the friends?" He laced his hands on his belly and closed his eyes, apparently unwilling to absent himself from this wake for a life more dear than Rye had realized.

"Will you write to her?" Alasdhair asked. "To Miss Pearson, I mean. Mrs. Dorning will send her husband to hunt you down if you neglect to correspond with your sister."

How Rye would miss these friends who'd stuck by him through everything. "Go to hell, MacKay."

"I might have to, if I want to look in on you. Have another nip?"

Getting drunk never solved anything. Staying sober hadn't exactly resulted in a quick victory either. "Half," Rye said. "And then I must be going."

Otter would be furious at leaving London, but then he'd settle down and accommodate what could not be changed. When Otter had reconciled himself to the inevitable, the other boys would too.

Rye's list of worries expanded as the fire mellowed: the horses, the cats in the stable—Hannah would fret over them—and Hannah herself, though Jeanette could keep an eye on her. Mrs. Murphy would need a character, and whoever was hired to share warehouse guard duty would have to understand that Nicolas needed looking after as well.

In his head, Rye made a list of tasks to do before leaving, people upon whom he must call, affairs to put in order. He could even in his imagination conceive of how he'd take leave of Ann. A swift, fond farewell, a kiss and a smile, soldier-fashion, and then march off to battle, head held high.

All very well for the part of him that had wrangled recruits, mules, horses, and artillery, but in his heart, he felt as if he would be deserting the regiment, the one betrayal a loyal officer would never commit.

~

ANN STEPPED BACK to admit Orion, and even Miss Julia and Miss Diana for once had no comment. Colonel Sir Orion Goddard in dress regimentals was a sight to strike a lady speechless. His eye patch made him look only more imposing, and his smile... oh, his smile was all the spice and sweetness Ann could have wished for.

"Miss Julia, Miss Diana, good evening." Orion bowed, then took Ann's hand. "Miss Pearson, my vineyards at harvest time pale beside your beauty."

She curtseyed. "And your splendor outshines my most delicate double consommé."

"Besotted," Miss Julia muttered. "The pair of you."

"Oh, to be besotted," Miss Diana said. "Colonel, you must be very attentive to our Ann tonight. I do not care for these relatives of hers. They never call upon her, and they—"

"Enough, Sister," Miss Julia cut in. "The young people must be off to display their finery."

Finery had nothing to do with why Ann wanted to be off. "Don't wait up for me," she said. "If the evening goes quite late, I might stay with my aunt."

Miss Diana looked ready to launch into one of her well-reasoned, politely withering diatribes on the undeserving nature of relatives who never called, while Orion draped Ann's cloak over her shoulders and fastened the frogs for her.

"Ann, take care of our colonel," Miss Julia said. "I've spent enough time around officers' wives to know where the worst ambushes come from."

Orion passed Ann her bonnet. "We are away to enjoy one of the most impressive banquets ever served in London, and that is saying something. Try to contain your envy."

Miss Julia touched his sleeve. "Young man, you had best get out that door while you still can. Sister and I are quicker than we look."

Something wistful passed over Orion's expression, and then he was offering Ann his arm and escorting her to the walkway.

"I borrowed the Dorning coach," Orion said. "The occasion seemed to call for it. Do you mind?"

The conveyance was splendid, the horses matched grays. "Because we will travel in a closed carriage after dark without a chaperone?"

Had Ann any intention of pursuing the much-vaunted advantageous match, had she any aspiration to socialize with high society rather than to cook in its kitchens, she might have hesitated.

"As I keep telling my aunt, I am not a young lady new to Town intent on attaching the interests of a well-off spouse. We'll keep the shades down."

"Will we really?"

"Yes, and if anybody asks, your sister accompanied us, but nobody will ask."

Orion handed her up and settled on the forward-facing seat beside her. "I will tell John Coachman to let us off before we reach the brigadier's front door, in case anybody thinks to make a fuss."

What does it say about me that I like even sitting beside this man?

Like watching the light of the coach lamps turn his features stern—more stern—and complicated?

"I hope the guests make a fuss about the *sauce velouté* I devised for the fish and the *sauce béarnaise* to be served with the beef."

Orion took her hand as the coach glided forward, and Ann wished they weren't wearing gloves. "Are you trying to make me hungry?"

"If you don't kiss me in the next thirty seconds, I will make you—"

He kissed her. Gently, then with a combination of heat and tenderness that had Ann longing to take off far more than her gloves. She let go of him reluctantly long minutes later, because even she would not arrive at her aunt's house looking tumbled.

"Are you nervous?" Orion asked as Ann finger-combed his hair back into order.

"Yes. I've never partaken of the banquets I prepare or plan. My aunt is right about that. I'm torn between wanting to simply enjoy good food and wanting to keep paper and pencil handy to note any room for improvement."

"Enjoy the food, Annie. God knows you've earned the right. If Melisande is merciful, you won't be seated too far away from me, and I can enjoy you enjoying your creations."

Orion's entrance into the guest parlor was met with some raised eyebrows and a few murmured asides, but then Emily Bainbridge took him by the arm.

"We have an expert, ladies," Mrs. Bainbridge said, drawing Orion to a group of women. "Colonel, you can settle a dispute. We are debating the meaning of the French verb *courtiser*. You must translate it for us."

A lull in surrounding conversations coincided with the lady's question, and more eyebrows went up. As the gentlemen exchanged glances, and Melisande's expression edged close to a grimace, Orion smiled down at Mrs. Bainbridge.

"The verb does mean, in present French parlance, to court,

tracing its origins to the courtiers who paid their polite attentions to the sovereign and thus attempted to win his or her favor. That is a very fetching fan, Mrs. Bainbridge. Do you recall how you came by it?"

Conversation resumed, and Melisande was soon pairing up her guests to process into the dining room. Ann found herself on the arm of a magpie lieutenant, one who patted her hand needlessly and wore far too much Hungary water.

The lieutenant seated her, then moved around the table to take the place opposite, which ensured, at least for the early courses, Ann would hear him chattering, but would not have to engage him in conversation herself.

Orion was seated next to the lieutenant, surely a form of penance, though when Ann felt a boot nudging against her toe, she looked across the table to see Orion regarding her with the veiled humor so characteristic of him.

The canapés were brought out, and the conversation barely paused. Ann had agonized over the choices, weighing appearance, cost, flavor, ease of preparation, and availability of fresh ingredients. Mrs. Spievack—she'd nearly shouted her name to Orion—popped a little serving of ham, Dijon mustard, and cornichon into her mouth, all the while nodding vigorously at whatever Orion was saying.

Up and down the table, guests behaved similarly. The first course disappeared while the talk grew louder. Emily Bainbridge's laughter occasionally sliced through the din, and those sly, measuring glances from the officers passed over Orion and occasionally rested on Ann.

Dexter Dennis, who'd accompanied his sister to the gathering, sent Orion a particularly venomous look, which Uncle and Aunt pretended to ignore.

Ann stuffed a canapé into her mouth—brie topped with chopped green olives and a garnish of parsley and ground black pepper—and wished she were back in the Coventry's kitchens, melting butter for her white sauces.

All the pretty delicious courses in the world could not disguise the fact that something nasty and mean was being served up exclusively to Orion Goddard, and Ann had been wrong to insist he escort her into this company.

~

THE FOOD WAS GLORIOUS, the table magnificent, but most wonderful of all was the chance to sit and merely behold Annie Pearson amid the bounty she'd created. From the artful little canapés to the delicious soup, to fish in a sauce so scrumptious it defied description, Orion had never partaken of a meal half as impressive.

Ann belonged here, laughing and chatting with the officers, quietly outshining all the ladies in their formal best. She deserved to hear the occasional compliments regarding the food, including a rhapsody by Lieutenant Colonel Mornaday about the beef roast. He actually asked for the sauce recipe, and Orion waited for Melisande to acknowledge Ann's contribution.

"The sauce isn't that complicated," Melisande said, smiling self-consciously. "I'll send along the particulars before the week is out."

"Send them to me too," Mrs. Bainbridge said. "And I'm sure Mrs. Haines would like them as well. You have quite outdone yourself with this meal, Melisande, but then, you always outdo yourself with your menus."

Across the table, Ann sipped her wine and said nothing. At a formal meal, one conversed exclusively with the dinner companions on one's left and right, but the wine had been flowing for well over an hour, and this was a company of officers.

Formality was slipping by the wayside as each course was removed and more wine was poured.

"I commend Upchurch for inviting you, Goddard," Lieutenant Haines said as the main dishes were taken away and the greens brought out. "The war is over, I say. We were all a little mad back then, all happy to flirt with anything in skirts, but we showed Boney our mettle, and that's what ought to matter most."

He lifted his glass of claret, toasting his own sentiments. Across the table, Ann had apparently heard him, her expression a cross between veiled curiosity and not-as-veiled ire.

Mrs. Spievack, a widow whose husband had been struck down by a carriage a year after Waterloo, leaned closer. "The military has always excelled at two things, fighting and talking, and the less it does of the first, the more it does of the latter. You seem a perfectly agree-able sort to me, Colonel. Heaven knows some of the younger wives weren't always circumspect on campaign."

Rye was spared a response to that odd comment by the arrival of the vegetable dishes, beautiful, colorful, spicy individual servings that put Rye in mind of the baked *tians* served in his mother's native Provence.

The meal went on, with conversation eventually flowing in all directions, and again, somebody offered a compliment, this time to the cheese course.

"Can't say I usually care for fig jam," a tipsy captain observed, "too grainy, but this is outstanding. Makes the Camembert... more cheesy. My missus loves the fruit-and-cheese bit and would love to have the recipe."

That profundity merited a toast to smooth fig jam, and then the toasts to the ladies began, the toasts to His Majesty, Wellington, and fallen comrades having already been dispensed with. Rye dutifully lifted his glass and pretended to sip, all the while calculating how many bottles of wine were being consumed and what profit could have been made off them if Upchurch had deigned to place his wine order with Orion.

A petty sentiment. By the time the dessert course arrived, Rye's only thought was to say his good-nights and take full advantage of a long, slow carriage ride back to Ann's house.

The world's best pear compote was the finale to a grand meal, the flaming brandy sauce earning a round of applause.

"Melisande is a genius at this sort of thing," Emily Bainbridge said. "I vow her dinners would put the great Carême to shame, and she concocts all these recipes herself. To our Melisande and her exquisite menus!"

A round of *hear, hear* and *to Melisande* followed with the more inebriated banging spoons against glasses and fists upon the table.

Across the table, Ann's expression became a blank mask. Rye had seen the same shock on the faces of men wounded in battle, when the mind could not grasp the reality of the blow despite both pain and welling blood proving that a wound had been suffered.

The din died down, and Rye decided to fight one more battle before he withdrew to France.

"Mrs. Bainbridge," he said, rising with his wineglass in hand, "I would never argue with a lady, but you are much mistaken. The recipe for this most delicious sweet, in fact all the recipes we've enjoyed tonight, are the creations of Melisande's niece, Miss Ann Pearson. I know this because I have seen the recipes written in Miss Pearson's own hand. I've had the pleasure of sampling this very compote on a previous occasion, and I can assure you, Miss Pearson has put much consideration and effort into the food we've enjoyed this evening. To Ann Pearson, ladies and gentlemen, the true culinary genius."

He lifted his glass and waited for the other guests to do likewise. Only then did he take a taste of the champagne served to accompany the final course of the meal.

THE FINE MEAL, one of the best Ann had ever devised, sat in her belly like so much bad ale. All heads turned in her direction, save for Uncle Horace, who was glowering dire retribution at Orion.

"Perhaps you are confused, Colonel Goddard," Mrs. Bainbridge said. "I know for a fact that Melisande puts enormous effort into planning these dinners. She has even assisted me with a menu or two. If there's a culinary genius at this table, then that honor goes to Mrs. Upchurch. Tell the colonel he has misspoken, Melisande."

Part of Ann was reeling under the realization that Melisande had played her for a fool. For years, Melisande had apparently taken credit for Ann's work, all the while insisting that Ann should leave the role of professional cook. Years when Ann had been putting in eighteen-hour days, subsisting on limited wages, enduring Jules's spite, and Melisande's sniping.

How could you do this to me?

But then, Ann knew how.

What did Melisande have? One child she visited in the nursery, this exceedingly tiresome company, an aging busybody of a husband... No wages, no freedom, no rogue officer willing to take on the regiment for the sake of her compote. What Melisande and the Emily Bainbridges of the world had was an insipid, bland, tepid frustration of a life, and they were supposed to be happy with it and even grateful.

Those thoughts swirled through Ann's mind in the time it took Mrs. Bainbridge to offer her taunt. Emily Bainbridge was the mean girl at boarding school, the young lady who convened the gossip sessions in the retiring room, and the regimental wife who caused more trouble than Napoleon.

A wise general was generous in victory. Orion had said that. If Ann claimed ownership of the recipes, Emily Bainbridge would win another skirmish, while Melisande would be humiliated before the regiment.

"Perhaps you can shed light on this conundrum, Miss Pearson," Mrs. Bainbridge went on. "We are all agog to know whose gustatory expertise to commend."

If Ann took credit for the menu, she would lose the family she had. She wanted and deserved to have her ability publicly acknowledged, but was it justice to humiliate a woman because she longed for some recognition in life? Because a husband and child weren't the sum of her ambitions?

"Colonel Goddard is correct that the initial ideas are mine," Ann said, "but you are also correct, Mrs. Bainbridge, in that Aunt

Melisande and I collaborate. I send my recipes to Aunt before I show them to anybody else, and the first to prepare them for company dinners is her cook, under her supervision.

"One cannot simply toss together ingredients," Ann went on, "and know a dish or a meal will be successful. A sense of the guests, of their preferences and tastes, is invaluable when planning any menu. One has to know what's popular this Season, what has been overdone by other hostesses. Aunt Melisande has an instinct for such matters, while all I know are the sauces and spices. We make a formidable team. Uncle, perhaps you would lead us in a toast to Aunt Melisande."

Emily Bainbridge looked as if somebody had flung mud on her pinafore, while Orion was beaming at Ann. *Beaming* at her. When Uncle had offered a long-winded panegyric to Melisande's myriad virtues, all glasses were lifted, and Melisande blushed prettily.

Ann had hoped that by having Orion included on the guest list, she could see him sent off to France with some vestige of regimental acceptance. If her wildest dreams were to be exceeded, perhaps a gracious welcome by his fellow officers would prevent the need for him to decamp to France altogether.

The sly glances and sniffy asides weren't being aimed at Orion at the moment, but for Ann, that wasn't enough.

Uncle resumed his seat amid much cheering and smiling.

Ann dove into the moment before another tipsy cavalier could offer an even more long-winded toast. "Uncle, while we are commending deserving members of the company, we must compliment you on your choice of champagne. Colonel Goddard's wine is by far the best of its kind I've tasted, and I have tasted many."

Lieutenant Haines, who had imbibed his way to a state of great jollity, raised his glass. "To Colonel Goddard's champagne. Best thing to come out of France, if you ask me."

Up and down the table, glasses were raised once again, though in Uncle's case, the gesture was a bit slow and devoid of conviviality.

Orion's great good cheer had also left the table, for he was peering at his glass as if it contained wormwood and gall. Melisande called for another round of champagne before the ladies left the gentlemen to their port, and still, Orion remained silent.

"You must escort me to the parlor, Colonel," Ann said when the ladies rose to take their leave. "Lieutenant Haines is too busy communing with his wineglass."

"He never did have much of a head for spirits," Orion said, coming around the table to offer Ann his arm. "Brave, though," he muttered. "Foolishly brave. I commend your compassion, Miss Pearson. Mrs. Upchurch did not deserve it."

The company made a slow procession along the corridor to the guest parlor, some of the ladies not very steady on their feet. Orion Goddard, however, exuded all the sobriety of an officer facing massed armies in the morning. He was once again the remote, burdened man Ann had met months ago at Mrs. Dorning's bedside.

The evening had doubtless been trying for him in the extreme, while for Ann, it had gone surprisingly well. Not as expected, but well.

"Melisande," Ann said, "did not deserve to be told at the ages of six and eleven and sixteen that her only chance for happiness lay in enticing some man to offer for her. I did not exactly lie, and if I do publish a cookbook someday, Melisande can ensure it has many subscribers. What is wrong, Orion?"

They waited for the assemblage to thread the bottleneck into the guest parlor.

"I all but begged Upchurch to buy my champagne," Orion said quietly. "I could have supplied most of the wine consumed at this supper—at all of his fancy dinners—but he refused. I badly need the business, and he disdained to send it my way. But somehow, a considerable quantity of my champagne found its way to his table."

Mrs. Spievack glanced at them, as did Dexter Dennis. The lady's expression was merely curious, while Dennis was again glaring daggers.

"Uncle Horace did serve your champagne," Ann said. "I am sure of that."

"I was too busy wanting to throttle the Bainbridge woman," Orion said, "to notice that I drank my own vintage. Had you not said anything..."

Mrs. Bainbridge, who was fixed to the brigadier's arm like a barnacle clinging to the last ship in the harbor, chose then to laugh.

"Orion, listen to me," Ann said, keeping her voice down as well. "I will make my peace with Melisande—she owes me an apology, at least—but if I had to choose between the man who noticed my recipes and the relatives who've spent years being ashamed of me while exploiting my talent, I would choose the man."

The footmen had neglected to light enough candles in the guest parlor, and the entire company remained milling about in the corridor, escorts and ladies alike.

"I cannot ask you to choose between France and England, Ann. I know how hard you've worked, and—"

"I'm not choosing between France and England," Ann said, the words coming slowly. "I sat among these people tonight, watching them pick at food the cook spent hours concocting from a menu I've spent years crafting. Some of the guests noticed a particular dish, some of them even complimented a course here or a wine pairing there, but, Orion, to them it's merely food. Most plates went back to the kitchen more full than empty. A guest might recall a particular dish if they see something like it again, but it's not... A menu doesn't mean what I thought it meant."

What she'd hoped it meant.

"They appreciated the meal, Ann. I certainly did. I've never tasted anything like it."

The crowd resumed shuffling toward the parlor door. "And your appreciation matters. For the others, this was a passing pleasure, and for some of them, the gossip provides more sustenance than the food. I see that now."

Orion peered down at her by the flickering light of a mirrored sconce. "You are blowing retreat?"

"No, Orion. I am transferring to a different regiment, if you'll have me. I don't want to end up like Melisande *or like Jules*, and those are not my only choices. I want to end up like your sister, well loved by a worthy, if occasionally vexatious, man. I want to be an extremely busy woman who enjoys most of what she does."

"Dorning is more than occasionally vexatious."

"You like him, and you respect him, and I more than like and respect you. What will you do about Uncle Horace's thievery?" For that had to be how the champagne had found its way to his table.

"There's more to it than thievery, Ann. Horace Upchurch has much explaining to do."

"Then have your explanations from him, Orion, but know that my loyalty and my heart are yours and always will be." Ann kissed his cheek. "Be gracious in victory, for Uncle is surely facing defeat."

Orion bowed and left her at the parlor door. Ann sent up a quick prayer that Uncle was smart enough to surrender to superior forces before the battle turned into a complete rout.

CHAPTER SIXTEEN

"I want to know why." Orion chose to accost Upchurch in the library rather than give the brigadier time to concoct defenses or take evasive maneuvers.

The other officers filed past, some going immediately to the chamber pots set out by the sideboard, others settling into the comfortable chairs before the roaring fire. Two footmen stood at the ready, holding trays of port by the window.

"Not now, Goddard."

"You make my life a misery for years, bring shame upon my name, and try to destroy my business. You will explain yourself *now*, Upchurch, or you will find this gathering turned into a drumhead court martial."

Orion could do it too. He had Ann's support, though he also had her admonition to be gracious in victory.

Upchurch nodded at the footmen, who began passing out servings of port. "It's complicated. Call on me tomorrow, and I will explain all."

"Not good enough." Not nearly good enough, when Orion considered that he'd almost walked away from Ann, from the children, from his sister, from the émigrés, his cousins... "Your lies and scheming have brought me to the brink of ruin, Upchurch, and involved innocents in your battles. You owe me not only the truth, but justice."

"I'll buy your damned champagne, if that's what you want, though the expense will beggar me. You were never supposed to attend this dinner."

"I was never supposed to dine in company with a fellow officer again."

Across the room, Lieutenant Haines had embarked on the retelling of some vignette that had doubtless become a fixture of the after-dinner port session. Most of the other guests clustered around him, but for the few cadging naps before the fire.

"You were supposed to slink off to France," Upchurch said. "I thought when you went this summer that you were gone for good. Your own in-laws had joined in the talk, and I believed I had finished you at last."

"They are my sister's in-laws, and they only rode the coattails of the scandal you created for me. For the last time, tell me why you betrayed a fellow officer, Upchurch, one who never showed you anything but loyalty and respect."

The group across the room descended into laughter, while Orion's temper was threatening to slip the leash. He cared nothing for the bonhomie Haines and the others were enjoying. He simply wanted peace, a future with Ann, a chance to raise excellent grapes, and an opportunity to live out his life with dignity.

"I did it..." Upchurch waved a footman away. "I did it for Melisande, of course. What other motivation could possibly justify so much unbecoming conduct? She was young, she was foolish, and I... I was foolish too."

Orion thought back to years of boredom and battles. "You flirted with Mrs. Bainbridge, among others."

"I more than flirted, and that was badly done of me. Melisande retaliated accordingly, as any worthy opponent would." Upchurch scrubbed a hand across his brow. "Let us repair to the office, shall we?"

If a lady's good name was to be under discussion, that was the only gentlemanly course. Orion followed Upchurch through a paneled door into a stuffy room adorned with portraits of stuffy fellows in overly decorated uniforms. The fire had been lit, but none of the candles, adding to the sense of gloomy masculinity.

"Melisande was charming," Orion said, choosing the word carefully, "but I never played you false with her. None of us did, that I know of."

Upchurch used a spill to light a branch of candles, though they did little to dispel the shadows. "You fellows knew better, but Deschamps did not. He was exotic, gallant, and forbidden, and if a woman is determined to twit her husband for neglecting her—and Melisande was devastated by my errant ways—how better to do that than to sleep with the enemy? She had no idea—no earthly intimation—of how serious a transgression that was. She liked his accent and his kisses, and he was simply a lonely fellow whose army was being defeated, mile by mile."

Were the situation not so sad, it would be ridiculous. "What have your past marital woes to do with me?"

"My superiors became aware that I was dealing with an unhappy wife."

"Because Emily Bainbridge could not keep her mouth shut, even in defense of the realm."

Upchurch sank into the chair behind the desk. "Emily is troubled, and she is not to blame. I am."

The air of wounded gallantry was too much. "And yet, it's not your champagne being stolen, or your good name that receives an annual trip to the regimental latrine. I have held my only sister at a distance because of you, lost substantial business, and nearly parted from friends and allies here in London." And as bad as all of that combined, he'd nearly parted from Ann.

"I know, and I am sorry, but if you'd been content to take a repairing lease in France... You were promoted, and you were knighted, and I meant for those measures to be some compensation for the gossip, but no, you wanted your blasted honor."

Were Upchurch not sitting at his desk, looking old and tired, Rye might have hit him. "I go to France frequently, and just when I think I'm finally to be allowed the peace we all fought so hard to secure, my friends tell me I'm the object of talk again at Horse Guards."

A burst of laughter came from the other room, reminding Orion that the ladies expected the gentlemen to rejoin them before too much longer.

And Ann expected him to be gracious in victory, damn the luck.

"The other culprit in this melodrama is Deschamps," Upchurch said. "He saw a lonely young woman following the drum for her older husband, and he should have kept his damned Frenchie hands to himself."

Deschamps's hands were not the problem. "What did you do?"

"My superiors saw an opportunity, where I saw only infidelity. They would send me on reconnaissance to the north, though I was to tell Meli that I was scouting terrain to the west. She would very naturally take advantage of my absence to further her liaison, and in all innocence, she could well pass along to Deschamps the nature of my excursion."

"The nature and *direction* of your excursion, and the French would go pelting off to the west, frantically searching for what drew you there."

Upchurch nodded. "I would tell her I was away to secure more ammunition because our powder stores were low when in fact I was scouring the countryside for horses, and well stocked with powder. Another time, I explained that I was off to the coast to buy up medical supplies—we were amply stocked at that point—when I was in truth meeting with shepherds in the mountains to gain a sense of the little-used trails our scouts could take to pass into France unseen."

"And all the while, you knew your wife was..."

"I knew she was in very great danger, Goddard. I had to pass along enough accurate information to Meli that the generals' ruse was not detected. At the same time, I was to also send the French wrong information when it mattered, through a conduit who to this day has no notion of the extent of the intrigue her little affair engendered."

"I still don't see how I come into it." Though Orion had to admit that he did not envy Upchurch this contretemps.

"Deschamps and Meli grew careless, and Meli would sneak out of camp after dark to meet him. Not often, but frequently enough that I feared somebody would notice."

Between one tick of the mantel clock and the next, the whole puzzle came together. "Thus you sent me off on goose chases. Whereas some think I sold secrets to the French—hence my evening excursions—others suspect that my transgression was in some ways worse: I cuckolded my commanding officer. Or possibly I did both?"

Upchurch rose from the desk and took a key from beneath the clock on the mantel, opening the clock face to wind the mechanism.

"I put it about that you had tempted Melisande to stray and that somebody had passed information to the French, but I could not say you were that person."

"Because," Orion said slowly, "a man who will disrespect his commanding officer would not *necessarily* also disrespect the crown? No wonder your guests despise me."

Upchurch closed the clock face and returned the key to its hiding place. "I made sure, at appropriate times and places, to emphasize that I had only suspicions, Goddard. Nobody was to call you out or confront you directly, because we lacked the evidence to do that, and it's all getting to be very old news."

"But your men nonetheless disparaged me at every turn. You could not let this whole situation simply pass into the great miasma of bad memories we call the war?"

Upchurch gazed at a portrait of some old fellow in muttonchops and regimentals. "Deschamps haunts me. He comes around once or twice a year, and while I trust Melisande with my life, I do not trust that man."

"Because he's French? Because you turned his encroachment on your marriage against his country and made a fool of him?"

Upchurch shook his head, and another layer of complications sorted itself out.

"Because," Orion said, "the child in your nursery could be half French." Hence Deschamps lurking in the park, where most of London's best families would occasionally take their children for some fresh air.

"Melisande and I don't speak of it, and I am not a man given to excessive sentiment, but I would hate to lose either Melisande or our daughter. I could not have anybody connecting Melisande to Deschamps, not ever, and you were a handy if unwitting decoy. I do apologize for that."

Profanity came to mind and some blunt instructions regarding what Upchurch could do with his apology. "Why steal the champagne?"

"I am desperate to have you gone, Goddard, and that Frenchie cook at the Coventry occasionally has wine for sale at bargain rates. I strongly hinted to him of an opportunity, and his greed did the rest."

"You put a boy up to stealing my sword?"

Now, finally, Upchurch had the grace to look ashamed. "He was bragging to one of his mates at the intersection about your sword being nearly as long as he was tall, about how he guarded your stables at night. I made some inquiries at the corner pub. The lad's father has been taken up for sedition, and I agreed to look into the matter."

"*Have* you looked into the matter?" Of all the offenses Upchurch had committed, and he'd committed many, putting Victor at risk to hang was the worst.

"The man will be released at the end of the month. The boy was torn, Goddard, but loyalty to his family won out. I assured him the sword would be returned to you and that this was a prank between officers."

Some prank. The clock ticked on the mantel, the hum of conversation came from the library, and Rye mentally scheduled a difficult discussion with young Victor.

"You should call me out," Upchurch said. "I'm not the dead shot I was as a younger man, but I could still give a good account of myself, if that's why you hesitate. My affairs are in order."

"My affairs are not," Orion said. "Much to my surprise, I am entangled with everybody from little old French ladies to street urchins to in-laws connected to an earldom. Besides, you would delope, noble old hypocrite that you are, and you've already apologized."

Then too, Rye had promised himself to eschew attempting to solve problems with violence, and the noble old hypocrite was *Ann's uncle.*

"My apology is sincere. I concocted the scheme of scapegoating you years ago, Goddard. The whole affair took on a life of its own when Deschamps kept circling the camp, as it were, and certain generals recalled you by name. I am glad we've cleared the air."

All personal vows aside, Orion dearly, dearly wanted to meet Upchurch on the field of honor, but if the choice of weapons were swords, a bad hip and an eye sensitive to bright light could see him killed. Then too, Upchurch had been caught up in a war, spying, marital difficulties, and the demands of command.

And finally, if all went according to Rye's wildest dreams, Upchurch would become family.

"We have not cleared my name," Rye said, "but you can tend to that detail now."

"I refuse to compromise Melisande's reputation, Goddard. Her socializing is all she has. But for Ann's kindness earlier this evening, even that could have been taken from her. This ends now, between us as gentlemen."

"If you had been more attentive to your wife when she was a new bride, you could have spared us all years of stupidity. I have no intention of dragging Melisande's reputation anywhere, but neither will I have my own bride inconvenienced by your schemes."

"You and Ann intend to marry." Upchurch sighed a defeated man's sigh. "Melisande and I will leave Town, then. Meli won't like it, but winter approaches and—"

"You can leave Town if you like, though retreating to France never did anything to resolve my own troubles. Before you tuck tail and run, however, you will impart a few salient facts to that pack of sots and buffoons in your library. Listen closely, for I don't intend to repeat myself."

MIDNIGHT APPROACHED, the magic hour at the Coventry when guests who'd put in a duty appearance at Godmama's ball or musicale came to treat themselves to some wagering and flirtation in less genteel surrounds. The champagne became free at midnight, and the laughter became freer.

Because Ann Pearson was not on the premises, Sycamore Dorning's anxiety also rose as the evening hours advanced, and the club's gambling floor became more crowded.

"The buffet needs attention," he said to a passing footman. "The roast won't last another quarter hour, and the sculpted potatoes are nearly gone."

The footman, one Henry Broadman, was young and fit, and yet, he looked exhausted. "Apologies, Mr. Dorning, but the kitchen isn't at its best tonight. Nan is trying to get the potatoes to look like those little ducks Miss Pearson makes, and it's not going well. Pierre didn't put the second roast on until about an hour ago, so we might well run out of beef. Hannah has a ham in the bake oven that should be ready to go soon."

This was not good. A scullery maid sculpting potatoes, an apprentice tending the ham, the sous-chef forgetting to spit a roast...

"Come along," Sycamore said, heading for the kitchen.

"Mr. Dorning, I don't mean to get above myself, sir, but you'd best not... That is..."

Sycamore pushed through the swinging doors, and where the happy bustle of a busy kitchen should have been, all was pandemonium. Somebody had spilled flour near the pantry, and white tracks formed random patterns on the floor tiles.

The girl trying her hand at potato sculpture also looked as if she'd been crying, and the new fellow—Pierre—was washing wineglasses at the wet sink.

Hannah, Miss Pearson's apprentice, was at the cook stove, stirring something that at least smelled enticingly like ham gravy.

"What is *he* doing here?" Sycamore asked. One of Orion Goddard's half-grown reconnaissance officers sat on a stool by the window, paring apples with a knife that did not look to be standard kitchen issue.

"I'm helping," the boy replied. "Colonel said to keep an eye on things, and I took that t' mean I was to keep an eye on Miss Ann's kitchen. Hannah put me to work." He bit into a pale apple quarter. "I like this kinda work."

"Theodoric," Sycamore said, the boy's name popping to mind. "Did you at least wash your hands before you took up that knife?"

The boy pushed off his stool and came close enough to hold out two exceedingly clean hands. "Hannah said everything in the kitchen starts with washing. I wasn't keen on that notion until she made us some crepes."

The sous-chef, who should have been bringing some order to the chaos, remained bent over the tub of glasses as if praying for their souls.

"Where the hell is Jules?"

Hannah, Theodoric, and Henry all glanced in the direction of the cellar door.

Unease climbed closer to panic. "How long has he been down there?"

A waiter came dashing through the doors. "Bloody guests are hungry tonight, and we're already out of soup."

"You," Sycamore said, "please trot across the street and ask Mrs.

Dorning to join us here in the kitchen. She's to come as she is as soon as she decently can. You three," he went on, gesturing to Henry, Hannah, and Theodoric, "come with me."

Hannah set her pot to the side of the burner and followed him, Henry came next, and Theodoric helped himself to another quarter of apple before falling in line.

"What the hell is going on in my kitchen?" Sycamore asked when they had gained the marginally cooler surrounds of the corridor.

"Miss Ann isn't here," Henry said. "We manage better when Miss Ann's here."

"Miss Ann asked to have the night off a week ago," Sycamore retorted. "Why hasn't Jules stepped in?"

"'Cause he's a drunk," Theodoric said. "And a mean drunk. He goes to the wine cellar, and the rest of the kitchen would just as soon lock him down there. He helps himself to your wine, by the way, and anything else he pleases to have around here. If Henry so much as took some day-old bread home without permission, he'd be sacked, but old Jules isn't even earning his wage and—"

Hannah elbowed her friend in the ribs. "It's worse than Otter says."

"What could be worse than a buffet that offers only mashed potatoes shaped to resemble horse droppings?"

"We can serve the mashed potatoes *en casserole* garnished with parsley, ham gravy on the side," Hannah said. "Miss Ann told me that before she left, but Jules ordered the tatie pigeons, and we haven't anybody to make the tatie pigeons."

"Henry," Sycamore said, "tell Nan to do what Hannah said. Make a casserole of the damned potatoes, sprinkle parsley on top, and set the ham gravy on a warming light beside them. What else did Miss Ann say?"

"Tell him what Jules said," Otter prompted, finishing his apple quarter. "Or I will."

Hannah wiped her hands on her apron. "I understand French. Otter does too. We heard Jules talking to Pierre, bragging about having a lot of excellent champagne in his personal inventory, and telling Pierre it's for sale at very attractive prices."

"*Champagne magnifique*," Otter muttered. "I know where he got it, too, because I recognize the cases."

"He's keeping stolen property here?" Sycamore asked.

"Nah." Otter stepped back to allow a footman to rush past with an empty platter. "I followed him. He keeps it at his place, in the cellar, which is bloody stupid. His cellar is damp and stinks of coal."

Resolving that situation would require Orion Goddard's participation. The immediate challenge was the buffet.

"Hannah, what else did Miss Pearson say about tonight's menu?"

Hannah withdrew a wrinkled paper from her pocket. "She left a list, but Jules tore it from the pantry door and crumpled it up. I picked it up when he wasn't looking. I was about to start on the apple cobbler. It's simple and quick."

"Start on the cobbler, get Nan to help you when she's done with the potatoes. What can we do about the roast?"

"You can make those curled-up things," Otter said. "You slice off strips of meat from the part of the roast that's done and roll them up on little skewers. Looks fancy, fills a plate without using up much meat, and you don't have to wait for the whole roast to cook."

"How long have you been lurking in my kitchen?" Sycamore asked.

"We did that last week," Hannah said, "when Pierre got here late. We used a cooked ham that only needed heating. I could use the ham in the oven, and Miss Ann says thyme, rosemary, and tarragon can wake up a plain ham."

"Go wake up the damned ham, then," Sycamore said, "and tell the waiters to make double the rounds with the champagne, starting immediately."

"It's not midnight yet," Otter replied as Hannah marched off. "The champagne ain't free until midnight."

"Isn't," Sycamore retorted, "and I'm the owner of the place, so if I say it's free, then it's free starting now. Jeanette, my dearest, thank you for coming."

Sycamore's wife emerged from the kitchen in an old morning dress, slippers on her feet, thick shawl around her shoulders.

She peered at the flour tracks leading to and from the kitchen. "The footman said you were well, but you should know that Jules is nigh insensible down in the cellars. I left him there singing French Christmas carols."

"The kitchen is a rudderless ship without Miss Pearson, apparently, and Jules disdained to follow the instructions she left."

"What of the sous-chef?"

"He don't know a butter knife from his arse," Otter said. "Beg pardon for my language, missus. Pierre's a nice enough chap, and his papa were a butcher, so he can cook a roast, but he ain't no chef."

"Go make yourself useful to Hannah, please," Sycamore said. "I need privacy if I'm to be reduced to tears."

Otter sauntered off, while Sycamore tried to read Miss Pearson's crumpled list by the light of a flickering sconce. "She left instructions. Half the words are French. My French is pathetic."

"Mine is excellent," Jeanette said, taking the list from him. "Tend to the guests, I will see what's to be done in the kitchen."

"I love you," Sycamore said, gathering her in a quick hug. "I love you and adore you, and I owe you a pineapple feast for this, Jeanette. I have a club full of hungry guests and apparently no chef worth the name."

Jeanette smoothed her hand down his back, and half the worry in Sycamore drained right out of him, but only half.

"Has Miss Pearson found another post yet?"

Sycamore made himself step back. "Not that I know of."

"Then we aren't without a chef. Not quite. Go flirt with the dowagers, and I will man the saucepots."

Sycamore kissed his wife, sent a silent curse in the direction of the cellars, and adopted the relaxed smile of a host without a care in the world. Tomorrow, he would promise Ann Pearson the sun, moon, and a new set of knives.

Tonight, he would be as cocky and charming as that dreadful little rascal Goddard had assigned to patrol the kitchen.

"GENTLEMEN, YOUR ATTENTION," Horace Upchurch said, striding into the library. "You must all take part in a celebratory round with me and Colonel Goddard before we rejoin the ladies. I'll be brief, but the occasion is too important not to remark in the company of good friends."

Rye had to concede the old warhorse was putting on a convincing show of manly good cheer. Maybe Upchurch was that intensely relieved to have his scheme unravel, or maybe he'd learned while at war how to put on creditable performances.

"What could the likes of Goddard possibly have to celebrate?" Dexter Dennis sneered. "He's the next thing to a traitor, and yet, he struts around with a damned knighthood."

"The ferocity of your temper does you credit, Dennis," Upchurch said, "for that's exactly the sort of contempt you were meant to direct at our Colonel Goddard. You have all—with your grumbling in Goddard's direction, your avoidance of his company, and general suspicion of him—assisted our government to perform a favor for a foreign entity faced with a delicate dilemma. The port, if you please."

Rye had demanded that Unchurch exonerate him of wrongdoing, but Upchurch was turning a brief explanation into some sort of Banbury tale.

While the footmen topped up glasses, the looks sent Rye's way became speculative.

"What sort of favor has Goddard been involved in?" Lieutenant Haines asked owlishly.

Upchurch considered his drink. "I must choose my words carefully, for utmost discretion is required, but I can tell you fellows this.

One of the nations with whom we were allied on the Peninsula became aware that some of its officers behaved in an untrustworthy manner. If the French learned that those officers—let's call them Hessians, for the sake of discussion—were being investigated, then evasive maneuvers would result, and the truth would never come out."

"So Goddard was a decoy?" Mornaday said. "A distraction?"

"He was perfect for such a role," Upchurch said, regarding Orion as if he'd won top wrangler honors three years running. "French on his mother's side, fluent in the language, and wounded badly enough to carry off a convincing grudge toward the military. Then there were his periodic trips to the Continent after the peace. He certainly had all of you fooled, for which on his behalf I do apologize."

"So he never sold secrets?" Dennis asked, sounding utterly crestfallen. "Never took coin to keep his French lands safe?"

Upchurch snorted. "Don't be ridiculous. Goddard had no need to safeguard his family's French holdings when they were miles away from any fighting. Plundering that far afield was too much effort for even the Grande Armée, but the rumor certainly served its purpose. Goddard suggested it himself."

The hell he had.

"Is that why Fat George tossed a knighthood at him?" Dennis asked. "Because of service above and beyond?"

Upchurch allowed a dramatic silence to build. "Imagine that you are the *Hessian* spies and along comes an English officer dwelling under a cloud of suspicion. If that officer were to suffer a fatal accident, all and sundry would assume a traitor had finally met with justice. The colonel's death could even have served as proof of his supposed guilt. All the while, Goddard's role was to march about like a man impervious to scorn. The real culprits enjoyed a false sense of security, convinced Goddard was blamed for their crimes. They grew careless and have been apprehended."

"Goddard did his marching about bit quite well," somebody muttered.

"Not an easy role," Upchurch said, "when you know men capable of the lowest conniving wouldn't mind seeing you dead. For us, the war ended at Waterloo, not so for Colonel Goddard. I am happy to say that our friends on the Continent have finally resolved the situation to their satisfaction, and thus I can entrust you gentlemen with the truth."

This complete taradiddle had been so convincingly rendered, Rye himself was tempted to believe it.

"A toast, then," Haines said, "to our Colonel Sir Orion Goddard!"

The usual cheering and thumping resulted, and Rye acknowledged the good wishes with a nod. "Thank you all. I am pleased to be once more in your good graces." Only pleased, oddly enough. Not elated, triumphant, jubilant, ecstatic or any other superlative.

Pleased. Relieved. Nothing more. To have won Annie Pearson's heart, though, was cause for profound rejoicing.

"Always said you were a decent sort," Haines replied. "Your men spoke well of you, and even the Frenchie prisoners respected you."

"That board of inquiry was just for show, then?" Dennis asked. "A farce?"

Upchurch peered at his drink. "We went to great lengths to make Goddard look both culpable and understandably bitter. Took away his field command, sent him out skulking about the countryside under the quarter moon. Made sure to breathe new life into old rumors every few months. He bore it all without complaint, and at long last, the whole business can be put to rest. Not a word in the clubs, though, gentlemen, and you cannot share what you've learned here with the fellows at Horse Guards."

And thus did Upchurch ensure the story would spread faster and farther than the flames of the Great Fire.

"My sister likes you," Dennis said. "She claims you have the air of a brooding hero. It's the eye patch, makes you look ruthless. I envied you that damned eye patch, Goddard."

"And the way you speak French," somebody added. "The ladies love a fellow who can offer sweet nothings in French."

The list of Rye's enviable qualities grew as the port in the glasses disappeared, until somebody suggested Rye was deserving of a monument in Hyde Park. He let them maunder on, listening with half an ear.

Upchurch's fabrication neatly cleared Rye's name without implicating Melisande or Upchurch himself in wrongdoing, and that was cleverly done. But Upchurch's loyal officers had believed one set of lies about Rye all too easily, and now, just as easily, they were convinced by another set of lies.

The good graces of such sycophants didn't, in fact, mean all that much, *and never had.*

This realization was a greater relief than knowing Rye would never again have to tolerate Dexter Dennis's righteous glowering. The regard of men like Alasdhair and Dylan mattered far more, as did the respect of the children. They cared nothing for gossip and everything for the fact that Rye kept his word and treated them decently.

Jeanette had never turned her back on her disgraced brother, and Ann had taken a man scorned into her bed and into her heart.

Rye stripped off his eye patch and rubbed at his forehead.

"You wear it for show?" Dennis asked, peering at the scrap of black silk.

"I wear it because bright light gave me terrible headaches for the first few years after I mustered out, and it still occasionally bothers me. I also wanted to spare others the sight of my scars, but those have faded."

"I don't suppose you'd be willing to stand up with my sister at some point this Season?"

The request was made ever so casually, and Rye wanted to laugh. "I have a bad hip, Dennis. I might occasionally try a waltz, but something as lengthy as a quadrille is beyond me. You won't see me dancing much." And when he waltzed, he'd waltz with Ann or not at all.

"But if you do take a notion to *trip it as ye go, on the light fanta-stick toe*, you'll keep m'sister in mind?"

"Of course, and speaking of the ladies, it's time we rejoined them." Rye was hungry for the sight of Ann and the sound of her voice, and weary of the company he'd so long yearned to join.

"Quite right," Dennis said, finishing his drink, "and the brigadier seems to be of the same mind."

The footmen collected glasses, and some of the company made further use of the chamber pots as Upchurch decreed the interlude at an end.

"And remember, lads," he said, "not a word to the ladies."

Dennis all but charged down the corridor and was whispering to his sister in a corner before the first gentleman was served his tea.

Rye tarried at the parlor door with Upchurch as the other guests greeted the ladies and found chairs and sofas to lounge upon.

"Was any of that fairy tale true?" Rye had told Upchurch to explain that his loyal subordinate had been following orders when on reconnaissance in the countryside, nothing more complicated than that.

Upchurch's gaze rested on Melisande, who made a graceful picture presiding over the tea tray. "Most of it. I am not the only officer for whom the generals charted a hard course, Goddard, but I wasn't permitted to tell you. Word came down from Horse Guards recently that the problem on the Continent had been resolved. I'd hoped you could simply slink off to France none the wiser—what soldier wants to know that he's been used in such a manner?—but then we had that little chat in my office."

"The chat where you explained that because you and your spouse did not honor your vows, I have been made to dance on a string for years like the generals' puppet."

Upchurch watched his wife, who laughed at some inanity from Dennis.

"I have danced as well Goddard, and in addition to my marital woes, there was that little business about all of Europe being embroiled in warfare. Nobody wants to see us reduced to that sad pass again. Though you are right: You deserve to have your good name cleared and your future secured. I will doubtless be taken to task for disobeying orders—unreliable dodderer that I have become— but the war, thank Providence, is finally over."

Not quite. "You will pay for that champagne, Upchurch. Every crate and bottle. To the penny."

Upchurch nodded.

"Then I will collect Miss Pearson, bid my hostess good evening, and make a night of it."

"Let me say this, Goddard, because you won't hear it from anybody else: Thank you. A lesser man would not have withstood the slings and arrows of outrageous fortune half so stoically, but a whole ring of bad actors has been brought to heel because of your sacrifice."

I don't care. Rye would care, maybe a little, soon, but right now, all he wanted was to be alone in a coach with Ann.

"You and the generals are not welcome," Rye said. "You had no need to keep me in the dark as you did. You did that to spare yourself humiliation. I would gladly have played the role assigned to me, but I wasn't given a choice."

"Understood," Upchurch said. "You might find yourself flooded in the coming weeks with orders for champagne."

That, Orion did care about. "I live in hope." He strode off to find Ann holding forth near the hearth about the wonders of *herbes de Provence.* She concluded her rhapsody as Rye offered her his hand.

"Miss Pearson, I am felled by fatigue. Would you mind very much if we took an early leave?"

Ann rose gracefully. "Of course not. I am unused to such enter-tainments myself and would gladly bid our hostess good night."

Countless eternities later, Rye had Ann bundled into the Dorning town coach.

"What happened?" she asked. "The men stalked off to the library glaring daggers at you. In less than thirty minutes, you become the toast of the regiment."

"I'll explain later. The whole tale approaches farce, but suffice it to say, I *am* the toast of the regiment at present, and I do not care one moldy cheese or wilted leek that it should be so. Kiss me."

Ann obliged, and as lovely as the meal had been, her kiss was a greater source of sustenance.

"Will you spend the night with me, Ann?"

"Yes."

"I haven't even told you what Upchurch had to say behind a closed door. I'm not going to France, not to stay."

"Then neither am I. Kiss me."

Rye obliged, at length, enthusiastically, and when Ann finally cuddled next to him on a contented sigh, he could honestly agree with Upchurch about one thing at least.

The war was over. The war was finally, absolutely over.

"YOU WANT me to take on the post of chef at the Coventry?" Ann asked.

Mr. and Mrs. Dorning had called upon her at her home, and Ann had no doubt Miss Julia and Miss Diana were listening at the keyhole.

"I do," Mr. Dorning said. "We do, rather. Jules Delacourt has succumbed to a serious bout of homesickness and is packing up his effects as we speak."

Sycamore Dorning could exaggerate a point for the sake of emphasis, but he wasn't given to outright lying. "Why is Jules leaving in such haste?"

Mrs. Dorning sent her spouse a look.

"I could tell you," Mr. Dorning said, "that Jules is at pains to avoid an awkward interview with the magistrate, and that much is true. My fancy French chef colluded with Brigadier Horace Upchurch to steal four hundred cases of champagne from Colonel

Goddard, though I believe Upchurch will see most of the goods returned and pay the purchase price for any missing bottles."

"He had better," Ann muttered, getting up to pace. "Does Colonel Goddard know of Jules's involvement?"

Orion had escorted Ann to her doorstep at dawn. They'd spent the night loving, talking, and drowsing, but he had neglected to mention Jules's hand in the theft of the champagne—if he'd been aware of it.

"He should know," Mr. Dorning said, "but the champagne isn't the half of it, Miss Pearson. You haven't been to the Coventry today, have you?"

"Not yet. I planned to look in on Hannah this afternoon." Orion was paying a call on Deschamps this morning, and then he'd promised Ann he would call on her too. They had more to discuss.

Much more.

"We saw firsthand what happens in the kitchen when you aren't there," Mrs. Dorning said. "Pandemonium wrapped in chaos tied up with mayhem. Hannah and Henry were of more use than Jules or his so-called sous-chef. That the guests were fed at all is only because you left instructions and set enough of a good example that some of the staff could carry on in the face of utter uproar."

The Dornings had declined a tea tray, which was fortunate, because at that moment, Ann was so muddled, she could not have managed the sugar tongs.

"The staff works hard," she said, resuming her seat. "Jules is truly leaving?"

"He'll be on a packet headed for Calais on tonight's outgoing tide," Mr. Dorning said. "Will you take the post of chef?"

A year ago, that question would have embodied every hope and aspiration Ann's heart held. A year ago, she would have answered with an unreserved yes, and part of her still longed to.

"May I have some time to think about it?"

Another look passed between husband and wife, one suggesting that Mrs. Dorning had predicted that Ann would not immediately accept the post.

"Provided you continue running my kitchen in the meanwhile, you may ponder the question as long as you please," Mr. Dorning said, getting to his feet and offering a hand to his wife. "My soul shrivels to contemplate the state of the kitchen last night, Miss Pearson."

"As does mine," Mrs. Dorning added. "Matters were truly dire, but Hannah rescued your instructions from the rubbish bin, and we muddled along with extra champagne rations for the guests. There is many a sore head in Mayfair this morning thanks to your departure from the kitchen, Miss Pearson. We really do need you."

Ann saw her guests to the foyer and was just offering them a farewell curtsey when a hard rap sounded on the door. Mr. Dorning performed the butler's office and stepped back to allow Orion to join the small crowd in the foyer.

"Dorning." Orion's bow was little more than a nod. "And Nettie." He kissed his sister's cheek. "A pleasure to see you, but what brings you to Miss Pearson's abode so early in the day?"

Mr. Dorning drew in a breath as if to hold forth about pandemonium and mayhem, but his wife passed him his hat before he could launch his diatribe.

"We came to ask Miss Pearson to take pity on our kitchen," Mrs. Dorning said. "I fear we are too late, for it appears she's had—or is about to receive—a better offer. We'll bid you good day. Come along, Sycamore."

She all but pulled her husband with her through the front doorway.

Orion set his hat on one hook and draped his cloak over another. He looked well, if tired, and he wasn't wearing his eye patch.

"You are upset, Annie. If Dorning offended you, I will have a very stern word with him. He's my brother-in-law, so I can't thrash him outright, but a short discussion—"

Ann wrapped her arms around Orion and held fast. "They asked me to be the chef at the Coventry. Jules helped to steal your champagne, and I gather last night did not go well in the kitchen."

"Jules is not my brother-in-law. He'd best be on his way back across the Channel, or I will take a potato masher to his handsome French phiz. Let's sit down, shall we? I've a need to hold you in my lap."

"Orion," Ann said, not turning loose of him, "Sycamore Dorning *offered me the post of chef* at the Coventry." She needed to hold on to him while they had this conversation.

"You already are the only chef worth the name at the Coventry. What you mean is, he's offered to pay you what you're worth. Come." Orion took Ann by the hand and led her not to the guest parlor, but to the family parlor.

"Orion, be serious."

"You did not get enough sleep last night," he said, closing the parlor door and scooping Ann into his arms. He settled into a wing chair with Ann in his lap and rested his cheek against her temple. "I apologize for that, but when we marry, you might occasionally go short of sleep. You can turn Dorning down, you know. Just because you will be family to him by marriage doesn't mean you have to indulge his little dramas. There are other cooks in London who can put on a fancy buffet—though, of course, none as talented as you."

"You speak as if I could accept his offer."

"Do you want to accept his offer?"

The previous night should have made it plain that Orion Goddard liked to leaven complicated discussions with affection. He'd told Ann the details of Uncle Horace's situation, including Aunt Melisande's straying and Emily Bainbridge's role.

"I thought you and I were to be married, Orion."

"I desperately hope we are. But what has making me the happiest man on earth to do with making profiteroles to inspire envy from the angels?"

He did not sound as if he was being purposely obtuse. "This is not France. If I am your wife, people will expect me to stay home and have your babies."

"I already have half a dozen babies of the half-grown variety, and no wife stays home with them. Melisande has a child in the nursery whom she doesn't even see some days. What do you want, Annie? What would make you happy?"

"I love to cook, and I want to be your wife."

"Then cook and be my wife. Dorning had better pay you what he paid that inebriated *bouffon*, or—"

Ann kissed him. "Gentlemen's spouses don't typically work for a wage."

"I am not a gentleman. I am a humble wine merchant who wants his wife to be happy. I thought you dreamed of writing a cookbook? If last night's meal is any indication, Annie, your recipes will sell better than Byron's naughty poems."

"I do want to write a cookbook, and I've had an idea." This idea had come to her in the middle of the night, between bouts of loving and talking.

"Do tell. I've had a few ideas, too, and one of them involves a special license and a wedding journey to Provence."

"I want to write a champagne cookbook. Meals for every occasion featuring champagne." She braced herself for laughter, or for gentle teasing.

"A champagne cookbook?"

"Champagne and pineapple juice for breakfast with pear crepes and ham with orange glaze. The Dornings have a pineapple venture. Did you know that? Champagne with raspberry liqueur for a Venetian breakfast and a selection of cheeses to include—"

"Hush, or you will make me hungry. Did you know that Deschamps's mama is a cousin to the King of France?"

"What has that to do with my cookbook?"

"With your brilliant cookbook? When I send along a case of my finest vintage to Deschamps's dear mama, I could tuck in a copy of your book, signed by the author. The Coventry could feature your recipes and offer subscriptions to your second book. Your next project might be a book about sauces made with wines, and I suppose Fournier will want copies to pass around because the idea of such recipes is actually his. As your adoring husband, I will do your French translations. Mrs. Radcliffe's husband managed all of her literary ventures, and—"

Ann put her hand to his mouth. "Then you can love a woman who wakes up dreaming of sauces? Who longs to cook all day? Who is a bossy and very-well-paid chef up at all hours and forever spouting ideas for new dishes?"

She took her hand away, and Orion regarded her with such tenderness, she felt as if she'd drunk a serving of the finest champagne a bit too quickly.

"Can I love such a woman?" Orion asked. "Annie Pearson, I already do."

"But can you love her if she works at the Coventry, for a wage, with her hands?"

"Of course I can love such a woman. I will say it in French, just so you are certain. *Bien sûr, je peux aimer une telle femme.* Can you love a man with a foot in each of two cultures that are more often at war than at peace? Who likes the company of impertinent children and aging destriers? Who is likely to be creaky before his time and who comes with a herd of meddlesome in-laws and honorary godmothers?"

"Can I love such a man?" She sank against him, cuddling close. "Orion Goddard, I already do."

EPILOGUE

The noise beggared description.

Between the celebration in the kitchen and the wedding breakfast hosted by the Coventry, Ann had to bend close to her new
husband to hear him speak. They shared the head of a long table, the
detritus of a midday banquet strewn before them.

"Dornings like champagne," Orion said, "and they love your
quiches and custards and fruit and cheese pairings."

Dornings loved each other, too, if this display of familial loyalty
for Sycamore Dorning's in-law was any indication.

"They appear to be taking quite an interest in your cousins,
Orion." Margaret Dorning, who had an encyclopedic knowledge of
herbs, was over by the window in earnest discussion with Alasdhair
MacKay, whose family distilled whisky. Willow Dorning was similarly engrossed in conversation with Dylan Powell. A mastiff leaned
against Dylan's leg, the dog looking as if he, too, was engrossed in
what Dylan had to say.

Various children scampered about, most of them with food in
hand, while Aunt Melisande and Uncle Horace, looking somewhat
dazed, were being entertained by Lord and Lady Casriel.

"The Dornings have taken an interest in us," Orion said, "for Jeanette's sake, and, Annie, it's a bit like being in the army before all the gossip started. I am surrounded by goodwill, and I don't know how to respond. Worth Kettering has agreed to meet with us to discuss investments, and Margaret and Hawthorne want to talk about growing culinary herbs commercially."

Across the room, Otter was making a pest of himself to Mr. Valerian Dorning, who was showing the boy how to execute a formal court bow for Hannah's amusement.

"I don't know anything about growing herbs commercially," Ann said.

"But you know how they're used in the kitchen, while Margaret has thus far only advised her husband regarding medicinal properties. These people have become family connections, Annie. If they'd like to chat with us over a glass of claret, I'm happy to oblige."

Somebody in the kitchen started singing Handel's "Hallelujah Chorus"—several somebodies—and the result was lovely.

"Henry has quite a voice, doesn't he?" Orion asked.

"He does, as does Nan. Margaret Dorning advises her husband?"

"Hawthorne claims the Dorning botanical venture would be lost without her. Why?"

Ann took Orion's hand, because it was their wedding breakfast and because she was already in the habit of reaching for him when her courage wanted fortifying.

"You said you feel as if you're back in the army, before all the intrigue and gossip stole the goodwill of your fellow officers from you. I have no frame of reference for a family where Mrs. Valerian Dorning is the first editor of her husband's books and Mrs. Margaret Dorning tells her husband which herbs to plant and where to plant them. Jeanette was the first person Sycamore Dorning turned to when the kitchen was in a panic. They aren't like Melisande and Horace, and I begin to see that much of the world isn't like Melisande and Horace."

"The brigadier and his lady are devoted, in their way."

Were they, or were they devoted to some manual of marriage for senior officers? "They have secrets from one another."

Orion brought Ann's hand to his lips. "I will make you a promise, Annie Goddard. When I am flummoxed by this vexatious old world, when I am overjoyed by some unforeseen turn of events, when I have a difficult problem to solve, or a simple pleasure to share, the first person I turn to will be you. I will find you in the kitchen, or the herb garden, or the nursery if we should be so blessed, or wherever you bide, and I will share my hopes, fears, dreams, and delights with you."

Those words settled around Ann's heart with a warmth and rightness the old church vows had not.

"And I promise you, Colonel Sir Orion Goddard, that when I am frustrated, or puzzled, or rejoicing, or pleased, I will turn first to you, no matter if you are in your office, the warehouse, the stables, or our bedroom. Kiss me."

"Your obedient servant, Mrs. Goddard." He kissed her on the cheek, and that somehow became Ann kissing him on the lips, and a round of applause started up, followed by a demand that the toasting begin.

While tables were rearranged, and the kitchen serenade careened into jolly melodies, Orion refilled Ann's champagne glass.

"Sycamore Dorning made me an offer, Annie."

"What sort of offer?"

"He wants a manager for this club. Somebody with a head for business who gets on well with *madame le chef*, as he put it. Dorning excels at charming the customers, but he also longs to spend more time charming his wife. He wants to develop his Richmond property into market gardens, in the Dorning horticultural tradition, and he doesn't feel free to do that without dedicated eyes and ears on the club."

Just like that, Orion was sharing his heart with her, even here, amid this happy din.

"You need to be free to travel back and forth to France."

"Dorning can spell me for those few weeks here and there, but

I'm more concerned that you might not want your husband underfoot at your club, Annie. I won't necessarily be in evidence every evening, but I'll be here a lot, if I take Dorning up on the offer."

Ann thought back to earlier discussions with her husband. "What's your compensation to be? The Coventry is a jealous mistress, Orion, and hasn't had a dedicated manager before. You will find that what the Dorning brothers did not enjoy doing often went undone. Mrs. Dorning has made some inroads on things like the linen inventory, but all is not in order."

"My compensation is to be a share of ownership that increases over time, if Dorning offers suitable terms in other regards. The original owner, a fellow named Tresham, has been gradually bought out, and now Ash Dorning is similarly easing away from the business. Dorning would like to ease us in."

"Let's think about it," Ann said, tucking an arm around her husband's waist. "We are soon to be toasted at length with the finest champagne in the world, and I would like to enjoy that pleasure with my new husband."

"Twenty minutes," Orion muttered as Sycamore Dorning got to his feet with glass in hand. "I will put up with this nonsense for another twenty minutes, and then I'm taking my new wife away for a few toasts made in private."

"Surely nobody can offer twenty minutes' worth of toasts?"

The toasts lasted nearly twice that long, and when Orion was inclined to let good manners prevail still longer over marital priorities, Ann took her new husband by the hand and stole away for many toasts made in private, only a few of them involving the finest champagne in the world.

TO MY DEAR READERS

To my dear readers,

I devour well written biographies of writers from days gone by, and in the course of my reading I came across a recounting of the life of Victorian author Thomas Hardy.

His mother, Jemima Hardy (née Hand), harbored a girlhood aspiration to work in the kitchen of a fancy London club, though her ambition was never realized. She saw such a post as well above the options available to her in rural Dorsetshire, and as sufficiently remunerative that she could enjoy life in the big city. Her unfulfilled dream made enough of an impression on young Tom that when he had the chance to see London for himself, he took it.

Jemima Hardy's wistful ambition stuck in my mind, as did memories of my childhood. My mom made dinner every night for a family of nine, and she regularly fed whatever shirt-tail cousins, neighbor children, or stray colleagues of my father's needed a meal that day. Her dinner parties were legendary, and she collected recipes with a passion. She made sure each of her daughters had a copy of *The New York Times* cookbook, though among my six siblings, my brother Tom is probably the most dedicated cook.

As much as my mom knew about keeping a gang of people fed, it was my father who was the tenured professor of food science. With all due respect, Dad could just about make an edible omelet. Later in life, Mom pointed out to him that he had retired from the professorship, but she was still on KP day after day, decade after decade. He agreed to take over responsibility for half the meals, and this resulted in my octogenarian parents eating a lot of Don Bravos' carry out fish tacos.

Which are *wonderful*, but still...

I got to thinking about these matters when I met Ann Pearson in **The Last True Gentleman**, and I already knew Orion Goddard had some tricky personal matters to sort out. So what if the colonel and the cook took a shine to each other? Wheee!

And if you're wondering what's up with Alasdhair MacKay and the ladies of the night... So am I! His story, ***Miss Delightful***, is book two in the **Mischief in Mayfair** series. Excerpt below.

If you'd like to stay up to date on all my new releases, pre-orders, or works in progress, you can sign up for my **newsletter** (comes out about monthly, easy to unsubscribe, and I never sell, swap, or otherwise give out my mailing list), or follow me on **Bookbub.** I also have a **Deals** page on my website, where I note any titles on limited-time discounts or scheduled for early release in the web store.

Happy reading!

Grace Burrowes

Read on for an excerpt from ***Miss Delightful***, book two in the Mischief in Mayfair series!

MISS DELIGHTFUL—EXCERPT

Miss Delightful, Mischief in Mayfair, book two

Dorcas Delancey, preacher's daughter, spinster, and do-gooder at large, has seen her late cousin's infant son ensconced in the household of his new guardian, Major Alasdhair MacKay. The wee lad has kept Alasdhair (and the whole household) up all night for several nights running. When Dorcas visits to look in on the baby, Alasdhair all but collapses at her feet. Modern folk might say Alasdhair is prone to hypoglycemia, but Dorcas apparently thinks he's swoony...

Mr. MacKay had switched sides of the bed, but not roused. Dorcas took the reading chair when she should have left him to slumber on in solitude.

She was merely resting her eyes when an annoyed Scottish burr roused her.

"Have they gone? I know Powell and Goddard were here, or did I dream that?"

She sat up to behold Mr. MacKay sitting up amongst his pillows, his hair sticking up on one side, his gaze disgruntled.

"Your cousins have traveled on to the Aurora Club, where they await you, though you are not to hurry to join them. A tray is on the way, and I forbid you to leave the house until you eat something."

Mr. MacKay sank back and nuzzled his pillow. "I love it when you give me orders."

Was he still half-asleep? "I do not love it when a grown man in otherwise apparent good health collapses in a heap at my feet. I don't care for that at all."

"Every woman should have a grown man collapsing at her feet in a heap from time to time. Keeps us grown men humble."

"Mr. MacKay, you frightened me." Dorcas hadn't meant to say that. Hadn't allowed herself to think it, but if anything happened to Mr. MacKay, where would that leave the baby John?

He sat up, scrubbed a hand over his face, and swung his feet over the side of the bed. "You for damned sure intimidate the hell out of me. You are fearless, woman, and I apologize for my language, but profanity is another indication that I need to eat."

"I am not fearless." Far from it.

"Then you bluff exceedingly well. I ought to shave, and I refuse to do that with you glaring daggers at me."

"Your cousins said you weren't to bother, that they'd seen you looking far worse."

He sighed and looked around the room as if he expected those cousins to pop out of his wardrobe. "What else did they say?"

"Not much. That you needed to eat very regularly or you got into difficulties. They weren't worried."

"They were worried. They are my nannies, those two. In Spain, they carried extra rations at all times..." Mr. MacKay rose, stretched, and gazed down at Dorcas. "I did not mean to frighten you, but that's part of the nature of the beast. I don't realize I need to eat, and then I get too muzzy-headed to think through the situation. I always come right, so please don't fret. My cousins admonished me not to shave because when I'm peckish, my hands shake too badly to manage a razor. I could always shoot straight though."

"I can shave you. I have shaved my father from time to time, when he's ill, or once when he sprained his wrist. I will be careful."

"One suspects you are always careful. Has the wee fiend gone to sleep?"

He thought of the boy, even now. "I don't know. The nursery is quiet and I gather John enjoys a full belly." Dorcas *was* always careful, because she had to be. The offer to shave Mr. MacKay was not one a careful woman would have made. Charitable, perhaps, but not careful. "Shall I shave you?"

"I'll be fine once I eat something. You have my thanks for your concern."

Harrison arrived then with a tray of sandwiches and a pot swaddled in a thick linen towel. Dorcas poured out, the coffee aromatic and strong.

"You are to eat before you swill the whole pot." Perhaps she liked giving him orders, a disturbing notion.

He saluted with his cup. "A sip to revive the dying. You want to leave me some privacy, but you are worried, Dorcas Delancey, because you think I will try to back out of my promise to house John here for the next fortnight."

She resorted to making the bed, the only bit of busyness available. "I am more concerned you forgot that you made that promise. You were half-swooning at the time."

"And yet, you badgered me into an agreement. I admire your tenacity." He consumed a sandwich and poured a second cup of coffee, this time adding cream and honey.

"Swoony men should not be held to account for their delirious declarations."

"I do not swoon," he said. "I grow light-headed. I become vertiginous. I am prone to syncope—a French doctor patching up British troops taught me that one—and presyncope, but I do not swoon. Perish the thought."

Dorcas went to the wardrobe and began laying out a suit of morning clothes. "You *fell* upon me. I could not stop you from collapsing. You must promise me to leave the nursery to Timmons tonight. She can sing as well as the next person, while you cannot... lactate."

"My dear Miss Delancey, you are blushing."

I am not your dear anything. "Have another sandwich."

He did, this one disappearing more slowly. "Now, I can tell I'm hungry, but this will hold me for the present." He rose and surveyed the outfit Dorcas had chosen.

"I would not have paired that mulberry waistcoat with a blue morning coat."

"Too showy? A touch of gold—cravat pin, cufflinks, watch chain —will pick up the gold embroidery in the waistcoat. You must have a care with your appearance to reassure your friends that you are back on your mettle."

He stood improperly close, but then, what was propriety when she'd offered to shave him? When she'd seen him snoring on the floor? When she'd badgered him—his word—into keeping John here for the next two weeks?

"*You* put me back on mettle," he said, "and I state only the somewhat surprising truth."

Dorcas moved away, for she was blushing again. "Then I am no longer needed here. If you have any news to impart regarding John's situation, please call on me at the vicarage."

She wanted distance between herself and Mr. MacKay, or that's what she *should* want. What Dorcas truly wanted shocked her.

To touch his hair again.

To see him without his shirt.

To watch the transformation from bearded ruffian to cleanshaven *Master of Abercaldy* and former officer.

To ensure that he did not again grow peckish because he was too worried about a teething baby.

Perhaps she was the one grown light-headed and unsteady.

Mr. MacKay escorted her as far as the bedroom door. "I will keep John for the next fortnight, and I will not part with the lad until I'm certain he'll be well cared for. If possible, I'll send Timmons along with him, and I make you a solemn vow, Dorcas Delancey, that he will never want for anything."

His gaze was utterly serious, as if he were in fact taking a solemn vow.

"I should not have carped at you as I did," Dorcas said. "That's why they call me Miss Delightful—because I am *not* delightful. I am tiresome and difficult." She made that confession staring at the bare skin of Mr. MacKay's throat. She was tempted to collapse against him, to give him the weight of all her disappointments, and forget for a time who she was and where the line lay between propriety and folly.

He really had given her a bad turn.

"You are delightful," he murmured, very near her ear. "I keep my promises, Dorcas, and I do not lie. You are maddening, brilliant, determined, and as tenacious as a seagull at a picnic, also entirely delightful. The boy is lucky to have a champion such as you."

Something warm and soft brushed Dorcas's cheek. *His lips.* He moved away behind the privacy screen with its intriguing collection of portraits.

She had just been kissed by the dour, unsmiling Alasdhair MacKay, *and she had enjoyed it.* On that startling revelation, Dorcas slipped out the door.

Order your copy of ***Miss Delightful***!